WRANGLED Love

ANN EINERSON

Paperback ISBN: 978-1-960325-12-9

Cover Character Art by @chelseakemp_art

Cover Design by @madicantstopreading

Dev Edited by @bryannareads, @probablyalovestory, @bookswithkaity

Edited by Emily McNish @EmilyintheArchives, Jenny Sims Editing4Indies

Proofread by Nikki Carrero @NikkiGetsLiterary, Judy Zweifel @Judy's Proofreading

Formatted by Champagne Book Design

For those who love a rugged man with a dirty mouth who traded in the boardroom for wide-open skies, muddy boots, and Wranglers—I introduce you to Jensen Harding, a.k.a. Urban Cowboy.

PLAYLIST

Somethin' Bout A Woman – Thomas Rhett
(feat. Teddy Swims)

A Bar Song (Tipsy) – Shaboozey

A Life Where We Work Out – Flatland Cavalry, Kaitlin Butts

After All The Bars Are Closed – Thomas Rhett

Cowgirls – Morgan Wallen (feat. ERNEST)

Speechless – Dan + Shay

Worst Way – Riley Green

Country Boy's Dream Girl – Ella Langley

What I Want – Morgan Wallen (feat. Tate McRae)

Love Me Like You Mean It – Kelsea Ballerini

you look like you love me – Ella Langley (feat. Riley Green)

She's Everything – Brad Paisley

Drunk On You – Luke Bryan

Thank God – Kane Brown, Katelyn Brown

AUTHOR'S NOTE

Hey, Reader!

Thank you for picking up *Wrangled Love*, where tension quickly turns to temptation in Bluebell, Montana, between a single dad and his nanny in this steamy age-gap, brother's best friend, small-town, cowboy romance.

Caleb, the MMC's son, stops speaking after his mom passes away. Every child processes grief differently, and this portrayal reflects one interpretation based on the story's unique circumstances. While inspired by real experiences, I've taken creative liberties to support the characters' emotional journeys. This is not intended to represent every child's experience with loss.

Wrangled Love contains explicit sexual content, profanity, mention of cancer, mention of foster care, mention of a parent's death, and mention of absentee parents.

Reading is meant to be your happy place—choose yourself, your needs, and your happiness first!

Xoxo,
Ann Einerson

WRANGLED *Love*

CHAPTER 1

Jensen

"**C**AN YOU REPEAT THAT?" I GRIP MY PHONE TIGHTER, waiting for a reply.

It was supposed to be a typical day at the office. My biggest worry this morning, as CEO of DataLock Systems, was overseeing the final round of testing for our upcoming cybersecurity product launch. As a major player in the tech world, my team is a well-oiled machine. Every detail is accounted for—no surprises or disruptions.

My career is my life. Yet, with a single phone call, everything I thought I knew has been turned upside down. I'm convinced this can't be real.

"My name is Tony Fletcher," the man on the phone repeats. "I'm a partner at Westbrook Law Group based in Chicago, and I regret to inform you that after a long battle with cancer, Amelia Campbell has passed away."

I didn't recognize the name at first.

We met at a club six years ago. Her quick wit and career-minded focus won me over. She was in town for a legal conference, and we spent a night together. When I woke up the following morning, she was already gone, and I never heard from her again. Amelia was just another beautiful woman from my past who I hadn't thought about in years—until now.

I draw in a deep breath. "Like I said before, Tony, I only met her once, and that was six years ago."

A knot forms in my stomach the moment the words pass my mouth. He's kept things vague so far, but I have a feeling I know what's coming, and I'm not sure I'm ready to hear it.

"Mr. Harding, I worked with Amelia for over ten years. She was meticulous in everything she did. In her will, she listed you as the biological father of her son, Caleb, and designated you as his legal guardian upon her death."

The words hit like a punch to the gut. My knees buckle, and I sink into my office chair, struggling to process the weight of it all. If Amelia knew I was Caleb's dad, why keep it from me? I've lived in New York this entire time. Hell, I even told her the name of my company the night we were together.

Is it really possible that I have a son and never knew it?

Pressure builds in my chest, my pulse hammering. "Where is Caleb now?"

He must be devastated after losing his mom, and I can only imagine the confusion he's feeling right now.

"Amelia passed two days ago, and he's been in a temporary foster home since," Tony says, his voice heavy with emotion.

"Why wasn't I called sooner?" I demand, rising to my feet to pace my office.

On several occasions growing up, I spent time in foster homes while my parents were under investigation. Their biggest offense was neglecting me during gambling sprees, but the houses I was sent to were never an improvement. They were always over-crowded, and the people running them were more concerned with collecting checks than taking care of the kids in their care.

"It took that long to access and review her estate documents." He pauses, blowing out a slow breath. "I was able to visit Caleb yesterday to make sure he's being properly cared for, and I can confirm he's holding up as well as can be expected given the circumstances."

I bite back my frustration. The man is just doing his job, and it's clear he's gone above and beyond, which I'm grateful for. But that doesn't ease the anger I feel knowing Caleb's in foster care, no matter if it's just temporary. I haven't even met him yet, but the instinct to protect him is already there. Whether he's biologically mine or not, I'd do whatever I can to help. No kid should be caught in the system, especially after losing a parent.

I wonder why none of Amelia's family stepped up to take him in after she passed, but I let it go for now. There will be time for questions later. My priority is getting to Caleb and advocating for him in person.

"I'm on my way." I glance at my watch. "I'll be at the Westbrook offices by four. Caleb better be there when I arrive. Am I clear?"

"Absolutely. I'll give his social worker a call to set it up." I hear the faint clicking of keys in the background. "Would you like to see a picture of him in the meantime?"

I pause, caught off guard. "Uh, sure."

"Sending it now. See you shortly, Mr. Harding," Tony says before ending the call.

I exhale shakily, dragging a hand down my face. Just as panic starts to set in, an email comes through from Tony with a photo attached. In it, Amelia sits on a picnic blanket at the park, holding a little boy in her lap with tousled brown hair and warm chocolate eyes.

I'll be damned.

It's like looking in the mirror at a younger version of myself, down to the gap in his smile. The only difference being is, he has

Amelia's eyes. I don't need a DNA test or other proof to confirm that Caleb's mine. Which means what Tony said must be true.

I have a son.

The gravity of the situation finally sinks in, and I realize there's no time to waste. I fire off an email to my assistant, instructing her to have the company jet ready at the airfield within the hour. I can't sit idly by while Caleb faces this alone for another minute. Whatever happens next, he's got me in his corner now.

Next, I call my lawyer, Dawson Tate. He's one of the few people I trust. We met early in our careers and have had each other's backs since. He's now the most ruthless lawyer in New York City with a reputation for turning even the toughest cases in his client's favor. He also grew up in foster care, so he knows how to navigate the system. If anyone can cut through the red tape and fast-track the guardianship so I can bring Caleb home, it's him.

"Harding, this better be good," Dawson answers. "I have a negotiation settlement in ten, and you know I enjoy watching the opposing legal counsel squirm before it starts."

"I just found out I have a five-year-old son," I blurt out.

"Come again?" He shifts gears to lawyer mode. "Who's claiming this, and what's she after?"

I wedge my phone between my shoulder and cheek, freeing my hands to pack my laptop.

"Her name's Amelia. Her lawyer just contacted me to say she passed away and named me guardian of her son, Caleb, and listed me as his father in her will."

"Fuck," Dawson mutters. "Is it possible?"

I look at the photo on my computer screen again. "He's mine," I state.

Dawson lets out a dry laugh. "You won't know for sure without a DNA test. Say the word and I'll get one set up."

"That's not necessary." I pause to add a stack of papers to the briefcase I'm filling to take with me. "I just saw a photo of him, and he's the spitting image of me as a kid. He's mine," I repeat with conviction.

I've never been so sure of anything in my life.

Dawson lets out a whistle. "Well, shit. What can I do?"

I exhale deeply. "Amelia lived in Chicago. Caleb's in temporary foster care, and I want to bring him back to New York as soon as possible. I'm headed there to get him now."

"Send me the law firm's details, and I'll call them within the hour. By the time you land, it'll be taken care of."

I sigh in relief. "Thanks, man."

"I'll send you the bill."

I chuckle. "Nice to talk to you too, Dawson."

It's always business first with him. Then again, I'm no different, but I have a feeling that's about to change.

As someone who treats research like a competitive sport, I spent the past two hours on the plane taking a crash course in child development online.

It started with a simple search: How to take care of a grieving child. That opened the floodgates to articles about night terrors, regression, and emotional outbursts—none of which I'm remotely prepared to handle. I found myself reading through forum posts from relatives stepping in after tragedy, most of them overwhelmed and heartbroken. I also came across several therapist-recommended guides for helping kids through loss, and I bookmarked all of them.

I've been alone my entire adult life. I left my hometown, Bluebell, Montana, when I was eighteen and haven't looked back since.

The one bright spot in my childhood was the Halstead family. They own a ranch near town, and I practically lived at their place thanks to my friendship with their oldest son, Heath. We've stayed in touch over the years, and I still consider them the closest thing I ever had to a real family, which is why I send Heath a message before landing in Chicago.

Jensen: Hey.

Heath: Long time, city boy.

I roll my eyes at his nickname for me. It's only been a few weeks since we talked last, but Heath always loves an excuse to give me shit.

Heath: Wall Street kick you out yet?

Jensen: Just missed your charming personality.

Heath: Everything alright?

Jensen: Got some unexpected news today, and I could use the help of you and your mom.

Heath: Whatever you need.

Jensen: Thanks. I'll call you tonight and explain everything.

Heath: We'll be here.

His mom, Julie, is the principal at the elementary school in Bluebell, and she's been wrangling kids longer than I've been alive. I may be in over my head, but if I trust anyone to steer me right, it's her. The Halsteads were my haven as a kid, and I'm hoping they can help me navigate this new chapter, too.

I arrive at the Westbrook Law Group's office building an hour later. The driver idles near the entrance as the weight of the situation settles over me. I take a deep breath, attempting to steady my racing heart before heading inside.

Following the directions from Tony's assistant, I take the elevator to the twentieth floor. A woman sits behind the reception desk, her fingers a blur across the keyboard. The moment she spots me, her hands still, and she greets me with a warm smile.

"Good afternoon. What can I do for you, sir?"

"I'm here to see Tony. He's expecting me."

She gives me a quick nod and stands. "You must be Mr. Harding. Right this way."

I follow her to the door at the end of the hallway with Tony's name on it. She knocks twice before opening it, motioning me inside.

"Thanks," I say.

"My pleasure," she replies with a smile.

I step inside and spot Tony at his desk across the large office. His salt-and-pepper hair is combed to the side, and his shoulders tense beneath his tailored suit. He looks up, his expression solemn as he pushes his glasses up the bridge of his nose.

He waves toward the chair opposite him. "Glad you're here, Mr. Harding. Although I wish it were under better circumstances. Please have a seat."

I sit down, crossing one leg over the other. "Has Caleb arrived yet?"

He nods. "He's in the conference room with his social worker. I wanted to review a few important matters with you before we join him. I'll make it as quick as possible."

"I appreciate it."

I understand we have to go over the logistics, but sitting here while my son waits in a nearby room makes me feel like I'm already letting him down.

Tony opens a desk drawer, takes out a thick binder, and sets it on his desk.

"I must admit, I'm impressed," he tells me. "You move fast. I've been on the phone with your lawyer, Mr. Tate, a dozen times already." He opens the binder, glancing down at the first page. "I'm not sure how he did it, but he got a judge to grant temporary emergency guardianship. You'll just have to meet with the social worker and give her a virtual tour of your residence."

"Does that mean I can take Caleb home tonight?" I question.

He nods. "As long as the social worker approves, I don't see why not. A formal hearing will be scheduled in the coming months to grant permanent custody if all parties agree and the court finds it in Caleb's best interest to remain with you."

"You haven't mentioned Amelia's family. Are they involved?" My biggest concern on the way here was that someone might challenge my guardianship or petition the court for custody.

Tony shakes his head. "Her parents are deceased, and she was an only child." He flips to the back of the binder, pulls out a document, and slides it toward me. "She listed a second cousin from Florida and a college friend as secondary guardians in case you declined, but we haven't been able to reach them."

"Has Caleb met either?"

"I don't believe so."

A sharp ringing pulses through my ears and a cold sweat breaks across my forehead. Even though I had made up my mind before coming here that I wanted Caleb, it's hard to accept that he has no one else. Now I understand why he was placed in temporary foster care. There wasn't another option.

Tony takes off his glasses and rubs the bridge of his nose. "There is one more thing I need to tell you before you meet Caleb."

I straighten in my chair, my brow furrowed. "What is it?"

"He hasn't spoken since Amelia was admitted to the hospital two weeks ago." Tony's voice falters, betraying the sadness beneath his professional exterior. "The social worker mentioned that some children stop talking as a way to cope with the trauma. Right now, his silence is the only thing that he can control. It's likely temporary, but it could take time for him to trust that it's safe enough to use his voice again."

Tears sting my eyes at the thought of my son carrying his pain alone, too heartbroken to speak. The hardest part is that I may never know what Amelia told him about me or if she even mentioned me at all. For all I know, he thinks I didn't want him or wasn't interested in meeting him, which is the furthest thing from the truth.

"I'd like to see him now if I can," I say.

"Of course." Tony nods. "Let's go to the conference room."

I'm about to meet my son. One I didn't know existed until today.

I follow Tony into the conference room, my eyes going straight to Caleb seated on the other side of the large table. He's holding a stuffed dinosaur against his chest, and when his big brown eyes meet mine, my heart skips a beat. The photo didn't come close to capturing just how much he looks like me. His shoulders are slumped, weighed down by a sorrow no child should have to handle on their own.

A woman with a blonde bob and wearing a powder-blue suit, sits beside him with a clipboard in front of her. I assume she's the social worker, so I offer a polite nod. There will be time for us to talk, but my priority is to meet my son and ensure he feels safe around me.

Caleb's lower lip quivers as I settle in the chair on the other side of him.

"Hey, buddy," I say softly. "I'm Jensen. It's really nice to meet you."

9

He blinks, his small hands squeezing the dinosaur tighter, gripping it like a lifeline.

"How are you doing?" I instantly wince when the words leave my mouth.

What a stupid question. Of course he's not doing well. He just lost his mom and now he's in a room with strangers, probably scared and unsure of what's going to happen next.

This is uncharted territory for me, and it shows. I've never spent time with a kid before, yet here I am trying to connect with my son while doing my best not to push him too hard. I don't know his favorite food, what makes him laugh, or how to earn his trust. The only information I have is his name and that he clings to a stuffed dinosaur as if it's the only constant in his world.

"I like your dino," I say, running my fingers along the spikes on its back. "I bet he has a mighty roar."

Caleb lifts his shoulders in a slight shrug, the only sign he's acknowledged me.

I lean in and whisper, "I heard dinosaurs love grilled cheese sandwiches, especially with lots of gooey cheese."

His mouth twitches in the faintest hint of a smile glancing at his dino.

"They're my favorite. In fact, one of the best ones I've ever had was from a deli a few blocks from here. Maybe we could get one together if you're hungry."

I watch with bated breath as Caleb's eyes flicker and his finger flexes around his dinosaur, revealing a small spark of interest.

"How about you nod if you like the idea, and shake your head if you'd rather try something else."

Caleb nibbles on his lower lip, studying me for what feels like ages. Just as I'm about to suggest other options, he gives me a hesitant nod.

I flash a grin, giving him a thumbs-up. "Great choice. How

about I talk to the nice lady waiting for us, then we can head to the deli? I'm sure you're as hungry as I am."

"That's an excellent idea," the social worker interjects with a smile. "It's been a few hard days for Caleb and he could use some normalcy. Let's head over there now and we can go over the questions I need to ask once we get back."

"Really?" I ask.

She nods, jotting something on her clipboard. "No reason why not."

I exhale in relief, grateful she wants to make this transition easier for Caleb. I'm eager to get back to New York and establish a routine. Every article I read stresses it as essential when caring for a child who's experienced loss. I'm also counting down the hours until I can speak with Julie Halstead. Hopefully, she can offer a new perspective and the kind of reassurance and wisdom that can't be found online.

No matter what comes next, I know the Halsteads will help Caleb and me through it. And until he's ready to let me in, I'll keep showing him that I'm here, and he'll never have to face anything alone again.

CHAPTER 2

Jensen

AFTER THE SOCIAL WORKER APPROVED CALEB'S STAY WITH me, we were on our way to New York. Somewhere between crossing state lines and returning to the city skyline, I wondered if I was in over my head. Thank god my assistant, Beth, stocked the fridge and set up the guest bedroom for Caleb before we arrived. It was one less thing I had to worry about, allowing my focus to be solely on him.

It's past midnight once we get to my place, and we head straight to his room—complete with a king-sized bed, gray walls, and a leather armchair in the corner. Not exactly kid-friendly, but it's the best we could manage at the last minute.

Caleb stands in the doorway, watching me with wary, sleep-heavy eyes as I move his things from the duffel bag he had with him to the dresser in the corner.

"We'll go to the store soon, and you can pick out whatever you want to decorate your room," I assure him.

Maybe it'll help him feel more at home and give me a glimpse of what he likes.

He blinks slowly as I pull a pair of pajamas from his bag and hold them up. "How about you get changed and brush your teeth before bed?"

He bites his lower lip, clutching his dinosaur tightly, and hesitantly shakes his head.

It's challenging to guess what he's thinking or feeling, but I know I have to be patient and let him open up in his own time. I blow out a soft breath. It's only been a few hours, and I already feel like I'm failing. I got in touch with Julie on the plane ride home, but *what to do if Caleb doesn't want to change into his pj's* wasn't one of the endless questions that I asked.

This confirms that I'm completely out of my depth. The truth is, I have no idea what to do next. I've never spent much time around young kids—especially not one coping with the loss of his mom.

Caleb looks exhausted—his eyes are half-closed, and he's barely standing. If letting him sleep in his clothes means there's a chance he'll get some rest, then that's what we'll do.

"Why don't we skip pajamas and brushing teeth tonight?" I suggest, putting the pj's in the top dresser drawer. "How about we read a book instead?"

I pull a picture book with a coconut tree on the cover from his bag—one that I saw earlier called *Chicka Chicka Boom Boom*.

Caleb rubs his eyes, and his grip loosens on his dinosaur. I feel a pang of relief when he gives me a slight nod.

I offer him a reassuring smile. "Hop into bed, and we'll start the story."

He shuffles across the room, climbs onto the mattress, and settles under the covers on the side closest to me.

I move the leather chair as close to the bed as possible before taking a seat. Caleb lays his head on the pillow, turning toward me, and his curious gaze studies me.

My throat tightens as I open the book with shaky hands, holding it out so he can see the pictures. I've never read a book to a child before, and I realize just how important this moment is. After everything he's endured, if there's a chance to give him even a few minutes of peace, I'll give it my all. So I put my energy into reading, wanting to make it as entertaining as possible.

A few pages into the book when D, E, and F tumble out of the tree, I pretend to wince. "Oof! D is going to need a giant bandage. Maybe even a whole box of dinosaur ones," I exclaim.

Caleb steals a glance my way, and the sadness in his eyes doesn't seem quite so heavy.

The social worker said it might take a while for him to warm up to me, and that's okay. Seeing him interested in the story is a small victory worth celebrating.

When we get to the part where the whole alphabet falls from the tree, I lean over, tapping the nightstand gently with a soft *thud-thud-thud* to mimic their fall.

"Oh no," I gasp in mock horror. "Those poor little letters."

Caleb rubs his eyes again, holding his dinosaur close to his chest. I soften my tone and read the last few pages in a hushed voice, letting the story wind down with him.

By the time we reach the final page—where A sneaks out of bed to climb the coconut tree again—Caleb has fallen asleep. I set the book on the nightstand and lean over the bed, pulling the covers around his shoulders.

My hand hovers over his head, and I gently push his hair back. He's the most perfect thing I've ever seen, and my heart swells with a fierce protectiveness.

"Don't worry, bud," I whisper. "You've got me now, and we'll figure this out together."

This past week has tested me in ways no one could've prepared me for. After the first night, Caleb withdrew, barely acknowledging me let alone willing to speak. Even getting him to respond with a simple nod or shake of his head has been a struggle.

He's in bed for the night, and I should be catching up on work, but I haven't managed more than staring blankly at the computer.

I grab my phone and call Julie. We spoke the night I brought Caleb home, and she shared advice to help him settle in. Now I'm hoping she has more to offer because I'm completely overwhelmed and could use her guidance.

"Hi, Jensen," she answers cheerfully. "How are you and Caleb holding up? I was starting to worry since I hadn't heard from you much except for a few texts."

I run a hand through my hair. "It's been rough. He's barely left his room since we got to my place. He's ignored the cartoons I've put on for him and steers clear of the toys and stack of kids' books I picked out, unless he thinks I'm not watching." I get out of my chair, pacing my office. "Hell, I haven't even been able to get him to show me what food he likes besides grilled cheese. I've had to order from several different places for every meal, paying close attention to what he eats and what goes untouched." I sigh in defeat.

"I'm sorry, Jensen," Julie says, her tone soft. "How is his therapy going?"

"The therapist has come over twice." I've had her come to the apartment because I was worried about taking Caleb to another unfamiliar place so soon. "I asked if it might be helpful to start teaching him sign language or give him a tablet with a communication app, but she said to give him more time to adjust."

She reminded me that grief doesn't follow a schedule and said introducing other forms of communication too soon could overwhelm Caleb or make him feel pressured. Which could actually delay his comfort in speaking again, and that's the last thing I want.

"That makes sense. It sounds like you're doing the best you

can to make him comfortable given the circumstances, and like the therapist said, it'll just take a little time," Julie reassures me.

"The therapist also recommended that he spend time with other kids. Even if he only watches at first." I stand at my window overlooking Central Park. "She thinks it'll help him warm up to playing and interacting when he's ready."

I tried looking for local playgroups and classes earlier, but it turned into a rabbit hole of options and conflicting parenting advice. Eventually, I had to step away to take a breather. I usually enjoy doing deep dives into a subject, but this felt more like an emotional endurance test than a fact-finding mission. Honestly, it's a miracle neither my browser nor my brain short-circuited.

"What if you and Caleb come to Bluebell for the summer?" Julie suggests. "I think it would be good for both of you."

I come to a standstill, my fingers tightening around the phone. "You're serious?"

"I am. Next week, the elementary school is kicking off a summer camp focused on outdoor learning. It's run by some teachers and volunteers, and includes activities like painting pine cones, visiting local farms, and learning how vegetables grow. I'm sure Caleb would enjoy it." She pauses briefly, letting me absorb her recommendation. "The camp is full, but I can squeeze him in. That's one perk of being the principal," she adds brightly.

My gut reaction is to immediately decline. I haven't set foot in Bluebell since I was eighteen. It's a reminder of my shitty childhood and the struggles I endured early on. Even though my parents have passed, the scars they left still haunt me—etched into every corner of that town.

New York City is my home now, and I've fought to build a successful career and the stable life I missed out on as a kid. So, returning to a past I've tried to leave behind feels like a step in the wrong direction.

"I know coming back here isn't what you want," Julie

continues, seeming to read my thoughts. "But the sunshine and slower pace could do Caleb some good. A child therapist retired to Bluebell last year, and I often recommend her to parents at the school. So, Caleb can continue in-person therapy. I've always thought of you as my own, and I'd love nothing more than to support you right now. They say it takes a village and you have one here on the ranch, ready to help."

As much as I hate to admit it, that does sound like the perfect setup. The truth is I'm isolated here in the city. I have my own business and employees, but not much support outside of work. Back in Bluebell, I'd have Julie and the whole Halstead family to help Caleb and me navigate this unexpected new chapter. Even though it would mean swallowing my pride and confronting my past.

"Where would we stay?" I ask, unsure why I'm still entertaining this idea.

"Briar lives in the cottage now, and there are two extra bedrooms. You can stay with her," Julie answers without skipping a beat. "The cabins are full all summer, and the ranch house is too chaotic for Caleb. This way, you'd get separate rooms and a bit of privacy."

Briar was only ten when I left town and we haven't spoken since. She'd be twenty-four now, and I doubt she'll be thrilled about sharing her space with her older brother's best friend and his kid.

"It's a lot to ask. Are you sure that's something she'd be okay with?" I question.

"Oh, I'm sure she'll be fine with it," Julie chirps. "Especially when she hears about your situation. I wouldn't suggest this if I didn't think it's what's best for you and Caleb."

She stops there, leaving me to stand in silence, weighing my options. Julie knows a thing or two about raising kids, and I believe her when she says she wouldn't suggest Bluebell unless she truly believed it was the right move for us.

My chest tightens, knowing what I have to do.

"Alright. We'll come, but just for the summer."

"Really?" Julie exclaims. "That's the best news."

I exhale slowly. "I'll need some time to get everything in order, then we'll be on our way."

There's nothing I wouldn't do for my son, even if that means going back to the small town I vowed never to return to.

CHAPTER 3

Brian

I WIPE THE SWEAT FROM MY BROW AS I APPROACH THE cottage, squinting against the sun. My brother Heath is sitting on the porch swing with his arms crossed over his chest. I'm surprised to see him here. He rarely shows up on this side of the ranch unannounced, especially not in the middle of the day when there's work to be done.

I lower myself onto the spot next to him. "What are you doing here?"

"Nice to see you too, sis." He smirks as he bends to pick up a bag from Prickly Pear Diner I hadn't noticed before and hands it to me. "Figured you've been fixing the AC in cabin six since dawn, and might want something more than stale chips and a soggy sandwich for lunch."

He knows cooking isn't my area of expertise and that pancakes are the only thing I can make without setting off the smoke alarm. Since I usually spend my days outdoors, I stick to peanut butter and jelly sandwiches or whatever snack I have stashed in my Jeep or back pocket.

I blink in surprise when I open the bag and find a barbecue pulled pork sandwich and loaded cheese fries—my favorite.

If Heath is hand-delivering food, it's either because Mama Julie sent him or he's about to ask for a favor. My suspicions are confirmed when I catch him drumming his fingers against his jeans-clad thigh. His brow is creased as he watches me, waiting for the right moment to ease into whatever request he has up his sleeve.

"How about you tell me why you're really here, so I can enjoy my bribe." I don't bother pretending I don't know he has an ulterior motive.

He shrugs. "What? Can't a guy drop by to check on his favorite sister?"

I roll my eyes. "I'm your *only* sister."

Many in town would argue that's not exactly accurate since I was adopted at fifteen. Before that, I lived on the other side of town in a run-down trailer park with my mom, who bartended at the Blue Moon Tavern and was always chasing her next high— whether it came from pills or the fleeting attention of whichever man happened to be around.

My biological father was just one in a long line she never bothered to remember, and I doubt she could've if she tried. I never knew his name. He was merely an empty space where a dad should've been.

Julie Halstead, Heath's mom, was my elementary school teacher at the time. She took me under her wing when she realized my home life wasn't stable. I spent most evenings at her house where she taught me how to tie my shoes, garden, and ride horses. Her husband, Samuel, and their two sons made me feel like I was part of their family from the start, no questions asked.

When I was a teenager, my mom skipped town and never returned. However, before she left, she found the time to visit the local law office and sign away her parental rights, paving the way for the Halsteads to adopt me. It didn't take long for me to start calling Julie "Mama Julie" and Samuel "Pops." It felt right since they had been more parental figures to me than my own mother ever was.

Heath rubs the back of his neck, avoiding my gaze. "Do you remember Jensen Harding?"

I nod. We grew up in the same trailer park, and I used to see him at the Halsteads all the time—he was always with Heath, and Julie watched me after school most days. We had an eight-year age gap, so I was only ten when they graduated from high school, and Jensen left town. He hasn't been back since.

"Do you still keep in touch with him?" I ask.

"Yeah. He runs a tech company in New York," Heath replies.

I set the takeout on the side table next to the swing, and turn back to Heath. "That's quite a change from Bluebell, Montana."

"No kidding. It's not going to be easy for him to adjust when he gets here," he mutters.

My eyes widen in surprise. "Jensen's moving back?"

"Yeah. For the summer. That's what I wanted to talk to you about." Heath drags a hand through his hair. "He recently found out he has a five-year-old son."

"Seriously? What's the little guy's name?"

"Caleb. Still wrapping my head around the fact that he has a kid."

"I can imagine! Do you know why they're coming to Bluebell?"

It's been fourteen years since Jensen's set foot in town, and I can't help but wonder why he'd come back now.

"Caleb's mom recently passed, and he hasn't spoken since," Heath says solemnly. "He's been staying in Jensen's penthouse but hasn't uttered a word. Ma's convinced the ranch might be a better environment for him while he adjusts to his new life. She thinks the summer camp hosted by the elementary school will help him get some social interaction with other kids and ease him back into a routine."

I'm sure Jensen's decision to come was influenced by the fact that Mama Julie is now the school principal, which means she'll be around to look out for Caleb. Kids can be cruel toward those who are different and don't communicate like they do.

"I agree. It sounds like the best possible thing for Caleb, but I don't understand what that has to do with me?"

Heath clears his throat. "They need a place to stay. All the guest cabins are booked through the summer, and Jensen and Caleb won't have any privacy if they stay at the main ranch house."

Heath and our brother Walker live there with our parents. They each have their own wing, which gives them their own space, but there isn't another area available that would offer Jensen and Caleb the same.

Mama Julie and Pops offered to add another wing for me, but I always declined. I don't want to burden them since they've already done so much, and taking more doesn't sit right with me. That's part of why I jumped at the opportunity to manage the cabins. It gives me a way to contribute around the ranch and show my appreciation to the family who's given me everything.

"I can't cancel any of the reservations. People booked two years in advance, and I wouldn't feel right doing that to them..." It occurs to me that's not what Heath is suggesting. "Please don't tell me you're proposing Jensen and Caleb stay here." I groan.

Heath shrugs. "Why not? You've got the room. Plus, you're the only one, besides Ma, who might be able to help Caleb come out of his shell."

I shoot him a glare, annoyed that he's right. After everything I went through as a kid, I've made it my goal to be there for other children dealing with their own trauma. Someday, I want to open a nonprofit where kids can heal, surrounded by fresh air, open fields, and animals that love without judgment.

"The cottage is a work in progress," I remind Heath.

"Please, Briar. I wouldn't ask if this weren't important," he pleads.

I bite the inside of my cheek, frustrated by how easily he's backed me into a corner. I've spent most of my adult life living alone and prefer it that way. After high school, I convinced the Halsteads to let me move into the cottage on the far side of the ranch. It's a fixer-upper, but I'm slowly bringing it back to life while juggling the cabin rentals, repairs, and my volunteer work. Once fully renovated, it'll be converted into another rental, since the current ones have a long waiting list.

"You waited until the last possible second to ask me, huh?"

I admit, it was clever. Heath knew that after hearing Caleb's story, it would be impossible for me to turn him and Jensen away.

"Let's not dwell on the timing," he says with a sheepish smile. "What do you say? Can they stay?"

My big, tough-as-nails brother silently pleads with his eyes, causing the last of my resolve to crumble. He's always been there for me, so how could I say no? Even if it means opening my home to Jensen, who I haven't seen in over a decade.

"Fine," I sigh. "They can stay here, but the next time the septic tank gets clogged, you're fixing it." I dread that chore, so I'm cashing in on this favor while I can.

Heath smirks, putting his hat on his head as he stands. "You've got it, sis." He leans down to kiss my forehead. "I'll call Jensen and share the good news. You won't regret this."

I want to believe him.

But something tells me I might have signed up for more than I bargained for.

Once Heath gets in his truck and leaves, I take out my phone to call my best friend, Charlie. I sigh when it goes to voicemail. She's probably with a customer or taking her lunch break. She owns Timeless Threads, a vintage boutique in town where she gives secondhand clothes and home decor a new lease on life.

Briar: Why aren't you answering?! It's an emergency.

Charlie: What kind of emergency?

Charlie: Are we talking about a "ran out of Cheetos" kind of crisis, or a "your vibrator ran out of batteries" kind of disaster?

Briar: What's the difference?

Charlie: One can be fixed with a snack run. The other requires a glass of wine and some elbow grease.

Charlie: If it involves a stray animal, a tractor, or you trying to DIY your bangs again, I'll need coffee first.

Briar: Your emergency contact status = pending review.

Charlie: The number you're trying to reach is no longer in service.

Briar: Wow. Abandoning me when I'm in crisis mode.

Charlie: Better spill what's so urgent before the next customer comes into the shop to argue with me over the price of a vintage vase.

Briar: Jensen Harding found out he has a five-year-old son, and they're staying in Bluebell for the summer.

Charlie: And that's an emergency because...

Briar: Heath said they could stay at the cottage with me.

Charlie: That son of a Mama Julie.

Charlie: Do I need to come over and bring a shovel? I think there's one in the storage closet.

Briar: That escalated quickly.

Charlie: I just looked up Jensen.

Charlie: He's hot.

Charlie: And a tech whiz.

Charlie: At least when he moves in, you'll never have Wi-Fi issues again.

Charlie: Oh, and according to the internet, he's rich. Do you think he has one of those black credit cards that's super heavy?

Briar: Upon further review, your emergency contact status has been revoked.

Charlie: You tell me he's not good-looking in a three-piece suit.

A photo pops up of Jensen in a charcoal suit, standing in front of a skyscraper with his hand in his pocket and an unreadable expression. It's hard to believe this sharp-dressed businessman was once a cowboy, wearing boots and flannel, with dirt under his nails, who spent his summers working on the ranch.

The longer I stare at the image, the harder it is to look away.

Aren't tech geniuses supposed to wear graphic tees, have bedhead, and squint through smudged glasses? Not look like a walking *Forbes* cover. It's criminal that he could be brilliant *and* ridiculously attractive. No wonder he left Bluebell after high school. It's clear city life has treated him well.

Charlie: Busy setting the photo as your new wallpaper?

Briar: The cottage is a dump compared to whatever fancy penthouse he lives in.

Briar: He probably has multiple.

Charlie: The cottage is charming.

Briar: Yeah, if you look past the creaky floors, drafty windows, and the ancient appliances. He can't stay here.

Charlie: Alright, fine. He can stay with me if he must.

Briar: You live in a studio apartment.

Charlie: Your point being...

Briar: Where exactly do you plan on putting him? The cereal shelf?

Charlie: Please, I have standards. He gets the closet. It's private and cozy. Total upgrade.

Charlie: But seriously, if you need anything from the shop or a hand with getting the cottage ready, let me know.

Briar: Thanks. Love you!

Charlie: Love you more!

I remind myself that when Jensen comes to Bluebell, it won't be for a vacation. His life has been flipped upside down after finding out he's a dad, and his main focus will be on Caleb, not on the condition of my house or what kind of bed he sleeps in.

Despite my initial hesitation about them staying here, my priority is to make sure they feel welcome when they arrive and to create a space where Caleb feels at ease. He lost his mom and *just* met his dad. This additional change could be overwhelming for the little guy, and I want the transition to be as smooth as possible.

CHAPTER 4

Jensen

A FEW DAYS AFTER MY CONVERSATION WITH JULIE, CALEB and I are in the only taxi in Bluebell on our way to Silver Saddle Ranch. It's early June, and summer is in full swing around here, with a bright blue sky and fields of gold and green stretching in every direction.

"Jensen Harding. A face I never thought I'd see in these parts again," Earl remarks from the front seat. "I heard you made a fortune selling gadgets to protect rich folks' homes. Don't reckon we have much use for that kinda thing around here." He motions to the surrounding countryside, the car veering off the road when he does.

My fingers curl around the door handle. "It's not that kind of security," I mutter.

Heath had to bail on airport pickup duty because a calf arrived ahead of schedule, and the vet couldn't get there fast enough. I called Julie, but she was tied up at the school, leaving me with one option—Earl Barnard.

He's been Bluebell's taxi driver for the past forty years and often drives guests to Silver Saddle Ranch, since it's the only tourist destination in town. The trouble is he drives like he's racing a tornado and also has advanced cataracts in his left eye. Heath told me that the town council decided to look the other way last year when he ran over the mayor's prized rose bushes. Despite his tendency to confuse the gas pedal with the brake, he's a fixture in Bluebell.

Growing up, Julie's marigolds at the ranch entrance never made it through the season with Earl's station wagon making a habit of turning them into mulch every spring. Seems some things never change.

"You and the tater tot staying at the ranch house?" Earl asks, glancing over his shoulder at us crammed in the back seat.

"No. The cottage."

He lets out a low whistle. "Well, now, I didn't see that coming. You and Briar a couple?"

"Nope," I say, trying to end the conversation so Earl will focus on the road and not town gossip.

"That won't stop the ladies at the diner from talkin' about this for weeks," he says, wagging his finger.

"I have no doubt," I mutter under my breath.

If Bluebell's residents love one thing, it's a good rumor. And the kid from the trailer park, coming back after fourteen years with a five-year-old son, *and* moving in with his best friend's little sister? The whole town will buzz over coffee and lemon meringue pie at the Prickly Pear Diner for at least a week.

Earl swerves sharply, nearly taking out a mailbox. I instinctively wrap an arm around Caleb, bracing him against me until the car straightens out. When I pull back, I glance down to find his gaze fixed out the window, unfazed by the abrupt movement.

"By golly, them mailboxes must be gettin' closer to the road these days." Earl chuckles, shaking his head.

"It's definitely the mailboxes moving and not your steering," I deadpan under my breath.

He swivels his head. "What'd you say, city slicker? My hearing ain't as good as it used to be."

"Said you've got catlike reflexes. I'm impressed." No harm in letting him think I mean it.

Earl grins. "All those years of dodging potholes and raccoons have paid off."

"Looks that way," I say, tightening my grip around Caleb.

I sigh in relief as we pass the welcome sign to the ranch. It's the only place that's ever felt like home. As soon as the taxi pulls up to the cottage, I help Caleb out before grabbing his booster seat.

Earl's already unloading our luggage and stacking it on the porch. "Remember, cash only," he reminds me.

It figures he's holding on to the old-school way of doing things. I take out a hundred-dollar bill and hand it to him when he finishes with the bags.

"Thanks for the ride," I say.

Earl stuffs the bill into his front pocket, not bothering to ask if I want change.

"Mighty kind of you, city slicker." He takes out a crumpled business card and hands it to me. "Call me the next time you need a lift, you hear?"

"Sure." I slip the card into my pocket.

Right after I get a root canal and volunteer for a wasp nest removal with my bare hands.

Thank god Heath's loaning me one of his trucks for the summer so I don't have to ride with Earl again. His heart is in the right place, but the same can't be said for his lane position.

I watch him hop into the driver seat, his car rattling when he turns it on. As he drives away, he lives up to his reputation, clipping a fence post on his way out.

It's a miracle we made it here in one piece.

Caleb and I are left alone on the front porch. He stands behind me, holding his dinosaur to his chest as he takes in his surroundings. Silver Saddle Ranch is a world away from the suburbs of Chicago and my penthouse overlooking Central Park. I take a deep breath, hoping I did the right thing by bringing him here.

Taking a step forward, I knock on the door, frowning when there's no answer. I check my watch, noting it's a quarter past one. Heath said Briar spends her mornings handling cabin maintenance, and I wonder if she's behind schedule today. After knocking again, I jiggle the knob and find it's unlocked.

I stick my head inside. "Hello? Anyone home?" I'm only met with silence.

I glance down at Caleb with a smile. "Why don't we go inside and look around?"

He stares at me, blinking slowly, his expression unreadable. I exhale and hold the door open, motioning for him to follow me into the house before closing it behind us.

Becoming a father overnight has been a shock to the system. The constant disconnect with Caleb has me questioning if I'm failing him as a dad. But when I look at him, I remember I'm all he has, and giving up isn't an option.

When we step inside, I take a look around. The space looks like a snapshot of the nineties. Pastel wallpaper lines the entryway walls, and vinyl tiles cover the floor. There's even popcorn texture on the ceiling.

I glance into the living room off to the right, which is similarly styled. The walls are a faded beige, and a worn floral-patterned couch is positioned in front of a circular coffee table. A built-in curio cabinet against the far wall displays a mismatched collection of teacups.

The place hasn't changed one bit since the last time I saw it. Julie and Samuel lived here briefly after they got married but quickly outgrew it. Since then, several ranch hands lived here until a few years ago, when Briar moved in. Julie told me Briar has plans to fix it up, but it doesn't look like she's made much progress.

When I enter the kitchen, the linoleum floor creaks and the scent of pancakes and cinnamon lingers. The faded yellow wallpaper is covered with decorative plaques with sayings like "Farm Fresh Eggs" and "Rise and Shine." A bulky white oven with worn dials sits against the far wall, and an ancient fridge leans slightly to one side, propped up by a folded piece of cardboard under one foot. A rooster-shaped clock ticks away on the wall, its tail feathers forming the pendulum.

I'm definitely not in New York anymore.

Despite the downstairs being outdated, it's spotless. No dishes are in the sink, the counters have been wiped down, and the floors are impressively clean, which is remarkable, considering we're on a ranch, and dust has a habit of tracking into the house. I spent enough time at the Halsteads' ranch house to learn that the hard way.

Caleb and I are still in the kitchen when I hear the front door open, followed by hurried footsteps in our direction. Briar rounds the corner, panting as if she sprinted the whole way. She rushes past us to the sink, her back turned, so I don't get a good look at her.

"Sorry I wasn't here when you arrived," she says over her shoulder, her voice slightly muffled. "One of the cabins had a clogged drain, and of course, it had to be the one with a couple who had nothing better to do than supervise. The husband, Carl, must've asked a dozen times if I knew what I was doing—bold of him, considering it was his brilliant idea to pour baking soda and vinegar down the pipes." She dries her hands on a towel covered in cartoon chickens.

"I wasn't expecting you to..." I trail off when Briar turns around, and I finally get a good look at her.

The last time I saw her, she was a freckle-faced ten-year-old with a wild mess of curls who was curious about how everything worked. She followed Julie around like a shadow, determined to prove she could do anything the ranch hands could, even if that meant hauling hay bales half her size and wearing her blisters like a badge of honor.

Fourteen years later, she's nearly unrecognizable. The woman before me has long, brown hair tied back into a ponytail, a few loose tendrils framing her face. Her tanned skin has a natural glow from countless hours spent under the sun, and her brown eyes sparkle with curiosity as they meet mine.

Damn, she's stunning.

Heath talks about her often but conveniently left out the part where she's drop-dead gorgeous. Why couldn't I be sharing a house for the summer with someone less distracting—like a retired librarian or a male ranch hand—instead of a woman who looks like she stepped out of a country music video and right into the chaos that is my life?

"Earth to Jensen." Briar waves a hand in front of my face, her brow creased with worry.

I clear my throat. "Sorry, what did you say?"

"How was your flight?"

"All right." I glance down at Caleb, who's quiet and withdrawn. "It's been a long day for us both."

She crouches to Caleb's level, offering him a warm smile. "Hey, Caleb, I'm Briar. It's great to meet you." She gestures to the stuffed dinosaur in his arms. "Looks like you've got a loyal friend there. Is it an Ankylosaurus?"

I'm about to explain that he won't respond when he gives her a small nod. It catches me off guard since he hasn't had this response with anyone else in the past week. Then again, no one else has guessed what kind of dinosaur it is—myself included.

"That's really cool. Your stuffie looks like a strong and brave protector. You two make a great team." She reaches out to ruffle the top of the dinosaur's head, and I swear Caleb's lips twitch to a hint of a smile. "Since you're a fan of dinos, I think you'll like your new room. Want to see it?" Briar extends her hand toward him.

Caleb's whole face seems to brighten as he tentatively places his hand in hers.

This is the most emotion he's shown since I've met him. A wave of jealousy hits me, knowing that Briar managed to get this kind of response from him within the first five minutes. It's an irrational thought, and I should feel relieved that he's warming up to her so quickly, especially since we'll be living together for the summer. Still, it serves as yet another reminder that I'm falling short as his dad, and I wonder if he'll ever look at me with that same kind of light in his eyes.

CHAPTER 5

Brian

CALEB'S SMALL HAND GRIPS MINE AS WE CLIMB THE STAIRS to the second floor. He keeps stealing glances, clearly still unsure of the situation. I don't fault him for being cautious—he's in an unfamiliar place with someone he's only just met. That's enough to make anyone uneasy.

The pain in his brown eyes breaks my heart—it's raw, unspoken, and far too much for a kid his age. If I can ease even a fraction of it, or find a way to give him a moment of peace, I will.

"We're almost to your room," I say, giving his hand a reassuring squeeze.

His only response is to clutch his stuffie to his chest and trace its worn belly with the pad of his finger.

"You've done some work on the place," Jensen remarks from behind us.

I glance back to see him motioning toward the wall I painted cream last year and the light fixture I added shortly after.

"Yeah, I've been updating things when I can, but between

managing the cabins and keeping up with repairs, it's a slow process."

Every time I fix one thing, two more break, and it feels like an endless cycle I can't escape.

"Tell me these creaky stairs made the renovation list," Jensen says, testing each step like it might give out at any moment.

Okay, sure. The stairs creak a little, and the handrail wobbles if you lean on it wrong, but it's nothing dangerous. I'd never invite someone into a place that wasn't safe. Still, I make a mental note to grab some screws tomorrow. Jensen can live with it for one more night.

"They are," I assure him. "It's no New York City penthouse, but it's got plenty of character."

"What makes you think that because I live in the city, I can't appreciate rustic charm?" he says with a tired smile.

"You've been away so long, I figured you'd gotten used to fancy city life." I flash him a playful smirk as we reach the landing. "Might want to consider blending in while you're here unless you're hoping to be the talk of the town."

"They'll talk no matter what. That's Bluebell for you. Lots of nosy-ass charm packed into a tiny zip code," he says with a dry chuckle.

I widen my eyes, nodding toward Caleb.

"Right. Sorry," Jensen whispers under his breath.

My conscience is quick to step in, reminding me they've only been recently acquainted despite their striking resemblance to each other. Caleb isn't the only one struggling to adapt to the situation.

From what I've learned from passing comments between my brothers, Jensen never settled down, fully immersed in growing his company. I can't imagine the shock of finding out he missed five years of his son's life that he'll never get back, no matter how many resources he throws at it.

It's ironic—people like my mom actively chose to walk away from parenthood, while others like Jensen would sacrifice everything for a chance to reconnect with their child.

When we get to Caleb's bedroom at the end of the hall, I pause at the threshold.

"I had a limited amount of time, so I couldn't remodel everything, but I tried to make it special," I say as I open the door.

I glance down at Caleb to see his reaction. His eyes widen as he looks around, taking it all in. A twin-sized bed with a navy-blue comforter sits in the corner, with a white nightstand beside it. Across the room, I mounted a bookshelf and filled it with children's books from Mama Julie's collection. Three walls are painted a light gray, while the fourth is covered in blue wallpaper printed with T. rexes and Triceratops. A plush area rug shaped like a Stegosaurus footprint, courtesy of a hidden gem at Charlie's shop, covers the hardwood floor.

Decorating the room was one way I thought would help Caleb feel more comfortable while he's staying here this summer. I assumed Jensen would bring more of his favorite books, toys, and other things, but I wanted to make a good first impression.

He lets go of my hand, his movements slow and purposeful as he circles the room. When he reaches the dinosaur wallpaper, his hand brushes against it, a faint smile tugging at his lips. His reaction tells me he's happy with his new space, leaving me with a quiet sense of pride. It was a stroke of luck that dinosaurs are his favorite, making the reveal that much more meaningful.

However, my joy is short-lived when I peek over at Jensen, where he's lingering in the doorway with a scowl plastered on his face.

His gaze sharpens when his eyes meet mine. "Can I talk to you in the hallway?"

"Sure," I say.

It's clear that something I've done has upset him, and I'm

willing to hear him out. But that doesn't mean I'll let his sour mood ruin Caleb's positive reaction to what I've done.

"We'll be right back, buddy," Jensen says to Caleb.

He gives a quick nod before returning his focus to the wallpaper, tracing each dinosaur at eye level.

I follow Jensen down the hall, leaving the bedroom door open a crack.

"Did I offend you somehow?" I keep my voice low. "Because you're looking at me as if I committed an unforgivable crime, like putting pineapple on pizza."

Jensen shakes his head in disbelief. "You're joking, right? Pineapple on pizza is elite."

I wrinkle my nose, rolling my eyes. "Fantastic. Now, I have to second-guess every choice you make. What a devastating discovery."

He offers a faint smile before his expression falls, sadness settling over his face. "I was disappointed when I saw Caleb's room. I'd imagined us decorating it together since the one he stayed at in my apartment was a guest room." Jensen leans against the wall, shooting me a regretful glance. "I only found out he's my son less than two weeks ago."

"Less than two weeks?" I ask, struggling to hide the shock in my voice. I'd assumed it had been longer.

"Yeah. I was hoping to create a memory with him while making his new space special."

"I'm sorry," I apologize, hating that I might have overstepped. "I don't mean to pry, but Heath didn't share a lot of details…" I trail off, letting the question hang in the air.

"His mom, Amelia, and I had a one-night stand a few years ago, when she was in New York for a conference. She was gone the following morning when I woke up."

"And she never reached out to you?"

Jensen shakes his head. "I had no idea about Caleb until her lawyer called to say she'd passed away after a long battle with cancer and left me full custody."

I press my hand to my mouth, blinking back tears. "God, Jensen, that's awful. I can't imagine how hard this must be for you."

My chest tightens at the thought of what Caleb must be going through. I know what it's like to grieve a parent, even if mine left by choice. The difference is I had the Halsteads to rely on. Caleb's world has been turned upside down, and now he's been placed in the care of someone he doesn't know—who happens to be his dad.

It hadn't crossed my mind that something as simple as decorating a room might be important to Jensen. I acted on instinct, wanting to do something nice, but after hearing more details about the situation, I believe I have overstepped.

I shift my weight from foot to foot, tucking a strand of hair behind my ear. "I didn't mean to interfere. I just wanted to make sure Caleb felt at home when he got here."

Jensen sighs, rubbing the back of his neck. "It was a thoughtful gesture, and I appreciate you wanting to make things easier for him. I really do."

"Of course, but I know you've already missed out on a lot with him. Next time I want to do something for him, I'll make sure to run it by you first."

I can admit when I've crossed a line, and I'd rather we talk things out now than spend the next three months walking on eggshells because we couldn't agree to move forward.

"Thank you for understanding. This is all so new to me," he says as he blows out a deep breath. "I was surprised to see how quickly Caleb warmed up to you when I've had to practically drag out the smallest response from him."

Jensen's admission tugs at my heartstrings. This can't be easy for him either. He built a successful tech firm in New York and had a life there. Now, he's had to leave it all behind and move back to a place he barely tolerates while navigating fatherhood for the first time. I suspect his frustration has less to do with me and more to do with how powerless he feels, caught at the mercy of forces beyond his control.

"You're doing your best, Jensen. It will take some time, but Caleb will adjust. Keep showing up like you have been, and he'll get there."

He pushes off the wall, stepping toward me. "Thanks for the vote of confidence. Now if only I believed it," he whispers.

I rest my hand on his shoulder, giving him a soft smile. "Don't worry. I'll keep believing for both of us until you do."

"Sorry again for being such an ass—" He pauses as noise drifts from Caleb's bedroom.

We're both quick to move down the hall, and I quietly push the door open a few inches to investigate. Caleb sits on the floor by the bookshelf, flipping through a picture book, his dino nestled in his lap. Jensen moves in behind me, close enough to feel his breath against the nape of my neck.

He leans in and whispers, "He looks happy."

Caleb really does, and I only hope Jensen realizes it's not all because of the decorated room. His happiness comes from Jensen's unwavering devotion since finding out he was a dad. You can see it in the way he looks at his son and his commitment to giving him the best life possible. When all is said and done, no dinosaur wallpaper will make Caleb brave and strong again. It'll be Jensen's strength and courage that will carry them through to better times, even when he questions if he's up to the task.

I meet his eyes over my shoulder. "You're not alone in this. Not anymore."

He studies me, his expression softening. "Thank you, Briar. This wouldn't have been possible without you."

"You don't have to thank me," I reply.

Somehow, I know Caleb and Jensen will find their rhythm.

"One red velvet latte with sugar-free syrup and almond milk, as requested." I slide the cup across the table to my friend Charlie, then slide into the booth across from her with my own coffee and bagel.

She grins. "You're a lifesaver."

After taking a sip, she leans back in her seat, sighing in satisfaction.

"I'm pretty sure you're the only reason Lasso & Latte keeps sugar-free red velvet syrup in stock," I tease.

Charlie shrugs. "As they should. I'm a VIP customer."

She's earned the status.

In high school, we stopped by every morning before class, and as adults, it's still one of our favorite hangout spots. The owner, who has diabetes, made sure that when Charlie was also diagnosed at sixteen, she could still enjoy her go-to drink without worrying about her blood sugar spiking. Though I have it on good authority that she orders it with regular syrup when she comes in alone.

She's always been stubborn. Not even a serious diagnosis can convince her to give up her favorite coffee.

"Okay, spill it. Did Jensen survive the big move, or did he ask for a personal assistant to unpack?" she asks, chuckling at her own joke. "I'm disappointed you didn't text me a play-by-play yesterday."

I normally would have, but after my conversation with Jensen, I spent the afternoon helping Walker check the irrigation system. By the time I got home, it was late; both Jensen and Caleb were asleep. I was too tired to do anything but crash into bed.

"Caleb is a sweetheart," I say fondly. "He's shy, and it could be a while before he speaks again, but I'm confident he'll open up when he's ready."

I think spending time with the animals on the ranch will do him good, and maybe he can even ride one of the ponies eventually. But I'll have to run it by Jensen first. I don't want a repeat of last night, or to upset him by making decisions for Caleb without consulting him.

"What about Jensen?" Charlie's question has me looking up to find her staring at me with an amused expression. "The ladies from the walking club said he's easy on the eyes but wouldn't last a day hauling hay. What do you think? Is he as good-looking in person as he is in the photos?"

Yes.

He looks so different from what I remember as a kid. He's ridiculously hot in business clothes, but there's no question he'd be downright dangerous in Wranglers and a white tee. The last time he wore anything like that, I was too young to appreciate it. There's something about a man who can trade in his designer suit for dusty boots and who has the kind of smile that makes me forget every rule I've made for myself.

I need to get a grip—preferably not on him.

I avert my gaze from Charlie, running my finger along the rim of my coffee mug. "I didn't pay much attention. My focus was on getting him and Caleb settled in."

Charlie snorts. "Right. If Miss McGregor, who can't see two feet in front of her without her inch-thick glasses, noticed how handsome he was passing by in Earl's taxi, you sure as hell could with him under your roof."

My cheeks turn warm, and I scramble to think of a way to explain myself without admitting she's right. It doesn't help that I keep replaying the way his breath grazed against my neck when he stood behind me at the door of Caleb's bedroom. Luckily, I'm spared from answering when Charlie suddenly freezes, her gaze locked on Heath, who's picking up an order from the counter.

She frowns, narrowing her eyes in his direction. "What's *he* doing here? Last time I checked, this was our spot."

I arch a brow. "You do know this is the only coffee shop in town, right?"

"Why can't he go to The Screwy Nut?" she asks like it's a viable solution. "They have a coffee machine and vanilla creamer pods at the back of the store."

I spread cream cheese on my bagel as I answer. "Just to be clear, you want him to go to a *hardware store* to get his coffee so he'll stop coming to Lasso & Latte?"

"It's a brilliant idea, right?" Charlie beams. "Most of the tools in there are small and unpowered. Just like him in bed, according to Beverly Smith."

I scrunch my nose in disgust. "I did not need to know that."

Charlie and Heath have never gotten along, and things have only escalated over the years. Now, I'm stuck dealing with their constant bickering whenever they're in the same room, which I try to keep to a minimum. Unfortunately, it looks like it's unavoidable today.

I take a quick bite of my bagel, bracing myself for the drama brewing between them.

Heath strolls over with his thermos in hand. The shop doesn't allow outside cups, but one flash of his crooked grin and the baristas fall over themselves to fill it. He's broody by default, but turns on the charm when it suits him. Plus, as the owner of a thriving ranch, he could wear a burlap sack and still get any woman he wants—except Charlie.

"Hey, sis, fancy seeing you here," he says, his voice light with amusement. "I spoke with Jensen this morning, and he told me you decorated Caleb's room. That was really nice of you."

I smile. "I'm happy I could do it."

"Thanks again for letting them stay at your place."

I give him a sideways glance. "You didn't exactly give me a choice," I retort.

"Heath doesn't concern himself with how his actions will impact others," Charlie interjects, sending him a sharp look.

He glowers back. "Maybe you should start charging for that

47

unsolicited advice, Charlie. Too bad no one's interested in your greatest hits of passive-aggressive commentary."

"Oh, now you're a wisdom guru?" she asks smugly. "Weren't you the one who got stuck in a fence last week trying to untangle that stubborn pet cow of yours? Not exactly the kind of person I want to take professional advice from, but thanks anyway."

"Petunia isn't my pet," Heath grumbles.

Our friend Birdie is an animal activist. She's not exactly a fan of my family's ranch, since we raise cattle for beef. When she was visiting last year, one of the cows died during labor. She begged Heath not to raise the calf for meat, saying it was too tragic. When she started crying, he caved and agreed to keep it in the barn for a while. Fast-forward a year, and he has a full-grown cow named Petunia. He totally treats her like a pet, but I'm not about to get involved in this debate.

Charlie tilts her head, wearing a self-satisfied grin. "Uh-huh. Because hauling in that fancy hay she likes from two towns over, even though you've got plenty of the regular stuff at the ranch, makes total sense," she says sarcastically.

Heath's eyes flicker with surprise, but his expression is quickly replaced with an unreadable mask. "How the hell do you know about that?" he snaps.

Charlie smirks. "It's shocking how chatty people are when they're browsing my shop. I hear all sorts of things."

"I didn't think you had time for idle gossip," Heath says dryly.

Charlie takes a drink of coffee before responding. "I prefer facts over fiction. Now don't you have a ranch to run or some-thing?" she asks, waving toward the door.

"God, you're insufferable," he mutters.

"Right back at you, *cowboy*." She winks.

Heath tightens his free hand at his side, before glancing in my direction. "Do you want to leave with me? I can barely stand five minutes with this one." He nods toward Charlie who rolls her eyes. "I don't know how you've put up with her all damn morning."

I chuckle. "Thanks for the offer, but after we finish, I have a few errands to run."

My plan is to swing by the hardware store and the grocery store to pick up a few essentials. Jensen was still in his room when I left the cottage this morning, so I didn't get to ask what he might need. Judging by the protein powder, blender bottles, and electrolyte tablets he left on the kitchen counter, I'm betting he eats pretty clean, so I'll make sure to stock up on fresh produce. I also want to make Caleb pancakes soon since it's my specialty. I'm not sure what kind he likes, so I'll make a few different options and let him choose his favorite.

"Okay, but call me if anything comes up," Heath says.

"Does the same go for me?" Charlie asks in a singsong voice.

He shakes his head. "Keep dreamin', sweetheart."

A flicker of hurt flashes in her eyes, but she blinks it away in an instant.

"Knock it off, Heath," I warn. "Charlie might have more patience than you, but don't test her."

Charlie folds her arms, shooting Heath a smirk.

She's perfectly capable of standing her ground, but I can't help stepping in when I catch the smallest crack in her armor. Not when she rarely lets anyone see that side of her.

Heath raises his free hand in mock surrender. "Alright, alright, no need to get your feathers ruffled, sis. I'm heading out. See you later." He tips his hat and heads for the exit.

Once he's left the coffee shop, I turn to Charlie. "Are you ever going to tell me why you dislike my brother so much?"

"Didn't you say you had errands to run?" she asks, dodging my question with an expertise only she can manage.

I glance at my watch, nodding. "You're right. I've only got an hour before I have to be back at the ranch. The guests in cabin four are checking out today, and I have to fix the leaky faucet before Ethel comes. She doesn't like me there when she's cleaning. Apparently, I'm too much of a distraction." I grab a napkin, wiping a few crumbs from my face. "It's not like I can control her sharing all the gossip she's picked up from Earl during their last sleepover."

Ethel's been the housekeeper for the cabins at Silver Saddle Ranch for twenty years. She's always denied that she's in a relationship, but Earl is often seen coming out of her house early in the morning. And any gossip he gets from driving people around is usually circulated by Ethel the next day, so it's safe to assume they're knocking boots most nights.

Charlie sighs. "It's depressing that she has a better sex life than we do."

"Speak for yourself."

She arches a brow. "It's been months since you've gone home with someone after a night at the bar."

"Are you forgetting we live in Bluebell with a population of four thousand? The dating pool isn't exactly overflowing with options."

"You're in luck. The local law firm just brought on a new partner, and I caught a glimpse of him at the bank yesterday. Those blue eyes had every woman in the place ready to risk it all for a five-minute detour into the supply closet."

"If he's such a catch, why don't you date him?" I suggest playfully.

"I wish," Charlie mutters. "Unfortunately, my taste in men is the broody-cowboy type who has a habit of never sticking around long enough to make it worth my while."

"You do have a knack for picking the ones who love the chase but run at the first hint of commitment."

"At least I go out with them more than once," she quips.

"It's not my fault no one can keep my interest for long."

I don't intentionally set out to have one-night stands or leave halfway through a first date. I just prefer not to get invested in someone I can't see a future with. Growing up, I watched my mom waste her time on countless men who weren't good for her. They fueled her addictions, then left her behind after getting what they wanted. I refuse to fall into the same cycle. When I finally commit, it'll be because the person has proven they're worth the effort, willing to make sacrifices for those they love.

"Why not take Daddy Jensen for a ride?" Charlie smirks. "He's hot, emotionally unavailable, and right down the hall. Sounds like the perfect no-strings setup, if you ask me."

"Because I prefer being able to walk around my house without post-hookup tension clinging to the air like Febreze."

"Oh, please." She waves me off, taking another sip of coffee. "Awkwardness builds character and makes for the best stories."

I roll my eyes. "I'll stick to being a good host and not accosting my roommate; the man has enough going on as it is." I glance at my watch again. "I really should get going."

After popping the last bite of my bagel in my mouth, I move around the table to give Charlie a quick hug.

"Have a great day," I say.

"You too. Don't drool over Daddy Jensen too hard," she calls out, her voice carrying enough to turn a few heads.

I lower my gaze, hoping no one notices the warm flush spreading across my cheeks. Charlie's only teasing, and there's no chance I'd ever let my attraction to Jensen interfere with his and Caleb's time here. I'm sure by tomorrow, I'll have moved on and will be busy fantasizing about someone else.

As I step outside, my thoughts drift to Caleb. I wonder how his first day in Bluebell is going. Mama Julie was supposed to give him and Jensen a tour of the school today before the summer program kicks off tomorrow. It's surreal to think they'll both be at the house tonight. After living alone for so long, it'll be an adjustment—but my heart goes out to Jensen and Caleb, and I'll do everything I can to help them feel at home.

CHAPTER 6

Jensen

"ARE YOU SURE CALEB WILL BE OKAY BY HIMSELF?" I ASK.
Julie looks up from the stack of papers she's sifting through. "He's not alone. The two camp counselors outside will keep an eye on him." She walks around her desk to stand next to me at the window. "Caleb's gone through a lot, but he's resilient. It might take him some time to engage with the other kids, but he'll warm up to them eventually. Like the therapist said, if watching them from a distance makes him feel safe, that's perfectly okay."

We're at the elementary school for an open house, and Julie was kind enough to drive us and give us a private tour. She's briefed the camp staff on Caleb's situation, and in the few interactions he's had so far, they've gone out of their way to make him feel at ease and included.

While we were outside earlier, he was intrigued by a group of kids on the playground and stayed put when I asked if he wanted to come to Julie's office with us. Now I've officially entered helicopter parent status—eyes glued to him through the window, ready to swoop in if he needs me.

Caleb remains standing on the edge of the playground but has moved closer to the sandbox where a few kids are playing. I watch as he takes a tentative step forward but then hesitates, pulling back like he's decided against getting closer.

"It's hard not to feel like I'm letting him down by leaving him out there. What if the other kids start bullying him when they find out he doesn't speak?"

Julie gives my arm a reassuring squeeze. "I wouldn't have recommended you move to Bluebell if I didn't believe it was the best place for him. Once he gets into the swing of things and starts meeting with his new therapist, he'll find his footing."

I know she's right, but my instinct is to keep Caleb in a protective bubble, away from anything that could hurt him. Part of me wonders if we should've stayed in New York and hired private tutors and nannies to come to the house so he wouldn't have to socialize. It's not a practical solution, but that hasn't stopped it from crossing my mind.

I sigh. "Why does everything have to be so complex?"

Julie gives me a knowing smile. "Welcome to parenthood, where second-guessing every decision is a full-time job. It doesn't end, even when your kids get older. If anything, it only intensifies."

"Fantastic," I deadpan.

I'm glad I get to spend a lifetime overthinking every decision regarding my son. Exactly what every new parent wants to hear.

"What happens when I make a mistake?"

"Every parent does, more than they'd like to admit, but kids forgive easily. All they want is to feel loved and safe."

"I love Caleb," I state.

More than I thought possible in such a short amount of time.

We have a long summer ahead, but I'm committed to proving he belongs with me long-term. I'll move heaven and earth to make it happen, because now that I have him, there's no way I could ever let him go.

"He's lucky to have you," Julie says with conviction. "We'll get through this, I promise."

Moments like this remind me why I love her and the Halstead family. They were there when my parents gambled away their life savings, and we had to move into the trailer park. Julie converted her sewing room into a bedroom so I could have a peaceful place to study and sleep when my parents' arguments became too chaotic at our place. Even after being gone for fourteen years, the Halsteads still treat me like one of their own, and I'll forever be grateful.

"How was your first night at the cottage?" Julie asks, making me appreciate the change in topic. "It's definitely a fixer-upper. The plan is to renovate the space and turn it into another rental, but Briar is determined to do it herself, and it's taking longer than she'd like. Between the cabins and her volunteer work, she hasn't been able to give it much attention."

"Yeah, she mentioned that yesterday. Sounds like she's got her hands full. But even though it's an older house, she maintains it well." I glance over at Julie, who's listening intently. "She went out of her way to give Caleb's room a makeover to surprise him when we arrived."

Unlike his remodeled room, mine is bare bones with an old twin mattress, a rickety nightstand, and pastel pink wallpaper that appears to be original to the house. I rub my neck, remembering my uncomfortable night on a lumpy mattress. It's a drastic change from the memory foam bed at my penthouse. The grandfather clock in the hallway chimed every fifteen minutes, each one dragging me further from rest.

Even with my lack of sleep, I realize in hindsight that Briar's gesture meant more than I gave her credit for. Last night, I couldn't help but wonder if Caleb would have opened up more if I'd been the one to hang up the wallpaper or install the shelf of books. But now I understand that it's not a competition. The whole reason I came to Bluebell was to have a support system. Not to prove that I can do it all alone. If the past week has taught me anything, it's that I can't.

Julie takes a seat on the edge of her desk. "That sounds like Briar. She has a soft spot for kids, and I'm sure she was just trying to make the change feel less overwhelming for him." I lean against the wall with my arms folded, unwilling to move from the window and lose sight of Caleb. "One thing you'll learn quickly is that it takes a village to raise a child," she says, holding my gaze. "You may want to handle it all yourself, but it's okay to accept help. It doesn't mean you love Caleb any less."

I swipe a hand across my face. "He's still guarded around me, and it threw me off to see how quickly he warmed up to Briar."

The thought's crossed my mind that he might be more at ease with her because she's a woman. His mom raised him, and from what I know, she wasn't in a serious relationship during the past five years. It makes sense he'd be wary of me, but that doesn't make it sting any less.

"I'm afraid he'll decide he doesn't want me as his dad and beg not to stay with me after the summer." It's my biggest fear.

Julie's mouth curves into an amused smile. "Jensen, he's five. Only a week ago, you were strangers. Besides, even if he didn't want you—tough luck. You're the only dad he's got, and that's a permanent deal."

I like the sound of that last part.

When I look out the window again, Caleb is sitting at the edge of the sandbox, his fingers tracing patterns in the sand while he observes the other kids building a giant mound using their buckets.

"All I want is for him to be happy," I say to Julie.

When I glance over, she's grinning. "And that's how I know the two of you will be just fine."

She has more confidence in me than I have in myself.

"Have you thought about who is going to look after Caleb in the afternoons? I wish I could take him, but starting tomorrow, I'll be at the school until four on weekdays."

"I haven't. My priority was getting here and making sure we got settled in. If I have to take more time off until I figure it out, I will."

I'll have to return to work sooner rather than later, though. With a new product launching soon, I'll be heavily involved in the final stages of development. Fortunately, being the boss means I can oversee things remotely until we head back to New York at the end of the summer. In the meantime, Carlton, my chief operations officer, will manage any in-person meetings while I'm away.

"There's a daycare on Main Street that offers pickups from the summer program. I'm friends with the owner if you'd like me to put in a good word," Julie offers.

I wince at the idea of leaving Caleb in another strange environment with unfamiliar faces and limited staff to give him the patience and attention he deserves.

"At the school, I know he's in good hands because you're here," I say, gesturing around us. "I can't say the same for a daycare I don't know or trust."

"Don't worry, we'll find another option," she promises me. "It might just take a while since most Bluebell residents work full-time, so finding a nanny or babysitter could be challenging."

That's one perk of living in the city—there's no shortage of nannies, and finding someone with a flexible schedule is a breeze. My assistant had a baby last year and told me how lucky she was with all the options available when searching for childcare.

Julie clasps her hands together, an idea sparking in her eyes. "What about Briar? She's usually finished with cabin repairs by early afternoon, and I'm sure Heath could give her a break from helping around the ranch."

I instantly shake my head. "I couldn't ask her to do that."

She probably isn't inclined to do me any favors after my initial reaction to her thoughtful gesture last night. Yes, I was quick to apologize, but that doesn't undo the fact that I got upset when she was only trying to help. I might be a family friend, but that doesn't mean she owes me anything. Besides, she already has more than enough on her plate without me asking her to drop everything to take care of Caleb.

Julie rises and joins me at the window again, smiling as she looks out at Caleb. "Don't overthink it. Just an option to keep in mind."

I loop my arm around her shoulders, drawing her into a side hug. "I'd be lost without you."

"We're all here for you, Jensen."

"Thank you."

I can't imagine where Caleb and I would be without the Halsteads.

Julie drove Caleb and me to the ranch after the open house, music playing through the speakers. Caleb stayed quiet in the back seat, but I noticed him in the rearview mirror tapping his fingers along his dinosaur's stomach, keeping in time with the rhythm. I'll have to try out different types of music to see if he has a similar reaction.

When we pull up to Briar's place, I get out of the car and help Caleb out.

"Thanks for the ride, Julie."

"Anytime. Enjoy the rest of your day," she calls through the window. "Once you're settled, I want you to join us for dinner at the ranch house."

"We'll swing by later this week." I want to give Caleb a few days to acclimate to school before adding anything else to our routine. "See you tomorrow."

"You bet." Julie waves at Caleb as she pulls down the road.

She'll drive us to the school in the morning for Caleb's official first day. Heath will bring me back to the ranch on his way home from picking up supplies in town. The truck he's letting me borrow is still in the shop but should be ready soon. It'll be nice to have the freedom to come and go without relying on others to drive us around.

We're halfway to the front porch when I hear a high-pitched bleating noise coming from behind the house. I didn't think Briar kept any animals at the cottage, so I have no idea what it could be. When we hear the sound again, Caleb's eyes dart between me and the backyard.

"I wonder what that is. Should we go check it out, buddy?" I ask.

Julie suggested that I explain things to Caleb before acting so he has a chance to react if it's not something he wants to do.

Caleb fidgets with the hem of his shirt, his other hand clutching his stuffed animal. It comes with us everywhere. Julie made a special cubby for it in her office today, and once she told Caleb that dinosaurs have to go to school too, he accepted the idea of leaving it with her for a few hours each day.

He hugs the dino against his chest, letting out a shaky breath before taking a few tentative steps toward the backyard. I follow his lead, inching along the side of the house, the noise getting louder.

We round the corner and find Briar crouched beside a baby goat, holding a bottle to its mouth as it kicks its legs and head-butts at the nipple.

"Really? All this drama for milk?" she scolds, shaking her head. "I'm just trying to feed you."

The goat bleats again in protest, stomping its tiny hooves.

My pulse kicks up as I take in Briar—a white-and-pink floral shirt tucked into her tight blue jeans, paired with a white cowboy hat and worn boots. She's the type of beautiful that doesn't ask for attention, but demands it. She's trouble wrapped in denim and sass, and I'd be smart to keep my distance. I have enough going on without lusting after a woman I have no business ogling—especially with jealousy gnawing at me when my son looks at her like she strung up the stars just for him.

"Looks like he's giving you a run for your money," I note with a smirk.

Briar's head snaps in my direction, her brows raised as if daring me to say more.

"You try wrangling this little guy. He's as stubborn as a mule." She adjusts her hold on the squirming goat.

When Briar spots Caleb next to me, her expression softens; a genuine smile spreading across her face.

"Thank goodness you're here," she exclaims. "Our friend here arrived an hour ago and still won't take his bottle." She tugs it away from the goat to stop him from knocking it out of her hand. "Would you mind helping me?" she asks Caleb.

His eyes widen as he looks between us, lingering on the baby goat. He shifts his weight, then lets out a soft exhale as if building up the courage to say yes.

Briar releases the goat from her hold, and it springs into action, racing around, its hooves pounding the dirt. The little ball of energy is a blur of black-and-white fur, weaving in and out of Briar's legs like it's an obstacle course.

It hadn't paid Caleb or me any attention before now, but suddenly, its gaze locks on me. Without warning, it stiffens, its legs rigid as it collapses to the ground with a dramatic flop that leaves us frozen in disbelief. Panic flickers in my chest. What if something's seriously wrong with the goat? How am I supposed to explain that to Caleb after he witnessed the whole thing?

I frown when Briar bursts out laughing, holding the bottle to her chest.

I'm about to argue that this isn't funny when the goat twitches, lets out a snort, and springs to its feet like it didn't just scare years off my life.

I roll my eyes. "You've got to be kidding me."

The goat turns its head toward me, letting out a soft bleat before dropping to the ground again, toppling over like a tipped statue.

"Guess we have a fainting goat on our hands. Clearly, he's not your biggest fan, Jensen," Briar says, shooting me a teasing grin before leaning over to stroke its side.

I'm unsure whether to be offended or amused that the goat has pegged me as some kind of danger, thinking playing dead is its best defense.

When it pops back up again, I stay quiet, not wanting to scare Caleb any more than I'm sure he already is. But instead of reacting with fear, he bursts into a fit of giggles, the sound growing louder when the goat trots over and bumps him in the leg. It's the first time I've heard him laugh, and it's music to my ears.

The goat stretches its neck to investigate the dinosaur that Caleb holds loosely at his side, rubbing its nose against his pant leg.

"When were you going to tell me you were a goat whisperer?" Briar winks at him. "Maybe he'll let you feed him. Want to try?"

Caleb's head bobs up and down as he sets his dinosaur on the ground before going to sit beside her, cross-legged.

"Great."

Briar guides his hands around the bottle. Together, they offer it to the goat, who nudges it curiously before finally latching onto the nipple and taking a few eager gulps. Briar slowly moves her hands away, letting Caleb feed it by himself.

She shakes her head in amazement. "Looks like you've got the magic touch, Caleb."

He grins, his cheeks flushed with pride as he holds the bottle steady. His unguarded reaction makes me second-guess my initial reluctance to accept Briar's efforts to help him feel at home. It still stings that he gravitates toward her, but I can't deny she's getting through to him in a way I haven't yet.

"Pretty sure you didn't have a goat yesterday," I say to her. "Was he an impulse buy, and if so, is there a return policy?"

She chuckles. "I'm afraid not. My friend Birdie owns an animal sanctuary and found this little guy abandoned by the railroad tracks this afternoon." She stands up, brushing off her pants. "She's busy with a litter of kittens and a lamb that requires frequent feedings, so she asked me to foster him."

I grunt, folding my arms across my chest. "Does this friend often ask you to take in strays?"

"Only when she's got her hands full."

"Do you ever tell her no?"

"Not usually." Briar shrugs. "I guess that means I'm a pushover, right? After all, I did agree to let you stay too, didn't I?" She leans over to nudge me playfully.

"To be fair, I don't chew on shoes or headbutt furniture."

Briar bites her lip, trying—and failing—to hide her laugh. "Was that a joke? I thought stoicism came with a no-humor policy."

"Even brooding types have layers." I look away, hiding the smirk tugging at my lips. "Like onions. Or emotionally repressed ogres."

The only movie Caleb has shown the slightest interest in is *Shrek*. It played on a loop for days, and all I got out of it was a head full of quotes and a kid who still wouldn't say a word.

Briar narrows her eyes in mock suspicion. "Careful. That was dangerously close to a dad joke. Next thing you know, you'll be wearing white sneakers and khaki shorts."

I roll my eyes, pretending to be offended. "Hey, white sneakers are timeless."

She laughs, shaking her head. "Just promise no cargo shorts, please."

"Fine, but I can't guarantee I won't wear socks with sandals," I tease.

The more I talk with Briar, the more I enjoy her company. She has a way of making even a mundane conversation interesting. Although part of it could be due to the fact that most of my adult conversations up until now have been centered around client meetings, stocks, and profit margins.

The goat has finished its bottle and is now resting its head on Caleb's lap, nibbling on his shirt.

"Since our friend will be sticking around for a while, we should give him a name. What do you think, Caleb?" Briar asks.

He nods as he pets the goat's head.

Briar flashes him a grin. "Great minds think alike."

She's unbothered by his silence and has found her own ways to connect with him. Watching them interact makes me feel more like an outsider than a dad. I'm doing my best to be patient, but it's hard when Caleb doesn't show me the same warmth and affection he's shown Briar, or even Julie during their brief interactions today.

"What do you think of Reginald?" Briar suggests.

Caleb scrunches his nose, shaking his head.

"No stuffy names. Got it." She taps her chin, her brow furrowed slightly. "How about something playful like Buster?"

He hesitates for a beat, mulling it over before shrugging.

Briar lets out a teasing sigh. "Not easily impressed, are you? How about Jensen? It's got a nice ring to it, don't you think?"

Caleb glances at me, his lips lifting in amusement at her suggestion.

The goat, still settled in his lap, bumps his arm as soon as he stops petting it, clearly wanting more attention.

"The only catch is that it might faint whenever it hears its name. Or imagine calling for the goat, and your dad comes running instead," Briar says.

Caleb giggles, his laughter bubbling up again at the absurdity.

I can't be upset at Briar for teasing me when it comes with the bonus of hearing my son laugh twice in the span of a few minutes.

"Hmm... what about Ziggy?" Briar asks.

Caleb tips his head, considering the name before giving us a thumbs-up.

Briar lets out an exaggerated breath, wiping her brow with a flourish. "Phew! I was afraid you wouldn't like that one. It's my favorite too, but Jensen was a strong contender," she says with a wink in my direction before leaning down to pat the goat. "Welcome home, Ziggy."

One thing is certain—Julie was right. Between the way Caleb lights up around Briar, how naturally she connects with him, and the fact that we're living under the same roof, she'd be the ideal person to be his nanny. And frankly, the only person aside from Julie that I trust right now to leave him with, even for a few hours. Now I just have to hope she agrees.

CHAPTER 7

Briar

I T TURNS OUT THAT SAYING YES TO BRINGING ZIGGY HOME was the right decision. I almost told Birdie no when she called in a panic on my way home earlier, since I wasn't sure how Jensen would feel about a goat running around. But when she started to beg, and her voice wavered as she fought back tears, I caved. She has the biggest heart, and when she's fighting for something small and helpless, it's impossible not to rally behind her.

Jensen and I are on the back porch watching Caleb and Ziggy play in the grass. Mostly, Ziggy keeps gently headbutting Caleb's shins while he laughs like it's the best game ever. Judging by the stunned look on Jensen's face, this is the happiest he's seen him.

"Thanks for introducing Caleb to Ziggy," he finally says, breaking the silence. "Who would've guessed a baby goat could get him to open up like this?" He motions to Caleb, kneeling on the ground as Ziggy climbs into his lap.

"It's good to see him easing into things," I say with a smile.

"Today's the first time I've heard him laugh," Jensen whispers, his gaze fixed on the ground.

I place a hand on his arm, waiting until his eyes find mine. "It's beautiful."

My heart aches for him. One minute, he was a bachelor, running a successful tech empire, and the next, he's raising a son he didn't know existed until a couple of weeks ago. He's at the mercy of circumstances he never saw coming and has been forced to figure things out as he goes.

Jensen's eyes flicker to my hand resting on his forearm, lingering for a beat before meeting mine with something unguarded and intense, sending heat to my cheeks. I ease my hand back, praying he didn't notice my reluctance to let go.

I clear my throat, forcing a casual tone. "How did the open house go?"

He leans back, bracing his palms against the concrete. "Fine. He didn't engage much with the other kids, but Julie thinks he'll come around."

"What do you think?"

I shift to face him, drawing my legs to my chest and resting my head on my knee while waiting for his reply. Jensen's face tightens, and just when I wonder if I've overstepped, he answers.

"It's tempting to shield Caleb from every challenge, but I know it won't benefit him in the long run. After talking with his therapist and from what I've observed myself, I think the most growth will happen when he's able to step outside his comfort zone and learn to trust again. Right now, everything around him is strange and unfamiliar, but I'm hopeful that he has the resilience to overcome the painful adjustment and can start his healing journey." He glances across the yard where Caleb grins as he pets Ziggy, now curled up in his lap. "It won't be easy to stand on the sidelines and let him spend hours at camp, but having Julie around if he needs anything makes it more manageable."

I'm not surprised by his sentiment. Julie has been a haven for so many kids in Bluebell—Jensen and me included. She's my inspiration for wanting to create a nonprofit where I can provide a safe, healing space for kids, including those with emotional scars.

I've offered a few pop-up events that have been at capacity, but the long-term vision is to offer seasonal camps and year-round therapeutic horseback riding at the ranch to help kids build trust, self-assurance, and learn emotional regulation. There's a vacant stretch of land near the cow pastures that Heath offered for the center I want to build on. But I'm holding off until I can fund the project myself. It's important that I prove I can do it on my own.

Given my mom's history of taking advantage of people in this town, the last thing I want is to be seen as someone coasting on the Halsteads' name or looking for handouts. This is why I live in the cottage in exchange for making improvements, save every penny I make from managing the cabins, and help out around the ranch.

Jensen pushes up from his hands, shifting forward, rubbing them together before folding his arms. "Listen, I have a proposition for you, and I want you to hear me out before you answer."

I sit up straight, resting my hands on my knees. "Intriguing. Do go on."

"I've been on leave since I learned about Caleb, but I can't put work off much longer. The plan is to work remotely from the cottage, which means I'll need someone to watch him in the afternoons once camp lets out at noon."

"Is this the part where you offer me a job I didn't apply for?" I say, though I'm only half joking.

Jensen runs a hand through his hair, looking uneasy. "I am," he admits. "Julie suggested you as a possibility and said Heath could probably spare you for the summer if you're open to it," he adds quickly.

"What about the daycare on Main Street? Mama Julie's friend runs it, and I bet she'd make room for Caleb."

He shakes his head. "I'm not comfortable leaving Caleb with someone who may not be sympathetic to his situation," he explains.

I bite down on my bottom lip, conflicted. "I appreciate you thinking of me, but I'm not sure that's a good idea."

It could be my imagination, but I swear Jensen's expression falters with disappointment. "Do you mind me asking what's holding you back? Is it the pay? I'll match what I'd offer someone in New York, so you don't have to worry about that."

I shake my head. "It's not about the money."

Heath pays me more than he should to manage the cabins and lend a hand around the ranch. Thanks to his generosity, within a couple of years, I should have enough to break ground on the first building of my children's sanctuary.

"What's your hesitation, then?" he questions.

"For starters, I've never been a nanny before. Sure, I've baby-sat, but the stakes were never this high."

Offering comfort to a grieving child in small doses is familiar territory, but stepping into a role where I'm partly responsible for their care is daunting. I know I'm capable, especially with my experience working with a local nonprofit that helps young children who've been through trauma, and have hosted several camps for kids at the ranch, but it's different with Caleb.

It's one thing to be with him under Jensen's watchful eye. It's another to be the person entrusted with his son's well-being when he's not around. Caleb's been through so much already and is the sweetest little boy. I would never forgive myself if I let him down.

Jensen's brows knit together, a subtle crease forming as if he's puzzled by my response.

"Don't sell yourself short, Briar. You're more than qualified in the ways that matter most. You can't fake the compassion and empathy you've shown Caleb," he says in earnest. "He doesn't need perfection. Hell, I'm far from it myself. But he does deserve someone who shows up every day and won't give up on him. And I'm convinced that person is you."

I blink at him, unsure if I heard him right. After admitting I lack the experience I figured he wanted, I expected him to dismiss the idea of me being Caleb's nanny. Not try to talk me into it like it's the only option that makes sense.

"I appreciate the vote of confidence, but I have to admit I'm not used to being on this side of a pep talk," I say with a chuckle.

Usually, I'm the one offering words of encouragement, not the one quietly soaking them up.

"I better keep going until I convince you that you're the right person for the job," Jensen states with a smile, undeterred from his mission at hand. "What are your other reservations?"

I hesitate, nibbling on my lower lip. "My schedule is pretty full. After I do my rounds at the cabins in the morning, I have a few ranch duties in the afternoons."

My plan for the summer had been simple: save every penny I could for my center and spend long hours renovating the cottage. I've only managed to tackle one or two projects every few months, and I was hoping to make real progress before the fall. But suddenly, that feels almost trivial compared to helping Caleb.

Jensen tilts his head, watching me carefully before answering. "I'd take Caleb to camp in the mornings and relieve you in the early evenings after work. And like I said earlier, Julie mentioned that Heath would understand if you couldn't help him in the afternoons for a while."

There's a hint of vulnerability in Jensen's eyes, something I assume is rare for someone used to getting his way. I'm sure he doesn't hear the word no often, especially with all the power and influence he must wield.

"You're sure you don't want to explore other options?"

He shakes his head, taking my hands in his. "I mean it when I say there's no one better suited to be Caleb's nanny. He deserves the best, and that's you." His gaze holds mine as butterflies stir in my belly. "I'll beg if that's what it takes."

My attention drifts to our hands clasped together, and the

undeniable chemistry simmering between us. The warmth of his touch is like a soothing balm, distracting me from staying focused on our conversation.

"I'm not asking for me," Jensen whispers when I don't respond. "This is for Caleb."

Damn him.

Of course he'd say the one thing guaranteed to make the rest of my resolve crumble. Saying no to someone who needs my help has never been my strong suit, especially not when it's a child who's already lost so much. That's why I'm one breath away from giving in, even if it means adjusting my summer plans and opening up my heart to a little boy who'll be gone by the end of summer. Because the idea of handing him off to someone else feels like an abandonment, and I don't think I can do that.

"If I'm going to be Caleb's nanny, I expect room to make judgment calls," I explain. "I'll always keep you in the loop, but I need you to trust that I have his best interests at heart, too."

Jensen moves one hand to his jaw, brushing his thumb against his scruff. "Of course, I trust you. I'll want regular check-ins when you're not at the cottage, but I'll do my best to step back and give you the freedom to make decisions."

The honesty in his voice is sincere, and I believe he's willing to make a real effort, even if giving up control doesn't seem to come naturally to him.

With his other hand still wrapped around mine, he gives it a gentle squeeze. "So does that mean you'll do it?"

I smile. "Yes, I'll be Caleb's nanny."

Relief washes over his face, the tension easing from his shoulders. "That's exactly what I was hoping you'd say. Caleb's going to be so happy when I share the news."

At that moment, my doubts fade away, replaced by a calm certainty that this is the right decision for all of us. Now if only I could ignore the way my stomach flips every time Jensen touches me.

CHAPTER 8

Briar

I'M UP BY SUNRISE TO CHANGE THE AIR-CONDITIONING filters in two cabins ahead of new guests arriving today. The last thing I want is for them to walk into a stuffy cabin and complain. I also finished setting up Ziggy's space in the old shed in the backyard, with fresh hay and a water trough. He's adjusting well, and after watching him and Caleb play together so well the past few days, I think having him around will be good for them both.

It's nearly one in the afternoon when I get back to the cottage. Jensen brought Caleb home after summer camp, wanting to ease him into the new routine with me as his nanny. When I get inside, I find Jensen pacing in the entryway, his hands clasped behind his back. There's a deep crease between his brows, and tension is etched in the rigid line of his jaw. He whips his head in my direction when I close the door.

"Are you okay?" I ask.

"Peachy," he replies curtly.

I raise a brow, resting my hand on my hip. "Really? Because

you're giving off more of a squeezed-lemon-left-out-in-the-heat vibe."

"Real cute. Should I expect a full medical report, or are you still working on a diagnosis?" he asks, trying to hide a smirk tugging at the corner of his mouth despite the tension in his jaw.

Julie called me earlier to warn me he might be on edge. He's spent the past three mornings hovering in her office during camp, convinced Caleb might need him. She told him he has to drop Caleb off tomorrow like every other parent. No exceptions. I'm guessing he's panicking about it, which is why I'm already thinking of ways to make the transition to me watching Caleb easier, so it's one less thing he has to stress about. It's like taming a wild colt—you don't win by brute force but by showing patience and persistence.

"Where's Caleb?" I ask.

"In his room, coloring a picture of a Triceratops they gave out at summer camp."

Someone brought a kid-sized activity table to Charlie's shop, and she set it aside for Caleb. I picked it up yesterday, stocked it with a bin of craft supplies, and now he has his own mini art station.

Jensen lingers by the front door, watching as I settle onto the bench and tug off my boots. I press into a spot on my right foot, wincing when I hit a tender spot that's been aching since this morning.

"You're in pain," Jensen observes.

I wave it off. "It's nothing."

He raises an eyebrow. "I spent my fair share of time wearing boots back in the day. I've never forgotten that working in them is its own kind of punishment."

I'm stunned when he lowers himself in front of me and takes my foot in his large hands. He removes my sock and gently cradles it.

"What are you—" My question is cut off by a low moan slipping out as his thumbs work into the sore spot, kneading the area, easing the tension bit by bit.

"Aren't you the one who tells everyone they don't have to do everything on their own?" he replies with a pointed look. "You've got a long afternoon with Caleb, so why not let me help lessen your pain before you have to get back on your feet?"

I fully intend to tell him it's not necessary, but the soothing pressure I'm experiencing has other plans. The pain begins to melt away under his touch, replaced by a calming relief that spreads like liquid warmth. My head falls back against the wall, and I bite my bottom lip to keep from groaning as he lifts my other foot, taking off my other sock and giving it the same attention as the first.

Jensen glances up at me, his green eyes low and heavy-lidded. Every touch lingers a little longer than his last, sending a slow-burning heat straight through me.

"Does that feel good?" he asks, his voice husky.

"Mm-hmm." I swallow hard as he curls his fingers around the arch of my foot, kneading a knot I hadn't realized was there until now. "Would it be alright if I took Caleb to the ranch house today? Mama Julie's got a playroom full of games and crafts, and I figured he would have fun feeding the chickens." I have to concentrate hard to keep my thoughts focused. "The dining room table has a clear line of vision into the playroom and outside. You're welcome to work from there this afternoon if you want."

Jensen is silent as he mulls over my proposal, never stopping his thumb's slow, deliberate movements.

My suggestion is one way I can soothe his concerns about Caleb and show him that stepping back doesn't mean letting go. It's a step toward balance that I hope he'll accept, but this has to be his choice.

After a minute, he nods. "Yeah, that works. Heath texted

earlier to say the truck he's lending me is ready. He's bringing it back this afternoon, so I'll meet him at the ranch house."

"Sounds like a plan."

Jensen's hands have stopped moving, but his fingers linger on my foot. His gaze meets mine, and for a moment, neither of us moves.

"Thanks for the massage," I say, my voice quieter than I intended.

His lips lift into a faint grin. "Anytime." He brushes his thumb over my ankle one last time before gently setting my foot down. "We should go get Caleb so we can head out."

I nod, tucking a piece of hair behind my ear. "Good idea."

I'm quick to stand and hurry toward the stairs, my pounding pulse revealing my body's response to his touch. It was just a foot massage. There's no reason for me to be flustered. He was only being nice, and I'm obviously turning it into something it's not.

I'm relieved when we get to Caleb's room, grateful for the shift in focus. He's hunched over the craft table in the corner, coloring a picture.

He pauses, glancing over to give us a small smile.

"Hey, little man." I crouch to his level and give his hair a tousle. "How'd you like to lend me a hand on the ranch today? I have to feed the chickens, and I could use a second set of hands."

He picks at the crinkled paper around the blue crayon he's holding, his eyes darting around the room until they land on Jensen.

"You can go if you'd like," Jensen says gently.

Caleb sets his crayon down and grabs his stuffie off the floor. He holds it tight, rubbing the belly as he considers his options. I wait patiently, giving him the space to process. He doesn't have much control over his life right now, so it's important to let him make choices in the areas where he can.

After a few seconds, he draws a deep breath and nods.

I grin, clapping my hands together. "Great. Your dad will ride with us to the ranch house and will be inside if we need anything."

I can't tell if that reassures Caleb or not. He's still adjusting to being around new people, and I wish I had a better read on what he's thinking—or what might help him feel more comfortable. I'm sure Jensen wishes the same thing.

After I change my clothes and Jensen collects his laptop, we all pile into my Jeep. He's already installed a booster seat for Caleb, so I'll have it ready whenever we go out when I'm watching him.

As we pull out onto the road leading to the ranch, Jensen points at the dashboard where more than fifty rubber ducks are scattered across the surface in a sea of yellow. "That's quite the collection. Do they judge your driving? I feel like that one's been side-eyeing me since I got in." He motions to the pirate duck with an eye patch.

"Oh, him? That's Captain Quackbeard. He's just protective. You're lucky he hasn't made you walk the plank yet," I tease as I pull onto the gravel road leading to the ranch house.

When Caleb giggles from the back seat, Jensen's smile is instantaneous; it softens his sharp features and takes the edge off his usual cool demeanor. It makes me want to find more ways to make Caleb laugh, hoping it'll help Jensen drop the walls he hides behind.

"The others are excellent copilots," I add, maintaining a straight face.

"Where'd they all come from?" Jensen asks.

"I got the first few from Tinker Toys, a toy shop in town. My friends thought it would be funny to gift me ones I didn't have yet, and it snowballed from there. Now, I have my own rubber duck empire." I motion to the dashboard of ducks.

One by the steering wheel is rocking a red polka-dot swimsuit, another's geared up for scuba diving with a tiny snorkel, and my favorite has gone full cowgirl with a pink bandana, hat, and sunglasses. Charlie got me that one from an airport gift shop in Texas, saying my collection wouldn't be complete without it.

The *Frozen* soundtrack plays as we drive. One of my friends, Wren, told me that her daughter Lottie listens to it on repeat, so I figured Caleb might enjoy it since they're close to the same age. When I glance in the rearview mirror, my breath catches when I find him mouthing the lyrics like it's second nature, his eyes fixed out the window.

I tap Jensen's arm, nodding toward the back seat. He looks back, blinking rapidly before his lips curl into a faint smile. There's something special about observing him as he watches his son slowly come out of his shell. It's a gradual process, but every little moment is a victory to celebrate.

He turns to me, mouthing the words "thank you."

I tip my hat in response as a silent "you're welcome."

When we pull up to the ranch house, the driveway is empty. This makes sense, given that Mama Julie is still at the school, Walker and Heath are running errands in town, and Pops is probably out feeding the livestock. Once I've parked, I check my phone, noticing several missed text messages.

Backroads & Bad Decisions Group Chat

> **Birdie: Briar, is it true you're nannying for Jensen Harding?**

> **Charlie: Briar Elise Halstead, I thought we didn't keep secrets from each other.**

> **Charlie: Besides, I thought you weren't into him?!**

> **Briar: I'm not.**

I bite my lower lip, thankful she can't read my expression.

> **Charlie: Uh-huh.**

> Briar: I agreed to do it for Caleb.

Charlie: Sure, and I'm the Queen of England.

> Briar: Who told you guys? I just started today.

Literally five minutes ago, if we're being technical.

Birdie: Apparently, Julie told Ethel, who shared it with Gladys from the walking club, and now all of Bluebell knows you're watching Caleb in the afternoons.

Wren: Sometimes I forget how quickly gossip spreads in a small town.

The four of us have been best friends since kindergarten and were inseparable through high school. I figured we'd all stay in Bluebell forever until Wren dropped the bombshell that she was moving to Florida with Cole, her boyfriend. I've never been a fan of his, but after they had their daughter, Lottie, I knew she wasn't coming back. At least our group chat keeps her in the loop on all the town gossip.

Charlie: The rumor mill has one thing right.

Wren: What's that?

Charlie: Jensen is hot AND single.

I hate it when she's right.

Birdie: Did you forget he's eight years older?

Charlie: Older men = more experience.

Charlie: Picture this. Having sex with a guy who treats minute five like a warm-up.

Charlie: Mind. Blown.

Most of the guys I've been with are my age, but she might be onto something. Having a man who knows how to take charge and has experience pleasing a woman is a tempting upgrade.

Birdie: I think I missed a chapter because when did you hook up with an older guy??

Charlie: It was field research. No one from town.

Birdie: Yet you kept it a secret. You know I have to live vicariously through you. *unamused face emoji

Wren: Do I have to book a flight to Bluebell so I can referee you two?

Charlie: Yes, you do. We might dissolve into total chaos without you.

Wren: Now you sound like Lottie when she's trying to talk me into letting her have a second cupcake before dinner.

Charlie: You should let her. Cupcakes are practically a food group.

Charlie: Sugar Pine Bakery's new red velvet ones are sinful. I had one yesterday.

Birdie: Didn't the doctor say you should cut back on sugar?

Charlie: Yes, Mom.

I chuckle. That girl lives by her own rules.

> Briar: As entertaining as this is, duty calls.

> Charlie: Try not to swoon too hard over Mr. Tall, Dark, and Daddy.

I let out an ungraceful snort, followed by a burst of laughter. "What's so funny?"

I snap my head up, meeting Jensen's curious glance from the passenger seat. My face flushes, warmth spreading over my cheeks when I realize he's been waiting for me to get out of the Jeep.

"Oh, nothing. Just something my friend Charlie said." I really hope he didn't catch a glimpse of my group chat, particularly not the last message. "We should go inside."

I hop out of the vehicle and stand nearby while Jensen helps Caleb out of his booster seat. I notice Caleb has left his stuffie in the Jeep. I'm not sure if it was on purpose or if he just forgot about it, so I don't mention it. We can swing back and grab it if he asks for it later. But right now, I'm taking it as a small sign that he's learning to be without it.

For the most part, Jensen left Caleb and me to our own devices this afternoon, though I did spot him peeking into the craft room between his calls, where we were painting rocks to put in the garden.

The real problem was me. I couldn't resist sneaking a glance at him every few minutes. His hair was tousled from running his hand through it, and he had on jeans and a crisp white button-up shirt. What really did me in was when he put on a pair of black-rimmed glasses. They gave him an irresistible edge, blending intelligence with a rugged appeal.

I never thought I'd be someone who'd swoon over a man in

glasses. Then Jensen showed up looking like a sexy nerd wrapped in sin. The stacks of parenting books scattered around the cottage only make him more irresistible. I've caught him several times this week with his nose buried in a book and scribbling notes as he reads.

He might not have experience as a parent, but he's determined to learn everything he can to be the best dad possible. It's just one of the many reasons he has me mesmerized. He loves Caleb and fiercely protects him at all costs. Not to mention the way he rakes his hand through his hair when he's deep in thought or his early runs at dawn, muscles flexing with every step. I can't resist watching him from the kitchen window every morning as I make breakfast, but it's hardly my fault it has a prime view of his workout route.

Even the way he massaged my feet earlier was addicting—his intense gaze locked on mine the whole time. It's too bad he's off-limits. The last thing he needs is any distractions from the reason he came to Bluebell.

I finally suggested to Caleb that we explore outside while our rocks dry, so I'd have some space to clear my head.

We've just returned from a walk by the pond when Caleb's attention shifts at the sound of a high-pitched whinny drifting from the pastures.

"Must be feeding time for the horses," I say.

His face lights up, and he stands on tiptoe to get a better view of the horses grazing in the field.

I'll have to ask Jensen if he's okay with Caleb riding soon. I doubt he'll object, especially if he's there to supervise and Caleb is as excited about the prospect as he seems.

I text Cooper to see if he can fit in a lesson for Caleb in the next few weeks. He owns a private security firm that employs vets as bodyguards for high-profile clients. In his free time, he trains the horses at Silver Saddle Ranch and occasionally offers riding lessons. He and Heath have been friends for years. They met when Cooper moved to Bluebell after serving in the military. He was searching for peace and purpose, and the horses gave him both. He's been the biggest supporter of my nonprofit and has already agreed to volunteer twice a week to teach kids how to ride once we're up and running.

"Why don't we go feed the chickens now?" I suggest.

My mouth falls open when Caleb slips his hand into mine. It's a simple act, yet his trust in me feels significant. I gently squeeze his hand as we walk toward the chicken coops, glancing over my shoulder when I sense someone is watching.

Jensen stands at the dining room window, his eyes fixed on my hand clasped with Caleb's.

I crouch beside Caleb and nod toward the house. "We should say hi to your dad. How about we give him a wave? I'm sure it'll make his day."

Caleb stands a little taller as he turns toward the house and flashes an enthusiastic thumbs-up, his grin stretching from ear to ear. Jensen's shoulders relax, his eyes softening as he waves. My chest tightens at witnessing the sweet exchange. It's a reminder that love can grow one small gesture at a time.

When Caleb looks toward the chicken coops at the sound of clucking, Jensen takes the opportunity to mouth, "thank you" in my direction.

I respond with a smile and a silent "you're welcome."

I mean it. Nothing is more rewarding than seeing the bond between father and son begin to blossom. I may not be able to hurry it along, but being part of the process feels like magic.

CHAPTER 9

Jensen

A Few Moments Earlier

I WATCH BRIAR AND CALEB WALK ACROSS THE FRONT YARD from the dining room window. Briar's talking, her hands moving fluidly through the air as she tells what must be an animated story. Caleb stays by her side, hanging on her every word.

A pang of longing hits me square in the chest when Briar lowers her hand, and Caleb puts his hand in hers. She smiles down at him, giving his hand a tight squeeze. They've only spent one afternoon alone together, and he's already reaching for her.

It's not Briar I'm frustrated with. It's me. I'm disappointed in myself for not knowing how to bridge the gap between me and my own son. For choosing a career that takes me away from him during such a critical time. I'm even doubting if I'm cut out to be his father.

I hated my parents growing up, and while the circumstances couldn't be more different, I still worry Caleb will eventually feel the same way—blaming me for not doing more to be a part of his life when he was younger and then taking him from his home.

Briar looks my way before crouching beside Caleb and saying something I can't decipher. Seconds later, Caleb turns to face me with a megawatt grin, throwing me a thumbs-up. I wave back, my throat tightening as I rub my chest. My earlier doubts fall away as I take in the rare bit of affection he offers me.

It has everything to do with Briar and her gift for drawing him out of his shell. Asking her to be his nanny was the best decision I could've made. She's as invested in his progress as I am, and with her help, I think we'll be okay.

It has me thinking about how to make the most of the time I *do* have with Caleb and be more attentive when we're together. Letting myself stew won't solve anything. That's why I've made early morning runs around the cottage a priority. The calm of watching the sunrise and the open fields helps clear my mind, so I can be fully present for Caleb once he's awake.

Though I never intended to come back to Bluebell, I can't deny I missed ranch life—riding horses, spending Saturdays patching up fences, and practicing my cattle-roping skills. I want him to get a taste of that world, even if it's only for a fleeting summer.

When his gaze shifts away from me, I mouth a "thank you" to Briar, who immediately replies with a quick, "You're welcome."

I watch as she guides Caleb along the paved path that disappears behind the fenced-in chicken coops on the other side of the yard. It's amazing how naturally my guard has come down around her.

Her cheery disposition and big heart are what draws people in, and Caleb is no exception, judging by how quickly he's taken to her.

My biggest challenge? Resisting the urge to let my mind drift, picturing what it'd be like to kiss her pouty lips.

Holding her hand the day I asked her to be Caleb's nanny hit me like an electric jolt, and that simple touch opened the damn floodgates. I blame my reaction on the fact that I haven't gotten laid in months, but I can't deny her smile and touch are getting under my skin. All I can hope is that it's temporary because my life is messy enough as it is.

My attention shifts when I hear a sharp metallic clank, and I see Heath pulling up beside the house in an old pickup truck, the exhaust spitting out a cloud of dust. The paint is a faded blend of sea glass and rust, with more dents and scratches than I can count. When he spots me at the window, he nods for me to come outside.

He smirks when I step onto the porch, giving me a once-over. "Not bad for a city boy. But if your goal is to blend in, you'll need more than a pair of regular ol' jeans."

My gaze drops to my white button-up shirt and pants. I don't get why he's giving me grief. This is downright casual compared to the usual three-piece suits I wear to the office. I didn't bother packing one since there's no use for them in Bluebell.

I'll admit, these jeans are a lot more comfortable than slacks. I had my assistant pick them up at the mall before I left the city, though they don't quite measure up to the Wranglers most folks around here wear. I think I've avoided them because it feels like stepping back into my old life. One I used to resent, but now am learning wasn't all bad.

"Guess I'll have to start wearing flannel and muddy boots again. Can't have anyone thinking I've gone soft," I say with a grin.

Heath comes over to clap me on the back. "One day tossing bales, and we'll see if you're still cocky."

I scoff, offended by the insinuation. I might not spend my days roping cattle or mending fences anymore, but I run daily and lift weights regularly. I'm sure I could take on a full day of labor hauling hay—or any other task—without breaking a sweat.

"This the truck?" I nod to the vehicle behind Heath.

"Yup." He tosses the keys in my direction, and I catch them

in mid-air. "I had the shop do a full-service check, including new tires, new brakes, and an oil change."

"Thanks, man; I really appreciate it."

I drove a truck just like this in high school, and honestly, I'd take it over any fancy SUV I could have shipped in or being chauffeured around by Earl.

"No problem." Heath leans against the truck, crossing his arms over his chest. "What are you doing at the house anyway? Shouldn't you be busy saving the world with an app or something?"

I chuckle, tucking the keys in my back pocket. "*Or something.* Briar's watching Caleb today, and I wanted to keep an eye on them." I grimace, aware I'm toeing the line between concerned and hovering.

Heath raises a brow. "Interesting. Be straight with me, Harding. Are you checking in on your kid or keeping tabs on my sister?"

I lower my gaze, nudging a loose rock with the toe of my shoe. "It's her first day with Caleb, and I figured I'd stay close by in case they needed me."

"I see." He rubs his jaw, looking out over the pastures. "You sure that's the *only* reason?"

I clear my throat. "I'm just keeping an eye out for Caleb, making sure he's settling into the routine okay."

"Uh-huh." He glances at me, a flicker of amusement in his eyes. "Have any ladies in town caught your interest?"

"Nope."

There is one woman I can't stop thinking about, but technically she lives on the ranch and not in town. Although I'm not about to admit to Heath that I'm attracted to his sister.

The fact that we live under the same roof only makes it harder to keep my feelings in check. I'm haunted by her big brown eyes, legs that go on for days, and the stubborn tilt to her chin that drives me wild. Has it been a challenge not letting my mind wander when I hear the shower running down the hall? Absolutely.

Would I ever act on said temptation? Absolutely not. She's Caleb's nanny now, and I know better than to cross boundaries, even if my imagination refuses to keep in line.

Heath pushes off the truck, tugging down the brim of his hat. "We'll see. I have a hunch you'll meet a nice country gal before summer's over." He grins.

"I don't think so. I'm here for Caleb, and in a few months, we're going back to New York, so a summer fling would hardly make sense." I leave it there, hoping Heath won't push further.

He presses his lips together, his features full of amusement. "Fair. But I'll tell you what. If it stays that way, I owe you a hundred bucks. If not, you owe me."

Sounds like an easy win. The fact that I'm attracted to Briar doesn't mean I'd act on it. I push aside the flicker of doubt that tries to take root and extend my hand.

"You've got yourself a deal," I say as we shake on it.

"We'll see if you're this confident by the end of the summer," he says, a smug glint in his eyes. "Are you and Caleb staying for dinner? Ma should be home soon and planned to make pulled pork sandwiches with slaw and cornbread."

I nod. "We'd love to."

My mouth waters just thinking about Julie's cooking. Despite all the Michelin-starred restaurants I've experienced, nothing beats a home-cooked meal at the Halsteads'.

Since we arrived in Bluebell, I've made simple dinners at the cottage, including mac and cheese and chicken nuggets. Briar's been out every evening, probably at the ranch house or with friends. Part of me worries that we've pushed her out of her own space, and I decide to bring it up to her later.

Caleb's bedtime routine is the highlight of my day. Since moving to Bluebell it's when he's most at peace, and now that the rest of his things have arrived from Chicago, there's a new sense of comfort in having his belongings here with him.

Everything else from Amelia's apartment has been boxed up and placed in storage where it'll stay until Caleb is old enough to go through it and decide what he wants to keep. She might not be around to watch him grow up, but the least I can do is preserve the pieces of her life that might one day help him feel closer to her.

After Caleb's bath, he picks out the pajamas he'll wear to bed, which are always one of three dinosaur-themed sets. Tonight, I offer him two choices: a blue set with smiling Stegosauruses, Triceratops in party hats and tiny volcanoes erupting with confetti, or a black pair covered in glow-in-the-dark dinosaur skeletons.

He's quick to point to the party hat pajamas.

"Can't go wrong with dinosaurs in hats." I smile, setting the others aside. "Arms up, buddy."

He does as I ask, and I pull the shirt down over his head. Then I kneel so he can hold my shoulders as he steps into the pants, one leg at a time. After our failed nighttime routine during his first evening in my penthouse, he's been more comfortable with me helping him get ready for bed.

When he's dressed, he scoops up his dinosaur stuffed animal from the ground and climbs into bed. I'm momentarily frozen in place when he scoots over to make space for me. This is the first time he's done that. Usually, he takes the center of the bed, leaving me to sit on the edge, trying not to crowd him. After the initial shock wears off, I settle beside him, swallowing down the lump in my throat as I wrap my arm around his shoulders, relieved when he doesn't move away.

Caleb's favorite part of our nightly routine is story time. He picks a book from the shelf, and I read it aloud. He's never asked for more, but I'd read every last one if he asked me.

Tonight's pick is *Dragons Love Tacos.*

I can't help but wonder if he did this with Amelia. Would she do the voices, and would he laugh at the silly parts? Did he have a favorite story they read every night? And does he think about her when I'm flipping through the pages of a book they read together?

I push the thoughts aside. There's no use in dwelling on what I can't change. What matters now is creating new memories and being here when he's ready to share the ones he had with his mom.

Once I've finished reading, I set the book on the nightstand, leaning down to kiss Caleb's forehead. "Good night, buddy. I love you." I've never meant anything more.

He doesn't respond. The only sound is the soft rustle of his sheets as he lies in bed, waiting for me to turn off the overhead light. The night-light in the corner glows enough to keep the darkness at bay.

I didn't believe in love until now. My parents never showed it, and I didn't stick around long enough in any relationship to experience it myself. Then came Caleb, proving that love does exist. It's fierce, exhausting, and unrelenting. I'm constantly questioning myself, convinced I'm not getting anything right. Still, when he looks at me with those innocent brown eyes, there's no question that being his dad is worth it all.

"Sweet dreams," I murmur, shutting the door behind me.

I close my eyes, letting out a sigh. Even though I wouldn't change any of it, being a parent is the hardest thing I've ever done.

Leaving my hometown without a penny to my name? Challenging.

Teaching myself to code? Brutal.

Launching a startup in New York with zero funding? Flat-out reckless.

All of it pales compared to raising a kid and the challenges that come with it. Still, now that I've had a glimpse of fatherhood, I realize I'd trade it all for more time with Caleb when he was younger.

It's a quarter past nine, and I should call it a night, but instead, after changing into sweats and a T-shirt, I venture downstairs to stretch my legs. Not because I'm hoping to catch a glimpse of a certain brunette.

Definitely not that.

The only light on is above the kitchen sink, and a sharp twinge of disappointment hits me when I realize Briar has probably already gone to bed—until I look out the window facing the front yard and see her sitting on the porch swing. Her legs are tucked beneath her, a steaming mug cradled in her hands.

In the brief time we've been in Bluebell, she's been constantly on the go. It's nice to see her relaxing and enjoying the peace and quiet.

A kettle is on the stove and the faint aroma of hot chocolate wafts in the air. I pour myself a cup, adding a generous pour of the whiskey on the counter. Looks like I'm not the only one needing a drink tonight.

Briar glances up when I come outside and join her on the swing.

She smirks. "I see you found my spiked hot chocolate."

I lift the mug to my lips and take a sip. "My whiskey-to-cocoa ratio highly favors the whiskey, but I'm not sorry about it."

She chuckles, scooting a little closer to nudge my leg playfully. "Maybe it'll soften that serious expression of yours."

"Let's hope so," I tease before glancing out at the fields ahead of us.

A deep breath fills my lungs with fresh air, the silence settling around me like a blanket. After the constant buzz of the city, I realize I missed the peace and quiet far more than I thought I ever would.

My body tenses when Briar's hand brushes mine as she pulls away. The warmth of her touch shoots straight through me, and when I meet her gaze, she's studying me—a silent acknowledgment that we both felt the shift between us.

She's the first to break eye contact, yet I can't look anywhere else. Her hair dances in the breeze, and the intoxicating scent of sun-warmed leather fills the air. Briar Halstead is undeniably beautiful, but part of what makes her so captivating is the warmth in her voice when she speaks to Caleb and the unapologetic boldness when she stands her ground.

"Am I making you feel like you can't be in your own house?" It's been on my mind since earlier this afternoon.

Her gaze softens, an inquisitive frown tugging at her brow. "What makes you think that?"

"You haven't been around much in the evenings, and I figured the cottage would be where you'd want to spend your time after a long day."

A smirk crosses her face. "Jensen Harding, have you been keeping tabs on me? If you wanted my attention, there are easier ways."

Heat creeps up my neck, and I tug my shirt collar loose. "What? No. I just don't want you to feel like Caleb and I are crowding your space. We're guests and don't want to overstep our welcome this early on." I stumble over my words, and I can see Briar hiding a small smile behind her mug.

God, this is embarrassing. I've never had trouble talking to women, but now I'm tripping over my tongue with zero finesse while Briar watches, clearly entertained by every second.

"I wanted to give you both the chance to settle in without getting in the way." She raises her hand when I open my mouth to speak. "But rest assured, you'll be seeing a lot more of me from now on."

"Good." I pause, trying to maintain a neutral expression. "Caleb will be glad to hear that."

So am I.

Briar wraps her blanket tighter around her waist, resting her cocoa in her lap as she meets my gaze. When she speaks, her voice is low. "Can I ask you something?"

"Sure," I reply.

"How are you doing? I know your world has been turned upside down."

My first instinct is to shut her down and say I don't want to talk about it. But she'll only feel more comfortable with me if I'm willing to meet her halfway and let down my guard. Besides, I appreciate her wanting to better understand my situation and how Caleb and I ended up here.

"That's a loaded question," I admit, pausing to knock back a long swallow of spiked hot cocoa, welcoming the heat hitting the back of my throat. "Finding out I'm a dad has been incredible, but it's also painful knowing that Amelia kept it from me for so long. Now I'm just trying to figure out fatherhood and find ways to connect with my son until he's comfortable speaking again. It's a lot to process." I run my thumb along the rim of my mug.

Briar rests her hand on my leg, her expression filled with compassion. "I'm sorry, Jensen. I can't begin to imagine what you've gone through or how devastating it must have been to find out you'd missed the first five years of Caleb's life."

I scoff, a dull ache settling in my chest. "That would have been the normal response. Yet all I felt was frustration and confusion toward the woman who kept my son from me. She robbed me of precious time with him, and I'll never get it back."

Maybe it's unfair of me to hold on to the disappointment. Amelia must have had a good reason to make the choices she did, but the fallout of those landed on my shoulders. I don't know the specifics of her cancer battle or exactly how long she was sick, but I do know this much: she had time.

Time to call.

Time to explain.

Time to give Caleb a chance to meet his father.

Hell, I would've been there for her during her battle with

cancer, taking care of Caleb while she fought. I may never know why she didn't reach out for help, and that haunts me.

There's so much I would've asked if I'd had the chance. When did Caleb's love for dinosaurs begin, what's his favorite color, and why does he prefer Swiss cheese over cheddar? All are things I may never get the answer to because Amelia kept my son from me, and Caleb may never tell me himself.

I wish I could make peace with what Amelia did, but every time I look at Caleb, I'm reminded of everything I missed—and the silence she left behind is utterly deafening.

Briar's voice draws me out of my haze, steady and soft, sensing that I'm seconds away from unraveling.

"Caleb's a bright, kind, and curious kid who didn't become that way by accident. His mom loved him with all she had, and it shows in every part of who he is," she states, her tone gentle. "Whatever her reasons for keeping Caleb to herself, he was her whole world, and in the end, she chose you to take care of him even after she was gone. That has to count for something."

She's right.

There's no doubt Amelia loved Caleb beyond measure, and the proof is in the small things. The handwritten notes in the children's books from her house, the way Caleb can color inside the lines, and the fact that he can tie his shoes already. All of it speaks to the hours Amelia must have spent with him perfecting those skills.

It doesn't erase the pain and frustration, but it does offer a new perspective—the hope that one day I might be able to forgive Amelia, even if I never get the closure I desperately wish for.

I rest my hand over Briar's, giving it a gentle squeeze. "I haven't thanked you properly."

"For what?" she asks.

"Caring about Caleb as much as I do."

CHAPTER 10

Briar

I T'S FRIDAY NIGHT, AND I'M CONTEMPLATING GOING TO BED early when I get a text.

Backroads & Bad Decisions Group Chat

> Birdie: SOS! I was at the diner earlier and overheard Mr. Grady say that one of his chickens is getting pecked on and she's not worth the trouble. He's going to put her down tomorrow!

> Birdie: We have to save her before it's too late.

> Briar: He's got thousands of chickens. How would we know which one it is?

> Birdie: She's in her own pen waiting for her execution.

> Charlie: Welp. Guess we're going on a chicken rescue mission.

Wren: Seriously! The FOMO is real.

Charlie: You left us unsupervised. This is on you.

Briar: Besides, you're our backup plan if this goes sideways.

Wren: Like when you tried rescuing a box of kittens from a dumpster that turned out to be baby possums, and one of them bit Charlie?

Wren: I still owe my cousin for meeting you at the clinic after hours to give Charlie that rabies shot.

I laugh at the memory. For living in a small town with four thousand residents, we sure do find ourselves in precarious situations quite often.

Charlie: I thought we agreed to never speak about that again.

Briar: So... what's our game plan to save this chicken?

Charlie: There's only one solution: Operation Feathered Freedom. We're breaking her out tonight.

Briar: I'm pretty sure this is illegal.

Charlie: Only if we get caught.

Birdie: You guys are the best!!

Wren: Better write my number on your arm so the cops know who to call for bail.

Charlie: Appreciate the vote of confidence.

Between Birdie's bleeding heart and Charlie's knack for finding trouble, it's a miracle we've stayed out of jail this long. It does help that Sheriff Matterson is Birdie's dad—he tends to look the other way when we get ourselves into trouble. Most of our past run-ins with the law involve unlicensed rescue missions or Charlie's disregard for "No Trespassing" signs.

Charlie: You want to save the chicken or not?

Charlie: Meet at my place at nine. Wear black.

An hour later, we're in Charlie's bright red SUV on our way to Mr. Grady's farm, all decked out in head-to-toe black. Anyone passing by might assume we're filming a low-budget spy movie with no money left for a wardrobe budget.

"This thing isn't exactly incognito," Birdie complains from the back seat.

"My orange Jeep would've stood out just as much," I say, tossing a handful of popcorn into my mouth.

Charlie came armed with snacks, as if we were on an FBI stakeout.

"We could've taken your car, but *someone* refused to drive," Charlie grumbles, glancing back at Birdie.

"It's not my fault a family of rabbits decided to make their home under my car," she protests, crossing her arms. "The mama just gave birth last week, and they won't be able to leave until the babies are old enough to hop and venture out on their own."

"What's your plan for getting around until then?" I ask.

"I have Earl on speed dial. He's got a punch card system, and I'm halfway to a free ride," she says proudly, as if it's a badge of honor, ignoring Earl's track record of turning flowerbeds into mulch.

"The man is a goldmine for gossip and animal rescue tips," Charlie admits.

I'm just glad Birdie has a positive outlook on the situation, because my guess is that those bunnies are one litter away from forming a permanent colony under her car.

Charlie pulls off the road onto a narrow gravel turnout, parking the SUV behind a grove of trees to avoid drawing attention. Around here, someone's bound to stop and check if we're stranded, so we have to be cautious.

"Let's take a quick picture to send to Wren," she says, leaning over and holding out her phone with one hand. "Everyone say, 'Free the chicken!'" She snaps the photo with her grinning from the driver's seat while Birdie and I squish into the frame, mid-laugh. The flash goes off, briefly casting a sharp glow on our faces.

Charlie leans back in her seat and fires off a text, my phone chiming seconds later. I glance down to see that she's sent the picture to the group chat with a message.

Charlie: Wish us luck, Wren. We miss you!

Once she's finished, we all climb out of the vehicle and make our way through the trees.

When we reach Mr. Grady's farm, we keep low to the ground, darting behind farm equipment and haystacks. Thank god he's behind the times and doesn't have cameras on his property—though, I wonder if that'll change after tonight.

Birdie and Charlie whip their heads toward me when my phone chimes, the screen lighting up.

"What the hell, Briar," Charlie hisses. "Do you want us to get caught?"

"Sorry," I whisper, putting my phone on silent. "Wren was responding to the photo you sent."

"She'll have to wait for a reply until after we finish this mission," Charlie says, her voice low.

We stick to the perimeter of the property before passing through a cluster of cottonwoods leading to Mr. Grady's house.

When we reach the maze of fencing and sheds that make up the chickens' enclosures, I spot a small pen off to the side, holding a lone chicken with patches of missing feathers. Birdie doesn't waste a second, bending down to unlock the latch, trying to coax the bird into the crate we brought to transport it. She's halfway in when a loud squawk suddenly echoes from the other side of the coop. The chicken panics and scurries back inside its pen.

We might not be able to see the other hens, but it's obvious they sense something isn't right when they all begin to cluck furiously. One particularly loud rooster lets out a battle cry, and the entire flock erupts into chaos, shaking the fence.

"Uh-oh," Birdie whispers.

I wince, my eyes darting toward the house, hoping we're too far away to be noticed. Spoiler: We're not.

Seconds later, the porch light flickers on, and Mr. Grady stomps out in his long johns and boots.

"What in tarnation is going on?" he hollers.

"Shit," Charlie mutters. "We have to get out of here before we get caught."

My adrenaline kicks in, and all I can think about is escaping undetected. If we don't, and Jensen finds out, he may never let me see Caleb again—especially if I get arrested for trespassing and stealing someone else's property. I can't let that happen.

"New plan," I say in a hushed tone. "Birdie, you're going to carry the chicken out of here. Charlie, you distract Mr. Grady. I'll take the crate." I'd leave it behind, but it has the Silver Saddle Ranch emblem on it, and the last thing we need is for this to become front-page news in the local paper.

"Why do I have to be the one to distract him?" Charlie hisses.

"Because Birdie panics under pressure, and you'd probably face-plant if you tried to run with the crate in those shoes." I gesture toward her black ankle boots. They're meant for a trip to the coffee shop, not a covert mission.

She lets out a sharp breath, brushing a stray lock of hair from her face, a determined expression setting in. "Fine. Let's just get it over with. I'm definitely going to need a drink after this."

We watch as she stealthily darts along the perimeter of the chicken enclosure, ignoring the hens that continue to squawk loudly.

Once she is out of sight, Birdie lifts the fragile chicken from its pen, cradling it against her chest. "Shh, I've got you," she whispers when it clucks.

We wait for what feels like an eternity, the sound of Mr. Grady's boots growing louder with each step. Just as he's about to round the corner, a loud commotion from the other side of the coop grabs his attention. I crane my neck to see hundreds of chickens scattering out of the enclosure, running in all directions.

That's one way to distract him.

"Goddammit," he shouts as he bolts toward the open gate.

My heart races, thumping wildly. Now is our chance to make a break for it.

I glance at Birdie, still holding the chicken, her brows furrowed in concentration as she tries to keep the bird from squawking its head off.

"Run. Now," I order.

She doesn't waste a second, taking off in a sprint across the yard. I grab the crate off the ground and follow. As we reach the tree line, I glance back, catching sight of Charlie, her hands pressed against her chest.

"Why didn't you tell me to wear a sports bra for this?" she whisper-shouts.

I bite my lip, fighting the urge to laugh. "How was I supposed to know we'd be sprinting for our lives? Was it necessary to let the other chickens out?"

"What did you want me to do, distract him with my impressive rack?" She motions to her chest. "Even that wouldn't have been enough to divert from the fact that we stole his chicken."

"Correction, we liberated her," Birdie adds, ever the optimist.

We don't stop running until we get to the SUV. I toss the crate in the trunk, then climb into the passenger seat, leaning back to steady my breath.

Charlie slides behind the wheel and starts the engine. She turns and points at the hen, who's now wrapped in Birdie's jacket, its head poking out and swiveling curiously.

"Listen up, clucker. If you even think about making a mess in my car, you'll be turned into chicken nuggets. Got it?" The chicken stares at her, nuzzling its head into Birdie's chest. "That bird is as sharp as a rock."

Birdie shoots Charlie a scowl. "Don't say that. You'll hurt Nugget's feelings."

Charlie throws her hands up in exasperation. "Oh, great. Now you've gone and named the thing."

"Yup. Nugget is here to stay," Birdie says with a toothy grin.

"As much as I love this feel-good moment, I think we should get out of here," I say.

"You got it." Charlie buckles up and pulls out onto the road. "Once we drop off the chicken, we're going to the bar to celebrate."

"Alright, but only if the bar has better music than your car," I tease.

Charlie wouldn't let us leave the bar until closing—too busy having the whole place cheering as she belted out songs about heartbreak, dirt roads, and bad decisions. Somewhere between her fifth margarita and grinding on every man who bought her a drink, I stepped in as her designated driver and got her home before things went too far with someone she might actually remember in the morning.

It's well past midnight when I get back to the cottage, so I'm surprised to find the lights are still on. I stop in the kitchen doorway, shocked to find soaked towels spread across the floor and Jensen lying on his back under the sink, my tools scattered around him.

"What happened?" I exclaim.

A clatter of metal echoes beneath the sink as Jensen drops whatever tool he was holding.

"Shit," he mutters.

He grabs the tool from the ground before moving out from under the sink. As he stands to his full height, that's when I realize he's shirtless. Every ripple and curvature of his bare chest is on display, a light dusting of hair trailing over the firm planes of his torso. His body is a sculpted piece of art and far more impressive than anything I've ever seen. My eyes drift to the waistband of his Wranglers.

Wait. What?

My jaw falls open, and I do a double take when I realize he's *actually* wearing a pair of worn-in blue jeans. Not the designer brand he's favored since he got here. The switch from his usual polished style makes my pulse quicken. It's absurd how sexy he is, and suddenly, I can't help but imagine him on horseback with a hat, every bit the cowboy he once was.

He clears his throat, and when our eyes meet, a smile tugs at the corner of his lips. "Something catch your eye, Briar?"

I force a laugh and avert my gaze, pretending I wasn't just ogling my shirtless roommate—who also happens to be my boss and my brother's best friend.

"What? No," I rush out. "I was just wondering how the kitchen floor turned into a splash pad while I was out."

"A pipe burst under the sink while I was upstairs putting Caleb to bed." He motions to the mess around him. "I came down to find water shooting out from under the sink like a fire hydrant. I watched a few tutorials online, figuring I could fix it before you got back, but it turns out I'm better at patching broken code than busted plumbing." He rubs the back of his neck with a sheepish shrug.

I nod to the tool in his hand. "Guess that explains the non-adjustable wrench."

He raises his hand in mock surrender. "It was either this or duct tape."

"And here I thought your most questionable decision was pineapple on pizza." I toss my purse on the counter and gather my hair into a messy bun. "You're in luck," I say, pulling out a hair tie. "I've fixed enough busted pipes to earn a gold star in plumbing disasters—no duct tape necessary. This is a walk in the park compared to when I had to crawl under cabin four during a snowstorm, with a raccoon giving me the stink eye like I was the intruder."

He arches a brow, intrigued. "A raccoon in a snowstorm? Sounds like something straight out of a movie."

If that's the case, I can only imagine what he'd think of the chicken rescue mission my friends and I managed earlier tonight. But I'm keeping that little adventure to myself for now.

I slide under the sink, my eyes adjusting to the dim light as I survey the pipes. Water's still dripping, so I grab one of the towels and blot the area dry. "Can you pass me the plumber's tape?" I call out to Jensen. "It's the silvery, fabric-like roll in the toolbox. Oh, and I'll need a clamp to stop the leak."

The toolbox lid clicks open, followed by the shuffle of footsteps. I'm not expecting Jensen to drop down next to me, the space between us shrinking as he holds out a flashlight, casting a beam on the pipes.

He holds out the plumber's tape and clamp. "Here."

"Thanks."

With the cold floor pressing into my spine, I crane my neck toward the pipe. My fingers tremble slightly as I thread the tape around the pipe, distracted by a shirtless Jensen lying beside me.

He's holding the flashlight like it's no big deal while I'm trying not to sneak another glance in his direction.

My heartbeat quickens when he tilts his head, his breath grazing my cheek as he leans closer.

"So, what's the damage?"

"Um… the joint's cracked, so I'm patching it temporarily. I'll replace the whole section tomorrow." Why is it so difficult to concentrate on the words coming out of my mouth?

Jensen smells like cedarwood and mint, and it's criminal how intoxicating it is. I don't notice that I've shifted closer until his bare chest is pressed against my arm, and a spark of electricity shoots through me. Thank god the flashlight's aimed at the plumbing and not the way I'm blushing like a teenage girl with her first crush. I remind myself I'm here to fix a broken pipe, not climb this man like a tree.

I only had one drink tonight, and that was hours ago—but with the way my body's reacting, you'd think I was tipsy and desperate. It's been way too long since I've gotten laid. Maybe I should take Charlie up on her offer to set me up with the lawyer. He's successful, charming, and most importantly, *not* the insanely attractive single dad currently watching me fix a leaky pipe like it's the hottest thing he's ever seen.

Yup. I definitely need to get laid.

I tighten the clamp, giving it one last look before wiping my sweaty palm on my jeans.

"That should hold until I can do the full repair in—" The rest of the words get stuck in my throat as I turn and catch Jensen staring at my mouth. The flashlight in his hand casts soft shadows across the cramped walls of the cabinet, highlighting the sharp cut of his jaw. When I shift, his gaze drops lower, lingering on the curve of my chest. I took off my flannel before getting to work, leaving me in a tight black tank top.

"That was kind of hot," he says, his eyes still locked on me.

I tilt my head, smirking. "Are you referring to the temperature of the space?"

His head jerks in a nod. "Yeah. That."

"Maybe we should get out from under here, then," I suggest.

"Good idea," he says, rubbing his chin thoughtfully before climbing out from under the sink.

I'm left disappointed when the warmth of his body is gone. I peek my head out to find his hand extended, and I can't help the flutter in my chest as he helps me rise to my feet.

"Thanks."

"You're the one who fixed the busted pipe. I should be thanking you," he says.

I like this side of Jensen. He appears more relaxed. His typically serious demeanor has faded, and I'm getting a glimpse of the playful side usually reserved for Caleb.

An expression I can't decipher flickers across his features, and my heart rate speeds up when his gaze flits across my face, settling on the spot just below my mouth.

"What is it?" I whisper.

He steps closer. "You've got a smudge—right here."

My breath hitches when he slowly reaches out and drags his thumb across my chin, grazing my lower lip, his fingers resting lightly on my jaw. My heart races as I imagine what it would be like if he leaned in and kissed me. Given the intensity in Jensen's eyes, I wonder if he's thinking the same thing.

"Am I making you uncomfortable?" His voice is barely above a whisper.

I swallow hard, my hooded eyes glancing up at him. "No," I say, hoping he doesn't hear how loud my heart is racing. "You're practically walking around naked, so it's hard not to stare." I don't bother hiding my smirk.

"Didn't exactly improve my repair skills now, did it?" he asks, his gaze shamelessly lingering on my mouth. "But you, on the other hand, were exceptional. Especially for someone who managed to fix a pipe without stripping." He winks. "I'm honestly impressed. You've definitely earned that gold star."

"High praise coming from the shirtless distraction committee," I tease.

He damn well knows the effect he's having, standing there all bare-chested and smug with confidence, close enough that I can feel the heat rolling off of him.

"Glad I could be useful," he quips, his eyes glimmering with fascination. Maybe it's my imagination, but I swear he leans in a fraction. "You smell like apples," he murmurs.

My knuckles turn white as I grip my hands into fists. "It's my body wash."

"It's nice."

I force myself to remain still, my body coming alive with him so close. My pulse is pounding in my ears as his breath whispers against my lips, the undercurrent of desire in his touch leaving me trembling. We're supposed to be roommates, friends at most, and I can't let my emotions get the best of me.

The adrenaline from the chicken heist is still coursing through me, and I haven't had a real release in a while. That's why I'm so hot and bothered—not because of the shirtless man in front of me.

On impulse, I reach toward his chest but catch myself before losing complete control, forcing my hands back to my sides.

"I have an early morning tomorrow, so I should get to bed," I say, forcing the words out.

Jensen runs a hand through his hair, blowing out the breath he must've been holding. "Yeah, me too."

I take several steps back toward the stairs. "Night."

Jensen's face is unreadable, but I catch the subtle flex of his hand, the fingers that brushed my skin rubbing together. I can't tell if he's trying to shake off the moment or if he's grappling with the same rush I felt when he touched me.

"Night, Briar," he drawls.

I offer him a quick wave before darting up the stairs, not stopping until I'm in the bathroom with the door shut. I turn on the faucet and splash cold water on my face, trying to calm my racing heart.

I must be ovulating.

That's the only explanation I can come up with for why I reacted the way I did. Sure, Jensen was shirtless, but I've seen plenty of men working bare-chested in the fields on a hot day, and not one of them ever made my knees go weak just by standing next to them.

I blame those damn Wranglers. Seeing him slowly start to embrace his cowboy roots is messing with my head, especially when that lazy Montana drawl slips into his voice, turning every word he says into a slow-burn seduction. It's absolutely unfair to my nervous system.

Jensen brought Caleb to Bluebell to ease him into his new life and provide him with a stable environment. The last thing he needs is to live under the same roof as a woman whose brain short-circuits when she sees a hint of denim or hears his drawl. Yes, there's mutual chemistry there, but I can't risk doing anything to mess up Caleb's stay at Silver Saddle Ranch. His happiness comes first.

Which means one thing is for certain: Jensen Harding is strictly off-limits.

CHAPTER 11

Jensen

"**Y**OU READY TO GO DOWNSTAIRS FOR BREAKFAST?" I ASK Caleb.

He nods and sets aside the magnetic tiles Julie gave him for making it through his second week of summer camp. Hard to believe it's already mid-June.

Between his twice-a-week therapy appointments and summer camp, he's doing much better than I could have anticipated. Just yesterday, he made space at his table during snack time for one of the other kids at camp and even shared the crayons without being asked. It may seem minor, but considering he used to avoid interacting with anyone, it's a big step.

There's no question Briar has played a big role in the shift. Caleb always comes back from their afternoons together smiling and more engaged. She shows him around the ranch, introduces him to the animals, works with him in Julie's garden, and even takes him on adventures in town. Thankfully, today is Saturday which means she should be here and not out doing rounds at the cabins.

As Caleb and I enter the kitchen, we're greeted by the sweet scent of pancakes. Briar stands at the stove, spatula in hand, dancing along to a country song on the radio. It's impossible not to watch her hips sway to the beat, her jeans clinging to her every curve. Her hair's pulled into a messy bun, the same as it was the night of the plumbing disaster last week.

Watching her fix that pipe was damn sexy. With grease on her chin and wisps of hair framing her face, I couldn't take my eyes off her.

I've replayed the moment countless times. The way her breath hitched as my thumb grazed her chin, her body flush with mine, wrapped in the sweet scent of apples and worn leather. Her doe eyes were soft and brimming with longing, making the urge to kiss her burn in my chest and difficult to resist. If she hadn't pulled away, I may not have had the sense to stop, which would make our situation more complicated.

Caleb's face brightens when he sees her and races over to wrap his arms around her legs. I watch, my chest tightening with gratitude for how she shows up for him.

Briar sets the spatula down and smiles, ruffling his hair. "Good morning, little man. You hungry?"

He tips his head, giving her a thumbs-up.

"Great. You boys better be ready to dig in, because I made pancakes. A whole lot of them. It's my one specialty, so I had to go all out."

Briar's normally gone before I wake up, so I stick to easy options like eggs, toast, cereal, or oatmeal. Caleb usually eats whatever I put in front of him, but he's never been enthusiastic about breakfast. Not like he is now, as he takes in the massive stacks of pancakes on the kitchen table.

Before joining him, I step behind Briar, brushing a hand against the small of her back as I lean in to whisper in her ear. "Morning, sugar. Those pancakes smell amazing."

We both blink at the unexpected nickname. It's totally fitting, though, since everything about her is sweet and leaves me craving more.

Before this summer, I was never big on affection—physical or verbal—but the way Briar is with Caleb, always hugging and praising him, must be rubbing off on me.

Maybe a little too much.

I've been on my best behavior this past week, but seeing her barefoot and at ease in her kitchen makes me want things I shouldn't—like pressing her against the counter and kissing her senseless. I pull back before I do anything reckless, relieved when she resumes flipping pancakes, pretending I didn't come close to crossing a line I shouldn't. I subtly adjust myself, wanting to hide how being close to her affects me.

I sit next to Caleb at the kitchen table, reminding myself that we came to Bluebell for him, and everything else comes second, including my inexplicable desire to be around Briar. She's a novelty. Someone forbidden who plagues my thoughts, but eventually the attraction will fade. Or at least I hope it will.

Caleb is eyeing the platefuls of pancakes. Next to each stack is a slip of paper with the flavor.

I lean forward, reading off the options. "We've got classic buttermilk, blueberry, chocolate chip, banana, and apple cinnamon. Want to pick one to start with?" I ask Caleb.

He gestures toward the bear-shaped chocolate chip pancakes with a grin.

"Great choice."

I slide a pancake onto his plate, top it with banana slices and a drizzle of syrup, then set it in front of him. He immediately digs in and takes a big bite, humming his approval.

I chuckle. "That good, huh?"

He quickly nods, already scooping the next bite into his mouth.

"I still can't believe you finished fixing the pipe without me," I say to Briar as I add a stack of blueberry pancakes to my plate.

The morning after the plumbing incident, I headed to the kitchen after my workout ready to help with the permanent repair—only to find Briar had already cut out the damaged joint and installed a new section, all before sunrise.

"If I hadn't, *someone* might've tried using a non-adjustable wrench again, or worse—duct tape," she teases, shaking her head.

"I figured a makeshift fix was better than turning the kitchen into a swimming pool," I reply sheepishly. "I'm usually good at improvising... most of the time."

She flips the final batch of pancakes and turns off the burner before glancing at me. "Just not the kind that involves tools." She winks, clearly enjoying this.

I smirk. "Guess I'm better with a hands-on approach."

"You keep talking like that, and I might start expecting daily maintenance." She clears her throat, probably realizing how that sounded. It seems we're both toeing the line between teasing and something more.

"Caleb, what do you say we pay Ziggy a visit after breakfast?" she asks Caleb, changing the subject. "I'm sure he'd love to stretch his legs and play."

His face lights up, and he nods eagerly.

"Sounds good. Once you finish eating, we'll head outside."

Briar opens the shed, and Ziggy bursts out with a happy bleat, hooves skittering as he zigzags across the yard. He's grown a lot in the past two weeks but still lacks direction. When he spots Caleb, he starts running toward him, but the second he sees me, he freezes. His little legs go stiff, and he collapses to the ground in an overdramatic swoon.

Caleb's lip quivers with worry as he watches Ziggy collapse. It's not the first time he's seen him faint, but it's been a few days. Briar and Caleb typically visit him in the afternoons when I'm working.

Briar kneels and puts her arm around Caleb. "I think Ziggy's read too many comic books and is convinced your dad's a superhero in disguise. He gets starry-eyed and can't help fainting on sight," she whispers the last part like it's a secret.

Caleb peers cautiously at Ziggy, his eyes widening as the goat suddenly springs up and trots toward him—full of energy and pretending I don't exist.

Briar brushes Caleb's hair from his face. "See? He just needed a second to regroup from seeing his hero. Now he's ready to play."

She releases Caleb and stands as he gently pats Ziggy's head, laughing when the goat nuzzles into his hand.

I approach Briar, leaning in so only she can hear. "What happened to the goat not being my biggest fan?" I smirk.

She shrugs, raising her hands, palms out. "Guess Ziggy decided you're not so bad after all."

Something tells me we're not talking about goats anymore.

While Caleb and Ziggy chase each other around the yard, Briar grabs the laundry basket she left on the back porch and heads to the clothesline along the side of the house. Several rows of clothes are hung across it, fluttering in the breeze.

The washer's out of order, and the part Briar needs won't arrive for another week. That means doing laundry at Julie's and hanging it out to dry since the weather is nice. As much as I've come to like the cottage, the constant repairs to the plumbing and appliances are a hassle. I've learned during our time here that Briar has a strong work ethic. Between helping with Caleb and the repairs on the cabins, not much time is left to make a dent in the cottage renovations.

Caleb and me being around hasn't exactly lightened her load.

If anything, we've added to it, and I've been wanting to do something to prove that I can be helpful. I may not be able to fix a leaky pipe, but I have a black card and a guilty conscience. It's time I started contributing around here, especially since I'm not paying rent this summer.

I pull my phone from my pocket to email my assistant a list of tasks, asking her to prioritize them first thing Monday morning. Once I hit send, I slip my phone back into my pocket, deciding to hold off on telling Briar. I'll handle any fallout with her once it's too late to undo what I've planned.

I join her, watching as she folds clothes straight off the line, stacking them into the basket at her feet.

"Need a hand?"

She glances up, shrugging. "Sure."

I take down a pair of silk pajama pants from the line, smoothing out the fabric between my hands, and fold them before placing them in the basket.

"It's been ages since I've hung clothes out to dry," I admit.

The last time was probably helping Julie hang all the bedding out at the ranch house the summer before I left for New York.

"Careful, or I'll start to think you miss the ranch more than you let on," Briar teases.

I look over at the pastures in the distance where the cows are grazing beneath a sky so big it swallows the horizon. "I did miss it. More than I realized before coming back."

I'm halfway down the line when my hand stops mid-air, hovering over a pair of pink lace panties with bows on the sides and the words 'All You Can Eat' stitched across the front.

A surge of envy sweeps over me as I imagine another man having the privilege of seeing Briar in these—or, god forbid, acting on what they imply. It's an unreasonable reaction, especially since she's supposed to just be my son's nanny and my roommate.

But that doesn't ease the tightness in my throat at the idea of her being with someone else.

"Jensen, did you hear what I—" Briar's voice falters when she sticks her head around a pair of jeans separating us, and her face turns beet red when she catches me holding her panties. "Oh my god. Give me those." She snatches the underwear from my hand.

She glances over to make sure Caleb isn't looking before bending down to shove them into the bottom of the basket.

"I can finish my laundry." She pulls a shirt from the clothesline, avoiding my gaze as she folds it. "You should go inside and write some code or whatever it is you do."

I step forward and cover her hand with mine, holding it there until her eyes find mine. "Why are you blushing, sugar?"

"I'm not. Just don't need you staring at the underwear I got from a bachelorette party I went to last year. Everyone was asked to bring party favors, and Charlie bought a bulk pack of lacy panties with cheeky sayings on them. She gave the bride a pair that said 'Grab Life by the Buns.'"

The corner of my mouth twitches into a smile. "I prefer 'All You Can Eat,' even if it causes heart palpitations just thinking about it."

All I can picture is those lace panties hugging her creamy hips, begging me to taste her sweet pussy. And if that weren't enough, she had to go and mention lacy panties, causing my second hard-on in an hour. God help me. Fantasies of this woman now live rent-free in my mind, and damn if I know how to stop them.

I draw closer, gently tucking a strand of hair behind Briar's ear, feeling her shiver beneath my touch. "Most guys would need a roadmap and those panties to spell out what they're supposed to do," I say, my voice low.

"You included?" she taunts.

"I'm not one of your country *boys*, Briar. I'm a man who

doesn't need hints to know what my woman needs." I shoot her a confident grin as she rests her hand on my pec, her chest rises and falls in quick, shallow breaths. "Every woman deserves to be claimed by a man who's not afraid to make her beg for more and show her what she's been missing."

Her fingers curl around the collar of my shirt, her gaze locked on my mouth. When she swipes her tongue across her lips, the flicker of desire inside me turns into something undeniable, pulling me closer. I'm inches away from claiming a kiss when Caleb's laughter erupts from the other side of the yard.

Just like that, whatever was building between us vanishes, and we both pull away. I look around the wall of clothes to check on Caleb and see Ziggy has fainted again. Caleb is now lying beside him, mimicking the goat's stiff posture. My heart swells seeing my son playing without a care in the world. Now, if only I can figure out how to get a goat in our penthouse, because he will be heartbroken if he has to say goodbye to Ziggy at the end of the summer.

When the goat sits up, it starts licking Caleb's face, leaving a trail of slobber down his cheek.

"I guess that's one way to bond with a goat," Briar laughs.

I wrinkle my nose when Ziggy moves to Caleb's head, nibbling on his hair. "I'd better go rescue him before the goat decides he's a walking tasting menu."

"Good call," Briar says.

Our eyes meet for a split second before I jog toward Caleb and Ziggy. Damn, she's incredible, and that near-kiss only makes me crave her lips on mine even more.

CHAPTER 12

Briar

N O MATTER HOW HARD I TRY, I CAN'T FORGET THE IMAGE of Jensen seconds away from kissing me this morning. Despite the distraction, I still managed to paint a wall in the living room, though the memory of our *almost*-kiss played on repeat in my head.

I can't explain why, but a part of me wanted him to kiss me—to find out what it would feel like to have his lips on mine. Thinking about him gazing at me with those green eyes as he traces my jawline makes my pulse quicken.

I blame those damn panties.

They've opened a door I'm afraid can't be closed. Until now, my attraction for Jensen had been set to a simmer, and I've tried everything to stop my desire from boiling over. It made it easier when I assumed his occasional flirting was a product of loneliness and isolation on the ranch. But now, our *almost*-kiss has upended that theory, and I fear I won't be satisfied until he kisses me. The problem? It could unleash a whole host of complications we're better off avoiding, but I'm unsure if I can pretend it didn't happen.

After a trip to Tinker Toys, Jensen and Caleb spent the afternoon at the ranch house with Mama Julie and Pops. Caleb's obsessed with the craft room, especially the dinosaur paint-by-number set they got him. He hasn't been in Bluebell long, but he's already getting the grandparent treatment. They already adore him as if he were their own.

They invited me to dinner, but I politely declined. Instead, I stayed in my room until the boys got home, and once Jensen went to put Caleb to bed, I slipped out to sit on the front porch. I love the peace that comes with quiet nights on the ranch, including the rustling grass, the chirping crickets, and the distant lowing of cattle settling in for the night.

My favorite part about living here is the slow pace. We all work hard but always make time to enjoy the little things.

My phone buzzes repeatedly, and of course, it's the girls blowing up the group chat.

Backroads & Bad Decisions Group Chat

> **Charlie:** Ran into Mr. Grady at Lasso & Latte.

> **Charlie:** He's got half the coffee shop convinced someone's out to sabotage his chicken farm because they're bitter over losing to his wife in the pie contest last year.

> **Charlie:** Even showed Sheriff Matterson a photo of a boot print like it's CSI: Country Chicken Edition.

> **Birdie:** Oh. My. God. We might actually go to jail this time!!

> **Briar:** For rescuing a chicken? Highly doubtful.

Wren: Technically, it was a bird-napping.

I shake my head, amused with their concerns.

Charlie: I can't go to jail. Do you know what orange does to my complexion?

Wren: Montana's state prison issues dark green uniforms.

Charlie: Whew. I was worried I'd clash with the walls.

Birdie: You're worried about matching your cell?!

Birdie: Did you miss the part where WE COULD GO TO JAIL?!

Wren: I promise to write you letters weekly.

Charlie: Birdie, stop panicking. Your dad's the sheriff—he'd never arrest you. Me and Briar? Different story.

Briar: We saved a chicken from being slaughtered. That has to count for something.

Birdie: Shh! Keep the murder talk to yourself. Nugget is still processing.

Wren: I still can't believe you named the chicken.

Birdie: Of course I did. She's part of the family now.

I smile. Her fierce loyalty to animals never ceases to amaze me.

Charlie: She better not expect a phone plan.

Birdie: Too late. She already picked out her ringtone.

Briar: We need to lie low. No more rescue missions for a while, okay?

Birdie: Copy that.

Charlie: Why do I get the feeling Birdie's version of "lying low" means a herd of sheep on her porch by sundown?

"Looks like someone's enjoying their conversation." I lift my head when I hear Jensen's voice. He's propped against the doorway, watching me. "Maybe I'd stand a better chance of getting your attention if I text you, too."

"Depends. Are you any good with emojis?"

"Nope, but I have some pretty good pickup lines that'll make you laugh."

"Go ahead, hit me with your best shot," I challenge.

I lift a brow, puzzled when he pulls out his phone and starts typing. A second later, mine buzzes with a new message. We exchanged numbers on my first day nannying for Caleb in case he ever needed to get in touch while we were out.

Jensen: Are you a parking ticket? Because you've got "FINE" written all over you.

I shake my head, fighting a grin. He was right. Funny but ridiculously cheesy.

Briar: If I'm a ticket, you're about to get fined for that terrible pun.

Jensen: I deserve a redemption line, don't you think?

Briar: Well?

Jensen: Do you have a Band-Aid? I just scraped my knee falling for you.

Briar: I have a Band-Aid, but it's not enough to patch up your delivery.

Jensen: You wound me.

Briar: Your pickup lines started it.

I steal a look at him, his mouth twitching as he holds back a smile while typing a reply.

Jensen: How about this one...

Jensen: If you were a vegetable, you'd be a cutecumber.

I burst out laughing, an unladylike snort escaping my nose. "It's official. You've entered your dad-joke era, and I fear all hope for redemption is lost."

Jensen tucks his phone into his pocket and comes to take a seat next to me on the porch swing. "Hey, I got you to laugh. That's a win in my book."

"If that's what you call winning, I'm afraid you're more out of practice than you think."

He smirks. "Guess I should thank you for tolerating my lack of humor, then. Maybe you should share what you thought was so funny on your phone when I came outside. Could be something I could learn from."

He's good, I'll give him that—steering the conversation back to the question he wants answered.

"I was checking texts from my friends' group chat. We mainly gossip and plot our next questionable decision," I respond, staying light on the details.

"Like?" Jensen presses.

I bite my bottom lip, contemplating how much to tell him. It's totally irrational, but a part of me still worries he'll judge me or decide I shouldn't watch Caleb after I admit that I committed poultry-related breaking and entering.

I face him, offering a look that's all business. "Promise you won't judge or call the sheriff?"

Jensen tilts his head, a playful smile curving at the corners of his mouth. "Now you have to tell me, or I'll assume the worst, like you getting in a bar fight or cow tipping."

I gasp in mock horror. "Birdie would never tolerate us messing with them. When Charlie suggested riding cows in high school, Birdie didn't talk to her for a month. She's all about protecting the animals at all costs."

As a kid, she was devastated when she found out the Halsteads owned a cattle ranch, and it took her years to come to terms with the idea that my family's ranch didn't mean I couldn't also support her and her passion for animal rights.

"If that's true, what in the world could you have done that might warrant a visit from the sheriff?" It's obvious Jensen's more curious than concerned.

I shift in my seat, tucking my hair behind my ear as I look him in the eye. "Remember the night we had the plumbing issue, and I was out late?"

He nods slowly.

"Well... we sort of trespassed on old man Grady's property to steal a chicken. We being me, Charlie, and Birdie," I say, trying to sound nonchalant.

To be fair, for us, it was a typical Friday night adventure.

Jensen blinks twice, his lips parting in disbelief. "You *what*?"

"He was getting rid of a chicken for being pecked on. So, we took matters into our own hands, snuck onto his property, and rescued her from being slaughtered. Had it not been for us, the poor thing would've ended up on Mr. Grady's dinner table." I exhale deeply when I finish, anxiously waiting for Jensen's response.

I don't have to wait long.

He throws his head back, laughing. "For a minute there, I thought you were about to confess to burying a body or robbing a bank. Does a chicken heist even constitute a real crime?"

I scoff, playfully swatting his arm. "Excuse me—poultry theft is serious business."

Jensen presses his lips together, amusement shining in his eyes. "Oh, I have no doubt."

"Birdie's dad is the sheriff, so we usually get a warning... and a lecture that always ends with him offering us his home-made peach cobbler."

We only had real consequences the time Charlie vandalized a minivan to create a distraction while we were saving a piglet with a limp. Turns out it was the pastor's vehicle used to deliver meals to homebound individuals and to shuttle the church's senior choir to rehearsals. That stunt bought us six months of community service, and the pastor still gives me the side-eye when I run into him at the grocery store.

"If you get hauled off to jail, I'll be waiting with bail money. No questions asked," Jensen states.

"My criminal career thanks you," I tease. "Honestly, I was half convinced you'd never let Caleb see me again if you thought I was a bad influence."

He scoots closer, his hand settling on my thigh. "By now, you should know I'd never think that, especially when you're out rescuing animals with your friends. And besides, you're far too important to Caleb, and—" He stops short, his eyes searching mine as if he wants to say more.

"I think we should talk about what happened this morning," I say hesitantly.

"Oh, you mean the part where I found your risqué panties hanging on the clothesline?" He smirks. "Yes, let's discuss that, shall we?"

I bite my lower lip. "No, the part where we almost kissed."

His grin widens. "Ah, that part. Must have slipped my mind."

I exhale slowly, my heart racing. "We were in the heat of the moment, that's all."

"Sure."

"A kiss would have been a disaster for us both."

Jensen nods. "The worst."

"It's good we stopped before it went that far."

His gaze drops to my mouth. "Definitely."

I sigh. "Will you stop agreeing with everything I say?"

His hand inches higher up my thigh. "Why? Would you rather I disagree and show you exactly what we missed out on?"

"What? No. We just agreed that it was a bad idea."

"If that were true, why is it all I can think about?" He tugs me closer, his breath skimming my lips. "Tell me I can kiss you, Briar."

It's not a question—it's an invitation to cross a line we've both been dancing around. Something real, unspoken, and long overdue. As much as I deny it, the truth is I want this... more than I should.

How much could one kiss hurt?

Tomorrow, we can go back to pretending there's nothing between us, but if I don't take this chance, I'll always wonder what could've been, and I refuse to live with regret.

"Well? What are you waiting for?" I whisper.

Jensen leans in, cupping my chin, his thumb tracing along my lower lip. His fingers barely graze my skin, but it's enough to light a fire in my nerves. It's only fair that he experiences the effect he has on me. His gaze stays locked on mine as I wrap my mouth around his thumb, my tongue swirling in slow strokes over the pad. Jensen's jaw tightens, restraint fraying at the edges, and I want it to unravel completely.

Slowly, I let his thumb slip from between my lips and lean forward until our mouths meet. I catch his bottom lip between mine, nipping just hard enough to make him groan. His breath is hot against my skin as his hand trails to my hip, gripping it firmly.

His mouth crashes over mine, my body surrendering to him with reckless abandon. I thread my fingers through his hair, dragging him closer as he deepens the kiss—claiming, consuming, devouring.

"Damn, you taste sweeter than I imagined, sugar," Jensen whispers.

He tugs me into his lap, guiding me to straddle him, his hands gripping my hips. Whatever restraint he had left snaps as he rocks up into me, his bulge rubbing against my core. My nipples grow achy, and my body hums with longing, and I'm tempted to beg for more when I remember this was supposed to only be one kiss.

What would happen if Caleb woke up and came downstairs? The thought hits me like a cold splash of water, and I lean back, breaking the trance we'd fallen into.

Jensen's chest rises and falls as his vivid green eyes meet mine, studying me as if gauging my reaction. His hair falls in tousled waves, thanks to my fingers running through it, and I long to lose myself in him again—unbothered by reason or restraint.

"Is this alright?" he asks.

"Caleb could wake up and find us out here," I say quietly.

He presses his forehead against mine, his eyes closing as he breathes me in. The quiet stretches between us, thick with words neither of us wants to speak. Caleb is our priority, and not only do we all share a living space, but I'm his nanny. What's already a complicated situation could easily spiral into a distraction Jensen can't afford and one I can't defend, no matter how my body betrays me whenever he gets close. Caleb's been through enough, and risking his stability for our own desires would be unforgivable.

When Jensen breaks the silence, his voice is low and gravelly. "That kiss was fucking incredible, and I'm not sorry it happened. In another life—one without my son asleep upstairs—I'd have taken you to bed, spread you out beneath me, and made you scream my name until your voice went raw." My thighs clench, betraying my body's desire. "But you're right, we can't let this go further."

"I guess sometimes the right things happen at the wrong time," I say softly. "But I don't regret kissing you either."

He opens his eyes, his thumb brushing my cheek. "You're so damn beautiful, darlin'."

"Careful now, with talk like that, you're starting to sound like a cowboy," I tease, a playful glint in my eye.

"One thing New Yorkers and cowboys have in common is that we understand a well-placed curse word is the most effective way to make a point."

He might not admit it, but there's a lot more country in him than he lets on, and the longer he's in Bluebell, the more that side shows. If I could get him in a pair of boots to go along with those Wranglers he's been wearing, I'd probably never be able to think straight again. That could be problematic since I'm supposed to be finding ways to dial down my attraction toward him, not make it stronger. A good first step would be getting off his lap and creating distance between us.

Yeah, definitely that.

I run my fingers through his hair, pressing a chaste kiss to his lips. "Had to sneak in one last one before going cold turkey."

Jensen gives me a soft smile as I climb off his lap and grab my phone from the seat beside us.

"Briar?"

"Yeah?"

"Had to get one more look at you standing in the moonlight with those bee-stung lips—before I go cold turkey," he teases, echoing my earlier words.

I brush my fingers over my mouth, giving him a wistful smile before slipping inside.

CHAPTER 13

Jensen

I TAKE MY GLASSES OFF, PRESSING MY FINGERS TO MY
temples as Carlton, my chief operations officer, drones on
about bug reports and sprint cycles. We have touch-base
calls semi-weekly so I can stay in the loop on what's happening
at headquarters. It's been a long morning reviewing upcoming
product changes before we move them into production for our
clients.

Before Caleb, my career was everything. It gave me control
and structure. I built DataLock Systems from the ground up,
vowing never to depend on anyone or risk losing what I'd built.
But the past month has shown me that money can't replace love
and family. Those things are earned, not bought, and require
time, patience, and a willingness to be present.

It makes me grateful for the support system we've built in
Bluebell. Thank god for Julie, who takes Caleb to the summer
camp, and Briar, who takes care of pickups. It allows me to concentrate on work during the day so I can give Caleb my full attention in the evenings.

The longer I'm away from the city and my office, the harder it is to remember why I was convinced success had to come with solitude. Now that I have Caleb, I finally understand why the silence in my penthouse used to echo so loudly.

These days, the quiet I've been feeling is for a different reason. Since that kiss with Briar a week and a half ago, we've managed to remain friendly, but there's been a distance between us. Every night, I see her on the porch, but I don't go out. If I did, I wouldn't trust myself not to pick up where we left off: with her lips against mine.

It would be easy to give in, but I'm afraid about the impact it would have on Caleb. He just lost his mom and the last thing I want is for him to think I'm trying to replace her or that he's not my priority.

To distract myself from my impossible dilemma, I glance at my phone, a chill running through me when I see that I've missed five calls from Caleb's school.

"Dammit," I mutter under my breath.

My mind races with a million worst-case scenarios. The last call I received related to Caleb changed everything, so now every unexpected one feels like it could bring life-altering news.

Carlton furrows his brow, sensing my panic. "Jensen, are you alright?"

I glance up at the monitor, shaking my head. "We'll have to finish this later. Something urgent has come up." I end our meeting, not waiting for him to reply.

Just then, the school calls again. I swipe to answer on the second ring, dread tightening in my chest.

"Hello, this is Jensen."

"Mr. Harding, this is Lisa, the summer camp receptionist from Willow Creek Elementary. I have Caleb here in the office with me. He was sent here because he got into an altercation with another student."

I straighten in my chair, running a hand through my hair. "What the hell happened? Is Caleb okay?"

"I was told he pushed another student to the ground." Her voice is hesitant, as if she's trying to soften the blow.

"Excuse me? You think *my* son, whose idea of confrontation is walking away, started a fight?"

"I'm sorry," she apologizes, her tone genuinely remorseful. "I'm just relaying what I was told. You'll have to speak to his camp counselor to get the details."

"I'm on my way," I say as I stand and grab my keys before heading to the front door.

"See you soon, Mr. Harding," Lisa replies before hanging up.

I wonder where Julie is. Even if Caleb had done something wrong, which I doubt, she'd be by his side if she could. I try calling her, but it goes straight to voicemail, so I focus on getting to the school as quickly as I can.

I've just swung open the truck door when I spot Briar walking down the lane. She breaks into a jog when she sees me.

"I was going to change and make myself lunch before picking up Caleb from camp. Where are you racing off to?" she teases.

"The school called. Caleb's been in an *altercation*." My voice tightens with every word, barely masking my anger.

Briar gasps, covering her mouth with her hand. "Is he okay?"

"They wouldn't give me many details. I'm heading there now."

"Would you like me to come?" she offers tentatively.

Do I?

In the past few weeks, she's become a fixture in Caleb's life, and she understands him as well as I do. I'm certain he would want her there, and honestly, I do too.

"Yeah, hop in."

The drive to the school is quiet. Briar and I are both too preoccupied with our thoughts to talk much.

As soon as we pull into the parking lot and I shut off the engine, we rush to the entrance. Once we're buzzed in, we head straight for the office but stop short when we see Caleb sitting outside the office on a bench next to Julie. My stomach drops when I notice the tears in his eyes.

When he spots us, Caleb jumps off the bench and bolts to Briar. She crouches, arms open wide, and he throws himself into her arms, hugging her neck tightly.

"It's alright, sweetie. Your dad and I are here. You're not alone." Her voice trembles, thick with concern.

As my son clings to Briar with his head buried in her hair, I know I made the right call bringing her along. It's not about *who* comforts Caleb—but about making sure he feels safe. And I'll never stop being thankful that we're surrounded by people who offer him that, without hesitation or condition.

As Caleb lifts his tear-streaked face, his lower lip trembling, I kneel beside him and gently wipe away his tears. I give him a quick once-over for any physical injuries and am relieved when I don't find anything visible.

"Briar's right, buddy. We're here now and will take care of everything." He's my whole world, and I'll do whatever it takes to protect him.

A lump catches in my throat as he presses his cheek against my hand, his trust anchoring me. I rub his back, trying to ease the tension from his small frame. These are the moments no one warns you about in parenthood. The ones that leave you powerless, wishing you could shield your child from the harshness of the world and promise them a life without pain or fear.

Julie approaches, her face heavy with regret. "I apologize for missing your call. I was interviewing a candidate for a fall teaching position and came as quickly as I could."

"What happened?" I ask.

"I'm not certain yet, but we'll get to the bottom of it. Michael, the other child involved, is with a camp counselor in one of the classrooms. His mom, Vickie, is waiting in my office now. I think it's best if we all sit down together."

This is one of those times I wish Caleb would speak. It'd be much easier if he could tell me exactly what happened. Instead, I'm left relying on another student and his mom, who are only looking out for their own interests.

"What about Caleb?" Briar chimes in.

"Lisa can keep him company in the front office," Julie says with a reassuring smile. "It shouldn't take long."

I've met her a few times since Caleb started summer camp, and I trust she'll look after him. Still, it's hard leaving him this shaken, but I have to get to the bottom of this.

"Caleb." I wait until he lifts his head to continue. "Briar and I are going to speak with Julie for a few minutes, but we'll be right back, okay?"

He burrows his face into the curve of Briar's neck, and she draws him closer.

"It's alright, little man. You'll hang out with Lisa for a little while, and I have it on good authority that she has a hidden stash of cookies in her desk drawer. I bet she'll let you have one." Briar's voice is gentle. "And when we get home, we can play with Ziggy. I'm sure he'd like some cuddles too. How does that sound?"

She waits patiently as Caleb sniffles, peeking up at her. Briar's face softens into a warm smile when he gives her a small nod.

"Sounds like a plan. We won't be gone long," she promises.

Caleb glances at me for confirmation.

"She's right, bud. We'll be right back."

"Come on, honey, we'll go find Lisa together, and I'll make sure she gets you a cookie," Julie says.

Caleb hesitates for a moment before pulling away from Briar. He slips his hand into Julie's outstretched one. As she guides him toward the front office, he glances back, and I give him a thumbs-up.

My heart shatters at the sight of him so upset, but I keep my emotions in check, not wanting him to witness me losing control. The best thing I can do is be strong and figure out what actually went down.

"You two go ahead to my office. I'll be right there," Julie says over her shoulder.

I nod, heading in that direction. Briar stays in step beside me, neither of us speaking. I don't bother knocking before walking in.

Julie's office is warm and welcoming with large windows letting in the sun. Framed student artwork lines the walls, and a colorful rug covers the center of the room, surrounded by beanbag chairs and a low table scattered with picture books.

Vickie is perched behind Julie's desk as if she owns the place. Her auburn hair is twisted into a messy bun, and thick eyeliner frames her eyes. She's dressed in a grease-stained jumpsuit with her name stitched on the front, which makes me think she came straight from work to be here.

"You must be Caleb's dad," she says, her voice clipped. "Mind explaining why your kid thought it was okay to hurt mine?"

I stiffen at her accusation but bite back my frustration. "That doesn't sound like Caleb."

She scoffs. "Oh, please. My Michael said he wanted a turn with the bubble wand, but Caleb wouldn't share. When he asked again, your son shoved him, and now he's got a big bruise on his left knee from the fall."

I exhale through my nose, willing myself to remain calm. It's probably best to wait until Julie gets here to continue this conversation, but I refuse to stand by and let this woman paint Caleb as a playground bully when I know he'd never show aggression like she's describing.

"Bullshit," I retort.

Vickie gapes at me. "Excuse me?"

"You heard me," I say, folding my arms across my chest. "I'm guessing you weren't around for this so-called altercation, so how can you be sure what really happened?"

"Michael doesn't have a reason to lie."

"And you know that how?"

"Because he's my kid, and I believe him. Besides, it's the only version of events we're going to get. It's not our fault *your* son *won't* speak," she says, rolling her eyes. "Maybe you should do a better job at home of preparing him to interact with other kids before sending him off to summer camp and then acting shocked when he causes problems."

My jaw tightens, and I fix her with a sharp glare as a hot surge of anger burns in my chest. No one has the right to talk about my son like that, least of all someone who doesn't know the first thing about him or what he's been through.

Vickie fails to understand that even if Caleb chooses never to speak again, it doesn't matter. He's perfect exactly as he is. If that means we work with his therapist and find someone to teach both of us sign language so we can build a new way to communicate long-term, then that's what we'll do.

Before I can respond, Briar, who's been silently observing until now, steps around me, leans across the desk, and points her finger at Vickie.

"Caleb might prefer not to speak, but he's still one of the brightest and most gentle kids I've ever met," she fires back, eyes narrowed. "Shame on you for putting down a child just to defend your own."

Vickie scoffs. "Last I checked, your job is maintaining cabins, not handing out parenting advice. And you're not Caleb's parent, so what are you even doing here?"

I often forget how small Bluebell is—where most people know each other's names and what they do for a living.

Briar pushes back from the desk, standing straight. "Caleb recently lost his mom, and unlike you, I know better than to shame a child for how they choose to grieve. Even after everything he's been through, I can say with certainty he'd never shove someone unprovoked."

My mouth falls open, captivated by the fierce way she defends him. She's sexy as hell, standing her ground, and the passion in her voice hits me harder than I expected. I'm grateful I didn't let my hesitations get in the way of hiring her as Caleb's nanny, because she's the best thing that could have happened to him... and to me.

Before things escalate further, Julie steps inside her office, pursing her lips as if she can sense the tension. Vickie's eyes widen, and she quickly rises from the chair, straightening her uniform.

"Is Caleb alright?" I ask.

Julie nods. "He's fine." Turning to Vickie, she adds, "I just reviewed the report log and found an interesting entry. Yesterday, a camp counselor documented that Michael fell on the concrete while playing tag and ended up with a large bruise on his left knee. She also noted that his dad was informed at pickup."

Vickie's cheeks turn red as she glances over at Briar and me. "That's my ex-husband for you. Never tells me a damn thing."

Briar shoots her a cutting look as if to say *I told you so.*

"Guess it's a good thing we cleared up this misunderstanding," Vickie adds.

Misunderstanding, my ass.

The only reason she's back-pedaling is because she's embarrassed to admit she was wrong.

Julie clears her throat, and motions to Vickie. "Why don't we go get Michael? We can talk more out in the hall if you have any other concerns you'd like to discuss."

"Yeah, okay," Vickie replies, clearly eager to leave.

I watch as she ducks out of the office, avoiding eye contact. Julie follows, casting a curious glance at me and Briar.

I let out a relieved sigh, grateful for how that turned out. Still, part of me wants to pull Caleb out of camp, even if I know that's not a viable solution. He should be around other kids and learn to resolve conflict. However, it's hard watching him get hurt and seeing other adults rush to judge him simply because he's different.

Briar lowers herself onto Julie's desk, eyes shimmering with unshed tears. I move beside her and slide my arm around her.

"What's wrong?" Her sadness hits me almost as hard as Caleb's.

She tries brushing it off, but her voice wavers. "It hurt to see Caleb so upset, especially when he didn't do anything wrong. How can anyone be so cruel to a kid? Vickie's a mom. You'd think she'd have more compassion."

I draw her into my side, wiping a stray tear away. "You have a beautiful soul, Briar Halstead. Thank you for loving my son as much as I do."

She offers me a feeble smile. "I'd do anything for him."

"He's lucky to have you... We both are."

With every kind word, selfless act, and sweet smile, she chips away at my resolve, making it harder to pretend I'm not halfway gone for her already. As I lean in, her apple-sweet scent surrounds me, and for a fleeting moment, I allow myself to hold her close, a calm I haven't experienced in days washing over me.

"Let's go get Caleb, and then we'll stop by Sweet Spur Creamery for ice cream," I say.

"He'll love that," Briar replies.

CHAPTER 14

Jensen

T HE NEXT DAY, I DECIDE TO KEEP CALEB HOME FROM CAMP and take the day off work. After what happened yesterday, I felt we could both use a chance to recharge and spend some quality time together.

We're perched on a fence alongside one of the pastures, sharing a peanut butter and jelly sandwich and watching Petunia, Heath's pet cow, nose her way through the grass. Lately, we've been visiting daily, and Caleb has become almost as smitten with her as he is with Ziggy.

I have one arm around Caleb to keep him steady as he eats. "Good, huh?"

He nods enthusiastically as he takes a big bite.

Before we set off on our adventure, I packed PB&Js, a bag of Cheez-Its, a carton of strawberries from the patch behind the ranch house, and some water bottles. I want each outing to be special and serve as a small reminder of how much he matters to me.

When a butterfly lands near Petunia, she stops and lifts her head, letting out a loud moo that only stops once the butterfly has flown away. Caleb bursts into laughter as she flicks her tail and turns in a slow circle to make sure the intruder is gone.

I lean over, nudging his side. "Guess she isn't a fan of butterflies sharing her grass."

He gives me a nod, his eyes crinkling with amusement.

These moments with him make me appreciate the slower pace of life. Summer is flying by faster than I want, and soon, we'll be back in New York with him starting kindergarten. I once viewed the city as my escape, convinced that ambition and status would erase my past. Funny how the very place I wanted to get away from is the one healing me and my son in ways I never expected.

It makes me wonder how I'll give up the routine we've created or the quality time we've spent together in Bluebell. Sure, I'm working now, but since we got here, I've learned to set boundaries. I take a break when Caleb gets home from camp before he and Briar head off for the afternoon, and by six, I'm done for the day. Our weekends are all about creating memories. We explore the ranch, play with Ziggy, and often stop by the ranch house to feed the chickens. Briar has dinner with us but usually leaves us alone the rest of the night. If I'm honest, we'd both love to spend more time with her.

I glance across the pasture when I hear a horse's neigh and see Heath riding toward us on a black quarter horse, its white blaze standing out against the dark coat.

Caleb scoots closer, leaning into my side. He's still unsure around the horses but enjoys watching them from a distance. Briar mentioned wanting him to take lessons, but if that happens, I've decided I'll be the one to teach him. I'm a bit rusty since it's been so long, but riding never leaves you. I've missed it—a lot. There's a quiet power in learning to move in sync with an animal that commanding, and I'd like Caleb to experience that when he's ready.

Heath tips his hat as he gets closer. "Howdy there, buckaroo. You making sure your dad stays out of trouble today?"

Caleb's lips tug into a smile as he gives Heath a thumbs-up before plopping the last bite of his sandwich into his mouth.

"Good man. Someone's gotta keep him in line." Heath winks.

"Give it a few more weeks, and he'll be running this place," I tease, ruffling Caleb's hair.

"If that's the case, we've got to get him a hat and boots of his own. No proper cowboy or rancher can go without them. Although, I bet Briar's already on it," he says with a glint in his eyes I can't quite decipher.

I brush a few crumbs off Caleb's face and grab the water bottle from the fence post. Once I uncap it, I hand it to him and he takes a long sip. He lets out a satisfied sigh, wiping his mouth with the back of his hand.

"What are you doing out here in the middle of the day?" I ask Heath. "Don't you have cattle to round up or chores to do?" I smirk.

He swings down from his horse and loops the reins around the fence post, pulling them tight. He grabs a small container from his saddlebag before coming to stand near where we're sitting.

"Walker and the ranch hands took a lunch break, so I came to check this part of the perimeter. When I spotted you, I figured I'd stop by to visit Caleb and Petunia."

I arch a brow. "Nice to know where I stand."

"Sorry, partner. The new model has better hair and my favorite snack. Hard to compete with that," he says, grinning at Caleb, who has a Fruit Roll-Up sticking out of the pocket of his overalls.

"I'll remember that when you want help digging a post hold or baling hay."

Heath rubs the back of his neck. "Actually, now that you mention it, I could use some extra hands with the latter soon if you're up for it."

I roll my eyes, laughing. "Oh sure, nothing says lifelong

friends like swapping me out, then backtracking when you realize you need me for manual labor."

Heath arches a brow. "So does that mean you're in?"

I shrug. "Sure, but only if I'm done by six. Saturday nights are reserved for pizza and cartoons with Caleb."

"Fair enough," he says before turning to Caleb. "I brought Petunia a treat. Want to give it to her?"

Caleb nods eagerly and reaches out as Heath helps him down from the post. It's not the first time he's fed the cow, and he always lights up at the chance. He waits nearby while Heath pulls a small container from his saddlebag, then follows him over to Petunia. Her eyes are glued to the treats in Heath's hands, her tail swishing with excitement. He'll deny it, but Heath definitely thinks of her as his pet. It's ironic, considering most of the cattle on the ranch are raised for meat.

"Hey there, sweet girl," he murmurs as he scratches behind her ear. "We brought you a snack."

Petunia moos softly, pressing her nose against his palm while he pets her. He pauses to open the container he brought, and Caleb is already waiting with his hands cupped. Heath pours a generous amount of oats into them, and Petunia dips her head to reach Caleb's hands, greedily eating from his palms.

"She's your biggest fan." Heath chuckles.

Caleb giggles when Petunia sticks out her tongue, sweeping up every stray oat. My chest tightens, the sound music to my ears. I'll never tire of hearing it, and I'm grateful that it's becoming more frequent. Julie was right about the ranch being good for him. Not only has being around Ziggy, Petunia, and the other animals been therapeutic, but having the Halsteads rally around him has made all the difference too.

Here, he has all the love, support, and encouragement I could've hoped for, and I worry about how we'll manage when we leave it all behind to go back to New York.

CHAPTER 15

Brian

I'M IN THE GENERAL STORE ON THE RANCH, RESTOCKING shelves. Ethel runs it most days since she only cleans a couple of cabins each day—majority of guests stay long enough that daily housekeeping isn't needed.

I'm halfway through stocking travel-size shampoo bottles when my phone buzzes. I've been at it for hours, so I take it as a sign to give myself a break.

Backroads & Bad Decisions Group Chat

Charlie: You'll never guess who came into the shop this morning.

Birdie: Mr. Grady!?

Wren: Heath.

Briar: The new barista who flirts with you at Lasso & Latte with the rattail mullet and another woman's name on his neck?

Charlie: Nope, thank god no, and eww, seriously???

Charlie: The new hotshot lawyer came into the shop today. He was asking about you, Briar. He wants to take you out tonight.

Briar: Did you tell him I was interested?

She better not have.

Charlie: You never said you weren't.

I sigh. Having a feeling I might not like where this is going.

Wren: Not that it would matter. Charlie would set you up either way.

Birdie: No joke. Remember the bartender she pushed me into seeing? Charlie knew he was a walking red flag and still gave him my number.

Charlie: How was I supposed to know he was collecting a Rolodex of women for casual hookups?

Charlie: You were the one who agreed to the date.

Birdie: I didn't want to be rude! Then he had to go and ask me to ride him halfway through dinner.

Birdie: I thought he meant horseback riding until I texted you. I had to sit through the rest of dinner, mortified, waiting for him to finish his cheesecake so I could bolt.

> Wren: Honey, the next time a man asks you that on a first date, you don't stay for dessert. Grab your purse and leave.

> Briar: Amen to that.

> Charlie: So, is the date with the hotshot lawyer a no-go?

> Briar: I didn't say that.

> Charlie: It's okay to admit you're waiting for Mr. Hot Single Dad.

> Briar: I'm not.

I looped the girls in on my kiss with Jensen and swore it was a one-time thing, end of story.

The problem is, my hormones haven't gotten the memo. The man's a walking thirst trap, especially when he has on gray sweatpants and the glasses he wears at night, and with him down the hall, I have to refrain from sneaking into his room, demanding he prove all my fantasies right.

It's a good thing I have my own bathroom, because lately my showerhead's been putting in overtime. Still, it's a poor substitute for the real thing—calloused hands, warm skin, and a deep voice growling every filthy thing he plans to do to me.

Jensen wasn't wrong when he assumed I'd only been with country *boys* before. They handled me like I was made of glass, fumbling their way around with no idea how to bring me pleasure. I crave to be manhandled, dominated, and pushed to my limits— shown what it means to be taken control of. The one person I'm confident could provide that is strictly off-limits.

> Charlie: What should I tell the hotshot lawyer?

What's the worst that could happen if I said yes? The guy ends up being a total bore—or talks about himself nonstop? But what if I have a good time and get a break from thinking about a certain *someone*. Worth a shot, right? I hit send on the text I've just typed out before I can second-guess myself.

> Briar: I'm in.

> Charlie: Holy plot twist.

> Briar: Tell him I'll meet him at the Prickly Pear Diner at 7:30 p.m.

She sends me a thumbs-up.

This is going to be great… I think. At the very least, I'm looking forward to a much-needed distraction.

Once I've finished at the general store, I head back to the cottage. I want to speak to Jensen before I pick Caleb up from the school.

I'm caught off guard when I don't find him in the dining area, where he's set up his makeshift office. Normally, he's glued to his computer during the day, and the few times I've been home while he's working, he only gets up to check on Caleb or grab a bottle of water from the fridge.

I'm about to head outside to see if he's with Ziggy when I hear footsteps on the stairs. A second later, I look over to see him in the doorway. His damp hair tells me he must have recently taken a shower, but all I can focus on are the dark-wash Wranglers he's paired with a white crew-neck T-shirt. As if that weren't enough, he's wearing his glasses too.

Fantastic.

It's official: the universe is conspiring against me. Good thing he's not wearing boots, or I might have forgotten all about Mr. Lawyer and jumped Jensen right here and now.

"Briar, are you alright?"

I blink up at his face, dazed. "Hmm?"

Jensen's mouth twitches, fighting a grin. "You good? You spaced out on me there for a second."

"Sorry. I'm still getting used to seeing you in pants," I blurt without thinking. "Jeans. I mean jeans." Heat floods my face as I scramble to correct myself.

Real smooth, Briar. You might as well admit you're picturing him sweaty, shirtless, and railing you in the back of the barn while you're at it.

"Looks like you're wearing them too," he notes.

"Yeah, but I've always worn them. Until recently, you wore slacks and a button-up," I reply, pointing out the obvious.

"Heath brought over a couple of pairs of Wranglers for me. I'm helping bale hay next weekend, and he told me if I showed up in slacks or sweats, Walker and the ranch hands would never let me live it down."

I have a serious bone to pick with Heath. Helping turn Jensen into cowboy eye candy is cruel and unusual punishment when I'm expected to pretend to be unaffected by his denim and bicep situation.

"You still good to pick up Caleb?" he asks.

I nod, grateful for the change in subject.

"Yeah. I was hoping I could get off a bit early today, say around five, if that works."

"That's no problem. I've got him covered. Everything okay? Or are you off to save some more chickens tonight?" he asks, nudging his glasses up his nose with a crooked smile.

I chuckle awkwardly, running a hand through my hair. "Not exactly."

"Let me guess, saving a lamb from ending up on someone's dinner plate?"

All I wanted was a quick yes and an easy exit. Now, I'm stuck having to tell him I have plans with a guy I'm not interested in, all in the name of trying to distract myself from him. The last part I'm keeping to myself.

"I'm going on a date tonight. We're meeting at the Prickly Pear Diner, and I want some extra time to get ready," I say quickly before I lose my nerve.

Jensen goes still, his posture going rigid as if carved from stone. His jaw slackens as a myriad of emotions flickers across his face before his features settle into a neutral mask.

He gives me a small smile that doesn't reach his eyes before moving around me to get to his workstation. "Have a good time."

Is he serious?

Part of me was convinced he would beg me not to go or at least show some sign that it bothered him. Maybe our kiss didn't mean as much to him as it did to me. Could he be waiting for me to move on so he wouldn't have to spell out that he's not interested? The thought stings more than it should, especially after spending the past few days thinking of nothing but him.

I swallow the lump in my throat, feeling the excitement drain away, thanks to his dismissive goodbye. Still, I'm determined not to let this dictate my mood for the evening. I have a date with a hot lawyer, and I intend to enjoy every minute, even if deep down, I'd rather be with Jensen.

CHAPTER 16

Jensen

IT'S SETTLED. I'M A GODDAMN IDIOT.

I pace the entryway as if that'll make time move faster. At this rate, I'll wear through the rug and my nerves by the end of the night.

Briar left for her date thirty minutes ago. She was wearing a blue floral summer dress that hit mid-thigh, paired with cream cowboy boots, making the outfit more seductive than sweet. She looked stunning, and all I could think about was it should've been me taking her out to dinner and making her laugh. Instead, I let her leave and told her to have a good time with another man.

I shouldn't have tried to play it cool when she told me she was going out. If she'd mentioned it was a date before asking to get off work early, I would've found an excuse to keep her at the cottage tonight. Petty? Maybe. But the thought of her out with another man is pure torture. Yes, I'm aware we've only kissed once, but that hasn't stopped this gnawing jealousy from sinking its teeth into my chest when I picture her with someone else.

The worst part? She had Earl pick her up. Nothing says "first date" like calling the town taxi instead of driving yourself. If she wasn't planning to go home with the guy she's out with, why not drive herself?

What am I going to do?

I can't just pick up the phone and ask her to come back. She'd ask why, and what am I supposed to say? That I'm jealous? Like I have any right? We agreed that nothing could happen beyond the kiss we shared.

However, if Briar gets serious with this guy, I'll be forced to watch him fawn over her, and she won't spend as much time with Caleb and me. That's not going to happen on my watch.

So much for keeping my distance.

I have to put a stop to her night out.

But how?

Julie and Samuel are visiting a friend a few towns over, and even if they left now, they wouldn't be back for another hour. That's enough time for Briar to finish dinner and be well on her way to falling for her date.

I dial Heath's number, cursing when it goes straight to voicemail, so I try Walker next.

"What's up, pretty boy?" he answers, his tone cheeky.

"Where's your brother?"

"Out."

I let out a frustrated sigh, losing patience. "Out where?"

"He was checking the cattle, so he should be back at the ranch house soon. Why?"

"I need you guys to come to the cottage and watch Caleb for a couple of hours."

He lets out a humorless laugh. "Good one."

"I'm serious."

"You must be desperate if you're askin' two guys with zero experience to look after your kid."

"Walker," I say, my tone sharp. "This is important. He's in bed, so all you have to do is wait downstairs until I'm back."

"What if he wakes up?"

"You give him a glass of water and read him a story. He hardly ever gets up once he's settled, so you shouldn't worry about that."

"And where exactly are you going out on a week night?"

You'd think I was being cross-examined based on his line of questioning.

"Prickly Pear Diner."

Walker lets out a low whistle. "Interesting. Isn't that where Briar's on her date tonight? According to the town gossip, she's gone out with a fancy lawyer from California who moved here to work at his uncle's practice."

I clear my throat to hide my jealousy. "A lawyer?"

"Don't worry, I doubt he'll last very long. He's a vegan. We don't have tofu and avocado toast around these parts. Although he does have dreamy blue eyes," Walker says with a swoony flair. "Come to think of it, why do you care so much who Briar dates? Aren't you a little old for her?" he jokes, not letting up. "I hear the lawyer is only twenty-six."

"That's five years younger than you," I point out.

"Yeah, but six years younger than *you*," he quips. "Plus, he's not family, so I can't question his intentions with Briar like I can yours."

I sigh, running a hand through my hair. The truth is, I don't even fully understand the feelings I have for her. Would the age gap stop me from going after her if that was even an option? Hell no. I'd even let Walker and Heath grill me on my intentions. But for now, my only focus is cutting Briar's date short. Unpacking my feelings will have to wait.

"Walker," I growl, "can you and Heath come or not?"

He chuckles, clearly getting a kick out of pushing my buttons.

"What's in it for us? I was going to swing by Blue Moon Tavern tonight and wasn't planning on leaving alone."

Son of a bitch. This is why I prefer Heath. He's straightforward and doesn't play games. Walker, on the other hand, has the reputation of a cowboy Casanova. Rumor has it he's been with half the women in town and left behind a trail of broken hearts.

"I'm helping bale hay next weekend," I say.

He scoffs. "If I'm giving up a night with a pretty girl, there's no way you're getting off that easy. I want you working three full Saturdays on the ranch." He pauses, giving me a chance to think about it. "Do we have a deal?"

"Fine." Whatever it takes to get him here and fast.

"Awesome." I hear a door creak open, followed by the low grumble of a truck engine. "Heath just pulled in. We'll be there soon. And if that kid wakes up while we're there, I'm cashing in another Saturday of hard labor."

"His name is Caleb, and that won't be necessary. He'll stay asleep."

Not a promise I should make, but desperate times call for desperate measures.

The whole drive into town, my mind runs through every worst-case scenario. What if Briar's angry when she finds out I'm here? What if she's making out with the guy? Or what if they've already left for his place? I'm a damn pressure cooker when I reach Prickly Pear Diner. The flickering neon sign has me clenching my jaw hard enough to crack a molar.

I slam the truck door and march inside. I'm relieved when I spot the "Seat Yourself" sign near the hostess station. It's a small victory to avoid an awkward interaction that could land me in the town gossip column. I'd rather not explain why I'm here to keep an eye out on my kid's nanny, who's on a date with another man.

Nothing odd about that, right?

I fall behind a group of patrons heading into the dining area, tugging the brim of Walker's cowboy hat lower to avoid drawing attention to myself. He insisted I borrow it on my way out the door, claiming I'd stick out like a sore thumb without it, and tonight, I'd much rather blend in.

I move slowly, scanning the room until I spot Briar at a corner high-top table. She's seated across from a man with wavy blond hair, wearing a colorful floral shirt that must have come from a beachside surf shop, paired with black skinny jeans that seem painted on. He sticks out like a sore thumb, and several patrons keep shooting him wary glances, clearly not used to his flashy style.

Walker was right about the cowboy hat. No one's given me a second glance so far. I'm almost to the bar, where I'll have a clear line of sight to Briar's table, when a voice cuts through the low buzz of conversation.

"Hey, urban cowboy. You're blocking my view."

I turn to find a woman sitting at a nearby booth with red hair pulled into a ponytail beneath a green baseball cap, sunglasses hiding most of her face. She's wearing an oversized T-shirt that says *Stakeouts are my Cardio*. Subtlety doesn't appear to be her strong suit.

"Can I help you?"

She motions to the empty side of the booth. "Take a seat before you ruin my surveillance."

I glance around, unsure what to do, but when she sighs, tapping her red-painted nails on the table, I figure it's best if I do as she says.

Once I'm seated, the woman pushes a glass of water my way. "This is yours. Took you long enough to get here. I was starting to think you weren't going to show up."

I take a cautious sip, frowning. "Who did you say you were?"

"I'm Charlie, Briar's best friend and your fairy god-matchmaker tonight."

I sputter into my glass before setting it down. "Sorry. Are you the one who saves chickens?"

Briar has mentioned her friends' names before, but I can't keep them straight. It would've helped if she'd had them over since Caleb and I got to Bluebell, but she usually meets up with them in town. Now I'm left at a disadvantage, sitting across from one of them, and I'm not sure if she's going to continue to make small talk or start an interrogation.

Charlie shakes her head. "That's Birdie. I'm the getaway driver and distractions creator when things go sideways and we need a quick escape."

I motion to her ensemble. "And what mission is it you're on tonight?"

"I thought you'd never ask." She slides her sunglasses off, tucking them in the V of her shirt. "I'm working double duty as a spy and a matchmaker. It's exhausting. Thank god I ordered an appetizer." She slides a basket of chili cheese fries between us that I hadn't noticed earlier and plops one into her mouth.

While she's distracted, I look over at Briar and her date. He's busy scanning his menu, but Briar's stays closed, her eyes darting to the clock on the wall every few seconds. Maybe she's not enjoying herself as much as I thought she might.

"They're taking *forever* to order," Charlie says, making me turn back to her. "The hotshot lawyer is from California *and* vegan, so he's had a million questions about the menu. He'd better plan on leaving a big tip because their server is ready to throw him out if he asks about the dairy-free options one more time."

"He sounds high maintenance," I say, doing my best to hide how pleased I am. "You still haven't told me why you're here or how you knew I'd show up." Hell, I only figured it out an hour ago. "Were you not a fan of her going out with the lawyer either?"

Charlie's smirk tells me I've admitted more than I should.

"Actually, I set them up," she says smugly, grabbing another fry.

"You *what*?"

She leans across the table, giving my arm a patronizing pat. "Relax, urban cowboy. It was for your benefit since you hadn't figured out what was staring you in the face."

"What is that supposed to mean?" My voice rises, earning a few curious glances from nearby diners.

"Word on the ranch is that you can't stop making googly eyes at our girl." She smirks.

I blink, my mouth falling open, but nothing comes out. My first instinct is to deny Charlie's claim, but images of Briar over the past few days flood my mind. Whenever I see her, I'm unable to look away, mesmerized by how damn beautiful she is.

"Who told you that?" I ask, narrowing my eyes.

Charlie shrugs. "A lady never reveals her sources, but you didn't deny it, and that says a lot. Now, shh." She presses a finger to her lips. "We're supposed to be flying under the radar here."

"Your wardrobe isn't doing us any favors," I mutter.

"I heard that," she says, sipping her drink. "You should be nice, considering I know where you sleep."

"God, you're terrifying."

She grins. "Thank you."

I roll my eyes. "It wasn't a compliment."

We're so caught up in our conversation that I almost miss Briar's date setting down his menu and reaching for her hand across the table. I grit my teeth, bracing for the possibility that she might be receptive. But before he can touch her, she lifts her glass, taking a drink of water and offers him a tight smile.

"Thank god," I mutter under my breath.

She obviously isn't interested in his attempt at physical contact and that makes me breathe easier.

Just when I think that's the end of it, the hotshot lawyer moves his hand under the table, leaning forward to rest it on Briar's leg. She stills, her smile faltering as her mouth forms the word "no." But when she tries to move away, he chuckles, tightening his grip and ignoring her protest as if he's entitled to her personal space without permission.

"That motherfucker," Charlie hisses.

She's halfway out of the booth, ready to raise hell, when I slide out first and step in her way, blocking her from getting out.

"I'll handle this," I say firmly.

I storm toward Briar's table, my fists clenched at my sides with retribution on my mind. I'm usually a level-headed person, but when a man crosses a boundary with a woman, all bets are off. Especially when he dares to touch the person who's become important to me.

"Give him hell, urban cowboy," Charlie calls out behind me.

I plan to.

My focus is locked on the lawyer, his hand still gripping Briar's leg. She shifts, angling her body away from him the best she can. With each step I take, the anger in my chest intensifies. As I approach, the asshole finally notices me, his smug expression starting to slip.

"You're at the wrong table, buddy." He scoffs.

"Take your hand off Briar."

Confusion flashes across her face when she hears my voice, but the tension in her shoulders eases when our eyes meet.

"Mind your own damn business," the lawyer snaps.

"Move. Your. Hand. I won't ask again," I warn, taking one step closer.

My threat works, and he yanks his hand back, planting both on the tabletop. But it's a little too late.

I glare at the jerk, silently promising consequences before turning to Briar. "You alright?"

Her brows knit together. "What are you doing here?"

I run my hand down her arm, my knuckles grazing her skin. "Tell me you're okay."

She smiles faintly, nodding. "Yeah, I'm fine. Are you?"

"I'd feel better if you got up from the table."

Briar doesn't argue and is quick to stand. The second she's beside me, I slip an arm around her waist, guiding her behind me, away from the lawyer's leering gaze.

"Who the hell do you think you are interrupting our date?" he demands.

My shoulders stiffen as I turn back to him, thrusting a finger into his chest. "I'm the guy making sure she's safe from pieces of shit like you," I spit in his face. "'No' is a full sentence."

He recoils, eyes narrowing. "Whatever. She's not worth the hassle anyway."

The last thread of my patience snaps, and I step forward, grabbing the asshole by the collar of his shirt. "Wrong. Any man with half a brain would see she's a fucking catch. You're just too foolish to see it." I tighten my grip, smirking when he grips my wrist trying to break free. "You're a fucking coward who threw away his shot with a woman who's smart, beautiful, and kind. She deserves respect, and I'm the one who'll make sure she gets it."

"You better let me go, or I'll make sure you never—" He doesn't get the chance to finish before a splash of water hits his face.

It splatters across my arm, but I couldn't care less. I'm satisfied as I watch the spineless coward gasping for air, his smugness finally wiped clean.

I glance over at Charlie, who's now standing beside me with one hand on her hip, the other holding an empty water glass. "No one touches my friend without permission," she snaps. "I should have known that a man who wears skinny jeans can't be trusted."

She has that right.

I give the lawyer's collar another tug before releasing him. "If you ever touch Briar or any of her friends for that matter, you'll have me and her brothers to answer to." I'm one second away from throwing a punch when Briar's fingers brush my shoulder.

I look back to find her watching me with cheeks flushed and a soft smile. "Why don't we get out of here?"

Her words snap me out of my rage, and I nod, leaning over to grab her purse hanging from her chair. I place my hand on Briar's back, ushering her to the exit with Charlie following us close. My sole focus is on getting her as far away from the jackass lawyer as possible.

Once we get to the entrance area, Briar pulls away. Folding her arms she looks between Charlie and me. "Would you like to explain what the two of you are doing here?"

"I was just minding my own business, staking out to make sure your date wasn't a serial killer, when the next thing I know, urban cowboy here showed up all frustrated and territorial about you going out with someone else." Charlie waves a hand toward me. "The audacity of him, right? But thank god he showed up when he did, or I might've ended up getting arrested for roughing up that idiot for touching you without permission."

One thing is for sure. Charlie's not subtle, but her heart's in the right place. I'm glad Briar has a friend so fiercely in her corner, and who doesn't hesitate to protect her.

Briar turns to me, concern etched in her features. "Where's Caleb? Is he alright?"

"He's fine," I assure her. "He's at the cottage with Heath and Walker but should still be asleep."

"Ten bucks he's not when you get home," Charlie teases.

Briar shoots her a playful glare. "You're not off the hook, sister. We'll talk later."

Charlie grins. "If it weren't for me, urban cowboy wouldn't have rescued you from Mr. Grabby Hand. Just saying."

Briar chuckles, pulling her into a hug. "You might have a flair for dramatics, but I'm grateful you were here."

"Love you, babe."

"Love you more."

Charlie steps back with a smile. "Alright, that's enough drama for one night. Go be with your man and check on the little guy."

Briar shoots her a pointed look.

Charlie holds out her hands. "Hey, just saying. Have fun, lovebirds," she hollers as she steps outside, causing everyone waiting to be seated to look in our direction.

Before Briar and I follow, I crane my neck, getting one last look at the pathetic lawyer. He's still standing by the table soaking wet, now arguing with the server. Let that be a lesson for trying to touch what's mine.

CHAPTER 17

Briar

J ENSEN OPENS THE TRUCK DOOR FOR ME LIKE THE PERFECT
gentleman, and when he circles to the driver's side, I check
my phone and notice a string of missed texts.

Backroads & Bad Decisions Group Chat

Charlie: Mission: Date Night with Hot
Lawyer = Successfully Aborted

Charlie: PS. He turned out to be a handsy
creep with no concept of personal space.

Wren: Wrong message thread, Charlie.

Charlie: Shit!

I shake my head with amusement.

Briar: Wow. So we're doing secret group
chats now. Noted.

Birdie: Only for tonight!

Charlie: Snitch.

I have a good idea what it means, and truth be told, I'm not mad about it.

My date was a train wreck from the start. Sure, the lawyer was good-looking, but that lost its charm the second he launched into a ten-minute tirade about how awful small towns are. The only reason he's living in Bluebell is because he couldn't land a job in California, and his uncle owns the only law firm in town.

Then he picked a fight with our server over the lack of vegan options on the menu and bad-mouthed her the second she walked away when she refused to get the manager. If that weren't enough, he made us wait almost an hour to order because he wanted to let his drink settle before eating and then couldn't decide what to order.

I had every intention of taking a page out of Birdie's book and powering through until dinner was over, but that flew out the window when he put his hand on my leg and refused to let go after I'd already dodged his attempt to hold my hand.

Just as I was about to cause a scene, Jensen strode over wearing Wranglers *and* a cowboy hat, channeling Rip Wheeler from *Yellowstone*, all brooding hero and silent fury. It was sexy as hell. I didn't even care that he wasn't supposed to be there. I was just grateful that he was, and I didn't hesitate to go to him when he held out his arms.

Wren: Can we go back to the part where the lawyer was a handsy creep with no concept of personal space?

Charlie: He put his slimy hand on Briar's leg and acted like it was his god-given right.

Birdie: Did you or Briar mace him?

Charlie: Damn, that would have been so much more satisfying than tossing water at his face.

Charlie: Urban cowboy did get totally possessive and drew Briar into his arms before telling the lawyer off.

Not going to lie, it was a swoon-worthy moment.

Wren: Jensen sounds like a keeper.

Briar: Charlie, is now a good time to remind you that you practically begged me to go out with the lawyer?

Charlie: Momentary lapse in judgment. Now back to the group chats...

Briar: I still can't believe you started a new one without me.

Charlie: You're never going to let that go, are you?

Briar: Not a chance.

Birdie: Even if she had good intentions?

Charlie: Zip it, Birdie!

Briar: Don't listen to Charlie. Tell me!

Now, I'm determined to get to the bottom of this.

Birdie: She set up that date, hoping Jensen would get jealous and show up.

Wren: And sent us updates in real time.

Birdie: Up until the lawyer got handsy, apparently.

Charlie: You're both dead to me.

Charlie: And you're wrong. I knew urban cowboy would show up. It's obvious he's smitten with our girl.

Charlie: I was hoping for a more dramatic ending like him punching the lawyer in the face.

Briar: OMG.

"Texting your friends?" I jolt slightly, caught off guard when Jensen speaks.

Briar: This isn't over, but I have to go.

Charlie: Remember, save a horse...

"Yeah." I jam my phone into my purse and set it on the floor by my feet. "Charlie gave Birdie and Wren a full play-by-play of what happened in the diner as if it were *Monday Night Football*."

"Did she at least give them a decent halftime show?" Jensen smirks.

"Afraid not. She wasn't impressed with the material she was given and would have preferred if you'd have punched my date to make it more entertaining," I say, half-teasing.

I skip over Charlie's theory that he came to the diner because he was jealous and my growing suspicion that she might be right. His earlier indifference makes his sudden appearance feel more calculated than coincidental, and we both know he didn't show up with a sudden craving for the best chili cheese fries in town.

"I considered it but figured the chance of a night in jail wasn't worth missing even five more minutes without you." I blink, stunned by his unexpected honesty, but don't have a chance to reply before he speaks again. "Why did you have Earl drive you?" The question comes suddenly like it's been weighing on him all night.

I'd plead the Fifth if I could. I was angry at how little he seemed to care, and I figured if anything would push his buttons, it would be taking the taxi into town. I wanted him to wonder if I was spending the night with someone else. I even considered crashing at Charlie's or Birdie's to see if I could get a reaction out of him. Turns out, I didn't have to go that far.

I fidget with the hem of my dress, avoiding his gaze. "No reason. I just wasn't in the mood to drive."

When I risk a look at Jensen, he's frowning. "Oh, so we're lying to each other now?"

I scoff. "Rich, coming from the guy who crashed my date and won't tell me why."

"From where I stood, you seemed rather receptive to the interruption."

I narrow my eyes, exhaling sharply. "That's not the point."

"Then what is?" Jensen claps back.

I smooth out my dress, angling toward him to make sure I have as much of his attention as I can while he's still focused on the road ahead.

"You don't get to be upset with me," I state firmly. "When I told you I was going out, you had a chance to stop me, and you didn't. Honestly, you looked relieved when I left. What was I supposed to think?" My hands tremble, so I clasp them in my lap before Jensen notices. "Or what about when you kissed me, then pretended nothing changed, and suddenly appeared when I went on a date? Totally normal, right?" I ask, my voice dripping with sarcasm.

Jensen casts me a glance, regret etched into his features. "You're right, Briar. I fucked up. Big-time." He shifts in his seat, his posture rigid. "You seemed so damn eager to go out tonight, spending hours getting ready, putting on that pretty dress, and wearing perfume that smells like apples and amber."

My heart skips a beat at the word *pretty*—and again at the mention of my perfume. Normally, I wear jeans and a T-shirt and put on my scented lotion, but tonight, I wanted to go all out. Now, it feels ridiculous that I dressed up for a guy I have zero interest in seeing again, and who turned out to be a total creep to boot.

But it was never for the lawyer.

"I didn't put all that effort in for him," I admit, feeling vulnerable.

"You didn't?" Jensen asks.

I shake my head, letting the silence linger between us.

I'm disappointed when we pass the sign leading to Silver Saddle Ranch, my stomach dropping as the cottage comes into view. The porch lights shine bright, welcoming us home. But I'm not ready for this conversation to end.

When Jensen parks the truck, I slowly unbuckle my seat belt, not ready to get out yet. I peek over at him, his hands still gripping the steering wheel, shadows playing across his face. God, he's so handsome. Ever since he pulled me to his side at the diner and held my hand on the way out, I've wanted the chance to touch him again.

Before I can make a move, he looks over and pats the seat between us. I don't hesitate to slide over, and I exhale in relief when his hand lifts to gently cup my cheek. His eyes soften as they lock with mine, and I melt into his touch, feeling a sense of peace I've been missing all day.

"I showed up at the diner because I haven't been able to stop thinking about our kiss." He leans forward, pressing his forehead to mine. "I've regretted saying it should be a one-time thing ever since. I know I don't have a claim on you, but watching you go out with another man drove me wild, and I knew if I didn't do something, I'd regret it."

"What are you saying, Jensen?" I whisper.

"The truth is I want you all to my—"

He stops short when the front door of the cottage swings open, and we both turn to find Caleb dashing outside in his glow-in-the-dark dinosaur pajamas.

"What the hell," Jensen mutters under his breath. "He's supposed to be asleep."

I grab my purse from the passenger side floor, then climb out of the truck. When I circle to the front, Jensen's already gotten out and has scooped Caleb into his arms, ruffling his messy hair.

"Shouldn't you be asleep?" he asks, his tone amused.

Caleb nods shamelessly.

"If that's the case, why are you awake?"

Caleb scrunches his nose as he twists his head to the side, pointing toward Heath and Walker, who've just stepped out onto the front porch.

Walker whistles when he looks at Jensen. "The cowboy hat suits you, Harding."

"Thanks. I think it's safe to say I look better in it than you do." Jensen smirks.

Walker shoots him a mock glare. "You wish."

"Don't worry, Jensen, he's just jealous that you've got the whole rugged-charm thing going better than he does," Heath interjects with a grin.

Walker steps off the porch, heading straight to Jensen. He plucks the hat from his head and places it back on his own with exaggerated flair.

He grins. "Now that's more like it."

Caleb lets out a giggle, and Jensen shoots him a playful side-eye as he wipes what looks like cookie crumbs from his face.

"Is there a reason why my son's face is covered in crumbs?" Jensen asks.

Walker raises his hands in defense. "The kid probably heard you leave because he came down shortly after. He seemed confused, and we were worried he'd start crying, so Heath gave him some of the chocolate chip cookies left on the counter."

Heath shoots him a glare. "Oh, come on. You were totally on board. You're the one who said yes when he wanted to watch *Shrek*."

"You try saying no to that face," Walker says, gesturing at Caleb, who's smiling at his antics.

Jensen readjusts Caleb in his arms, pinching the bridge of his nose. "Would it have been so hard to give him some water and read him a story like I suggested?"

"Maybe next time you'll think twice about leaving him with us. And don't forget, now you owe us four Saturdays working on the ranch." Walker smirks.

"It's a good thing you didn't make the deal with me," Heath says to Jensen. "I would have had you out there for the whole damn summer."

"Watch your language," I warn, glancing at Caleb, resting his head against Jensen's shoulder. I'm guessing the sugar's finally catching up with him.

"My bad," Heath says, holding his hand out in surrender as he moves inside behind Jensen.

Before Walker can follow, I hold out a hand to stop him.

"How did Jensen get roped into ranch duty?"

"He agreed to help out in exchange for Heath and me watching Caleb. Didn't even try to negotiate. That's how desperate he was to stop that date of yours."

He did that for me?

CHAPTER 18

Jensen

WALKER AND HEATH QUICKLY MAKE THEIR EXIT AFTER Briar and I get back. I'm no doubt grateful but I may never ask them to babysit again. Granted, I still appreciate that they were here so I could bring Briar home, and I have no regrets about agreeing to four Saturdays of hard labor, since it means I didn't have to spend the whole night wondering if she was still with her date.

After tucking Caleb in again, reading him two bedtime stories, and leaving a glass of water on the nightstand—just in case—I head downstairs. It's late, but I can't go to bed until Briar and I finish our conversation.

The kitchen is quiet when I walk in. I wash my hands at the sink, my gaze shifting out the window, where I spot her on the front porch. She's changed into flannel pajama pants and a cardigan, her hair falling in soft waves around her face.

She's so damn beautiful; it takes my breath away.

I decide to make a batch of hot chocolate for us, adding a

generous splash of whiskey into each cup once it's ready. We could both use something strong to take the edge off.

When I step outside, Briar looks over. "Did Caleb fall asleep okay?"

"Yeah, he's out cold."

"Good." She smiles when she notices the mugs in my hands. "Please tell me that's hot chocolate."

"*Spiked* hot chocolate," I correct her.

Briar accepts the mug I hand her, and cradles it against her chest. "Even better. Hot chocolate is my comfort drink, even in the summer. When I was little, Mama Julie would make it on the nights I stayed at the ranch house. I had trouble sleeping, and it was her way of making sure I felt safe and warm."

She slides over, leaving space for me to join her on the swing. I've come to think of this as our meeting spot. A quiet place where we can be ourselves and the rest of the world fades away.

Sharing what's on my mind has never come easy, and I've always been the type to work through my problems alone. But with Briar, she picks up on the things I'm afraid to say out loud, and somehow, that makes me feel more confident than I ever have.

"Yeah, the Halsteads' place always felt like a safe haven. For me, nothing beats Julie's rolls and honey butter."

"Everything Mama Julie makes is good," she says wistfully.

"I couldn't agree more." I lean back, taking a drink, savoring the heat that hits after the sweetness fades. "If you don't mind me asking, how could you stay here when this town holds so many painful memories? Didn't you ever want to leave and start over?"

That's a question that has been on my mind since Caleb and I arrived. I don't have all the details of her past, but enough to wonder how she could stay here, surrounded by reminders of everything she's been through.

Briar nibbles at her bottom lip, lost in thought for a moment.

"To be honest, no. Bluebell's always been home, and the first time I stepped foot on this ranch, I wanted to build a life here."

I look out over the open fields, the lights from the guest cabins dotting the horizon.

We were both lucky to have the Halsteads when everything else around us was crumbling. I drifted between here and my parents' trailer, dreaming of escape and swearing I'd never set foot in this godforsaken town once I got out. Whereas Briar found a permanent home here, taking solace in the ranch, and building a life in the very place I wanted to forget.

"You're lucky," I say, a bitterness creeping into my voice. "Growing up, I wanted to be anywhere but here. I hated being the kid whose parents were gambling addicts, living in a shitty trailer because the bank foreclosed on their house."

"I never asked to be the daughter of a bartender who exchanged favors with men, but somehow, we both made it through, didn't we?" Briar offers with a small smile.

Her upbeat attitude has me returning her smile. I may harbor hard feelings about my past, but that doesn't mean I should let negativity weigh down our conversation.

"We did," I say. "Has your mom ever reached out since she left?"

Her shoulders slump, and the light in her expression fades as she gazes at the ground. I hate that what I thought was a harmless question immediately darkens her mood.

"No. For a while, I held on to the idea that my mom would come back for me, but after she missed my graduation, I knew she was gone for good." Briar's voice falters as she finishes.

After setting my mug on the porch table beside me, I turn back to her. I extend my hand to gently squeeze hers, offering what comfort I can without crossing any boundaries, unsure if she's ready for anything more until we've talked.

"I'm sorry. You deserved more from your mom."

Our parents failed us in different ways.

"Your situation didn't turn out any better," she says, eyes glossy with emotion.

No, it didn't. My dad died of a heart attack five years ago. I paid for his funeral despite our nonexistent relationship. I meant to be there, but my mom called, furious I hadn't wired her the money directly, and told me I wasn't welcome. A year later, she died alone in some casino hotel in Mesquite, Nevada, still chasing the high that destroyed her and my dad.

"You're a better person than me. While you grieved the loss of your mom, I was relieved when my parents passed," I confess.

"They might have let you down, but you've turned that pain and suffering into something good for Caleb," Briar states with conviction.

It's uncanny how easy she is to talk to. She doesn't interrupt or offer platitudes. Instead, she listens and gives me space to express my true feelings. Even from the beginning, she's made it easy to open up to her. Maybe it's because we come from similar backgrounds, bonded by the fact that our parents cared more about their addictions than they ever did us.

This is one of those rare times I wish Briar and I were closer in age. If we'd gone to school together, maybe we would've become close sooner, and I could've shielded her from some of the pain she had to carry for so long. She had the Halsteads, but I wish I'd been there for her too. We crossed paths almost daily at their place, but she was just a kid following Julie. I didn't pay her much attention, since I was too buried in my own problems.

What matters is that now we're both able to be here for Caleb.

"He deserves unconditional love, and I'll do everything I can to make sure he never goes without it," I say.

"That little boy is certainly spoiled." Briar chuckles. "I still can't believe you left him with my brothers tonight. I'm shocked that giving him cookies and watching a late-night movie was the worst they did."

"I don't have room to judge. Just the other day, I promised him ice cream if he ate his vegetables, and yesterday, I let him watch cartoons for two hours instead of the half-hour limit I set."

She gasps, feigning horror. "A real tyrant."

I smirk. "Guess I won't be winning any Parent of the Year awards."

Briar's laughter fills the air, a melody I wish could play on repeat. I'm not expecting it when she leans over me to set her mug on the table. Her hair brushes against my cheek, and I freeze—the soft scent of her perfume invading my senses, and I have to remind myself to breathe.

She pulls back just enough to look at me. Our thighs are touching, and neither of us moves, waiting to see what the other will do.

"Briar," I whisper.

"Hmm?"

A soft breeze picks up, and her hair falls across her face. I brush it behind her ear, and she shivers at my touch. My hand lingers as I trace along her cheekbone with my thumb, memorizing the curves of her face.

"I went to the diner tonight to see you, but what I should have done was stop you from going altogether." The overdue confession tumbles out, leaving me with a sense of relief and wishing I had found the courage to speak up earlier.

Briar's eyes go wide, her lips slightly parted. "Oh, and why is that?"

"Because I like you."

She grins, leaning into my touch, her face still cradled in my hand. "That's unexpected, given how few people you can tolerate."

"I guess I'm a glutton for punishment."

"We can't all be as accommodating as me," she teases.

"Like I said earlier, I haven't stopped thinking about you since we shared that kiss. The way you moved, the way you sounded—I want to experience it all again." I pause, trailing a finger down her neck. "Watching you at the diner just proved I should've asked you not to go. Because the only guy you should be out with is me."

Briar tilts her head, her eyebrows knitting together. "If that's the case, what are you going to do about it, *cowboy*?"

Damn, this woman has me twisted in knots, and all I want to do is draw her close and never let go.

I reach down to her lap, taking her hands in mine. "This summer, you're mine. I want you in *my* bed, moaning *my* name."

"But we have to be quiet," she says with a gleam in her eye.

"I can think of a few ways to make that happen," I whisper, trailing my thumb across the inside of her wrist.

What I'm proposing is a gamble. Briar could easily turn me down or tell me to leave. Even if she says yes, things could get messy fast if we're not careful. But after thinking it through, I see no other choice, since I can't let her be with someone else while I'm around. There's no reason for us to be miserable for the rest of our time together when we could enjoy each other's company.

"What about Caleb? I don't want whatever this is"—she motions between us—"to affect him negatively. He always comes first. It's probably best if he doesn't know about us, especially if it's temporary." That last word puts a bitter taste in my mouth, but I swallow it down, not wanting to spoil the mood.

"Sneaking around could be fun. Although your brothers definitely know something is going on between us. Walker grilled me earlier when I called and had the nerve to claim I'm too old for you." I scoff.

"Oh, he did, huh?" Briar smirks, grazing her fingers across my temple. "Good thing I've always had a thing for vintage collectibles."

"Don't worry, sugar, I've still got the endurance advantage." I grin, giving my bicep an exaggerated flex.

"Looking forward to you proving it." She leans closer, her eyes sparkling. "But remember, this is just for the summer."

"Just for the summer," I repeat.

"Promise me that however this plays out, you won't use it against me. I want to be Caleb's nanny until you leave… if you'll have me," Briar says with a hint of vulnerability.

A heaviness settles in my chest at the thought of us going back to New York, but I force the emotions aside.

I press a gentle kiss to her forehead. "I'm afraid you're stuck with us until then."

"Oh no, how will I ever survive?" she asks with a twinkle in her eye.

"Besides, we can't have Caleb revolting if he doesn't get to see you every day. He's smitten."

Just like his dad.

"He's not the only one," she says, trailing her fingertips along my knuckles.

"Listen, the county fair is next weekend, and I was thinking of taking Caleb. Would you want to go with us?"

Sure, we agreed to keep our new development under wraps with him, but that doesn't mean we can't all enjoy a day out together. He'll probably enjoy himself more if Briar is there. It's been ages since I've been to the fair, so I could really use her expertise to find the best food and attractions for Caleb.

Briar nods enthusiastically. "I'd love to."

I cradle her cheek in my palm, brushing my nose against hers. "I'd like to kiss you now, sugar."

Her grin widens. "Better not keep me waiting."

I lean in and capture her mouth in a slow, teasing kiss.

The way she melts into me has me looking forward to our first night together. I want it to be memorable, not rushed by sneaking around worrying that Caleb might wake up and end it abruptly. Briar deserves so much more than a hurried moment, and I'll make sure she gets it.

The only issue? Waiting will be the hardest part.

CHAPTER 19

Brian

THE COUNTY FAIR HAS BEEN A STAPLE IN BLUEBELL FOR as long as I can remember. The fairgrounds are thirty minutes outside of town, and every year, they're packed with locals, tourists, and enough fried food to give a cardiologist nightmares. I've been going since I was a kid.

My friends and I would scrape together our money for funnel cakes and caramel apples, then dare each other to go on the scariest rides. Charlie loves adrenaline and would always suggest the most intense ride first, whereas Wren and Birdie made a sport of stalling her with pleas to start with the carousel or the bumper cars.

On the other hand, I was more than willing to go along with Charlie's impulsive adventures if it meant delaying the inevitable Ferris wheel ride at the end of the night. It's not the height that scares me, but the idea of being stuck at the top with nothing but a flimsy metal bar between me and the ground. Now, the Tilt-a-Whirl? I could ride it on a loop without breaking a sweat.

I'm here with Caleb and Jensen this year, so our time has been spent on kid rides and the game booths. I'm hanging out near the front entrance, waiting for them to return from their snack run, when I get a text from Charlie.

Backroads & Bad Decisions Group Chat

Charlie: I can't believe you're cheating on us, Briar.

Briar: It's the county fair. Not an affair.

Charlie: Excuse you. Our friendship includes annual traditions and a sacred oath to ride the Zipper at least three times.

Wren: I'm queasy just thinking about it.

Charlie: Now I'm stuck with Birdie who won't even do the bumper cars because she's too busy stalking the animals.

Briar: Spending time with her can't be that bad.

A video flashes across my screen of Birdie standing by the livestock barn on the far side of the fairgrounds. Her lips are pressed into a worried pout as she watches a horse pace restlessly in a nearby corral. The livestock auction is tomorrow, and we usually make a point of steering clear of the event to prevent Birdie from buying every animal in sight.

Charlie: We should be on rides, but thanks to you, I'm forced to follow Birdie around a smelly barn.

Briar: What happened to laying low?

Birdie: There's a baby cow with a limp and a donkey with the saddest eyes. I can't let them be auctioned off to the highest bidder.

> **Wren:** This is why you're supposed to avoid the livestock auction.

> **Charlie:** Maybe I could have if Briar hadn't abandoned us.

> **Briar:** If you didn't want me to go to the fair with someone else, maybe you shouldn't have set me up with the lawyer, plotting for Jensen to show up and tell me he didn't want us to see other people.

> **Charlie:** How was I supposed to know the urban cowboy doesn't know how to share?

> **Briar:** Rookie mistake.

I set my phone aside when I glance up to see Caleb running toward me, clutching a stick of cotton candy bigger than his head. Wisps of sugar cling to his face, evidence that he's already gotten in a few bites on his way over here.

I let out a low whistle. "Wow, that thing's massive. You sure that's cotton candy and not a pillow in disguise? Maybe you should share so you don't get a stomachache," I say playfully.

Caleb giggles and tears off a giant piece, holding it out for me.

He's the sweetest little boy, and his thoughtful gesture melts my heart. I accept his offer and pop a bite into my mouth, letting the sugar dissolve on my tongue.

Caleb watches me with those big, eager eyes, waiting for my reaction.

"It's so good," I exclaim.

"Couldn't wait another minute for your own treat?" My gaze drifts past Caleb to where Jensen is heading toward us, holding a deep-fried Oreo and funnel cake, one in each hand. Caleb must've sprinted ahead on their way back from the food stands.

"Caleb was kind enough to share a bite of his, and I couldn't resist."

He's now on the bench beside me, busy demolishing his cotton candy, his face buried in it as the sugary strands stick to his lips.

I can't resist stealing another glance at Jensen. He's wearing Wranglers, a plaid shirt with the sleeves rolled up, and a pair of cowboy boots that showed up on the doorstep this morning with a scribbled handwritten note.

BETTER START BREAKING THESE IN NOW, PRETTY BOY. WE CAN'T HAVE YOU BAILING ON YOUR FIRST DAY OF HARD LABOR. - WALKER.

I'll have to thank him, because Jensen in these boots—looking all rugged and giving off a cowboy-next-door-vibe—is dangerous to my control, which was already hanging by a thread. Since our conversation on the porch, things between us have, unfortunately, been strictly G-rated—mostly time with Caleb and chatting outside for a few minutes before I crash for the night.

These days, I start my mornings diving into research and planning for my nonprofit. Taking care of Caleb has been the push I needed to take real steps toward launching it. Even if it'll be a while before I have a dedicated space built, that doesn't mean I can't start making an impact now.

Jensen takes the spot next to me, passing over the deep-fried Oreo.

"Thank you. I've been waiting for this moment since last year's fair."

"You're braver than me." He laughs. "That thing should come with a warning label."

"Says the guy about to scarf down a deep-fried cholesterol bomb." I gesture toward his funnel cake topped with chocolate syrup, whipped cream, caramel, and powdered sugar.

"Don't knock it till you've tried it," he says with a grin.

I watch him warily as he pulls a piece of the funnel cake off with his fingers, my eyes widening when he lifts it to my mouth, cupping his other hand beneath to keep it from dripping on me.

"You want me to try it now?"

He arches a brow, his lip twitching with amusement. "Yeah, I do."

I try not to overthink it as I lean in and take a bite. It's warm and crispy around the edges. He was right. This thing is good.

My stomach flutters when I find his eyes fixed on my mouth.

"What is it? Do I have something on my face?"

His eyes twinkle under the county fair lights. "You do," he says, moving closer. "Lucky me."

He wipes the corner of my mouth, slow and deliberate, a sprinkle of powdered sugar and chocolate syrup on the tip of his finger when he pulls back. Without looking away, he slips his finger into his mouth like it's the most natural thing in the world.

"Delicious," he drawls.

Nothing should be remotely sexy about sharing greasy food, but the way Jensen watches me like I'm next on the menu has me blushing.

"Hey, y'all. You kids having fun?" Mama Julie hollers.

She and Samuel are heading over from the pavilion, where the pie and jam contests are being set up. Judging starts tomorrow, and Julie refuses to leave her entries out of sight longer than necessary—there's been sabotage before, and folks around here treat those contests like high-stakes poker.

"Yeah. Caleb went on the merry-go-round and the kiddie roller coaster." Jensen glances at Caleb, smiling with pride.

He has taken a million photos to document every second of Caleb's first fair.

"How about you?" I ask Mama Julie. "Everything set for the competitions tomorrow?"

"Your mother insisted on sealing the jar lids with wax and

marked them with our initials, and left a pointed note by her pies warning against sticky fingers and sabotage," Pops interjects with a smirk.

Julie folds her arms and sends him a warning glance. "You laugh now, but I'm not risking another fiasco like the Great Peach Debacle of '02."

Pops moves to her side, wrapping an arm around her waist. "You're right. We wouldn't want Missy Daniels getting another blue ribbon she didn't earn. She's never used a crust that didn't come frozen."

"Oh look, you can be sweet on occasion," Mama Julie teases, kissing Pops on the cheek.

They both grew up in Bluebell and have been together since high school. Their lives haven't been easy, but they've built a lasting love that's weathered every storm and only grown stronger over the years.

"We're going to head back to the ranch now," Mama Julie says. "Our eggs in the incubator were starting to pip before we left, so come morning, we should have a new brood of fluffballs chirping their little hearts out."

Yesterday, I took Caleb to check on the eggs, and he could barely contain his excitement when I mentioned that the chicks would hatch soon.

"How would you like to spend the night at the ranch house and be the first to check on them tomorrow?" Julie asks him.

Caleb nods enthusiastically, looking at Jensen for permission.

He runs a hand through his hair, and I can sense his hesitation. This would be the first time he'd be away from Caleb overnight, even if it's just up the road.

"I guess that would be alright," he finally answers. "But his pajamas and the dinosaur he sleeps with are at the cottage."

Julie waves him off like that's no big deal. "We'll stop by and grab them on the way home." She pulls a wet wipe from her purse, kneeling beside Caleb. "Let's get you cleaned up, and we'll be on our way. We don't want to miss any of the action if any of the chicks decide to make an early entrance." He squirms but doesn't complain while she cleans his face and hands, tossing the used wipe in the trash. "Don't forget to tell your dad and Briar goodbye."

He darts over, wrapping his arms around my neck, and I'm quick to return his embrace.

"Have fun, little man. We'll see you in the morning," I whisper in his ear.

Next, he gives his dad a big hug. Once he leans back, Jensen pushes Caleb's hair from his face and kisses his forehead. "Love you, buddy. We're only a phone call away, okay?"

Caleb nods before taking Julie's outstretched hand.

Pops tips his hat. "See you in the morning."

"Yeah, have fun, you two," Julie adds, glancing between Jensen and me like she knows more than she lets on.

As they walk away, disappearing out of view, Jensen sighs. "Why does it feel like I'm watching my son leave for good?" he asks, his voice tinged with uncertainty. "I should be happy he's coming out of his shell, but part of me can't shake the worry about not being there if he needs me."

I place my hand in his, intertwining our fingers. "Mama Julie and Pops will take good care of him, and we'll only be five minutes away if something comes up later."

Jensen lets out a long breath. "You're right. He'll be fine." The reassurance seems more for his benefit than for mine.

He tightens his grip on my hand, and I don't miss the sideways glances from those passing by. With half of Bluebell here, it won't take long for word to spread that, just days after Jensen interrupted my date at the diner, I'm here holding hands with him. Let them talk. At least now, it's not speculation.

"Should we head out too?" I ask.

As much as I'd like to stay, if he'd rather go back to the cottage to be available in case Caleb needs us, I understand.

Jensen hums, rubbing his chin. "If you're game, we can stay a while longer. There are still plenty of rides we haven't gone on yet."

I smile. "What ride did you have in mind?"

"We should do the Ferris wheel. It'll be dusk soon, and the view from the top will be incredible."

My face blanches as I let out an awkward laugh. "Figures you'd pick the one ride I wish didn't exist."

"Are you afraid of heights?"

I shake my head. "I don't like the idea of hanging, suspended in the air."

"So, you must be afraid of the Zipper too?"

"Actually, no. That one's fine because there's a cage *and* I'm strapped in. On the Ferris wheel, you're free-floating in a metal box, praying it doesn't tip over." I playfully swat Jensen on the arm when he stifles a chuckle. "I didn't say it was rational."

He tips his head as he studies me. "A ride in the sky with me might just surprise you. I'd make it worth every second." His tone carries a double meaning that sparks my curiosity.

"That's a bold claim. Hope you're prepared to back it up."

He smirks. "Give it a chance, sugar, and I'll show you exactly what I mean."

My heart flutters at the term of endearment. The thought of belonging to Jensen, even if it's temporary, sends a rush of anticipation through me.

"Okay. Let's go on the Ferris wheel, but I'll be sorely disappointed if you don't live up to your promise."

He brings my hand to his mouth for a kiss. "You couldn't stop me if you tried."

CHAPTER 20

Jensen

O N OUR WAY TO THE FERRIS WHEEL, I SPOTTED A GIANT
stuffed dinosaur at the ring toss booth. I knew Caleb would
love it and had to get it for him. After several failed rounds
trying to win it, the attendant offered to sell it to me for a steep
price. He must have overheard me telling Briar I wanted to get it
for my son and assumed I'd pay whatever it took.

He was right, and now I'm left carrying a stuffed animal
through the fair.

When we reach the Ferris wheel, there's only one couple
ahead of us in line.

Briar drums her fingers against her leg, eyes flickering to
the towering ride turning lazily overhead. When she told me she
wasn't a fan, I assumed she was exaggerating, but her death grip
on my arm says otherwise.

We could skip it and find another ride, but I want to show her
she can trust me, and that she's safe with me. I'd never let anything
hurt her. Besides, sometimes the best memories are made when
you step outside your comfort zone. Here's hoping Briar agrees.

When the Ferris wheel slows to a standstill, she moves her hand further down my arm.

"It stopped," she blurts out. "That can't be good, right?"

I chuckle softly, kissing her temple. "That means it's almost our turn to get on."

"Oh."

I run my thumb along her palm. "You're safe with me; I promise."

She leans into me, briefly resting her head on my shoulder.

The people in front of us shuffle into the waiting car, and the attendant rotates the wheel, bringing another empty car to the loading platform. When he glances in our direction, he shakes his head.

"You can't bring that thing on board." He nods toward the giant dinosaur. "Two per car max."

I raise an eyebrow. "Seriously?"

"I don't make the rules. I just enforce them," he replies flatly.

With a sigh, I pull another ticket from my pocket, handing him three. "Okay. Put it in its own car, then." He stares at me, stunned, awkwardly accepting the dinosaur when I push it into his chest.

I rest my free hand on Briar's back, guiding her past the attendant. She releases a quiet shudder when the gate swings shut behind us. Frosted panels line the lower half of the car, providing a sense of privacy.

"Enjoy the ride," the attendant says flatly.

He pushes a button on the control panel to move our car forward. I look back to see him tossing the dinosaur onto the seat of the car behind us, closing the door just as we start our slow ascent.

A gentle breeze drifts through, carrying the buttery scent of popcorn. I settle in beside Briar, the cushioned seat creaking under our weight, but remain silent. I don't want to give her another reason to worry.

The past week dragged on forever, and every night, I was tempted to go to her bedroom to give us both what we've been craving. But time has been scarce between work and taking care of Caleb. I'd started thinking I'd have to take matters into my own hands and find a way to steal a few hours alone, but Julie and Samuel came to the rescue before I had to.

Letting Caleb go without me wasn't easy, but the fact that he wanted to go was significant, and I couldn't say no. Besides, it gave Briar and me a chance to explore this thing between us without interruptions, and I wasn't about to let that opportunity slip by.

I glance over to find her huddled in the middle of the bench, hands clasped in her lap, her eyes darting between the ground and the sky.

I drape my arm around her shoulders, pulling her to my side. "You alright?"

She lets out a dry laugh and shakes her head. "I'm trapped in a metal cage, spinning on a giant wheel of terror. How do you think I'm doing?"

"I've got you, sweetheart."

The wheel spins in a rhythmic motion, and as we reach the top, Briar's fingers grip my leg, her eyes squeezing shut.

"Remind me again what kind of person thinks this is enjoyable," she mutters.

"Probably the same people who think pineapple belongs on pizza," I tease.

Briar cracks one eye open, shooting me a mock glare. "I should have figured putting fruit on pizza and using a non-adjustable wrench to fix a leak weren't your only questionable life choices."

"At least I'm consistent." I shrug. "Should I have the attendant let us off when we get to the bottom?"

She sits up straighter. "Oh no. You promised this would be worth it, so I'm sticking it out. No take-backs."

I smirk. "Never."

She exhales slowly as I rub her back, and the tension in her spine eases with each rotation. Still, at the peak of every climb, her grip on my leg tightens, making my cock twitch. I bite the inside of my cheek, reminding myself this is about making her comfortable. But as she shifts beside me, her hand slides higher, making it damn near impossible to ignore the way my body reacts to her, every brush of her skin fanning the flames.

The Ferris wheel lurches to a sudden stop, snapping my attention away from Briar's hand on my leg, and I'm instantly on edge when I realize we're suspended at the highest point.

Shit, I don't think that's supposed to happen.

"Oh god, what's going on?" Briar asks, panic rising in her voice. "Why are we still up here?"

I flash her a comforting smile and give her hand a squeeze. "It's probably just taking longer than usual to let the other riders off."

I lean over the edge to watch the attendant at the controls. The Ferris wheel is small enough that I can clearly see him, yet high enough that we're still tucked away from the crowds below. He's frantically pushing buttons, eyes darting nervously around the fairgrounds. His lips move, and I'm pretty sure I catch a string of curse words under his breath.

Fuck, that's not a good sign.

Bringing attention to the problem will only trigger Briar's panic, and I might not be able to calm her down while we're stuck up here. My best bet is to distract her before she reaches that point, like I promised. My original plan was to make out on the Ferris wheel, but this calls for something drastic. I want to replace her fear with an unforgettable memory that leaves her breathless for all the right reasons.

Her teeth are clenched, and she's staring straight ahead. I cradle her face, caressing her cheek until her gaze meets mine.

"There you are," I say, trailing kisses along the delicate line of her jaw. "Have I told you today how beautiful you are?"

"Are you trying to distract me?" she murmurs.

"Maybe. Is it working?"

I follow the slope of her neck, tugging her earlobe between my teeth. She releases a soft moan, leaning in, her hand resting against my chest. The space between us buzzes with electric energy. I press a soft kiss to the sensitive spot beneath her ear, my hand sliding to the small of her back, drawing her closer.

"Do you trust me?"

Her breath catches, and she tilts her head to give me better access as her fingers curl into the fabric of my shirt.

"Yes," she whispers.

"Can I make you feel good, sugar?"

My hand drifts past her breasts, down her belly, fingers grazing the curve of her hip.

"Yes," she repeats, a shiver running through her.

"Take your panties off," I demand.

She blinks at me. "What if someone sees?"

"It's just you, me, and the stars." I nod toward the open sky. "The question is, can you stay quiet? Or are we about to give the whole county more to gossip about?"

She arches a brow. "Guess it depends on whether you bring your A game or not."

"Careful, darlin'. I play to win. Now…" I trail my fingers down her thigh. "Take. Your. Panties. Off."

Briar's breath hitches, and her eyes flicker with surprise before desire overrides everything else. She turns toward me and lifts the hem of her skirt, inching it higher to reveal smooth, sun-kissed skin glowing in the moonlight. When she has the fabric bunched at her waist, my eyes drop to the V between her legs, where I get a glimpse of her red satin panties.

She flashes me a cheeky grin as she lifts her hips, slipping them down her legs. Once they're off, she holds them in front of me, her sultry gaze locked on mine. My pulse is hammering as she holds me captive with her magnetic charm. I curl my fingers around her wrist and lean in, pressing the fabric to my nose, inhaling the scent of her musk.

"So damn sweet."

Her mouth parts as her fingers go slack. I catch her panties before they fall, sliding them into my shirt pocket.

"Lean back and close your eyes." I want her to forget the world around us, consumed only by my voice and the warmth of my hands on her.

This time, she doesn't hesitate to follow my command, tipping her head back, lashes resting against her flushed cheeks. Her chest rises and falls, each breath deep and measured as if she's already given herself over to what comes next, her legs falling open in invitation. The sight damn near undoes me.

My hand drifts along her side, brushing over her hips, leaving a path of goose bumps behind, before settling on her bare thigh. I slowly make my way to her core, running my fingers through her wetness.

"You're dripping wet for me, sugar."

Her eyes flutter open, giving me a mischievous smile. "Do something about it."

I answer by sliding a finger inside her tight pussy, her moan vibrates between us, drawing me deeper into her heat. My cock is painfully hard, but all that matters is watching her fall apart beneath my touch. My thumb finds her swollen clit, and when she groans, I'm torn between looking at her soaked center and the bliss written all over her face.

I drink in the sight of Briar's dilated eyes, parted lips, and the way her gaze tracks mine, dazed and hungry. Her frame quivers, melting into my side as I draw needy sounds from that sinful mouth of hers, and I'm unable to resist stealing a kiss.

The way she grinds against my palm is downright desperate, and she gasps as I slide in another finger and take my time exploring her.

"That's it, darlin'. Ride my hand and show me what a good cowgirl you are."

"Oh fuck," she cries out.

Mesmerized, I watch her circle her hips, gripping my wrist, urging me on. The car sways, but she doesn't notice. She's too caught up in the heat building inside her, chasing a high far more intense than her fear of being suspended in the air.

She squirms when my hand stills, furrowing her brow.

"Why'd you stop?" she croaks.

"Because I'm not done with you yet."

There's no telling how long we'll be stuck up here, so I intend to draw her orgasm out.

I give her another scorching kiss, my free hand working to unfasten the top buttons of her shirt, and tug one of her bra cups down to expose her breast. I lean down and wrap my mouth around her nipple, gliding my tongue across the pink bud.

"Jensen." My name falls from her lips like a prayer.

She inhales sharply as I alternate between flicking her nipple with my tongue and tugging it taut with my teeth. As I lavish her breast with kisses, I continue moving my fingers in and out of her, using short strokes, never going more than knuckle-deep. She gives a soft huff as she shifts, her body quivering beneath my hand.

Each movement fuels a craving only I can satisfy, and it's damn exhilarating to elicit this kind of reaction. She tips her head back, her brown eyes meeting mine as she lets out a breathless gasp.

"So good," she groans loudly.

"Easy, sweetheart; keep that up and the folks in the other cars might think we're putting on a show."

Her pupils grow wide, the flush on her cheeks deepening as she lets out another needy sound.

"You want everyone to hear how good I make you feel?" I growl in her ear.

Briar sinks her teeth into her lower lip, nodding as she clenches around me. She lets out another soft moan when my thumb moves back to her clit, and I catch her mouth with mine, muffling the noise. Her reaction to the idea of being heard is insanely sexy, but her sweet sounds are meant for my ears only.

I'm rock hard watching her wind tighter with every plunge of my fingers. Sensing that she needs a push over the edge, I apply pressure to her clit, sending her shattering around my hand. She lets out a strangled cry that I swallow with another kiss.

She's stunning, closing her eyes as she surrenders to the fading waves of ecstasy. I've imagined her coming undone with my hand wrapped around my cock more times than I can count, but no fantasy compares to the reality of witnessing it in person.

As she comes down from her high, she goes limp in my arms. I slowly pull my hand from her, bringing my fingers to my mouth, and suck them clean. I groan, savoring the taste of her sweet essence on my tongue.

Her eyes flutter open, a bright smile crossing her face. The fair lights bathe her in a golden glow as she tosses her head back, laughing. She looks so at ease, and I smile back, proud to be the reason she's so carefree.

Briar moves her hand to my pants, where the outline of my cock is visible, but I place my hand over hers.

She tilts her head, confused. "I want to take care of you."

I lift her hand to my lips and place a kiss to the back of it. "This was about *you*."

I fasten the buttons of her shirt, and just as I'm smoothing her skirt, the Ferris wheel lurches back into motion. Briar's hand shoots out to grip my arm.

"Still afraid of the Ferris wheel?" I murmur, taking her hand in mine.

"It's still not my top choice," she admits, leaning closer. "But I wouldn't have minded being stuck with you for a bit longer."

I lean my forehead against hers. "Don't worry, darlin'. That was only the beginning."

We have the rest of the night to ourselves, and I plan to make the most of it.

CHAPTER 21

Brian

"I STILL CAN'T BELIEVE YOU PAID THREE HUNDRED DOLLARS for that." I nod to the stuffed dinosaur under Jensen's arm.

"It's not my fault the attendant swindled me," he grunts. "Hell, the kid probably pocketed the money for himself."

"Caleb's going to be so excited."

"Worth every penny." Jensen grins. "Even if we totally got hustled."

When we reach the truck, he opens the passenger door and helps me in with a hand at my waist.

"Thank you," I murmur.

He gives me a quick kiss. "Anytime, sweetheart." The way his deep, smooth voice says those words has me weak at the knees.

He hands me the giant dinosaur, then closes the door and jogs around to the driver's side. I place the stuffed animal in the middle seat and pull out a tube of lip balm from my pocket. My mouth still tingles from his kiss, the warmth lingering.

I've just finished applying it when I feel Jensen watching me. He cranes his neck around the dinosaur, eyes fixed on my lips.

"Want some?" I ask, holding the balm out with a smirk.

He blinks, giving me a sheepish smile. "Why is there a giant stuffed animal playing third wheel?" He gives the thing a playful shove.

I laugh as he tosses the dinosaur into the back seat and pats the spot beside him. I slide over, and his hand finds my leg, tugging me in until I'm snug against his side.

He dips his head, kissing me softly. "That's more like it."

"Somebody's possessive tonight," I tease.

"You have no idea what you do to me," he whispers, giving me another kiss. "I can still hear every breathy sound of yours as you rode my hand."

I flick my tongue along his mouth. "Whatever will you do about it?"

He groans. "Once we get home, I'm going to show you all the ways I can make you come."

A spike of anticipation pulses through me when the engine rumbles to life and his hand moves to my upper thigh.

As the truck hums along the old country road, we settle into a comfortable silence. His presence is electric, like whiskey running through my veins—warm, smooth, and dangerously addictive. When I'm with him, it's easy to forget that this has an expiration date and I'm not supposed to get attached.

Jensen drums his fingers on the steering wheel, humming along to the country song on the radio. I take a moment to study him—the scruff framing his face, his bronzed skin, the subtle crow's feet around his eyes, hinting at a summer full of laughter and smiles.

When he first returned to Bluebell, his small-town roots were buried beneath a big-city mindset. But now, he seems more at peace in his Wranglers and boots than he ever did in a suit and tie, and I can't help but wish this version of him was here to stay.

My muscles tighten as he moves his hand in lazy strokes

against my thigh, reminding me of our moment on the Ferris wheel—his mouth claiming mine, and his fingers pressing inside me as I came apart beneath his touch. I bite the inside of my cheek, willing my breathing to stay even.

Jensen glances over at me. "You're awfully quiet."

I nod, playing it cool. "Mm-hmm. Just taking in the view." I motion toward the sky full of stars I hadn't noticed until now.

"That so?" he replies coyly.

I gasp when his fingers slip beneath the hem of my skirt, his knuckles grazing the inside of my thigh. All I want is for him to move his hand up a few inches. My panties are still in his shirt pocket, and the only thing between me and another release is his refusal to move higher. Unfortunately, his touch is featherlight—maddening in its restraint. Jensen knows it's not enough to satisfy me, but it's more than enough to set fire to my skin.

Two can play this game.

I slide my hand across his lap, his grip tightening on the steering wheel when I graze over the thick bulge pressing against his jeans. A low groan slips from his throat when I add pressure, circling the outline.

"Briar, what are you doing?" Jensen's voice is hoarse.

"Call it retaliation for all your teasing," I say sweetly, feigning innocence.

His eyes darken as he glances at me. "You're going to pay for that, darlin.'"

"Promises, promises."

At this rate, the rest of the ride home will be one big test of restraint for us both.

By the time we reach the cottage, my body is a live wire, every nerve strung tight. Jensen's hand hasn't left my thigh, and if he doesn't give me more soon, I might combust. Who knew edging with clothes on could be so erotic? It's a mix of sweet torture and desperate want. The inevitable crash after weeks of wanting him—close enough to touch but just beyond reach in all the ways that mattered.

The engine cuts off, and I exhale slowly, protesting when he lifts his hand from my thigh.

"Don't move," he says.

I open my mouth to respond, but he's already getting out and jogging around to my side. He flings open the passenger door and reaches forward, carefully sliding me across the seat until I'm on the edge, my legs dangling out of the truck.

Jensen slides his arms around my waist, pulling me against him as he dips his head, kissing me with an urgency that matches my own. I swipe my tongue along his bottom lip, and his groan vibrates through me, low and desperate. He deepens the kiss, his hands sliding down my back as I weave my hands into his hair, tugging him closer, unable to get enough.

I'm lost in him, every part of me yearning for more, and I'm powerless to resist. Not that I'd want to, even if I could.

I flick my tongue against his, and he lets out a low groan.

"God, the things I want to do to this mouth." He grabs my hand, guiding it down to his jeans, where his hard-on is visible and pressing against the fabric.

I trace the outline with my fingertips, relishing Jensen's shudder beneath my touch.

"You're the one taking your sweet time getting me to the bedroom," I murmur, my tone sultry.

Maybe teasing him isn't the best idea when my impending orgasm is at his mercy, but I want him to experience a fraction of the delicious torment I endured on the Ferris wheel and way home.

But I need him *now*.

As if he can read my mind, he bends down and effortlessly

hoists me over his shoulder. My hands shoot out to grip his waist, my fingers curling around the belt loops on the back of his jeans to steady myself.

I gasp. "Jensen Harding, put me down this instant."

He swats me playfully on the ass. "Behave, woman."

A moan catches in my throat as I arch my neck to look at him. "Did you really just spank me?"

"Sure did, and I'll do it again if you don't stop squirming." His voice rumbles, sending a thrill through me.

Jensen slams the truck door shut and carries me up the porch steps. Once inside, he heads straight for the stairs, his boots scraping against the wood floors as he moves without breaking stride. When he reaches my bedroom, he heads straight for the bed, tosses me onto the mattress, and I bounce against the soft surface.

God, the sheer force of his confidence is ridiculously sexy. I've always wanted a man who's not afraid to take control, and all I want is for him to fuck me right this instant.

"Take your clothes off. I want to look at you," he says, the intensity of his gaze pinning me in place. "*All* of you."

I shift to the edge of the bed, kicking off my boots and slipping off my socks, letting them drop to the floor. Next, I unbutton my top slowly, and when the lace trim of my red bra comes into view, Jensen inhales sharply.

Wearing lingerie is a small indulgence I reserve for myself. After long, sweaty days in the sun, slipping into silk and lace helps me feel human again. Jensen being here to admire my effort tonight is a bonus.

I reach for the hem of my skirt, but he steps forward, covering my hand with his.

"Let me."

He lifts me to my feet, his hand resting on my waist as he slowly drags the fabric down. His finger grazes my leg as the material slides past, and I gasp when he gets on his knees. He raises his eyes to meet mine, his pupils blown wide.

"You're so damn sexy. It should be criminal for you to go without panties."

I quirk a brow. "You mean the ones *you* confiscated?"

"Guilty as charged."

The air between us crackles with tension as he tightens his grip on my legs. His fingers brand my skin as heat shoots through me, settling low in my belly.

"Take your bra off, baby," Jensen orders.

I swallow hard, my lips parting slightly as I reach around to unfasten the clasp. The straps fall from my shoulders, cool air brushing against my nipples as I toss my bra to the floor.

Jensen gazes up at me as he leans forward, kissing my stomach. "You're so fucking pretty," he praises me.

"And you're still dressed," I say with a pout.

I'm trembling with need, my body strung tight. Only his touch can ease the ache between my thighs, and all I want is to peel off his clothes and finally see what I've fantasized about more times than I can count.

He stands to his full height, his voice low and rough. "Go lie on the bed, darlin'. Since you had to be quiet on the Ferris wheel, I plan to make you scream now."

I shoot him a playful scowl before turning around, letting out a squeak when he gives my ass another light smack.

"Twice in one night? I think you have a developing obsession."

"Can you blame me? That ass is a masterpiece." His reply sends a spark flickering through me.

I climb onto the bed and lie on my back like he told me to. When I tilt my head toward Jensen, he's already stripping out of his clothes. His shirt strains across his shoulders as he yanks it off and tosses it to the ground. The flex of his abs as he moves is enough to steal the air from my lungs. It should be a crime how hot he is, and I'm the lucky one he's staring at like he's ready to devour me.

A trail of hair runs down his stomach, drawing my eyes to the waistband of his jeans. I lick my lips as he drags down his pants and boxers, revealing his thick cock, the veins pulsing. His stare pins me in place, and it's a good thing I'm lying down because my knees would've given out if I were still standing.

Jensen pushes his discarded clothes aside, and joins me on the bed. He kneels at my feet, settling at the end of the mattress, his palms gliding slowly up my calves. I gasp when his lips brush my knee, but he doesn't stop. He moves higher, his stubble dragging along my bare skin with every inch he claims. My hands twist in the comforter, struggling to stay still as heat coils low in my belly.

When he reaches the apex of my thighs, he hovers, glancing up at me with a wicked smirk.

"Fuck, baby. I've been starving for you."

I'm mesmerized, unable to speak as he pushes my legs open, and a strangled cry falls from my lips as his warm, wet tongue laps at my clit. Each stroke unravels me, pulling me apart thread by thread.

Jensen lifts his head. "Another taste and you've totally wrecked my self-control."

I lost all control the second I saw him naked. Every ripple and curvature of his well-defined abs are on display, and his hard cock is dripping precum.

Understanding my unspoken plea, he returns his tongue to my clit, teasing the aching bud mercilessly. His movements alternate between quick, sharp flicks and slow, languid caresses. Each change in tempo leaves me gasping, edging me ever closer to climax.

He runs his fingers along my seam, circling my opening before pushing one inside. My back arches off the bed, sweat beading on my forehead as the pressure builds from within. He draws out my wetness with his finger and brings it to my clit, circling it with the perfect amount of pressure.

Jensen alternates, moving his mouth back to my core, and as I lift my head and catch sight of him buried between my legs, it pushes me past the brink. I grind against his face, my vision blurring as the pleasure crests and sends me into free fall, a whimper falling from my lips. My head falls back on the pillow, my chest rising and falling in shallow pants as the tremors fade.

Jensen pulls back. "Eyes on me, baby."

When I meet his gaze, he's watching me with a heat that threatens to unravel me completely.

"I don't think—"

I'm stopped short when he runs his tongue along my overly sensitive clit. My whole body jerks, but he doesn't ease up. Electricity rips through me, sharp and consuming, as he draws another whimper from my throat. I roll my hips, grinding against his face as I thread my fingers through his hair. He groans against me, lapping at my pussy like he's starved for it, the slick evidence of my first orgasm coating his tongue. The sensation is sin incarnate, making my toes curl.

His fingers circle my aching clit, sparking a second orgasm to ripple through me. I cling to him as my body shudders uncontrollably, my breaths coming out uneven and shallow.

He lifts his eyes upward, eyes smoldering with want. "I can't wait another minute to be inside you. Please tell me you have a condom. I would've asked sooner, but I was a little distracted." He grins smugly.

I nod to the nightstand, and he pushes off the mattress. Jensen grabs one from the drawer and rips the package open with his teeth. Once he rolls it on, he gets back on the bed and crawls over me.

"Ready for me?"

"Don't hold back."

"Give me that mouth, woman." He fists my hair in his hand, tipping my head back to claim my lips. Every stroke of his tongue against mine sends another jolt of heat through me, and I grip his shoulders as I surrender to his searing kiss. His dick brushes against my stomach as he leans in.

Jensen takes hold of his cock, sliding it along my slit to coat himself in my arousal. I'm drenched and lost in the haze of insatiable desire, not expecting it when he lines it up with my entrance and pushes in to the hilt in one stroke.

"Oh fuck," I cry out.

Our intermingled groans fill the room. I'm so full, and my muscles clench as I adjust to his size.

He dips his head, pressing a soft kiss to my lips. "You alright, baby?"

I can feel him holding back while he waits for my answer.

"More, Jensen. I need more," I beg.

That's all he needs to hear before hooking my legs over his shoulders and bending me beneath him. The position allows him to push deeper, and I moan loudly as he picks up his pace, slamming into me in unrestrained thrusts. He's lost total control, and the buildup between us snaps like a ticking fuse, leaving only raw need in its wake.

"Oh. My. God."

"You take me so damn well." He growls.

I dig my fingernails into his shoulder blades, gasping for air as he drives into me with unrelenting force. His hips grind into mine—harder, faster—with each thrust. My heart races out of control, and there's no telling where I end and he begins.

I can sense he's close when he drops his head against my shoulder. His breath is ragged as his cock hits my G-spot. The sound of flesh slapping against flesh resonates in the air. Each stroke is more desperate than the last until we're nothing but sweat, need, and tangled limbs.

"Scream my name when you come for me," he grunts out.

I look up and am met with his heated stare, the vein in his neck pulsing hard. He reaches between my legs, rolling my clit between his thumb and forefinger. I shatter with a force so fierce that it steals the air from my lungs. Another cry is torn from my throat as his name falls from my lips.

"You're clenching my cock so good." Jensen tenses above me, his own climax rocking through him, and he lets out a guttural groan.

He's still catching his breath as he murmurs, "You did so good for me, baby."

I trail my fingers along the rough edges of his five o'clock shadow. "I think I'm losing my voice," I say, my voice raspy.

"I always keep my promises," he replies, giving me a quick kiss.

Sex with Jensen is unlike anything I've ever experienced. My hips are tender from where his fingers dug into them, and my thighs are still trembling. The aftermath is a blend of aching satisfaction and lust that refuses to fade. I can still feel him twitching inside me, and I can't help but imagine how it would be without a condom between us—skin against skin.

He kisses my forehead as he slowly pulls out. He climbs off the bed, discarding the used condom in the trash before slipping on his boxers. He disappears into the bathroom and returns with a warm washcloth to wipe me clean before tossing the towel into the dirty laundry hamper.

"Stay here. I'll be right back."

He leaves the room without further explanation. I hear the clanking in the kitchen downstairs, but stay put like he asked. While I wait, I slide under the covers, pulling the comforter tight around me. A few minutes later, Jensen walks back inside carrying a tray of food.

"I figured you might be hungry after that workout." He winks.

My stomach rumbles in agreement. I haven't eaten since breakfast—unless you count the deep-fried Oreo and giant pickle from the fair.

"That was very sweet of you."

His eyes darken. "More like strategic. We have the house to ourselves tonight, and I plan to make every minute count." A fresh wave of heat settles between my legs.

He walks to the side of the bed, leaning over to set the tray over my lap. The spread is simple but thoughtful: a bowl of strawberries, freshly cut pineapple, and an assortment of crackers and cheese.

"Thank you. This is way better than what I'd make for myself. I'd probably end up with a peanut butter and jelly sandwich."

Not only is he the first man to give me three orgasms in one night, but he's also the first to care for me afterward. He's the perfect balance of commanding passion and gentle affection, leaving me satisfied and cherished in ways I've never felt before.

"Anything for you, beautiful," he murmurs.

He slides into bed beside me, lifting a strawberry to my lips. As I take a bite, juice trickles down my chin, and he gently wipes it away with his thumb, his heated gaze never leaving mine.

I'm eager to see where the rest of the night takes us, and I can only hope that Jensen doesn't have regrets come morning because I intend to make the most of him being just down the hall for the rest of the summer.

CHAPTER 22

Jensen

I STIR AS MORNING LIGHT SPILLS THROUGH THE BLINDS, casting a soft golden glow across the room. I crack an eye open, glancing down to find Briar beside me, her hair a tangled mess on the pillow. One arm is draped across my chest, the other tucked beneath her chin.

The quiet stillness makes me want to remember every detail, from the way the sunlight dances along the curve of her cheek to the smattering of freckles on the bridge of her nose. I brush a loose strand of hair from her face, taking in how relaxed she looks. I'm not sure what I did to earn the right to wake up next to her, but I'm holding on to every second of it.

"No one else is ever going to compare to you," I whisper with a kiss on her forehead.

I've never known peace like this. I used to think relationships were a cycle of pain where couples tore one another down and enabled the worst in each other. I figured Julie and Samuel were the rare exception and that I'd never experience that kind of love. So I never made the effort to let anyone in.

I stuck to one-night stands and casual hookups, setting strict boundaries. There were no sleepovers at my place, no labels, and no promises. It allowed me to stay focused on growing my empire, and until recently, I never felt like I was missing out.

But with Briar, it's different. With her, it's easy to let my guard down, knowing she accepts me without judgment and inspires me to become the best version of myself. After just one night together, I fear I'm already hooked, secretly wishing this was more than the summer fling we've agreed to.

She shifts slightly in her sleep, her lips parting on a sigh. She must be exhausted from last night, where nothing existed beyond this room. No responsibilities. No complications. Just Briar and me.

She came alive beneath my hands, every stroke dragging a new sound from her lips until she was crying out my name. That raw, raspy voice continues to echo in my head. We didn't stop until she collapsed against me, spent and trembling. I drifted off with my fingers running through her hair, listening to the steady rhythm of her breath.

After watching Briar for a few more minutes, her lashes finally flutter open, and she blinks up at me with a slow, satisfied smile.

"Morning," she murmurs.

I brush a kiss across her lips. "Good morning, sugar. How did you sleep?"

She stretches, the sheet slipping down her bare breasts. "Hard to say. *Someone* kept me up most of the night."

I smirk. "You weren't complaining when you were screaming my name at two in the morning."

"That's because I was too busy seeing stars to form a coherent sentence."

"In that case, I'll have to make sure next time—"

We both freeze when we hear a sharp banging come from downstairs.

"Someone's at the door," she whispers.

I check my phone and see a string of missed texts from Heath and Walker saying they're on their way to pick me up to bale hay. The last one was sent twenty minutes ago.

Shit.

Judging by the noise, I'm guessing they've been waiting outside a while and have run out of patience.

"I think your brothers are here," I tell Briar.

She jolts up in bed. "What? Now?"

"Yeah."

I jump out of bed and pull on the Wranglers I wore last night, not bothering to look for my shirt. Briar's right behind me, throwing on a pair of sleep shorts and a flannel from a stool in the corner. She grabs a hair tie from the dresser, twisting her hair into a messy bun on the way out of the bedroom. We're halfway down the stairs when the front door swings open. Heath and Walker stroll inside, catching us stumbling into view, half-dressed and breathless.

Walker lets out a low whistle. "Looks like we missed one hell of a sleepover."

Heath smirks. "But we got here just in time for the morning-after special."

Briar's cheeks flush. "Did you guys ever think about waiting for someone to open the door before coming in?"

Walker shrugs. "It's not our fault it was unlocked. It's a good thing Ma is bringing Caleb over in a few minutes or you might've had to explain why his daddy and his nanny were conducting a *hands-on* team-building exercise."

As Briar and I reach the entryway, I shoot him a glare. "Not funny."

He chuckles. "I beg to differ. It's some of my finest work, if I do say so myself."

Whatever this is between Briar and me is fragile enough

without Caleb finding out and getting confused. He's already been through so much change, and the last thing I want is to add anything else that might cause him more stress. Not when he's made so much progress over the past month and a half.

Does that mean I'm done with Briar? Not by a long shot. But we'll have to be more careful, especially in the mornings, to avoid another awkward situation like this. There's no chance her brothers will ever let me live this down.

"Have you guys had breakfast?" Briar asks Heath and Walker, changing the subject.

"Nope. Ma was busy with the chicks, so we were hoping you were making those famous pancakes of yours like you usually do on Saturdays," Walker says with a grin.

Briar rolls her eyes. "Typical. You're lucky I'm in a good mood, or you'd be the one making pancakes."

"Yeah, well, we all know why you're so chipper this morning," Heath interjects with amusement. "By the way, love your outfit, sis."

Briar glances down at her mismatched clothes, her fingers tugging at the hem of her shirt as if that'll make her brothers disappear.

"Jensen's not exactly setting fashion trends either," Walker adds. "Pretty sure he's trying to flaunt his abs."

"Says the guy who looks like a lumberjack that got dressed in the dark," I say, nodding toward his half-tucked flannel.

He must have hit the snooze button three times before Heath dragged him out the door. Morning people are ruthless.

"As entertaining as this banter is, I'm going to make breakfast." Briar leans close, whispering, "I worked up quite the appetite last night." She shoots me a playful wink before slipping into the kitchen.

I plan to follow, but Heath stops me with a firm hand on my shoulder.

"What happened to not being interested in meeting a nice country gal this summer?" he asks with a raised brow.

I scratch the back of my neck, carefully considering my response. The last thing I want is to upset him and start a fight in Briar's entryway. It would be a surefire way to ruin the end of an incredible night, and I'm not willing to risk it being our only one. Briar's quickly become an important part of my life, and I don't want to go back to the way things were.

"It wasn't planned," I say defensively.

Heath tilts his head, rubbing his chin. "What happened? She trip and fall into your arms? Besides, don't you think you're a little old for her? After all, you wear reading glasses, and isn't that a gray hair in your stubble?" His expression shifts to smug satisfaction.

Walker laughs. "That's what I told him!"

I shoot him a mock glare, running a hand along my jaw. "Oh please. You've both dated women younger than Briar, and I haven't given either of you grief about it."

"It's different when it's our sister we're talking about," Heath points out.

"Convenient," I mutter to myself. "We've decided not to see other people the rest of the summer. If you've got a problem with us being together, you'll have to take it up with her because I'm not changing my mind."

I keep my hands at my side, bracing for Heath's anger, but he surprises me when he shrugs.

"Alright, I can live with that."

I furrow my brow. "That's it?"

"The guys at the coffee shop filled me in on the details of what went down the night of her date. You protected her from that jackass lawyer, and I appreciate it. Although if I'd been there, he would've left with a black eye."

"I didn't do it for you."

"Exactly." He moves forward, clapping me on the back. "You've got Briar's best interests at heart, which means you care."

"So, you're not mad?"

He wrinkles his nose. "It isn't my business what goes on behind closed doors. Briar's got a good head on her shoulders, and if she's set on you, I'll respect it. But if you so much as make her cry, you'll be answering to us both," he says, jerking his chin toward Walker.

"Damn straight," Walker adds with his arms folded across his chest.

"I'd never hurt her…" I trail off as Briar lets out a string of muffled curses from the kitchen. "I better go see if she needs help wranglin' the stove. It's been on the fritz lately."

As I turn toward the kitchen, I catch Walker leaning over to Heath and whispering, "There's no way he leaves after the summer."

I've thought about how difficult going back to New York will be, but until now, I haven't entertained the thought of making Bluebell our permanent home. The city is where the business I built from the ground up is, and I'm not sure I could give that up. Not when it provides the security and stability I lacked growing up.

Not to mention, Caleb starts kindergarten in the fall. I managed to get him into a highly sought-after private school with a top-tier early education program. The director of the board is a client of mine, and he owed me a favor for helping him with an emergency project a few months ago.

A nagging thought has me wondering if moving back to the city is the best thing for Caleb, but I dismiss it for now.

As soon as I'm out of view, I hear Heath's voice carry behind me.

"I'm not so sure. He abandoned his roots once. There's a good chance he'll do it again," he tells Walker.

That may be true, but I was trying to outrun the legacy my parents created back then. Now that I have a support system who genuinely cares about Caleb and me, the thought of saying goodbye is much harder.

Walker and Heath make themselves comfortable at the kitchen table with their coffee while eagerly waiting for breakfast. Briar shooed them out of the cooking area when they offered to help, insisting they were useless with food prep. However, once I put a shirt on, she had me washing and cutting fruit. Not that I mind—it's the least I can do since she's making the pancakes.

The stove's pilot light isn't working, and Briar hasn't had time to fix it, so she resorted to using an electric griddle to make pancakes. On the bright side, she won't have to deal with her appliances constantly breaking much longer. Not after she gets the surprise I've been planning. I've done extensive research to make sure it's tailored to her tastes, and I can't wait to see her reaction.

She's just finished the first batch of hotcakes when Julie arrives with Caleb.

I'm at the counter slicing strawberries when they come in, and I wipe my hands on a dish towel to say hello. When I turn around, I expect Caleb to rush to Briar, but instead, he runs straight to me. My heart swells as I bend down and scoop him into my arms.

"Hey, bud, I missed you," I say, pushing his hair back. "How was your night at the ranch house? Did any of the chicks hatch?"

He bobs his head, a smile stretching across his face.

"Caleb helped Samuel and me get the brooder boxes set up in one of the backyard sheds." Julie brushes past us, picking up where I left off, and finishes cutting the strawberries. "We're still waiting on a few to hatch, but most of the chicks should be dry and ready to move out of the incubator by tomorrow."

"Sounds like he had a good time. Thanks again for taking him," I say.

"Anytime. Hope you and Briar enjoyed yourselves," Julie replies, her eyes gleaming.

Walker snorts. "Did they ever."

I narrow my eyes, but he's unfazed, shooting me a cheeky grin before taking a drink of coffee.

Briar interrupts our silent standoff when she steps between us and sets a stack of pancakes on the table. "Dig in before they get cold."

Her brothers don't need to be told twice. They each pile three onto their plates and drown them in syrup.

Julie brings over a bowl of strawberries and bananas, setting it between Heath and Walker. "Add something healthy."

Without protest, they each add a generous helping onto their pancakes. Grown men or not, they know better than to disobey their mom.

I set Caleb down and he heads straight to the table, climbing onto a chair. His eyes light up at the sight of the food, and he licks his lips. Briar's breakfast has set a new standard, and I doubt he'll settle for cereal again.

"Want a pancake, bud?" I ask.

He nods.

"Here, I made this one special for you," Briar says, crossing the room to place a dino-shaped pancake with chocolate chips in front of Caleb.

It means a lot that she remembers his favorite and went out of her way to make sure there was one ready when he arrived.

"You bringing the little dude to help us bale hay?" Walker asks, talking around a mouthful of food.

"Don't talk with your mouth full," Julie chides.

"Yes, ma'am," he mumbles sheepishly.

I considered bringing Caleb along, but I don't think it's the best idea. It will be hot out today, and I don't want him getting overheated or too tired, especially since I won't be able to keep a constant eye on him. However, Briar has him every weekday afternoon, and I didn't want to ask her to give up her Saturday. Julie had him last night, so it wouldn't be fair to ask her again.

"Caleb can spend the day with me," Briar says before I can reply.

I glance over to where she's flipping another batch of pancakes. "Really? I don't want to inconvenience you."

She waves me off with a grin. "Of course. I'd love nothing more," she assures me. "I've been wanting to introduce him to the horses. Cooper, our horse wrangler, is here today, so there should be at least one in the corral for Caleb to meet."

"If Briar has other things to do later, Caleb's more than welcome to come with me to take care of the chicks once I'm back from town," Julie adds. "It's no trouble at all."

My heart swells with gratitude, amazed by the level of generosity we're surrounded by, and I'm certain now more than ever that coming to Bluebell was the right decision.

CHAPTER 23

Briar

AFTER JENSEN AND MY BROTHERS LEFT FOR THE FIELDS, Caleb and I spent time with Ziggy. We fed him oats and sweet potatoes, and when he finished eating, they played a game of tag. Ziggy would chase Caleb in short bursts, bleating as he ran, while Caleb darted between trees, laughing as he looked over his shoulder at Ziggy barreling toward him.

Our backyard adventure was followed by a walk, eventually making our way to the corral. Only one horse was there. The others were likely already out in the pasture for the day. With no sign of Cooper outside, we head inside the stable to find him tending to a saddle.

His face is hard-set, his piercing blue eyes scanning his surroundings, always alert to potential threats. He's wearing his favorite black cowboy hat and a short-sleeved tan button-down shirt that stretches across his muscular frame, revealing his inked forearms. Several visible scars peek out beneath, but he doesn't talk about them, and I've never asked, respecting his privacy. Some things are better left unspoken.

"Hey, Cooper," I call out with a wave.

He gives a quick nod. "Howdy, Briar." His hands move with precision, working the saddle soap into the worn leather in slow circles.

"It's been a while," I say.

"Yeah, I had to go on some business trips for the security firm. It's good to be back."

He sets the sponge and tin on the edge of the tack bench, wiping his hands on his jeans before approaching us.

He crouches down next to Caleb and holds out his hand. "You must be Caleb. Mighty glad to finally meet you."

Caleb chews on his bottom lip, staring at Cooper, and I brace myself for him to shy away or tuck himself behind me. However, to my surprise, he reaches out and shakes Cooper's hand. He's come a long way with me and the Halsteads, but this is the first time I've seen him interact with someone he's not familiar with.

"That's one heck of a grip you've got there," Cooper says, whistling low. "What do you say we feed Magnolia? She's the horse in the corral. I brought her favorites: carrots and apples. She can't get enough of 'em."

Caleb doesn't even look my way before nodding enthusiastically. He's been cautious around the horses up until recently, so this is another big win, and I can't wait to tell Jensen. I press a hand to my chest, my cheeks aching from smiling so hard. It's a privilege to watch Caleb come out of his shell, and it's further confirmation that he'll be just fine in the long run.

I follow at a distance as Cooper leads him to the corral, the sound of their footsteps crunching over gravel. The scent of hay and the earthy aroma of horses fill the air. It's one of my favorites because it reminds me of the simplicity and peace found on the ranch.

I still remember the first time Julie brought me here. I was in awe of the wide-open space stretching for miles in every direction, the opposite of the cramped, broken-down trailer I shared with my mom. Where my mom was sharp and indifferent, Julie was gentle and patient. That day she introduced me to the horses, and I remember one pressing its nose into my palm through the fence as if it could sense the sadness I carried. For the first time in a long while, I felt seen.

That moment planted the seed for wanting to offer other kids the same kind of refuge. To be a guiding light to them like Julie has been to me and show them the quiet comfort that can come from an animal's steady presence.

My phone chimes, and I pull it out of my back pocket to see who's texting me.

Backroads & Bad Decisions Group Chat

Charlie: I'm calling dibs on being godmother to your future kids, Briar.

Charlie: I did play matchmaker after all.

Briar: I don't know what you're talking about.

Charlie: Everyone at Lasso & Latte is talking about it.

Briar: About what?

Charlie: You and Jensen holding hands. At the fair. In public.

Charlie: Word is, you came off the Ferris wheel looking extra flushed.

It must've been Miss McGregor and her inch-thick glasses who started the rumor. She was conveniently walking by when Jensen and I stepped off the ride. How she manages to see anything through those lenses—let alone that I was blushing—is beyond me. Good thing Earl wasn't there. He'd probably have spotted us at the top of the Ferris wheel, and that rumor would be far more scandalous.

> **Wren:** I thought Briar was scared of the Ferris wheel.

> **Charlie:** Guess she's warming up to it. Or should I say to Jensen?

> **Charlie:** Fill us in… how was the rest of your night?

I laugh under my breath.

> **Briar:** You're far too nosy for your own good.

> **Charlie:** I prefer passionately invested in your dating life.

> **Charlie:** Now spill. Pretty please.

I had planned to tell her about last night, but I figured she'd rather hear it over the phone or in person. But since patience isn't her strong suit, the whole gang is about to get the rundown all at once.

> **Briar:** Jensen and I may have slept together.

> **Charlie:** And how was urban cowboy?

> **Briar:** I don't kiss and tell.

> **Charlie:** I wasn't referring to the kissing, so please do share. *drooling face emoji

> **Briar:** And you're done.

I look up from my phone to check on Caleb. He's standing next to Cooper near the corral, watching Magnolia. She's a bay mare with a shiny brown coat.

> **Wren:** Where's Birdie? She'd usually be all over this by now.

> **Charlie:** Birdie?! Show us proof of life, or we'll call for a wellness check.

> **Wren:** Weren't you the last to see her?

> **Charlie:** She wasn't feeling well, so we left the fair early last night.

> **Briar:** Has anyone gotten the town gossip this morning or checked the local paper?

There's no telling what kind of trouble Birdie stirred up overnight. Wouldn't be the first time she pulled a solo rescue mission, and we heard about her antics from the walking club or the local paper.

> **Charlie:** Holy shit. Check the home page of Bluebell Gazette's website.

I pull up their site on my phone. The home page loads, and the first headline jumps out at me: "Calf and Donkey Disappear Overnight from Local County Fair." I scroll through the article and learn they vanished between midnight and six a.m. Apparently, the fairground property has cameras, but the police haven't reviewed the footage yet.

I drop the link to the article in the group chat.

> **Briar:** Birdie, this better be a coincidence.

> **Charlie:** How is "lying low" such a difficult concept to grasp?

Wren: If you don't answer, we're launching a search party.

Birdie: I'm here!

Charlie: Where is here? In hiding?

Birdie: Someone did a nice thing by rescuing those animals, huh?

Charlie: Was that someone you?

Birdie: No comment.

As much as I want to get to the bottom of whatever trouble Birdie's gotten herself into, it'll have to wait. I put my phone in my pocket so I can give Caleb my full attention.

Magnolia pricks her ears at the sight of Cooper and trots over to the fence to greet him. He slides his hand through the wooden slats to scratch her forehead, and her nostrils flare as she nudges him.

"Hey there, sweet girl. I want you to meet my new friend, Caleb." Cooper glances over his shoulder where Caleb's watching from a distance. He motions for him to come closer. "This is Magnolia. She's as sweet as they come and would love if you pet her."

Caleb hesitates, shifting from foot to foot, his eyes dart from Cooper to the mare and back again. He finally takes a cautious step forward but keeps his hands at his sides.

It's clear that he's nervous, but before I can intervene, Cooper crouches beside him and gently takes his hand. "Try right here," he says, guiding it to Magnolia's lowered head, right between her ears.

She huffs softly, leaning into Caleb's hand. When her velvety nose presses against his shirt, he lets out a bubble of laughter.

"She's checking your pockets." Cooper chuckles. "I usually

keep a carrot or two in mine, so now she thinks everyone's hiding snacks. Briar, can you grab the bucket of apples and carrots in my truck?"

"Sure thing."

I jog over to his vehicle and open the tailgate to grab the metal bucket from the truck bed. It's filled to the brim, so I carry it with one hand under the base and the other gripping the handle to keep the contents from spilling.

"Thanks," Cooper says, taking the bucket from me.

He sets it on the ground, plucking out a handful of carrots and two apples. When he approaches the fence, Magnolia catches the familiar scent and stretches her neck over the rail.

Caleb watches, intrigued, as Cooper offers a carrot to Magnolia—her soft lips grazing his skin. She chomps it down in a few bites, juice dribbling from the groove of her chin.

Cooper holds out a carrot to Caleb. "You want to try, kid?"

This time, there's no hesitation. He takes the carrot and extends his hand the way Cooper did. Magnolia doesn't miss a beat, snapping it up with the same enthusiasm as she did the first. Caleb grins, pointing at one of the apples, ready to feed her again.

Watching Caleb and Cooper together, I'm reminded that pain doesn't care what stage of life you're in. It takes freely and without reason or mercy. Caleb lost his mom, and Cooper carries scars from his military service that he'd rather not talk about. Yet, here, in the stillness of this sanctuary, surrounded by fresh air and the calming presence of a horse, pain is forced to loosen its grip—if only for a moment.

This is why I believe that my nonprofit has the power to change lives. When kids are given the space to connect, they can begin to let go of what's been holding them back.

When my mom left town and I moved in with the Halsteads, I spent endless hours in my room, shutting myself off from everyone. In hindsight, I was struggling with depression and the loss of being left behind. One of the things that pulled me through my darkest moments was Heath and Walker making me go on weekly horseback rides. Each one brought me a sense of peace and allowed me to heal from my childhood traumas.

Horses offer healing rooted in compassion, patience, and trust. Just one piece of the larger vision I'm working toward, and Caleb is quickly becoming my biggest reason to keep going until my dream becomes a reality.

CHAPTER 24

Briar

ONCE CALEB FINISHES FEEDING MAGNOLIA, WE HEAD BACK
to the cottage. Mama Julie and Pops are in town running
errands, so I offered to make lunch for Jensen, my brothers,
and the ranch hands. It's sweltering hot, so I pack a cooler with
sweet tea and water to go along with their ham and cheese
sandwiches. It's a simple affair but should keep them fueled till
dinner. Mama Julie always hosts a big barbecue after a long day
of hauling hay or moving cattle.

I'm standing at the kitchen counter with Caleb beside me
on a stool, his tongue poking out in concentration. I slather mayo
and mustard onto the bread, and once I slide a piece his way, he
carefully lays down a slice of cheese.

"You're mighty good at this, Chef Caleb."

He grins, puffing out his chest.

After adding the condiments, I circle to his other side and
add the ham to each sandwich before putting the final piece of
bread on top of each.

"Alright, little man. Go wash your hands and put your shoes on so we can take your dad and the guys their lunch."

He hops off the stool and darts out of the kitchen. I finish wrapping the sandwiches and stack them into a reusable bag. I've already loaded the drinks into my Jeep, so the hard part is finished.

I've just put away the leftover ingredients when Caleb comes back in wearing a pair of boots Pops gave him. He stumbles every few steps, and I notice they're on the wrong feet. Each time he catches himself, he lets out an impatient huff.

"Thanks for listening, bud. Could I fix your shoes so it's easier to walk?"

He frowns, glancing down at his feet before nodding.

I crouch in front of him, his small hands gripping my shoulders for balance. While I switch his shoes, he absently twirls a piece of my hair. It's such a small thing, but it melts my heart to see how at ease he is with me.

No one could ever replace his mom, but I'm doing my best to show him a fraction of the safety and warmth I'm certain she did. I just hope that his time in Bluebell, surrounded by people who love him, has been enough to help him break through the walls he's built. He deserves to rediscover what it means to be a kid again without carrying the weight of the world on his shoulders.

When his boots are on the right feet, I give them a light pat on the top. "You're all set. Ready to head out?"

He gives me a thumbs-up before running over to the kitchen table to grab the basket filled with apples.

"You're the best helper," I say, grabbing the bag of sandwiches from the counter.

He bites his lip, eyes locked on the fruit in his hands, making sure he doesn't drop any.

Once we're in the car, I roll down the windows and tune into a local country radio station. It's become a tradition for Caleb and me whenever we drive together. He bobs his head to the music, one hand stretched out the back window, fingers catching in the breeze as we cruise through the ranch.

"I love my new rubber duck," I say over my shoulder. "Thanks for getting it for me. It fits right in next to the unicorn one from my friend Birdie."

Caleb looks my way with a smile.

After a trip to the toy store last week, he brought me home a lime-green duck shaped like a T-Rex, with orange spikes running down its back and a tail curling behind it. Jensen helped him pick it out, and it's touching that they went out of their way to find something I'd appreciate. Jensen's attention to my likes and dislikes means a lot, especially when he gets Caleb involved in turning a small gift into a meaningful memory.

My new dino rubber duck is the perfect addition to the collection and now holds the center spot on my console.

The tires crunch over gravel as I pull up beside the field where everyone is working. Heath is operating the tractor, glancing over his shoulder to make sure the rows are feeding evenly, clouds of dust rising behind him in thick plumes. Jensen, Walker, and the ranch hands work nearby with a front-end loader, scooping the bales and loading them onto a flatbed truck parked at the edge of the field near my Jeep. This operation is like a well-oiled machine.

My gaze drifts to Jensen, his white shirt soaked with sweat, clinging to his back as he lifts another bale onto the truck. The cowboy hat he's wearing is downright sexy, and I remember exactly what that body is capable of—his strong hands gripping my thighs and his mouth on mine, rough and urgent.

As soon as he spots my Jeep, he wipes the sweat from his brow and lifts a hand in greeting.

I exhale, forcing myself to rein in my fantasy. Now isn't the time or place to have lusty thoughts.

"Come on, little man," I say over my shoulder to Caleb. "They look like they could use a break, and your dad sure seems excited to see you."

I get Caleb out of the vehicle, and together we lay out the spread in the back of the Jeep so the guys can easily grab a drink and a sandwich when they're ready.

Walker and Jensen are the first to head over. Caleb runs straight into Jensen's arms, giggling as he lifts him and spins him in a circle.

"Appreciate you stopping by, sis," Walker says, grabbing a bottle of water from the cooler and drinking it down in seconds.

"Figured you could use backup in this heat."

"It's a scorcher today, that's for damn sure."

"Y'all making good progress?" I ask.

"We always do with Heath in charge. He's a tough taskmaster." Walker tosses his empty bottle in the garbage bag I brought and picks three apples from the basket. "Your pretty boy kept up, surprisingly, even though his gloves were more for gardening than hauling hay. Good thing we had extras or his hands would be toast." One by one, he sends the apples into the air, keeping them moving in a continuous arc as his fingers catch and release them with ease.

"Hey, you're just jealous that after all these years away, I still got it," Jensen quips, joining us at the back of the Jeep.

He moves next to me, his eyes dropping to my mouth as his fingers graze my hip. We both stiffen when he realizes his mistake, and he's quick to pull back. We glance at Caleb, who's too focused on Walker and his juggling act to notice.

"We'll see how cocky you are after a few more Saturdays in the fields." Walker smirks, looking between Jensen and me.

After a few more rounds, he catches all three apples, sets two in the basket, and sinks his teeth into the third.

"What have you two been up to?" Jensen asks as he gets a sandwich. "Anything fun?"

"We stopped by the stables and visited Magnolia, one of the mares. Caleb even got to feed her," I say.

He lets out a low whistle. "You did?"

Caleb nods enthusiastically, stretching out his hands to show how big Magnolia was compared to him.

"That's awesome. Can't wait to hear more about it later," Jensen says, ruffling his hair.

Caleb's therapist recommended we ask open-ended questions that encourage him to talk about his day. Just small openings so he knows we're here when he's ready to share. Jensen's taken every suggestion seriously, and has even started asking her for parenting books and podcast recommendations, now that he's gone through his pile at home.

When the ranch hands and Heath join us at the Jeep, I step back so they can grab their lunch. I've brought food out to my brothers more times than I can count, but with Jensen and Caleb here, it feels different. They're slowly weaving themselves into my heart, turning even the simplest tasks and routines into things I look forward to because they're around.

On the way back from the fields, Caleb and I swing by the ranch house to check on the rest of the newly hatched chicks. Mama Julie and Pops got back from town while we were out, and Caleb was more than eager to stay with them for a few hours while I went back to patch up a section of the corral that I noticed was damaged earlier.

As I mend the fence, I'm reminded that not long ago, my days were spent maintaining the cabins and working around the ranch. I mostly kept to myself aside from weekly dinners with Mama Julie and Pops, and the occasional rescue mission or girls' night with my friends. My focus had been set on saving for my children's sanctuary and renovating the cottage. For the most part, I was content, but restlessness had started to creep in, and I couldn't pinpoint why.

Then Jensen came to Bluebell and asked me to be Caleb's nanny. It brought a sense of purpose I didn't realize I was missing. I've volunteered with a local nonprofit that helps young children through hard times and hosted several camps for kids with trauma here at the ranch, but nothing has been as fulfilling as my afternoons spent with Caleb.

The crunch of gravel under tires pulls me from my thoughts. Heath's blue pickup rolls up with Jensen and my brothers inside.

"Finished for the day?" I ask as they climb out.

"Yeah. Just have to put away some of the equipment before we meet the ranch hands at the house for dinner," Heath mumbles.

He's always extra grumpy after a long day in the fields.

Jensen climbs out of the back seat, pulls off his hat, and wipes the sweat from his forehead.

"I just found out pretty boy here borrowed one of Heath's hats. It's like he doesn't know us," Walker adds with a mocking laugh.

"Excuse me," Jensen replies dryly. "I wasn't aware that not all cowboy hats are created equal."

"This is why you never should've left Bluebell. Living in the city for so long made you think any old hat would do. It's about finding one that fits *you*. Not swiping one of Heath's."

"Are you forgetting you let me borrow yours last month?"

"That was a one-time thing. You're working on the ranch again, so you need your own."

Jensen rolls his eyes. "If it's that important, I'll get a damn cowboy hat."

Walker claps him on the back. "Atta-boy."

I've been thinking about getting Caleb a hat, and now I can't stop picturing him and Jensen in matching ones. That would be downright adorable and would mean something special to them both. I tuck it away on my mental to-do list.

Heath shakes the truck keys, nodding to Walker. "Come on. We have to put away the rest of the equipment before it gets dark. Jensen, you stay here with Briar. Once we're finished, we'll circle back to pick you up and drive over to the ranch house together. Shouldn't take us more than twenty minutes."

Jensen nods. "Sure thing."

Heath and Walker head back to the truck.

Jensen glances around, his brow furrowed. "Where's Caleb?"

"At the ranch house with Mama Julie, visiting the chicks. He's smitten," I say.

He clutches his chest dramatically. "Great. First, Ziggy and Petunia, now the chicks. At this rate, I'll be lucky if he remembers I exist."

"Outranked by a goat, cow and some puffballs." I pat his chest with exaggerated sympathy, my lips curling into a playful grin. "You've got it rough. Poor thing."

"I think you're right. I definitely need some comforting." He draws me into his arms, nuzzling my neck, and I giggle when his scruff tickles my skin.

"I hate that our morning was cut short," I murmur.

"Me too. I missed you while I was gone." We just saw each other at lunch, but I know how he feels.

"I missed you too," I say softly.

More than I probably should after one night together.

After this morning, I half expected him to keep his distance. Sure, Caleb's not around, but I figured he'd only show affection when we're alone at night. Yet here he is, holding me, even with my brothers throwing not-so-subtle glances at us as they drive away.

"Heath said we had twenty minutes, right?"

Jensen nods. "Yeah, why?"

"Perfect. That should be plenty of time," I mumble to myself.

"For what?"

I don't respond, waiting until Heath's truck is out of sight before taking Jensen's hand and guiding him to the far end of the barn. I slide open the door and lead him into the closest empty stall, freshly lined with straw. The horses are all out to pasture, which means we've got the place to ourselves.

Jensen grunts when I back him against the wall hidden from the main aisle.

"What do you need, pretty girl?" His voice is strained.

"Something I've wanted to do for days," I confess.

Last night might have been our first time, but that doesn't mean I haven't had my fair share of fantasies since he arrived at the ranch.

I saunter closer, my fingers grazing Jensen's chest as our lips meet, the kiss starting slow and teasing. I keep the pressure light at first, brushing my mouth against his in soft, lingering touches, pulling back when he tries to deepen it.

I manage to keep my composure—until he groans.

My fingers curl around his collar, tugging him against me, and the initial tenderness shifts into something urgent and hungry. His hand slides to the back of my neck as he nips at my lips, his tongue slipping inside my mouth. Every touch is like a spark, igniting the tension simmering between us.

Our lips remain locked as my palms slide down his chest, moving lower until I reach his waistband. I work his buckle loose and undo the button of his jeans, our kiss never faltering. Once the zipper is down, I push his pants down to his hips, my breath catching at the heat radiating off his skin.

Only then does he pause, his breath ragged as he rests his forehead against mine.

"You're playing a dangerous game, baby," he warns.

"Good. I hate when the stakes are boring."

I drop to my knees, heat pulsing beneath my skin. My eyes

land on Jensen's cock straining behind his boxers. Not wanting to wait a second longer, I slip my hand between us and trace his dick with a featherlight touch.

The scent of sweat and hay clings to him, and it's ridiculously sexy. I bite my lip, aching with how badly I want him like this—dirty, rugged, every inch a cowboy.

His gaze remains locked on me as I slowly drag down his underwear, his cock standing at attention. He lets out a sharp inhale when I curl my fingers around it, giving it a gentle squeeze. I move my hand along his shaft in measured strokes, keeping my pace steady when precum leaks from the tip. I lean in, flicking my tongue over the tip before licking it clean.

"Fuck, you're driving me wild," Jensen groans.

I lift my hooded eyes, smirking. "I'm only getting started, cowboy."

"Show me."

He winds his fingers through my hair and pushes the tip against my mouth. I eagerly oblige his silent invitation, wrapping my lips around his cock and sucking the head.

"Holy hell," he curses softly, his hand tightening in my hair.

I groan, the sound reverberating around his dick. He rocks his hips forward, and I take in a sharp inhale through my nose. Sensing that I'm struggling, he strokes the column of my neck.

"Open that throat and take me deeper," he says, his tone guttural.

Jensen's commanding presence sets every nerve in my body on fire, leaving my panties soaked. It's electrifying to be with someone who knows exactly what I'm craving. He makes surrender a thrilling escape that leaves me wanting nothing more than to please him.

I hollow my cheeks, swallowing hard around him as his shaft pulses forward, pushing farther down until the head is at the back of my throat.

"Such a good fucking girl for me," he praises, and I hum around him.

Jensen lets me take control of the pace while I adjust, and it's unexpectedly sweet. His bottom lip is caught between his teeth as though it's taking every ounce of effort to keep himself in check—the opposite of what I want. No, I want to push him to the brink until he loses every ounce of control.

My fingers curl around the base of his cock, holding him steady as I run my tongue along his shaft, applying pressure to the vein. His body tenses as I swirl my tongue around the crown and back down his length, never slowing my pace.

"I'm going to come," he grunts.

I lean forward, pushing his head back down my throat. Tears sting at the corner of my eyes, but I don't let that deter me as he fucks my mouth with abandon, growling in approval as my swollen lips bob up and down around his shaft at the rapid pace we've set. I wrap my free hand around his balls, squeezing gently.

"Jesus Christ," he groans as his muscles tighten. "You're going to swallow every drop," he orders, his grip around my neck relaxing.

I nod the best I can as his cock jerks under my hand. He doesn't look away as I lap up every drop, licking him clean.

When I've finished, his cock springs free from my mouth with a *pop*.

"You're so damn pretty on your knees," he murmurs reverently.

I bite my lower lip, warmth blooming in my chest. I'm addicted to his praise and the way he takes charge, showing that he knows exactly what I crave and how to give it to me—right down to the commanding tone he uses when telling me to swallow.

Jensen draws me out of my thoughts as he wipes a bead of cum dripping down my chin. With my gaze locked on his, I grab his wrist and run my tongue over his finger, licking it clean.

"That's my girl," he croons.

When I'm finished, he reaches down and pulls me to my feet. Being with him leaves me dizzy, a rush from every possessive glance and touch, etched into my skin and impossible to shake. I crave his praise and the way his magnetic energy takes over when we're alone—it's everything I've imagined, but never experienced until now.

He tucks his semi-hard cock back inside his boxers and pulls up his pants, zipping them in place. His eyes meet mine as he smooths my hair with a tenderness that steals my breath, then kisses my temple.

"Coming back after a long day of baling hay is a whole lot more enjoyable when you're waiting for me. Now it's my time to—" Jensen cuts himself off at the sound of a truck pulling in front of the barn.

I sigh. I swear that was the quickest twenty minutes of my life.

"I owe you three more orgasms tonight," Jensen promises, a devastatingly handsome smile on his face.

"Three? How do you figure that?" I ask, intrigued.

Jensen lifts a finger. "You gave me the best damn blow job I've ever had." He holds up another one. "We were rudely interrupted this morning, and I don't believe in leaving a woman high and dry before starting her day. And last, I'm dying to taste you again," he says, raising a third finger as he leans in, brushing his lips against mine.

"I suppose denying you would be bad manners, and we can't have that," I tease, giving him a quick kiss.

We're halfway to the exit when Heath walks inside the barn. "Where the hell have you two been?" He gives us a once-over, arching a brow. "Seriously? You couldn't wait a few more hours? I swear, Jensen, if this ends with you as a dad of two, you can count me out of babysitting ever again."

"I second that or I'm charging double for emotional damages," Walker adds as he steps up beside Heath.

"Don't we have a dinner to get to?" I quip.

Jensen leans in and whispers in my ear, "I'm starving."

Butterflies stir in my belly as heat rises to my cheeks, and I find myself slipping further into his orbit with each passing minute.

CHAPTER 25

Jensen

"T HIS GAME IS RIGGED," BRIAR MUTTERS AS SHE TOSSES A piece of popcorn into her mouth.

"You're the one who shuffled the cards," I tease, leaning back against the couch.

"Guess we can't all be blessed with Caleb's winning streak," she says, grinning at him.

He's sitting beside me with Briar across the coffee table as we play our third round of Candy Land. When I got back to the cottage earlier, I found him in the living room setting up the board game. He found it in the toy chest at the ranch house, and Julie was delighted to let him borrow it. The way he expertly arranged the cards and set up the gingerbread men at the starting spot made it clear he knew what he was doing. It made me wonder how often he played with Amelia, and if they had regular game nights.

Despite my initial negative feelings about her keeping Caleb from me, I'm doing my best to preserve her memory for his sake, giving him pieces of her to hold on to that feel familiar. The last thing I want is for him to carry the weight of my frustration.

We've already played Candy Land twice tonight, and Caleb has won both games. That's why Briar broke out the popcorn and jelly beans to power through round three, saying she needed snacks to prepare for another inevitable loss.

She's still frowning at the peanut card that sent her back to Peanut Brittle House.

Caleb's blue gingerbread piece is seven spaces from winning, and his eyes dart between the card pile and me, silently willing me to pick a bad card.

I draw a double yellow, moving ahead of Briar, shooting her a smug look as I pass. After a string of unlucky draws, including being sent back to the Peppermint Forest, I think my luck is finally turning around.

"Better watch out, Caleb, I'm catching up."

He shoots me a mischievous grin and sticks out his tongue before drawing a single green and moving ahead one space. Only six away from winning it all.

"Here goes nothing," Briar sighs, flipping her card over and groaning when she's sent back to the Molasses Swamp. "Seriously? You both have all the luck. This game is out to get me."

Caleb shifts onto his knees, reaching over the table to rest a hand on Briar's arm. She covers it with her own, patting him.

"Thanks, little man. I'll be alright. Just make sure you beat your dad, okay?" she says, winking at me.

"We'll see about that," I reply, my tone playful.

I draw a double purple from the stack, closing the gap between Caleb and me. But when he pulls a double blue, it's game over. He slides his piece into Candy Castle, then leaps to his feet, arms raised in the air as he dances around in triumph. Briar and

I erupt in applause, cheering him on like he just won the Super Bowl. He ends with a dramatic bow that has us both laughing.

This right here is everything I've wanted for him—a home filled with laughter and love where we celebrate his wins, no matter how big or small. He's opening up more with each passing day, and I couldn't be happier.

When he yawns, a glance at the clock confirms it's well past his bedtime. No wonder he's tired. It's been a long day for everyone, myself included.

It turns out that hauling hay is a lot harder than I remember. After more than a decade behind a computer, even daily workouts can't hold a candle to the exhaustion of tossing fifty-pound bales in the summer heat. My back has already filed a formal complaint, and my hands are starting to show the beginnings of calluses, which, according to Briar, are sexy as hell.

Caleb rubs his eyes, stifling another yawn, the excitement of winning three times in a row finally catching up to him.

I reach over and rub his back. "Alright, champ, it's getting late. Time to head upstairs for your bath."

He gives a sleepy nod, but instead of leaving the room, he goes over to Briar. Wrapping his arms tightly around her neck, he rests his cheek on her shoulder. She draws him close, pressing a kiss to his temple.

"Sleep tight, little man. I'll see you tomorrow."

A lump rises in my throat as I watch them. Their bond has grown quickly, and Briar has become one of his favorite people. Every time she walks through the front door, he runs to greet her with a hug. The way he lights up when she's around makes it hard to imagine our lives without her.

Once Caleb and I go upstairs, I run a bath and get him settled with his water toys. He's added a dozen rubber duckies from Briar's Jeep to his bath time lineup, including his favorite—Captain Quackbeard. He'd stay in the tub forever if he could, so

I filled up his water bottle and laid out his pajamas to give him a few extra minutes.

He's recently added a pair of jammies with cowboy hats and horses to his regular rotation, wearing them nearly every night since Julie gave them to him. A month ago, I was convinced he'd forever be in his dinosaur era, but it appears the Wild West might give them a run for their money—a sign he's settling into small-town life more than I ever expected.

It's bittersweet. While I'm relieved Caleb is adjusting to life in Bluebell, I can't help but worry about what happens when it's time for us to leave. He's already been through so many changes, and the thought of putting him through another big transition makes me question if it'll undo our progress.

After he's finished bathing and changed into his cowboy pajamas, it's time for his bedtime story.

"Which book are we reading tonight?" I ask.

Caleb walks over to the bookshelf, his brow furrowed in concentration. He picks up a book about a pig and pancakes, skims the cover, then puts it back. Next, he pulls out one about a boy named Max and his adventure with wild creatures, but after a quick glance, he wrinkles his nose and sets it back on the shelf. Finding the right one is a tough choice, and I understand why he's taking his time to pick the perfect read.

His expression shifts to pure delight when he spots the newest book in his collection, pulling it from the shelf and confidently handing it to me.

"Excellent choice." I bite my lip, fighting back laughter, but a chuckle manages to slip out at the title—*Dragons Love Farts: They're More Fun Than Tacos!*

The name is just as hilarious as the first time I saw it. Walker spotted the book in the window of Tinker Toys on his way to the hardware store the other day and thought it was too funny not to get it for Caleb. Leave it to Walker to turn my kid into a fart-loving dragon enthusiast. But if it makes Caleb happy, I'm all for it.

He crawls into bed, leaving room for me to sit next to him. I sling my arm around his shoulders and pull him closer. This is still one of my favorite times of day, and he's grown more affectionate lately, sinking into me like it's second nature.

A few pages into the book, Caleb laughs as he points at a chicken and pig caught in the blast of a dragon's fart.

I let out a dramatic "Pfffft... BOOM!" Complete with an exaggerated arm wave. "If I were that pig, I'd be running for my life too," I say with a wink.

Caleb clutches his belly, shoulder shaking, and by the time we turn the page, he's doubled over in giggles as the dragons try to hide their farts in caves, only for them to explode like volcanoes.

I pinch my nose and gasp. "Whew! One of those dragons definitely had beans for breakfast." My voice sounds like a squeaky balloon, making Caleb snort before bursting into another round of giggles.

It's the most carefree I've ever seen him. Walker is welcome to send all the potty-humor books, if it means Caleb is this happy reading them.

I couldn't have pictured this would be my life a year ago—reading silly bedtime stories to my five year old and tucking him in each night. Fatherhood is downright humbling and the greatest adventure I've had the honor of experiencing. I wouldn't trade it for anything, not even for all of the success in the world.

That's why I've decided that I can't go back to how things were before. My work schedule needs to change long-term. Caleb deserves a dad who's present, and I plan to be that for him no matter what.

By the time we reach the last page with Estrella, the rainbow-farting dragon, his mouth curves in a smile, though his gaze is growing unfocused. I set the book on the nightstand and move him to lie down, resting his head back on the pillow. He reaches over to grab his stuffed dinosaur that he still sleeps with, though he's been leaving it in his room during the day.

"It was a busy day, huh? Mama Juile said you were a big help with the baby chicks. We might have to start calling you Farmer Caleb."

He nods, grinning wide as he gives me a thumbs-up.

"You'll have to tell me more about it later." I run a hand through his hair and bend to kiss his forehead. "Good night, buddy. I love you."

He blinks at me with those big brown eyes, half-lidded with sleep, and says, "Night, Dad."

Every part of me goes still, making sure it wasn't a figment of my imagination. It's not.

Caleb just spoke.

My heart pounds as his voice settles deep within my chest. I want to cry, laugh, hold him tight and never let go—instead, I grin and lean down to give him another kiss. What he needs from me tonight is to remain calm and steady even though my world has cracked open and put itself back together in the same heartbeat.

As I get up and tuck the covers around him, I notice Briar standing in the doorway, tears trailing down her cheeks. I turn off the bedside lamp and quietly exit the room. She steps out into the hall as I shut the door behind me.

My hand settles on her waist as I wipe her tears with my thumb, leaning my head against hers. Neither of us speaks, letting the weight of what we just witnessed settle around us. Since moving to Bluebell, we've carried the same fear that Caleb might never speak again or trust someone enough to use his voice. So to hear him say "night, Dad" is a monumental milestone I'll cherish forever.

"Thank you," I whisper.

"For what?" Briar asks, her breath warm against my lips.

"For helping make that possible." I nod toward Caleb's room. "He'd never have found his voice again without both of us, and I'll forever be indebted to you."

"Thank you for letting me be a part of this." She rises on her toes and brushes a kiss to my mouth. "You're a good dad, Jensen. The best."

A slow smile breaks across my face. Briar believed in me when I doubted myself most; I draw her closer, not ready to let her go.

It's hard to believe how far we've come since Caleb and I first arrived. He was scared of his own shadow, and I was bitter and lost. In such a short time, everything has shifted. Now, I can picture a future where Caleb isn't just surviving but thriving and embracing life the way every kid should.

Briar's grin stretches wide. "This calls for spiked hot chocolate on the porch. What do you think?"

"I couldn't agree more."

She kisses me again before slipping out of my arms. "I'll warm up the milk."

With her, I never have to ask for anything. She seems to know when I need a moment to myself before I do.

After she heads downstairs, I quietly push Caleb's door open a sliver, wanting to see him again. He's lying in the same spot, his eyes closed, already fast asleep.

"Thank you for being patient with me, bud," I whisper into the darkness. "I'm so lucky to have you, and your mom would be so proud. She may not be here, but you'll always have me, and I'll love you enough for both of us through every moment, big or small."

For the first time since learning about Caleb, I'm not angry with Amelia. What I feel now is gratitude. She trusted me with the most important person in her world and believed I could be there for him when she no longer could—and somehow, I have been. For Caleb.

I may never know the full story about why she kept him from me, but I forgive her. Because loving Caleb the way I do, I understand why she wanted to protect him, even if that meant keeping him a secret.

All that matters is that every sleepless night, every moment of frustration has paid off. My son *talked* to me, and I may never come down from this high. The best part? I got to share it with Briar.

CHAPTER 26

Jensen

W HEN CALEB WOKE UP THIS MORNING HE ASKED TO visit Magnolia, and of course, I said yes. It's only been a few days since he first spoke, and I'm already so proud of how far he's come.

Caleb holds out a handful of oats, laughter spilling from his mouth as Magnolia trots over. I know Briar would love to be here, but she's in town running errands.

Magnolia nudges her nose through the fence, lowering her head to eat from the palm of his hand. I watch, amazed by Caleb's confidence. Just a few weeks ago, he watched the horses from a safe distance. Now, he's at ease beside Magnolia as if he's done this a hundred times.

"Can I learn to ride a horse like Heath?" Caleb asks.

I blink, surprised by his question. This is the most he's spoken to me so far. The morning after he started talking, he only responded with one or two words. But in the days since, his sentences have steadily grown longer. Between the time spent on the ranch and his sessions with his therapist, his confidence is growing, and I'm beginning to see glimpses of the happy, bubbly boy I imagine he was before losing his mom.

"Of course you can, buddy."

"Will you teach me?"

I nod, fighting past the lump in my throat. "Absolutely."

Magnolia lets out a soft whinny once she finishes the oats, clearly asking for more. I pull the plastic bag I brought from my back pocket and shake a few into Caleb's outstretched hands. Magnolia doesn't hesitate, dipping her head for the second helping of treats.

This is what I've wished for since Caleb came into my life. For him to feel confident enough to ask for what he wants and comfortable enough to share his opinions. Even if he had chosen to stay silent, we would've kept finding other ways for him to express himself. But I'm thankful he's chosen to let his voice be heard, and I'll never take it for granted.

"Caleb?"

He gives me a curious glance. "Yeah, Dad?"

My chest tightens at the sound of him calling me that. Finding out I was a dad was life-changing, but hearing him say it aloud means everything.

"You can always talk to me, buddy. About anything. And if you ever don't feel like talking, that's okay too."

Magnolia's finished her second handful of oats, and Caleb wipes his hands on his pants. He averts his gaze to the ground and nudges a pebble with his foot.

"I miss Mom," he says so quietly I have to lean in.

My stomach twists, and I crouch down to his level. "She loved you more than anything, and I'm sorry she's not here." I draw him in for a hug, and he rests his head against my shoulder. "Would you like to tell me something special you two used to do together?"

He peeks up at me. "We used to go see the dinos at the museum."

"Sounds like a lot of fun."

"Mom did the best dino growls, kind of like yours when we read books," he says with a small smile.

I let out a shaky breath as a calm washes over me. I've often doubted if I'm doing enough for Caleb, so hearing that even the small things like reading books with all the voices brings him comfort is reassuring.

"That's so cool. Maybe you can show me how she did them sometime?"

He eases out of my arms so he can look me in the eyes. "If we read *Dragons Love Farts* at bedtime, I can."

I smooth back his hair from his face. "It's a deal. Can you tell me more about your mom?"

"She liked to put flowers in cups of dirt," he says.

I purse my lips, trying to figure out what he means. "She enjoyed planting flowers?"

"Mm-hmm. The red and pink ones were her favorite."

"How about we go to the garden shop today and pick some out? We can put them in pots and keep them on the front porch of the cottage." Magnolia leans her head through the fence, and I rub behind her ear, earning a soft huff. "You can tell me more about your mom while we plant them if you'd like," I suggest to Caleb.

"Thanks, Dad," he says quickly.

If flowers make him happy, I'll buy every red and pink one the garden shop has. These past couple of months he's had to sit alone in his grief, and now that he's speaking again, I want to give him every chance to share memories of his mom. His therapist said that encouraging him to open up when he's ready is an important part of the healing process and will reassure him that I'll keep the stories he shares safe.

I have Briar to thank for showing me this new perspective.

She helped me see that Amelia's actions or motives aren't important. Amelia was Caleb's mom, and he loved her with all his heart. She gave me the greatest gift I could have ever asked for. As much as I would have liked to have gotten closure from her before she passed, my own love for Caleb is more important. That means doing whatever it takes to guarantee his happiness and standing by my choice to forgive Amelia. The best thing I can do now is to help Caleb find ways to honor her memory and give him the kind of life she would have wanted for him.

After our adventure visiting Magnolia, we drove into town. Our first stop was the garden center where we picked out several pots and a variety of red and pink flowers, including snapdragons, petunias, and geraniums. Caleb was beaming the entire time, pointing out the supplies Amelia liked to use, and we made sure to get all of them. Gardening must have been one of her hobbies, and I'll do all the research I can to ensure I keep the flowers alive.

Next, we went to Tinker Toys so Caleb could pick out a few new books and some craft supplies. He found a new dinosaur coloring book that he's excited about. After that, we visited Milk & Honey Outfitters, the local clothing store, to get him some Wranglers and another pair of boots. I had planned to stop by the hat shop next, but he was getting restless after trying on his fifth pair of jeans, so I promised we'd stop by Sweet Spur Creamery before heading back to the ranch.

We've just stepped outside Milk & Honey Outfitters when a familiar, melodic laugh catches my attention.

I glance over to find Briar standing in front of Timeless Threads, a vintage boutique two doors down. Charlie is beside her, a crooked grin spreading across her face when she spots Caleb and me.

Briar's hair falls in loose waves from beneath her hat, spilling over her shoulders. She's wearing faded jeans that hug her hips, and a rose-colored blouse with lace trim and pearl buttons. She's so damn pretty that it makes it hard to breathe, and all I want is to close the distance between us and kiss her.

"Hi, Briar!" Caleb shouts, waving.

He drops my hand and takes off running, launching into her arms. She crouches to catch him in a warm embrace. It's obvious Caleb adores her as much as I do. The difference is, he gets to show it in public, while I have to stand back with my hands in my pockets resisting the urge to scoop Briar into my arms and kiss her until she's breathless. I can't deny I'm halfway gone for her already, and with each passing day, it's getting harder to stick to the rules we set when all I want is more.

"Hey, little man," Briar beams at Caleb. "Are you having a good day?"

He bobs his head. "Uh-huh. We bought red and pink flowers."

A smile lights up her face. "That's exciting. I bet they're beautiful."

"They were my mom's favorites."

A flicker of sadness crosses her features, but she masks it quickly for Caleb's sake. "That makes them even more special. I can't wait to see them when we get back to the cottage."

"Can you help us put them in pots?" Caleb asks.

Briar nods. "I'd love to."

He pumps his fist. "Awesome."

God, I could listen to his voice all day and never get tired of it. I worried that he might be selective with who he speaks to moving forward, but I shouldn't be surprised that he feels comfortable talking with Briar. Since we got to Bluebell, he's felt safe with her, and I'm so lucky she's a part of our lives.

"Swing by the shop with your dad next week, kiddo," Charlie tells Caleb, coming to stand beside him and Briar. "A few dinosaur lamps came in this morning, and I promised Briar you'd get first pick once I've fixed them up."

Caleb's face lights up. "For real?"

"You better believe it. I'd never joke about something so serious," she says with a hand on her hip. "You're officially the Head Dino Lamp Picker."

Caleb grins, tugging Briar's sleeve, making sure he has her attention. "Did you hear that? I'm getting my own dino lamp."

She chuckles, ruffling his hair. "Can't wait to see which one you pick out."

God, Briar is a saint. There's nothing she won't do to make my son happy, even when it means bringing in reinforcements to entertain his endless dinosaur obsession.

"Dad said we could get ice cream. Can you come with us?" Caleb asks her.

Briar's mouth rounds into a small O as she looks between us. "I wouldn't want to intrude on your day together."

"We want you there, don't we?" I ask Caleb.

He nods with a toothy grin.

"As long as you're free," I add.

"She is," Charlie replies for her.

"It's settled," I announce, not giving Briar a chance to argue. "We better hurry, or they might run out of chocolate with sprinkles." I wink at Caleb when his eyes grow wide.

As Briar stands, Caleb is quick to move between us, taking hold of both our hands, leading us down the street in the direction of the ice cream shop.

"Have fun," Charlie calls out behind us.

We draw plenty of curious glances from passersby. The town's still buzzing with gossip about Briar and me together at the county fair, and seeing us out with Caleb on a Sunday afternoon will no doubt only add fuel to the fire. But I don't pay them any mind because my full attention is on my two favorite people.

Sweet Spur Creamery hasn't changed much over the years. It still smells like fresh waffle cones and cherry syrup. The wooden floorboards creak under my boots, and the original vinyl booths are patched with duct tape. A chalkboard menu with the flavor of the day and other specials is displayed behind the counter.

Before my parents gambled everything away, this was our go-to spot. My dad's favorite flavor, black licorice, only came around once a month, so he made sure we never missed it. That is, until their addiction caught up with them and we lost the farm and ended up living in a run-down trailer park on the edge of town.

Until this summer, I never thought I'd set foot here again, let alone with my son. He's endured losing the person he loved most, but I'll make sure he never questions how deeply he's loved—surrounded by people who would do anything for him. It's a stark contrast to my own upbringing, but I'm grateful for my past because it showed me the mistakes to avoid and gave me a roadmap to become a better father.

Caleb makes a beeline for the ice cream case, pressing his hands to the glass and rising on his tiptoes as he scans the lineup of flavors.

A lanky teen in a Sweet Spur Creamery T-shirt, with a name tag reading "Beau," leans against the counter. "Welcome in. What can I get y'all?"

I glance at Briar. "What would you like?"

"Rodeo rocky road, please," she says, smiling at Beau.

"And a scoop of butter pecan, both in cups with a cone on top," I turn to Caleb whose nose nearly touches the glass as he studies his options. "Do you know what you want, buddy? Or do you want to try any samples?"

The last time we came in, he was too shy to ask to try any

flavors before ordering, so I'm not expecting him to make eye contact with the server and point at the cookies and cream.

"Can I try that one?" he asks softly.

"Sure thing, kid," Beau says.

He scoops a small sample onto a spoon and holds it out for me, and I pass it to Caleb. He takes a small bite, pursing his lips, and shrugs.

"Can I try another?"

"Sure. What'll it be?" Beau questions.

Caleb waves to the bucket of cotton candy ice cream. Beau hands me a sample, and this time, Caleb takes a generous taste, scrunching his face like he just licked a lemon.

"Not a fan of that one?" I ask.

He shakes his head. "Can I please have chocolate with sprinkles?"

No surprise there. That's what he got when we came in before.

"Great choice," I say with a grin. "Glad you tried other options before deciding. You wouldn't want to get stuck with a whole scoop of a flavor you didn't like, right?"

"Yeah. Chocolate is the best ever!"

"One chocolate with sprinkles," Beau says, handing me Caleb's order.

"Thanks."

I give Caleb his ice cream, and when I glance up, I find Briar already at the register, taking her wallet out of her back pocket.

"What do you think you're doing, sugar?" I ask, stepping in beside her.

"You and Caleb were kind enough to invite me, so I wanted to return the kindness."

"When we're out together, you don't pay," I state.

She ignores me, turning back to the counter and holds out a twenty-dollar bill. "Woman, don't test me, or I'll throw you over my shoulder."

She smirks. "Don't tempt me with a good time, cowboy. I happen to know that's the best view in town."

Beau sets our cups of ice cream on the counter, looking between us, ultimately making the wise decision not to accept Briar's money.

I slip an arm around Briar's waist and lift her clean off the ground. She squeaks in surprise as I carry her a few steps away from the register. Caleb giggles as he watches the spectacle, clearly entertained by my antics. Still stunned, Briar stares at me as I grab her cup of rodeo rocky road and give it to her with a kiss on her forehead.

"You and Caleb go find a table. I'll be right there."

"I could argue, but I'd rather not let my treat melt while I do." She lifts the cone from her cup, meeting my eyes as she takes a lick of ice cream.

God, there she goes again—teasing to get a rise out of me. It drives me wild, and when we're alone later, I plan to make sure that mouth of hers is too busy to sass me. For now, I'm going to enjoy the afternoon with my favorite duo, because nothing beats hearing them laughing together at an inside joke or watching Caleb smile at Briar as if she's made his day brighter.

After I pay the bill, I spot them at a booth in the corner, and take a seat across from them.

"This is so good," Caleb says, chocolate smeared across his mouth and cheek.

Briar chuckles. "I'm glad you like it, little man." She leans over to grab a napkin from the dispenser and gently wipes his face.

"I wish we could eat ice cream every day," he exclaims.

Briar's eyebrows shoot up. "Every day? If we did that, you might turn into a giant sprinkle." She tickles his side, and he bursts out laughing.

Simple moments like this make everything else fade away, showing me what matters most.

CHAPTER 27

Brian

I'M SUPPOSED TO BE INSPECTING THE GUTTER DRAIN ON cabin four, but I've been distracted, replaying the moment Caleb spoke for the first time.

I was on my way to grab a book from my room when I stopped outside his bedroom door, drawn in by the sound of Jensen reading. He throws himself into the stories, complete with the silly voices and dramatic pauses, and even if he doesn't notice, Caleb watches him with eyes full of quiet admiration. It was only fitting that his first words since losing his mom were for his dad, and it was a privilege to witness it.

Over the past few days, Caleb has grown more talkative and at ease, and the change in him is unmistakable. Watching him thrive on the ranch brings back memories of my own healing journey, and I'm glad to see him finding peace here too.

I'm further distracted from my inspection when my phone buzzes, and I check to see that I have a new message.

Charlie: The whole town's buzzing about your visit to the ice cream shop.

Charlie: Urban cowboy going full alpha when you tried to pay? That's hot AF.

Briar: NGL. It was super-hot.

I push my hair back, relieved she's not here to see the grin on my face. Once Jensen got Caleb to bed last night, we slipped into his room. As soon as the door clicked shut, he was already tugging at my shirt, nearly ripping a button off in his hurry. He whispered his admiration, calling me the most beautiful thing he's ever seen, and then he proceeded to break my record for the most orgasms I've had in a single night.

Briar: How come all the juicy gossip revolves around me lately?

Charlie: Because your situationship saga is the closest thing we have to reality TV.

Charlie: Until Ethel & Earl get caught canoodling in his taxi again.

Briar: Hands down the best edition of the town gazette.

I glance up from my phone, furrowing my brow when I spot a white speck in front of my cottage from across the ranch. I squint, able to make out it's a delivery truck, but it's too far away to discern any other details.

That's odd.

I haven't made any online orders, and Jensen hasn't mentioned any upcoming deliveries. After another thirty minutes, I toss my tool bag into the back of my Jeep and drive over to check it out.

When I pull up in front of the house, I spot the Iron Spur logo on the side of the truck, a local service specializing in out-of-town deliveries.

I hop out of the Jeep, frowning when I hear the distinct sound of a drill coming from inside. I must have left a window open this morning, but I'm not complaining since it gives me some idea of what to expect.

I head straight for the kitchen, stepping around several large boxes flattened and propped against the entryway wall. I freeze when I turn the corner into the kitchen and find several local handymen in the small space, installing a cream-colored refrigerator still wrapped in plastic. The old fridge is pushed to the side, next to the old stove and microwave. A second glance around the room confirms that *all* the appliances have been swapped out for new retro-styled ones.

"I think y'all might be at the wrong house," I say.

The men stop what they're doing, giving me puzzled looks, likely wondering why I'm standing here staring at them. Just then, Jensen emerges from the dining room, wearing his glasses and a startled expression when he sees me.

"Briar, you're home early."

I tilt my head with a hand on my hip. "I'm guessing that's a bad thing, considering the overhaul happening in my kitchen right now."

Am I upset? No. Just confused by the unexpected renovation taking place.

"Why don't we talk about this outside while the guys finish?" Jensen suggests.

I nod. "Lead the way."

He takes my hand and guides me through the laundry room, where a brand-new washer and dryer have already been installed, then out to the back porch.

Ziggy darts around the large pen I set up outside his shed, giving him plenty of space to play while still having access to shade whenever he wants. I plan to introduce him to more animals on the ranch soon so he won't be lonely while Caleb's at school. He's become a foster fail, and I'm not sorry. Birdie doesn't mind since it's one less animal she'll have to take care of herself.

When Ziggy spots Jensen, he freezes mid-step, letting out a squeaky bleat as he flops over like he's been unplugged. His legs stick straight out, stiff as twigs, and his eyes remain open, staring in our direction.

Jensen sighs in exasperation. "Seriously? Again?"

I bite back a smile. "Well, you are wearing your superhero glasses. The swooning was inevitable."

He takes a step forward, trailing his fingers along my arm. "Funny since you're still standing. I didn't think you were immune to my charm."

"Only when I'm on a mission to figure out why all of my appliances have been upgraded without my knowledge am I strong enough to resist temptation." I lean forward, our mouths only inches apart. "Any other time, we'd already be halfway to the bedroom."

"Then I guess I'll have them reinstall the prehistoric ones," Jensen teases, moving toward the door.

I catch his wrist to stop him. "Or you could come clean and tell me why you ordered the new appliances?"

"Because your stovetop's been on the fritz, the washer was out of commission, and you deserve the best."

Judging by his response, he obviously put a lot of thought into this plan, which sends my mind racing as I calculate the cost of each item I saw inside. I'm certain the number I come up with is far lower than what Jensen actually paid—especially considering the luxury brands. Even my estimate is astronomical, making my stomach churn.

"It's thoughtful, truly, but I can't afford that kind of upgrade," I admit.

Mama Julie and Pops would have replaced the appliances in an instant if I'd asked. Hell, Heath's tried more times than I can count. But the guilt kept me from agreeing to his offer. They've done more than enough—taking me in when I had nowhere else to go, making me feel like part of the family even before I was adopted, and letting me live in the cottage rent-free. That's why it's difficult to accept anything more, especially when it's the kind of upgrade I'd never justify for myself.

"You don't owe me a dime. It's a gift, plain and simple," Jensen says with conviction.

I shake my head. "It's too much."

He gently lifts my chin, making me meet his eyes. "Sweetheart, after everything you've done for Caleb and me, this is nothing. You deserve better than dragging your laundry across the ranch to wash it or flipping pancakes on a portable grill."

"But I don't—" Jensen places his finger over my mouth, stopping me mid-sentence.

"I *see* you, Briar Halstead. Always trying to shoulder everything on your own because you think asking for help is taking advantage. It's not. You're one of the most compassionate and loyal people I've ever met. Whether you're off on a chicken heist, helping a friend, or comforting someone in need—you always show up, no questions asked." A light breeze pushes my hair into my face, and Jensen tucks the loose strands behind my ear. "Let me take care of you for once," he adds softly.

I don't answer right away, weighing my options. I could say no on principle, but how can I when he flashes me his crooked smile and says the sweetest things? His grand gesture wasn't just about buying appliances. He went out of his way to pick ones that fit the cottage's style, another piece of evidence that he pays attention to the little things.

"Thank you," I whisper. "I have no idea how I'll repay you."

Jensen draws me into a hug. "Briar, it's a gift, not a transaction. All I want is for you to use that shiny new fridge and stove."

"I think I can manage that."

"Julie mentioned the other day that they've offered to hire someone to do the renovations, but you've declined. Is there a reason you prefer to do it yourself?"

It means a lot that he doesn't lecture me for not choosing the easier route. Instead, he wants to understand where I'm coming from, and that makes me feel seen in a way I never have before.

I tilt my head, looking him in the eye. "You were right earlier. Asking for help doesn't come naturally to me—especially not from the Halsteads. This is more than a small favor, and if they stepped in, I'd feel like I owed them something I might never be able to repay. Not when I've been saving for a children's sanctuary that I want to build on the far side of the property," I admit, my fingers tracing the button on Jensen's collar.

The Halsteads and the girls are the only ones who know about my ambitious plans. I'm reluctant to share them with anyone else, as many people are more interested in my past and how it relates to my passion for helping kids from trauma rather than focusing on the difference I want to make.

Jensen has become the exception. He's aware of my history and has seen firsthand how I've made a positive impact on Caleb through experiences on the ranch.

"A children's sanctuary? You've never mentioned that before," he says, trailing his fingers along my arm. "What will it be used for?"

"I'm in the process of starting a nonprofit for kids who've experienced trauma. The goal is to create a space where we can hold summer camps, horseback riding lessons, and other activities. It's been a dream of mine for a long time, but spending time with Caleb has made me realize how much of a difference it could really make."

I hold my breath, waiting for his reply. I'm confident he'd never make me feel inferior or discourage me from chasing my dream, but it's still not easy sharing this part of myself.

"It sounds like an amazing venture. Why haven't you broken ground yet?" He pauses, his gaze firmly fixed on mine. "Let me guess. You want to do this on your own, too?" The corner of his mouth quirks up into a knowing smile. "It's truly incredible what you're working toward. I hope you never forget you have a family who loves you—no conditions, no questions. Whether you're adopted or not, you're a Halstead, and they'll support you in whatever way you need, including me. Don't ever doubt that there's a group of people who will rally around you at any given moment. We're all here for you, sugar."

My heart swells with gratitude at his tenderness, and I rise on my toes to kiss him.

There's no hiding with Jensen, and as unsettling as it should be, it's oddly comforting that he's willing to speak the truths I've been too afraid to say out loud. He gives me the kind of reassurance I didn't know I was craving.

I've spent so long sitting in the shadows of self-doubt, convinced I didn't fully belong because I wasn't born into the family that chose me. But being wrapped in Jensen's arms has briefly silenced those fears, replaced with something steady and real. A reminder that I've always had the Halsteads' unconditional love and support, even when I've struggled to accept it.

"Thank you," I murmur. "I needed to hear those words more than you realize, and I'm beyond grateful for all the ways you've shown up for me."

"You've done more than enough, Briar. Honestly, I'm the one who should be thanking you." He leans in for another kiss. "How about we head back inside so you can oversee the delivery guys and make sure everything goes where it should."

"Sounds good. Plus, I want to offer them some sweet tea to thank them."

"Good thinking," he agrees.

CHAPTER 28

Jensen

I JOLT AWAKE, DISORIENTED, THE NUMBERS ON THE CLOCK glowing 2:00 a.m. I normally sleep through the night unless Caleb's had a nightmare and climbs into my bed—but he's not here.

I'm on the verge of dozing off again when the loud creak of the stairs cuts through the quiet. I sit up in bed, the hair on the back of my neck standing on end. Caleb always comes to me first, and he'd never venture downstairs in the dark alone, so it has to be someone else. Briar's never stayed up this late unless she's with me, so I can't imagine she'd be roaming around at this hour either.

She usually sneaks into my room after Caleb's asleep but slips back to her own bed before we drift off. Tonight though, Caleb went to bed later than usual, so she didn't come to my room. I'm guessing because she has an early start tomorrow. We've been careful not to let Caleb catch us together, but I wish she was here with me through the night.

I slide out of bed in nothing but boxers, not bothering with clothes. I tread lightly down the stairs, wincing at every groan of the steps. I don't want to alert whoever's down there. We live on a ranch, so it's possible an animal found its way inside, but that wouldn't explain why the noises started upstairs and are now coming from the kitchen.

As I round the corner, I'm met with the soft glow from the light above the sink. What I don't expect is to find Briar bent over the open freezer, her perfect ass in the air.

Fuck me.

She seems completely unaware of the show she's putting on, and watching her from a distance is my brand of torture. Her baggy T-shirt has ridden up, revealing the curve of her ass and leaving little to the imagination. The sight before me sends the blood rushing to my cock.

I step in behind her, my hands settling on her hips. She stiffens for half a second, then straightens. The startled look on her face shifts into a smirk when she looks at me. I tug her closer, my hands moving along her curves as I press a kiss below her ear. She exhales softly, melting into me.

"Why are you sneaking up on me in the middle of the night?" she asks.

"Heard a noise," I murmur against her ear. "But something tells me that you knew what you were doing when you came down here dressed like this, didn't you?" I lift the bottom of her shirt just enough to trace the lace of her panties.

"Maybe." She slowly spins around to face me, her palm trailing up my bare chest. "Or maybe I just had a late-night craving."

My gaze drags down her body, stopping when I realize she's wearing the panties that say 'All You Can Eat' across the front—and damn if I'm not ready to take that invitation literally.

"These panties say it all, sweetheart. And I'm starving," I say, dropping to my knees in front of her.

"Jensen." My name slips from her mouth on a shaky breath.

"Shh, sugar. Let me taste you."

A blush spreads across her cheeks as I kiss the strip of bare skin between her shirt and panties, then trail lower, dragging my mouth along the soft curve of her abdomen. I slide her underwear past her thighs, easing them down her legs. Once they're bunched at her ankles, I tap each foot, slipping the panties off and tossing them aside.

She gasps when I lean into the apex of her thighs, nipping at the sensitive skin.

Christ, this woman is going to ruin me.

She runs her hands through my hair, allowing me to hook her left leg over my shoulder, offering the perfect angle to claim what's right in front of me. My fingers dig into her skin as I glide my tongue along the seam of her pussy. Her body reacts on instinct, pushing my head farther into her thighs, chasing the electrifying pull between us.

After several shallow strokes, I run my tongue over her clit, causing her to buck her hips as she grinds on my face. Her enthusiasm is addictive, fueling me like a man starved as I lick her core.

"Damn, baby, you taste like mine," I say, coming up for air.

Briar whimpers when I insert a finger, pushing in and out in teasing strokes. She lets out a throaty moan as I set her nerves on fire but never give her enough to satisfy her craving. I push a second finger inside her entrance, moving them in and out in steady strokes, keeping her teetering on the edge right where I want her while tracing her clit with my tongue.

A bead of sweat trickles down her brow as she gasps for air.

"Oh god, please, Jensen," she mewls, her voice strained.

"You're so pretty when you beg," I croon.

Not letting up, I keep working her clit, swirling my tongue in languid circles, feeling as Briar's body coils tighter with each thrust of my fingers. When she's on the brink of release, I abruptly pull my hand away.

"Why did you stop?" Briar cries.

I rise to my feet, crowding her against the fridge, my hand gently covering her mouth.

"We have to stay quiet," I whisper, my lips grazing her jawline. "When you come, it'll be around my dick." I stop for a second, raking a hand through my hair. "But we'll have to take this upstairs since I didn't exactly come prepared."

The urge to have her without any barriers is strong, but that's a conversation she'll have to start, as I'd never pressure her into something she's not comfortable with.

Briar slips a hand into the side of her bra and pulls out a condom. "Oh, you mean one of these?"

"Sneaky little thing. You *were* hoping I'd come downstairs," I state.

She gives me a sly smile. "I wasn't going to take any chances."

Thank god for that.

I quickly strip out of my boxers, hanging on by a thread, just as close to losing control as Briar is. Once I'm undressed, I rip the foil package open, toss the wrapper on the floor, and roll on the condom in one smooth motion.

I shift us away from the fridge to the cabinets, spinning her around so her back is pressed against me, her palms splayed on the countertop. She bends forward, her pear-shaped ass lifted in the air, every inch a perfect invitation. I place one hand on her waist, the other guiding my cock into her from behind.

"Yes. Right there," she groans.

I clamp my hand over her mouth. "Shh, baby. We have to be quiet," I remind her.

She nods absently, each deep stroke drawing a ragged sound from her throat. I slide my hand up, palming her breast as she arches into me with a desperate push of her hips, meeting every thrust like she's starved for it. We're past thinking now, lost to the rhythm and pulse of something spiraling between us.

With Briar on the brink of release, I dip my head to her ear. "You're close, aren't you?"

She nods, her head tipped back as pleasure washes over her.

"Let go for me, baby." I growl, my tongue tracing her collarbone as I slam back into her.

With my other hand, I roll her clit between my fingers, dropping my head on her shoulder and putting all my energy into driving home.

"God, yes! Just like that," she cries out.

Her body shudders against mine, and I muffle my groan into her neck, staying locked to her through every wave. My arm stays tight around her waist, keeping her grounded as she comes undone, and part of me wishes I could freeze time and keep her here with me forever.

As she comes back to reality, I stroke her spine, pressing kisses along the nape of her neck. "Are you okay, sugar?"

She tilts her head, a sated smile curving her lips. "Mm-hmm. Amazing. I've worked up an appetite and have a serious craving for that chocolate ice cream I spotted in the freezer earlier."

I meet her warm brown eyes, lifting her hand to my mouth and kissing her palm. "We'll get you your ice cream, but after that, you're sleeping in my bed."

Briar glances toward the hallway. "What about Caleb?" she asks softly.

We've tiptoed around him, making sure he never catches us giving each other more than a hug or harmless touches. Tonight, we pushed the boundary, but the creaking stairs serve as a built-in warning and would have given us enough time to separate before Caleb might have seen anything he shouldn't. Thankfully, we didn't have to.

I brush a thumb along her hip, and she shivers beneath my touch. "You're usually gone before he wakes up," I say, my voice low. "Stay with me so I can hold you tonight."

She grins. "Only if I get to be the little spoon."

I laugh, pressing a kiss to her forehead. "Anything you want, sugar."

Even if all she wants to do is sleep, I still want her beside me. But after the mind-blowing sex we just had, keeping my hands to myself may prove to be challenging.

I'd keep her in my bed every night if I could, and that thought terrifies me. This wasn't part of the plan. We agreed to not get attached. I'm meant to be leaving Bluebell soon, and we're supposed to go our separate ways. What was meant to be uncomplicated and no strings attached now feels anything but. And the worst part? I'm starting to wonder if I'll be able to let her go.

For now, I push aside the chaotic thoughts swirling in my mind, choosing to be present and focus on the time Briar and I still have.

CHAPTER 29

Brian

THE PAST TWO WEEKS HAVE BEEN FILLED WITH NOTHING but happiness. It's now early August, and my days have been a perfect mix of ranch life, afternoons with Caleb, and late nights with Jensen, talking on the porch and tangled up in his sheets before drifting to sleep in his arms. It's been a little slice of heaven, and one that I'm clinging to as long as possible.

The three of us have gathered around the kitchen table. Caleb and I just came in from playing with Ziggy in the backyard, and now that Jensen's logged off work for the night, it's time for the surprise we have for him. Caleb's seated beside me with Jensen across the table. I slide the box I grabbed from my room toward Jensen and he raises an eyebrow in question.

"What's this?" he asks.

I nudge it closer. "Only one way to find out."

"Yeah, Dad," Caleb chimes in with a toothy grin.

Jensen smiles the instant Caleb speaks. In the past couple of weeks, Caleb's confidence has blossomed, and he's even made a new friend from summer camp, a boy named Jake. They've had a few playdates, and we have another one scheduled for this week-end. He occasionally clams up around strangers, but at home, he's chatty and curious and it's more than Jensen or I could've hoped for.

"Alright, alright." Jensen chuckles as he reaches for the box. "But if this thing has teeth, I'm blaming both of you if it bites."

Caleb giggles. "No peeking till I say."

"Cross my heart," Jensen replies, tracing an invisible X over his chest and averting his gaze as he lifts the lid with exaggerated suspense.

Caleb scoots to the edge of his seat, practically buzzing with excitement. He helped me pick out the gift and has been counting down the minutes until he could give it to Jensen.

"Okay, look now, Dad!"

Jensen sets the lid aside and blinks in disbelief as he lifts a honey-brown cowboy hat from the box. He traces the stitching along the brim, handling it like a prized possession.

He glances at me. "Did Walker or Heath put you up to this?" There's a hint of amusement in his voice.

I grin, shaking my head. "Nope. I've been wanting to get you one for a while, and Caleb and I figured it was high time you had one of your own."

Caleb leans over to tug on my sleeve.

"What is it, little man?"

"Can I show Dad the second surprise?"

I smile warmly. "You sure can."

"Awesome!"

He races from the kitchen, his footsteps echoing as he bounds up the stairs toward his room.

Jensen raises a brow. "There's more?"

"Trust me, you'll be happy there is."

A minute later, Caleb comes back into the room with a min-iature version of Jensen's hat perched on his head. Jensen grins, picking up his own from the table and putting it on.

"We match." Caleb beams.

Jensen scoops him into his arms. "Sure do, partner." He looks over at me with a cheeky grin. "We make a pretty great pair, don't we?"

"The most handsome cowboys around." When Jensen first got here, he might have scoffed at me using that term, but now he accepts the compliment without a second thought.

"You've got to wear them to the ranch house. Mama Julie's going to want a picture with you in yours, Caleb," I say.

"Can we leave now!?" he exclaims.

Mama Julie and Pops invited us over for another barbecue tonight. They've asked Caleb to come over several times in the past few days, and I'm pretty sure they've picked up on whatever is happening between me and Jensen. They haven't asked us outright; although, I'm certain Mama Julie will bring it up sooner rather than later.

I glance at the stove clock to see that it's almost six.

"Yeah, we should head out, or we'll be late," I say, pushing my chair back as I stand. "I'll get the macaroni salad from the fridge after I put my shoes on."

"Sounds good," Jensen says. "Caleb's boots are in his room. We'll get those so we can head out."

On my way to the hallway, I notice I have an unread text waiting.

Backroads & Bad Decisions Group Chat

Charlie: I'm filing a formal complaint against urban cowboy.

Briar: What did he do now?

Charlie: Kidnapped you, clearly. I've been caffeine-deprived and emotionally abandoned.

> Charlie: I've resorted to small talk with Heath twice this week. Dark times.

> Birdie: Why haven't you asked me to go to Lasso & Latte?

> Charlie: Birdie Mae, you've basically been in hiding since your livestock grand theft. Coffee dates aren't an option until you're off the wanted list.

Birdie's been paranoid since her "rescue mission" at the county fair. With her dad being the sheriff, and his office on the case, she's convinced they'll catch her on tape. She still won't tell us how she managed to get a donkey and a calf out of the fairgrounds and back to her place without a single witness. Good thing she lives alone, and her dad rarely stops by. Otherwise, her cover would've been blown already.

> Birdie: Enough about me.

> Birdie: Briar, are you and Jensen official yet, or still in denial?

At least one of the girls asks me that question every day, and I always find a way to deflect. Why? Because the truth is I am in denial, and I'd rather keep it that way a bit longer than face what's waiting on the other side.

> Wren: Seriously, if he doesn't lock you down, he's an idiot.

> Charlie: No chance urban cowboy is leaving.

> Wren: And if he even thinks about breaking your heart, we go full girl gang mode.

> Charlie: I'll go ballistic and watch him squirm.

I laugh under my breath. My friends are absolutely the best. They're always in my corner, no questions asked.

"There you are," Julie exclaims from the counter, where she's cutting peaches for her Dutch oven cobbler.

The ranch house's kitchen is my favorite space, with its wide-plank wood floors, vaulted ceiling accented by exposed beams, and a butcher block island at its center. A picture window above the farmhouse sink looks over the garden and the pastures beyond.

"Sorry we're late," I say, setting a bowl on the island. "I attempted macaroni salad but overestimated how much dressing I needed, so it's more of a soup consistency."

This is why I stick to pancakes. I can't be trusted with anything that doesn't involve a hot griddle and syrup.

"It's not as bad as she makes it sound," Jensen says. "In fact, I think she's created a new food trend—soup salad. Very innovative." He laughs, brushing a stray hair behind my ear.

Heat rises to my cheeks, and I flash him a grateful smile. This man might be a god between the sheets, but he's rather sweet and endearing when his walls come down.

"I'm sure it tastes divine," Mama Julie agrees, wiping her hands on a hand towel before coming over to greet us.

Her eyes widen when she notices Caleb's cowboy hat. "Oh my goodness, you look so handsome; I could cry." When her gaze shifts to Jensen, and she realizes they're wearing matching hats, real tears well up in her eyes.

She's always considered Jensen part of the family, and I can only imagine the rush of emotions she's experiencing as she's watched him go from hating this small town to making peace with his roots and embracing them. Especially now, with his son by his side.

"What's wrong?" Jensen asks Mama Julie, his concern evident.

"I'd cry too if I had to look at you in that hat," Heath says, stepping in from the deck with a smirk. "Caleb pulls it off like a champ. You? Not so much."

"Don't listen to Heath. You both look darling," Mama Julie coos, stepping in to defuse the situation as only she can. "Now hush and take this out to your father." She thrusts a foil-covered tray into Heath's hands. "The meat should be done soon."

"Yes, ma'am," he replies, wisely holding his tongue.

"Jensen, you grab the veggie skewers," Mama Julie adds, passing him a casserole dish full of them.

"Sure thing." He balances the dish in one hand and offers Caleb his free one. "Come on, bud. Let's go show Pops your new hat."

Caleb grins, taking his hand as they follow Heath onto the deck.

"I'll be there in a minute," I tell them, wanting to double-check that Mama Julie's all set before I do.

She's back at the counter, cutting peaches, and I stand behind her.

"Where's Walker?" I ask.

"He said he was going out." She rolls her eyes. "I'm guessing he's meeting the usual crowd at the bar. That boy strolls in at two or three in the morning like it's no big deal." She lets out a disapproving click of her tongue. "You think you're done when they turn eighteen, but truth be told, you worry even more once they're grown if they're making the right choices or getting mixed up in something they shouldn't."

"Not me, though. Right?" I tease.

Mama Julie leans over, pinching my cheek. "You're the exception, honey."

It's a missed opportunity that Heath and Walker aren't around to hear it, so I can brag that I'm the only one Mama Julie's not constantly worrying about.

Walker's the source of the most stress, hands down. He's always got some woman in a frenzy and has a habit of starting fights when he's had a few too many drinks. Heath, on the other hand, is all business and usually too rigid for his own good.

Sure, I have my flaws too, but they're not the kind that have kept Mama Julie up at night. My birth mom did enough of that for both of us when I was growing up.

A timer goes off, and she hurries to the oven, pulling out a tray of homemade rolls. The tops are golden brown, and the kitchen fills with the rich scent of butter, making my mouth water. She's a magician in the kitchen and she treats every meal like a special occasion.

"Jensen looks at you like you hang the moon," she says casually.

I should've seen this coming. Mama Julie's intuition is unmatched, and between the town gossip and how Jensen and I have been acting around each other, she's no doubt pieced it together. She's a hopeless romantic, inspired by her own love story with Pops, full of grand gestures and weekly flower deliveries.

"It's just for the summer," I say quickly, the words tumbling out as a knot tightens in my stomach.

She sets the tray on the stovetop, then faces me with one brow arched. "Honey, that man is head over heels for you, and judging by the look on your face, the feeling is mutual."

I move closer to the island, leaning forward to prop my elbows on the counter, and sigh. "I think I'm falling for him."

It's the first time I've admitted it out loud. I've been wrapped up in our blissful bubble, basking in the glow of the nights Jensen and I spend together in his bed and the quiet moments with him and Caleb, hoping I could ignore the truth. This was always meant to be temporary, and I was never supposed to get attached to either of them.

The truth is, I'm on the verge of a double heartbreak.

Somehow, in the span of a couple of months, an adorable five-year-old boy has woven his way into my heart. Caleb finds magic in the simple things and makes everything more enjoyable. What started as a favor to nanny him will end with me dreading the day I have to say goodbye.

What I hadn't anticipated was his dad slowly unraveling my defenses, too. Jensen showed up in Bluebell guarded and complicated, but his complete devotion to his son is what sparked my growing feelings for him.

It's unsettling to imagine a future where the cottage, once my peaceful refuge, becomes a lonely, quiet place without Caleb's laughter or evenings spent with Jensen on the front porch.

"Why does it have to end if you both want more?" Julie asks. "Have you told Jensen how you feel?"

I glance at the floor, shrugging. "What is there to say? I can't ask him to give up the life he's built in New York. His business is there, and Caleb will have opportunities this town can't compete with."

Mama Julie takes off her oven mitts and comes to stand beside me, lifting my chin so I have no choice but to meet her eyes. "Have you stopped to consider that what those boys need most is *you*? Schools, therapists, and jobs are a dime a dozen, but the kind of love and stability *you* offer? That's once in a lifetime."

"I'm scared," I admit. "What if this isn't enough for Jensen?" I motion around us.

When he arrived, he was set on staying just for the summer, and I'm afraid that no matter how strong his feelings are for me—and how at ease Caleb is here—it still might not be enough to convince Jensen they should stay. That's why I've avoided the conversation. Because pretending is safer than hearing him say that he and Caleb will still be leaving soon.

"You won't know unless you ask. You've never been afraid to speak your mind or back down from what you want. Don't start now, my girl. I'm so darn proud of you, and no matter what happens, you'll always have me and Pops in your corner." Her sincerity is evident by the smile on her face.

"Thank you. I needed to hear that," I say.

She draws me in for a bear hug. "That's what I'm here for, honey."

It's difficult to admit that Mama Julie is right. As much as I'd rather keep avoiding this particular conversation with Jensen, I'm going to have to talk to him about it and soon. Regardless of what he decides, I won't know until I ask. The hardest part will be facing the fallout if Jensen and Caleb do move back to New York. The truth is they've become my everything. And while I'll support what's best for Caleb, that doesn't mean it won't shatter me to let them go.

"How can I help with dinner? I'm sure those boys are about to eat us out of house and home," I say, wanting a lighthearted distraction.

Mama Julie doesn't press further. She busies herself with the rolls, piling them into a bowl before handing them to me. "Can you put these on the table outside? It's such a nice night. We're going to eat out on the deck," she says, handing me the bowl. "I'll join you once I put the cobbler in the oven."

"Absolutely."

I head out back, placing the rolls on the table set with plates and utensils.

"Howdy there, sunshine," Pops calls from the grill where he's flipping a rack of his famous huckleberry ribs.

I join him, squeezing his shoulder. "Hey, Pops. Where are the boys?"

He nods out to the yard where they've set up a game of cornhole. Jensen's lining up a toss with Caleb mimicking his stance behind him, while Heath heckles from beside the board, calling out exaggerated scores and grinning when Jensen misses.

"That little buckaroo is lookin' sharp in that cowboy hat of his," Pops says with a grin. "You've done right by him, stepping up like you did. You've got a good heart, and I'm mighty proud of you." He wraps his arm around me and presses a kiss to my hair.

Samuel Halstead doesn't show affection much outside of Mama Julie, so when he does, it's a precious moment that I never take for granted.

"Thanks, Pops," I say, resting my head against his shoulder. "It's because of you and Mama Julie that I know what love looks like, and I hope that I can pass that on to Caleb and other kids who might not have that kind of support."

Not a day goes by that I'm not thankful for the Halsteads and everything they've done for me. But it's taken me a long time to finally see what they've known all along—that it was never about blood. I was never a burden. Never a charity case. They've always considered me their daughter and loved me as their own. And maybe, for the first time, I'm starting to believe I deserve it. It's Jensen who finally helped me quiet the doubts and finally see the truth that this is where I belong.

As we gather around the table, the people I care about most beside me with the Montana mountains glimmering beneath the fading sun, I'm overwhelmed with gratitude. And it's almost poetic that it took someone like Jensen, carrying his own parental scars, to help me face mine.

CHAPTER 30

Jensen

THE DAY AFTER THE BARBECUE AT THE HALSTEADS', I asked Julie to watch Caleb for a few hours. It occurred to me that I hadn't taken Briar out on a real date yet. Until now, we've mostly only had nights together—sneaking in and out of each other's beds and sharing stolen moments in the dark. She deserves to be spoiled, and I want to show her that she means more to me than convenience and chemistry.

"Jensen, this is silly," she mumbles, tightening her grip on my shoulders. "I could walk if you'd let me take the blindfold off."

I adjust her position on my back, legs wrapped around my waist, and give her thighs a gentle squeeze. "Patience, sugar. We're almost to our first stop."

"Which is where?" she whispers, giving my earlobe a playful nip. "Let me guess, we're going to check the irrigation lines?"

I shift my head toward her, pressing a kiss to her nose. "Not quite."

"Are we going to fix the broken fence post in the eastern pasture?"

I chuckle. "I'd like to think what I have planned is more romantic than that."

"Well, I hope you know where you're going, because it feels like we're going in circles."

She's not wrong.

I met her at the ranch house after work so we could drop Caleb off. I told her we had plans but kept the details under wraps. I wanted to keep it a surprise up until the last minute. That's why I blindfolded her and gave her a piggyback ride around the garden and chicken coop a few times.

The goal was to disorient her before heading over to one of the storage sheds where I had Walker park a four-wheeler. They're used to check cattle, haul feed, and navigate through areas where the truck can't go—and it seemed like the perfect way to get us to where we're going for our date.

He gave me grief for asking for his help and even tried to rope me into another Saturday of free labor. But when I mentioned it was a favor so I could do something special for Briar, he begrudgingly agreed "out of the goodness of his heart." His words, not mine.

"We're here," I say enthusiastically.

I lower myself so Briar can get off, making sure her feet are on the ground before easing my grip on her legs.

She reaches for her blindfold. "Can I take this off now?"

"Not just yet."

I want her on the four-wheeler first so she doesn't see the cooler and bag strapped to the back rack and spoil the rest of what I have planned.

"Jensen Harding, are we about to go on a chicken heist? Because I'm pretty sure Charlie and Birdie will have *a lot* to say if we leave them out."

I cup her elbow as I guide her across the dirt pathway. "Trust me, I'd never dream of going on a rescue mission without your partners in crime."

I've been told Charlie's keeping score, and I'm public enemy number one for stealing all of Briar's time. How can she blame me when being with Briar is one of the best parts of my day? Whether we're with Caleb and Ziggy in the backyard, or it's just the two of us on the porch at night with cups of spiked hot cocoa, I've become addicted to her touch, her laugh, and the comfort she offers that feels like home.

"Will you tell me what we *are* doing?"

"Going for a ride," I say as I lead her to the four-wheeler. "Our destination is top secret, but I can promise there won't be any hard labor involved. Unless you count all the ways I plan to make you come."

"You keep talking like that, and we might not make it to wherever we're going," she murmurs.

"Normally, I'd say that's a good thing, but we've got a date to get to." I plant a kiss to her temple before bringing us to a stop.

"Okay, careful now. I'm going to help you get on a four-wheeler," I say, guiding her to the seat. I keep one hand on her waist as she swings her leg over. When she's settled, I slip the blindfold off and Briar squints against the light, her gaze bouncing between me and our surroundings.

"A shed? Wow, talk about getting in the mood." She smirks, grabbing my shirt and tugging me close for a kiss.

"I mean, you *are* kissing me, so I must've done something right," I reply, nipping at her lip. "We better get going before the sun sets."

"Ready when you are, cowboy."

I give her one more kiss before climbing onto the four-wheeler in front of her, her knees brushing against my thighs. The key is already in the ignition, and once I'm settled into my seat, I turn it, and the engine comes to life with a satisfying hum.

Briar winds her arms around me, holding on tight as I ease the four-wheeler forward. We follow a dirt trail that skirts the edge of the property. This section of the ranch isn't fenced, just open land stretching to the tree line in the distance.

The vast Montana landscape unfolds before us, with golden grass swaying in the breeze and wildflowers painting the fields with splashes of color. In the distance, jagged mountain peaks pierce the sky, which glows with a soft blend of gold and peach as the sun hangs low, casting a warm light across the pastures. The air is crisp, rich with the scent of earth and pine, and the gentle rustle of the wind adds a quiet soundtrack to the peaceful atmosphere.

Briar's body presses into mine with every dip and rise of the terrain, her front flush against my back. Her chin rests on my shoulder, and she glides her hands along my chest, the slow drag of her touch leaving a trail of warmth in its wake. I ease off the throttle, discretely adjusting myself, unable to control my physical reaction to her hands on me.

The hum of the engine dies as we come to a stop near a knoll where the land slopes toward a winding creek, sunlight glinting off the water's surface. Trees lean toward the bank, offering shade, and birdsong filters down from the branches, mingling with the stream's gurgling. It's the kind of place that makes you want to kick off your boots, stretch out on the grass, and forget the rest of the world exists, which is exactly what I intend to do—with Briar by my side.

I hop off first and turn around to help her off.

She looks around, already smiling. "Did you know this is my favorite spot on the ranch?"

I flash her a knowing look. "Julie might have mentioned it."

When deciding where to take her, I wanted to avoid the busy diner or the coffee shop, where half the town would eavesdrop while sipping their drinks. Instead, I looked for somewhere more intimate that she'd enjoy. Julie told me this is where Briar comes when she wants an escape. She brings a book or her sketchpad, filled with ideas for her nonprofit and lets her mind drift from the demands of everyday life.

I unstrap the cooler and basket from the cargo rack on the back of the four-wheeler and carry them toward the creek, setting them down on a flat rock.

Briar tilts her head, studying me. "What do you have there?"

"I thought we could have a picnic by the creek."

She watches as I pull a blanket from the basket and spread it out on the grass, taking out a plate from the cooler covered in plastic wrap. It's filled with thin slices of bread, brie, smoked turkey, an assortment of fruit, and a couple of peanut butter and jelly sandwiches cut into triangles.

Briar's eyes widen, her eyes flickering to the spread. "I can't believe you did all this."

"You haven't seen the best part." I pull out a thermos of hot chocolate and a mini bottle of whiskey.

She laughs, shaking her head in amusement. "Well, aren't you full of surprises today?"

"Only for my favorite girl."

"Charming and a sweet talker? That's a dangerous combination, cowboy."

"Can't help myself when you're around, darlin'."

After setting out the food and thermos, I ease onto the blanket, reclining on my side and propping myself on one elbow. I take off my hat and set it aside before motioning for Briar to join me. She lowers herself down, stretching out on her stomach to face me, her hand brushing against mine as she lets out a contented sigh.

She takes a grape and pops it into her mouth. "Can I ask you something?"

"Of course."

"Are you glad you brought Caleb to Bluebell?"

"Yes," I say without hesitation. "It's the best decision I've ever made."

In more ways than I expected.

Briar's been a guiding light for Caleb, offering him patience and love from the moment she met him. She'll never replace Amelia, but she's created space for him to grieve and heal, which I couldn't have done on my own. My feelings for her are a tangled mix of gratitude, admiration, and a magnetic pull so fierce it pushes the boundaries between reality and fantasy.

As much as we need to talk about what happens when summer ends, I've been avoiding it. The past few weeks have been incredible—both in terms of my time spent with Briar and the joy of hearing Caleb speak again. I have to make several big decisions, but for just one more night, I want to pretend that nothing is changing and this little world we've built is here to stay.

Briar toys with a loose strand of her hair before tucking it behind her ear. "I've been wanting to ask for a while... Why did you leave Bluebell in the first place? I know things were bad with your parents, but you had the Halsteads, too." Her eyes flicker to mine, and she quickly adds, "You don't have to answer if you'd rather not talk about it."

In the past, I would've shut down and gotten defensive, but it turns out Caleb's not the only one benefiting from therapy. After several conversations with his therapist, I've learned the value of being open to talking things through, even when the topics bring up old wounds.

"It's okay. I don't mind sharing," I say with a small smile. "My parents owned a small farm across town. It wasn't much, but it was ours. We had a cow, chickens, and ducks that would follow me around. I used to picture taking over the farm one day, making it into something as successful as Silver Saddle Ranch." I reach for a piece of bread and brie, using it as a pause to collect my thoughts. "That dream crumbled when we lost the place to foreclosure. The hardest part was how indifferent my parents were about it. They didn't care that we had to move into a mold-infested trailer with sagging floors and the smell of rat droppings or that the cupboards were always empty. As long as they could fuel their addiction to cards and slot machines, nothing else mattered."

Their addiction didn't happen overnight. It was a slow trickle, and our lives didn't drastically change until we lost the farm. They had done their best to hide the financial issues, so by the time I found out, it was too late. The one silver lining when we were forced to move was that the Halsteads took in my animals, so I still got to see them often.

Briar rests her hand on my arm. "I'm sorry, Jensen."

"The Halsteads were like family, but it stung watching their happiness while my life was falling apart." I shift my gaze to the stream, watching the water ripple over the rocks as I speak. "My parents didn't love each other, and I was an afterthought. I learned early on that relying on people only gave them the power to let me down."

"I can understand why you kept your guard up." She traces small circles along my arm. "Is that why you left? Was starting your own business always the plan?"

"Back in high school, I discovered my knack for computers. I knew if I wanted a future in tech, I had to leave Bluebell. So I worked summers at the ranch, saved every dollar, and after graduation, I moved to New York. It couldn't have been more different from here, and that's exactly what I wanted. I enrolled in a programming course and immersed myself in the tech world, learning as I went."

There was a time when I wasn't sure if I'd make it or be forced to return home, worse off than my parents. But I refused to settle and each risk pushed me forward, guiding me to the next hurdle until I got my lucky break. I fixed a critical bug for a small startup pro bono, and they hired me full-time, giving me the stability to eventually launch my own venture.

"I started my company from the ground up after talking to a friend in security who said the market was flooded with outdated systems." I take a bite of bread and brie, chewing slowly. "Those early days were exhilarating. I faced rejection at every turn, from investors to potential clients. Each 'no' only made me more determined to prove them all wrong and show them what I was capable of."

"Which you did, and then some," Briar says proudly.

"True, but success comes at a price." I blow out a deep breath. "Being CEO of a large corporation means nonstop board meetings, endless forecasts, and keeping shareholders happy. In the early days, it was about diving into code, solving problems, and chasing an idea until a solution worked. Somewhere along the way, I traded that for spreadsheets and approval chains."

That doesn't mean I'm ungrateful for my success, but it's made things feel less fulfilling, more about obligation than passion.

"I spent so long chasing success that I never stopped to appreciate the milestones I hit along the way. But then the call about Caleb came, and in an instant, everything I'd spent a decade building didn't matter much anymore."

Even before I found out about Caleb, my job had started to feel hollow, and I often questioned what success meant beyond the financial compensation and my title. I convinced myself that stability was essential because of my past, fearing I'd lose it all if I slowed down, but the truth is, I could've stepped back years ago and been financially set for life.

That's only been further proven since coming to Bluebell. My company thrives despite significantly cutting back my hours and delegating many daily tasks to Carlton and my assistant.

I assumed returning to my hometown would be unbearable, a sacrifice I made for Caleb because I couldn't handle it alone.

Now, I realize how much I've missed the peace and simplicity. It was once tainted by my parents and painful memories, but now that I've had a chance to create new ones, it's a place where I can finally leave the past behind and start fresh.

The one constant I've always had is the Halsteads. When I was younger, I didn't fully appreciate the connection I shared with them, but being back has opened my eyes to the love they've always shown me, even when I was away. And Caleb is now included in that bond, which I'm deeply thankful for. The one variable I didn't account for was Briar—and how my heart races whenever she walks into a room, or how natural it is to watch her hugging Caleb like he belongs in her arms.

We're both quiet as we eat, every so often bringing up our favorite moments with Caleb and Ziggy, along with stories about Briar's job maintaining the cabins. She has an endless supply of those. Between bites, I find myself touching her—brushing her cheek, wiping hot chocolate from her lips, and running my hand along her arm. I can't seem to keep my hands off her, but based on how she leans into me, it's obvious she craves my touch like I do hers.

Once we've finished with our picnic, and the plate and thermos have been pushed aside, we cuddle on the blanket. Briar is nestled against me, her leg draped over mine as I run my fingers through her hair. The sun dips below the horizon, casting the sky in shades of peach and lavender.

Fireflies begin to flicker in the grass, their tiny lights sparkling like distant stars. They only come out a few times a year, so we're lucky to see them tonight. We should be heading back to the ranch house soon, but neither of us wants to let the moment slip away, so we stay in the fading warmth of the disappearing daylight as long as possible.

Briar tips her chin to meet my gaze. "Tonight's been perfect."

"It really has," I agree, brushing a knuckle across her jaw. "You're stunning, baby."

My hand finds the back of her neck, fingers threading into her hair as I draw her closer. I press my lips to hers, and she tastes like strawberries and whiskey—a blend of sweet, bold, and intoxicating. My tongue dips into her warm mouth, tracing hers in a slow dance that speaks everything we haven't said out loud.

"Is this the part where you make me come?" she whispers.

"I was hoping it would be." I reach into my pocket and pull out a condom.

Briar places her hand over mine, shaking her head. "Jensen," she whispers.

"What is it?"

Her gaze meets mine. "I don't want anything between us tonight."

I freeze, unsure if I heard her right. "Are you sure? I was tested before coming to Bluebell, but if you're not ready, we can wait until we get back—" She places a finger to my lips, silencing me.

"Positive. I have an IUD." Her hand slides along my cheek, her fingertips grazing the stubble. "I want to feel you inside me. *All* of you."

My heart pounds in my chest as the weight of her words sink in. What was supposed to be temporary has turned into something far more consequential. We're both in deeper than we ever planned, but at this moment, all I want is to give Briar what she asked for. Because the truth is, I want it just as much as she does.

We move in tandem, peeling our clothes off between kisses and lingering glances. Once we're both naked, I wrap my arm around her waist, pulling us into a sitting position, my arm propped behind me to anchor us as I tug her into my lap to straddle me. I grab my hat from the edge of the blanket and place it on Briar's head.

"You're going to wear *my* hat while you're riding *me*."

She flashes me a sultry smile. "If you insist, *cowboy*."

It's not the first time she's called me that, but tonight, it carries a weight it hasn't before. When I got to Bluebell, I was trying to outrun my past, leaving behind anything tied to it, including my small-town upbringing. I hated admitting I came from a place full of ranches and cowboys, or that I used to be one of them. Yet, with Briar's help, I've learned to appreciate those roots more than I ever thought possible.

She puts her hands on my shoulders as she sinks onto my cock, her pussy clenching around me. The moonlight dances across her face, illuminating her features. Her hair spills over her shoulders, eyes dark with want, lips parted as she gasps my name. Our mingled groans fade into the hum of crickets and the trickle of creek water.

Fuck, she feels so damn good without a barrier between us.

"I don't think I'll ever get enough of you," I confess.

She dips her head, capturing my lips in a kiss. "Then let's make sure tonight is unforgettable."

I grip her ass, guiding her as she slides along my shaft, arching her back with every thrust. She drags her nails along my chest as we move faster.

"Damn, you ride me so good," I say, bucking my hips in time with hers.

"Jensen. Touch me, please," she moans.

I reach between us, circling my thumb over her clit until she's left gasping for air. She moves above me, her hips moving in time with my fingers, every motion edging her toward release. Warm and wet, and when she clenches tight, I know she's close to letting go.

"Come for me, sugar," I command.

She throws her head back, careening over the edge as she pulses around me. A guttural sound tears from my throat as I watch her come apart. She's the most beautiful thing I've ever laid eyes on. As we come down together, tangled and spent, it hits me.

I've fallen for Briar Halstead.

I didn't anticipate or plan for this, yet the truth is impossible to deny. I'm hopelessly and completely hers. And now I'm left wondering how the hell I'm going to survive if we have to say goodbye.

CHAPTER 31

Brian

LAST NIGHT FELT LIKE SOMETHING OUT OF A STORYBOOK. Jensen was romantic and charming, and meticulously planned every detail, right down to the peanut butter and jelly sandwiches he knows are my favorite. We stayed wrapped up in each other under the stars until the cool breeze had me shivering, and he insisted we go back to the ranch house to get Caleb.

It was the perfect date, and made one thing crystal clear: my heart belongs to a man who loves his son fiercely, and has shown tremendous strength in his vulnerability. What started as a fling has grown into so much more, and the thought of him and Caleb leaving ties my stomach into knots, making me wonder if he might feel the same way.

Mama Julie's words from the night of the barbecue have been on repeat in my mind: *you won't know unless you ask.*

Easier said than done.

Although I wanted to bring it up, I decided to hold on to one more carefree night without heavy conversations and difficult decisions. Instead, I chose to enjoy our evening under the stars, pretending we didn't have a care in the world.

But I know avoiding the subject any longer will only lead to regret. Which means we have to talk soon, no matter how much I fear the outcome won't be in my favor. Now I just need to find a time when Jensen and I are alone.

This morning, I had an early start with cabin maintenance and was out the door before Jensen went on his run. A family is checking into cabin one today, and I had to replace a light fixture that keeps shorting out.

It's nearly noon when I'm finished, and I swing by the general store with a crate of supplies to drop off, including coffee grounds, tea bags, and a few jars of local honey for the welcome baskets that Ethel swears are the reason the five-star reviews keep rolling in.

The last thing I expect to see when I walk in is Ethel perched on the counter next to the pastry display, legs locked around Earl, and the two of them making out like teenagers. Despite the bell chiming above the door, neither of them notices me. They're too busy putting on a PDA performance worthy of a reality dating show.

Ethel runs her hand down Earl's chest, and when it drifts dangerously southbound, he groans. I whip my head away so fast I almost drop the box in my hands.

I stumble backward, open the door again, then slam it shut more forcefully than necessary. Yet I still don't get any acknowledgement that I'm standing here as they round to second base.

You've got to be kidding me.

I clear my throat loudly. "Should I book you two a cabin?"

That gets Ethel's attention, and she glances my way with a lopsided grin.

"Hey there, sweetie." She waves. "Don't mind us. Earl's got

the stamina of a stallion, and our romp at my place this morning wasn't enough to tire him out."

"That's right, darlin'." Earl chuckles. "Can't keep my hands off you, even if I tried." He gives her another kiss before stepping back to look at me. "Heard the city slicker finally staked his claim. I knew you two would be an item." He wags his finger at me.

"He might be heading back to New York soon," I reply, side-stepping the question as another knot twists in my stomach.

"You sure about that?" Earl asks, grabbing a chocolate donut from the case and taking a big bite. "Saw the city boy in town last week wearing boots, Wranglers—the whole nine yards. That getup won't make it five blocks in the big city." I can't help but giggle, picturing Jensen strutting around New York, hat tipped low, as people give him curious glances.

"No, it wouldn't," I agree.

I've fallen for the version of him that belongs in Bluebell— dusty boots, cowboy hat, and worn-in jeans. The thought of him in his three-piece suit back in his high-rise office makes my heart ache.

Ethel approaches Earl, running a red nail along his collar. "Darling, stop pestering Briar. You have a pickup at the bank in thirty minutes. Why don't you get going so you're not late? We'll finish where we left off at my place tonight."

"Alright, doll; you've got yourself a deal. Just don't start without me." He winks.

Earl brushes his thumb over her cheek, stealing one last kiss before grabbing his hat that must have fallen to the floor during their impromptu rendezvous. On his way out, he tips it in my direction.

"If the city slicker had any sense, he'd see what's right in front of him and never leave."

He's not the only one hoping Jensen decides to stay.

"You're too sweet, Earl. Drive safe."

He might have a heart of gold, but I wouldn't want to be the passenger he's picking up. Let's hope he doesn't have any flower bed massacres or trash can mishaps today.

Once he's out the door, I carry the box I'm holding over to the counter where Ethel and Earl were getting frisky a minute ago.

I smirk at Ethel. "So... Earl's a stallion, huh?"

She watches him drive off through the window with a sigh. "Let's just say he's got stamina that would put a racehorse to shame."

I snort, covering my mouth. "Well, that's an image I won't be able to unsee."

"Honey, at my age, pleasure's a limited-time offer, and I'm not about to waste it on knitting and decaf."

I admire her confidence. She owns her sexuality and isn't shy about her desires or her relationship with Earl. They don't bother with labels, but they seem content, so who am I to judge?

I envy her ability to be unapologetically bold, not caring about the consequences. Me? I'm tangled in a no-strings-attached situation with a man I'm falling for but am too afraid to voice my feelings. When did my life get so complicated?

She grabs the box from the counter. "Thanks for bringing more honey and the other supplies. I'm going to put a few more welcome baskets together before the afternoon rush."

We typically have several guests stop by after their morning activities. Good thing I was the one who walked in on her and Earl. I doubt anyone else would've found that live show amusing.

"Sounds good." I check the clock on the wall to see it's later than I expected. "I've got to pick up Caleb soon, but I can swing by later if you need anything. Maybe next time, keep the Earl performance at home," I suggest with a giggle.

"No promises." She grins, strutting off to the storage room.

As soon as I step onto the porch, I pull out my phone and text the girls.

Backroads & Bad Decisions Group Chat

Briar: OMG. You're not going to believe who I just caught mid-make-out.

Charlie: If the next word is Heath, I swear I'm going to be sick.

Briar: Ethel. And. Earl.

Briar: They were making out at the checkout counter in the general store.

Wren: I knew it!

Charlie: Pretty sure they've been sneaking around since dial-up internet was a thing.

Charlie: Props to Ethel. Get it, girl.

Birdie: But in the general store?!

Charlie: Hey, when the mood strikes, location becomes a suggestion, not a rule.

Charlie: Right, Briar?

Briar: Oh, I'm the poster child for PDA now?

Briar: Last time I checked, Jensen and I weren't groping each other next to a shelf of pastries.

Charlie: It's only a matter of time.

Birdie: Wait! I just realized my punch card is full. Next time I ride with Earl, it's on the house!

I wonder when that'll be, considering she's still lying low. Her dad and the deputies have continued investigating the disappearance of the missing farm animals from the fair, and it's only a matter of time before they figure out Birdie's involvement. She's lucky law enforcement moves at a snail's pace in this small town, or she'd probably be in trouble already.

Wren: You're not serious, right? You have to stop riding with him.

Birdie: I'm not passing up a free ride. That's highway robbery.

Charlie: Not as bad as livestock theft.

Birdie: Too soon, Charlie. Too soon.

I walked to the cabins this morning, so I swing by the cottage to grab my car keys before heading out to pick up Caleb from camp.

I kick my boots off at the door before stepping inside.

"Anyone home?" I call out.

Jensen should be here, unless he's out with Heath and Walker. He's been meeting them for lunch once a week, and occasionally lends a hand in the fields during the afternoon if his schedule permits. He usually comes back covered in dust and sweat, but he always has a smile on his face. It's a world away from running his tech firm, yet it's obvious how much he enjoys working on the ranch with the guys.

His truck is parked out front, so he should be around. I head to the kitchen to find him seated at the table with his computer in front of him and his phone in hand, mid-conversation. It's on speaker, and I've heard enough of his calls to recognize his assistant Beth's voice on the line. She and Carlton, his chief operating officer, have been holding things down at DataLock Systems headquarters while Jensen's been away.

He glances over, his face lighting up when he sees me.

"Come here, sugar," he whispers, patting his thigh.

I eagerly obey, and when I get close, he pulls me onto his lap, winding his arm around my waist.

"Any other updates for me?" he asks Beth.

"Dawson had the hearing moved to this coming Tuesday," she replies.

Jensen blinks, pulling up his calendar on his computer screen. "Wasn't that scheduled for the end of the month?"

"There was a cancellation on the judge's docket, so he filed a motion to move it up, and it was granted."

"Your custody hearing?" I ask softly.

Jensen nods, pushing his glasses up his nose.

A sharp pang presses on my chest. He mentioned that he has temporary custody of Caleb, with a final hearing scheduled to grant full custody once they get back to New York. I never imagined the hearing would be moved up by several weeks. We were supposed to have the rest of August together, and now my mind spins with all the possibilities of what this could mean for us.

"I'll be in touch with the flight information once I have it, and make sure the penthouse is cleaned and fully stocked before you arrive," Beth informs him, pausing briefly, the sound of her keyboard clicking in the background. "That's all I have for you. Anything else you need?"

"Not at the moment," Jensen answers. "I'll reach out if anything comes up. Thanks, Beth."

"Always here to help, Mr. Harding."

The call ends, and he sets his phone on the kitchen table.

Neither of us speaks as he draws me into his chest. I wrap my arms around his neck, rest my head on his shoulder, and focus on steadying my breathing, trying to quiet the panic rising in my chest.

Jensen tilts my chin to meet his eyes. "I want you to come with Caleb and me to New York next week."

I absently trace the stubble along his jawline. "You do?"

"Of course." He lifts my hand to kiss my palm. "It's a big moment, and I want you there to share it with us."

"I want to be there more than anything. I'll just have to check with my brothers to make sure they can cover the cabins for me."

I've never taken more than a day off, let alone been on a plane, so this is a foreign concept to me.

"I understand. Talk to them and let me know if there's anything I can do to help make this happen. It would mean the world to Caleb if you were there… and to me. You're important to us both, and it wouldn't be right without you there."

It's the most honest he's been about his feelings, and his words send butterflies fluttering through my stomach. The fact that he wants me there for such an important day means a lot.

Yet I can't shake the idea that they might cut their time short in Bluebell and stay in New York after the court hearing, even though summer isn't officially over.

The conversation we're about to have was inevitable, and although I decided earlier that I wanted to address it sooner rather than later, now that it's here, I'm not sure I can bring myself to ask the questions I've been avoiding.

I exhale deeply, raising my eyes to meet Jensen's. "I need to ask you something first."

"Sure. What is it?"

"After the hearing, are you and Caleb planning to come back here?" I manage, swallowing past the tightness in my throat.

Regardless of his answer, I plan to go with them to New York for the hearing, but I couldn't wait a second longer to ask the question that's been lingering in the back of my mind for weeks.

Jensen runs a hand through his hair, waiting a beat to reply.

"Honestly? I don't know." His voice falters, and the conflict in his voice is unmistakable.

A flicker of frustration runs through me, but I rein it in, taking a deep breath to keep calm. He has only just found out about the hearing being moved and hasn't had a chance to think it through yet—or decide on his next steps.

"Have you considered staying in Bluebell... for good?" I ask, resisting the urge to squirm.

He takes my hand in his, running his thumb along my knuckles. "I have."

A flicker of hope rises in my chest, fragile but bright.

"What's holding you back?"

"When I left Bluebell, I had no intention of returning. I was determined to break the cycle I grew up in and create a better future for myself. New York quickly became my home, and it's all I've known for the past fourteen years. I threw myself into building something I could be proud of. Something no one could ever take away."

As a kid, he was powerless—collateral damage in the fallout of the chaos created by his parents. When they lost everything, so did he. It's no wonder he poured all he had into making a new life and leaving Bluebell in the rearview. And I can only imagine how hard it must be to consider calling the one place he vowed never to return to home again.

I shift in his lap to look him in the eye. "What you did took courage—starting over in a big city, learning everything you could about an industry you were passionate about, and turning a simple idea into a successful business. You did all of that despite your parents, and have proven that you're not destined to repeat their mistakes." I trail my fingers along the nape of his neck. "Caleb is living proof of that. You've become an incredible dad, standing by him through every challenge he's faced this summer."

"He's come so far, and I can't shake the worry that whatever path I choose won't be right for him." Jensen sighs, his shoulders slumping. "I've spent years proving I can stand on my own. Leaving behind everything I've built and stepping into the unknown terrifies me almost as much as failing Caleb."

Part of me wants to assure him that staying in Bluebell is what's best for them both, and that he should forget about the city and his career altogether. But how can I? He spent half his life waiting to leave Bluebell, and the other half creating a new life for himself. I can't be the reason he gives it all up, but I also don't have the heart to let him go.

"You should take some time to think about how you want to move forward." The suggestion sits heavy on my tongue, sharp-edged and difficult to get out. "Whatever you decide, I agree it has to be what's best for Caleb. He comes first always. Which is why no matter what happens, I'm coming with you next week."

As much as I want them to stay in Bluebell, it has to be Jensen's choice. He needs to see a future for himself and Caleb here and not feel coerced into it by me or anyone else, even if that means watching him choose a path that leads them away from me.

Jensen nods, pressing his forehead to mine. "Really? You'll come?"

I draw in a deep breath before responding. "No way I'm missing out on trying New York–style pizza. Just don't expect me to add pineapple to mine." My tone is playful, wanting to lighten the mood—even though my heart is heavy.

He flashes me a charming smile. "Never. It's bad enough that one of us puts fruit on pizza."

I chuckle. "You're lucky I'm the one who knows better."

I'll never tire of our teasing banter, especially when it gives us a break from heavier topics.

Putting the ball in Jensen's court could be the bravest—or the most reckless—choice I've ever made, and it has the potential to lead to devastating heartbreak. Still, I can't be the one to walk away, not when my heart belongs to both Jensen and Caleb. All I can hope is that he decides we're worth fighting for.

CHAPTER 32

Jensen

THE LAST THING I EXPECTED TO HEAR TODAY WAS THAT Dawson got my hearing moved up. The news is a catch-22—I'm eager to be granted full custody of Caleb, but it also forces me to figure out our future sooner than expected. It's why I froze when Briar asked if we were coming back after our trip to New York, and whether I had thought about staying for good.

What I want more than anything is for the three of us to be together—I'd do whatever it takes to find a solution that works for all of us. However, instead of explaining that, I hesitated, and now I'm afraid Briar took my response as a sign that this is goodbye.

Our conversation was cut short when she had to leave to pick Caleb up from school. They usually come back to the ranch, but today, they hung out in Julie's office doing crafts, and then she called to ask if she could take him to a new movie playing at the local theater and have dinner at the Prickly Pear Diner.

Briar knew without having to ask that I needed to think things through, and made sure I had the time to do so. That's the kind of person she is: thoughtful to a fault and always putting others before herself. It only makes it more obvious that I messed up, and all I want is to find clarity so I can make things right.

I worked late because everything took longer when I couldn't focus. Once I wrapped up, the air had cooled enough for a long run. I hoped it would clear my head, but when it didn't, I texted Heath to see if he was around. He replied almost instantly, telling me to meet him at the ranch house. He's always been a voice of reason, and I'm hoping he can help me put things into perspective and sort through my thoughts.

I walk over, appreciating the fresh air. On my way, I pass by the cabins and the general store, and I'm close enough to see the lights at the ranch house when my phone pings.

> Briar: Hey! We just got home. Caleb fell asleep in the car, so I tucked him into bed.

> Jensen: Thanks again for watching him tonight. I'm heading to the ranch house to talk to Heath but will be back soon.

> Briar: Take your time.

When I finally get to the house, Heath is waiting for me. He's kicked back in a rocking chair on the porch, his legs outstretched.

"Trying to butter me up, huh?" He nods at the two bottles of beer in my hand. "Whatever you want to talk about must be serious."

I shrug as I step onto the porch, leaning against the closest column to face him.

"A guy can't stop by to share a beer with his best friend?"

Heath smirks, one brow raised. "Let's not pretend you didn't steal that from my playbook."

Growing up, he always had a knack for getting what he wanted with a well-placed bribe. For Julie, it was flowers and butterscotch candies. With Samuel, a fresh bag of jerky did the trick.

And for Walker, Heath would take on the chores he hated most when he needed to get on his good side.

"You feel buttered up yet?" I ask, taking my hat off and placing it on the railing beside me.

"Hard to say when there's no beer in my hand."

I hook the lip of one bottle under the cap of the other and give it a twist. Once it pops off, I use it to pry open the second bottle.

Heath grunts a thank-you when I lean over to give him one.

I cross one boot over the other, glancing over my shoulder at the endless fields. At night, the ranch carries the hum of cicadas and the golden glow of the sunset stretching across the horizon.

"You've gone and fallen for Briar, haven't you?"

Heath's question makes me whip my head around to look at him, my eyebrows shooting up in surprise. "Why do you say that?"

He rolls his eyes. "It's obvious. You've been inseparable lately, and you get all googly-eyed when she's around." He pauses to take a sip of beer. "You have it bad."

Briar and I haven't exactly done much to hide things from anyone except Caleb. In my defense, it's damn near impossible to keep my distance when all I want is to have her close. Evenings have become my favorite part of the day, starting with reading to Caleb before tucking him in, then curling up with Briar on the front porch while sipping spiked hot chocolate out of chipped mugs. Most nights end with us in bed, limbs tangled up in her worn cotton sheets, whispering praises and talking till dawn.

"I do have it bad," I admit.

Heath shoots me a confused look. "Then what's with the long face? My sister's a damn catch."

She's that and so much more.

The way I handled things earlier weighs heavy on my mind, especially thinking about how she must've felt at the end of it.

"I found out earlier today that my custody hearing has been

moved up to next week, and Briar asked if Caleb and I were coming back to Bluebell afterward," I blurt out.

"That's quite the dilemma," Heath observes, rubbing his chin as he studies me. "I'm guessing you haven't decided?"

I hesitantly shake my head.

"Can I be frank?" he questions.

I chuckle. "When have you ever held back?"

He shrugs. "Never, and I won't be startin' now. You've spent most of your life running. First from your parents, then from everything that reminded you of them. I've only ever seen you truly happy in the past couple of months, and that's because of Caleb and Briar." He rests his beer on the ground beside his chair. "I think it's time you stopped running, Jensen. Sure, you have a high-powered job and a big-city life waiting for you, but is that what you really want? When you're old and gray—or should I say grayer," he adds with a wink, "is the size of your bank account or where you live going to matter, or is it the people beside you?"

My fingers tighten around the bottle in my hand. When I picture my future, many years from now, the first thing I see is Briar beside me on the porch swing, her head resting on my shoulder, our fingers intertwined. We look out across the yard as Caleb approaches, coming back from a long day of work on the ranch, wiping sweat from his brow as he joins us. Then another image surfaces of me, old and gray, in my penthouse, and all I see is silence and empty space. That vision isn't much different than it's always been.

The truth is, I was isolated in the city. I had my business and employees, but little support outside of work. Like Heath asked, is that what I want in the end? To be alone, surrounded by fancy things, with my son cut off from the people who love us most? Or to have them in our lives, and the privilege of falling asleep each night with the woman of my dreams in my arms, while Caleb is happy in the place where he belongs?

If hindsight is twenty-twenty, then mine is crystal clear. Before Caleb and Briar, I was going through the motions. Each day blended into the next, colorless and dull. Then they came along, transforming my life into Technicolor, and paved the way for me to find pieces of myself that I thought were lost forever.

I take my last swing of beer. "Since when are you so wise?"

"Somewhere between mucking stalls and mending fences," Heath jokes.

I pull out a hundred-dollar bill and hold it out to him.

He scrunches his nose, staring at it in confusion. "What's this for?"

"Betting that I'd meet a nice country gal before the summer's over. You were spot-on, and she's one of the best damn things that's ever happened to me."

"Guessing that means you've come to your senses?" He takes the money and tucks it into his flannel pocket with a grin.

"I have," I reply without hesitation.

"Then what the hell are you still standing here for?" He waves in the direction of the cottage. "Go get your girl."

I set my empty bottle down, then grab my hat, put it on, and tip it at him.

"Thanks, man."

On the walk back to the cottage, I run through every possible scenario. Briar might already be asleep, or worse, awake and ready to tell me she's changed her mind. I wouldn't blame her. She was looking for answers earlier, and instead of confessing my feelings and telling her she's my everything, I let her believe there's a good chance I'd leave her behind for my career and a life in the city.

I fucked up big-time.

I'm so caught up in my thoughts that I nearly miss her, curled up on the porch swing with a mug in hand. She's in sleep shorts, an oversized hoodie, and her hair is loose, tumbling over her shoulders.

She's gorgeous.

When she spots me, her eyes light up. "I wanted to wait for you to get back to make sure you're okay."

God, she's the most selfless person I've ever met. After how I left things, she has every right to be frustrated. Yet, her primary concern is making sure that I'm alright.

"Jensen?" she prompts when I don't reply.

I climb the porch stairs with purpose, striding toward her. She stares with her mouth parted, as I reach for her hand and help her to her feet. I set her mug on the side table and draw her close, burying my nose in her hair, breathing in the comforting scent of apples and sun-worn leather.

"What's gotten into you?" she whispers.

Having her in my arms confirms that I'm making the best choice. Nothing means more to me than her and Caleb, and though we'll have to figure out what our future looks like long-term, what matters right now is showing her how I truly feel.

"You're it for me, Briar Halstead, and I was a fool to ever think this was just a summer fling." I gently lift her chin, meeting her intrigued gaze. "I'm sorry it took me so damn long to tell you. From day one, you've treated Caleb as your own, and I'm in awe of your love for him. There's nothing I want more than for the three of us to be a family. That is, if you'll have us."

A flicker of hope flashes in her eyes, quickly masked by uncertainty. "What about New York?"

"My home is in Bluebell with you and Caleb," I state with conviction.

I've never been more confident about anything. The town I couldn't wait to leave as a teenager has become my haven. It's where my son and I healed together, and where I found the love of my life.

"But your company is in the city," Briar points out. "How is that supposed to work?"

"I've considered making changes at DataLock for a while now, and it feels like the right time to finally move forward with those."

Briar chews her bottom lip, shifting her weight from one foot to the other.

"And what happens if you change your mind?" she asks softly.

The concern in her eyes hits me square in the chest.

"That won't happen, sugar."

She furrows her brow. "How can you be so sure?"

I cradle her face in my hands, holding her gaze. "Because I love you, Briar. I love you so damn much, and I'll do whatever it takes to prove it to you. Even if it means waiting for you to figure out if you want the same thing. I'm in this for the long haul."

She melts into my touch, letting out a soft sigh. "There's nothing to think about, Jensen. I want nothing more than for you, me, and Caleb to be a family," she says, resting her hand over mine, her brown eyes shining. "I love you, too."

A light breeze blows a strand of hair across her face, and I tuck it behind her ear, brushing my fingers along her cheek.

"You mean it?" I ask.

Her fingers hook into my collar, tugging me against her. "I do. Despite your love for pineapple on pizza and lack of knowledge on plumbing tools, you've stolen my heart, and I never want it back."

"Say it again," I plead, desperate to hear it once more.

"Despite your enthusiasm for pineapple on pizza and lack of knowledge on plumbing tools, you've stolen my heart and I never want it back."

I shake my head with a chuckle. "No, what you said before that."

She rises on her tiptoes to kiss me. "I love you, Jensen."

I take a moment to soak in those three words. I'll never get tired of her saying them, and I'll make sure she hears them from me every chance I get. She'll never doubt how much she matters to me ever again.

"You know what this means?" I whisper.

She tips her head to meet my eyes. "What?"

"You're mine, sugar."

She smiles against my lips. "Then why don't you claim me properly, cowboy?"

I take my hat off, placing it on her head. "Gladly."

I tip her chin, leaning in to kiss her softly. My hands gliding along the curve of her hips as I draw her closer until her body molds perfectly against mine. Briar deserves the very best, and I intend to spend my life showing her how much I love her—with every touch, every word, and every action.

CHAPTER 33

Jensen

O N MONDAY MORNING, CALEB, BRIAR, AND I FLY TO NEW York. The city feels louder than I remember. The noise from the streets grated on my nerves during our car ride to my apartment, and I found myself missing the quiet of Bluebell—the sound of Caleb's giggles as Ziggy bleats, and the soothing rustle of wind through the trees as I work alongside the guys in the field.

I thought being back at my penthouse might settle the unease in my chest, but the moment I stepped inside, it felt foreign. The space is more showroom than sanctuary—professionally decorated but cold. This summer taught me that home isn't measured by square footage or decor, but by the people you share it with. The cottage is where Briar, Caleb, and I have made our most cherished memories, and being back in my apartment only reminds me of what's waiting for us back in Bluebell.

After ordering takeout for dinner, Briar and I tucked Caleb in together. He begged for extra stories tonight, and we read every one he requested. Having him nestled between Briar and me, listening as we took turns reading to him, gave me a glimpse into a life I never imagined could be mine—one where he has siblings and Briar isn't just the woman I love, but my wife.

I plan to soak in every moment as a family of three and figure out what life on the ranch will look like long-term. Still, it's nice to know the road ahead is bright and full of promise.

I'm currently in my home office, sending off a round of emails to my team. I've decided to officially step back from DataLock Systems and hand over the reins to Carlton, who will serve as interim CEO until I determine my future involvement with the company. At present, I have a more pressing priority that will require my full attention in the months ahead.

I'm proud of the company I've built, but somewhere along the way, I lost sight of what truly matters. It's time I shift my energy toward helping one of the people I love most chase her dreams. Once I've ironed out the details, and we're back in Bluebell, I'll share with Briar what I've been working on. For now, I've told her that I'm taking a much-needed break from corporate life, which is also true.

I hit send on the last email and close my laptop. After Caleb went to bed, Briar went to take a shower and call her friends, but she should be done by now. We haven't had any alone time today, and I'm looking forward to cuddling on the couch while we take in the skyline—one of the few things I will miss about living in New York.

I'm halfway to the door when I pause, my gaze drifting to the banker box in the corner. Tony, Amelia's lawyer, had it delivered the morning after we left for Bluebell. He didn't say what was inside, only that it held personal items Amelia set aside for me. I'd told my assistant, Beth, to put it in my office so I could go through it once I returned.

I guess now's as good a time as any.

I carry the box over to the couch along the far wall, and slowly open the lid, bracing myself for whatever Amelia left behind.

The first thing I see is a photo album labeled *Caleb's First Year*. My hands shake as I take it out and lower myself onto the couch before opening to the first page. There's a photo of Amelia in a hospital bed, cradling a newborn swaddled in a white flannel blanket with pink and blue stripes. She's staring down at Caleb with tears shining in her eyes. I flip to the next page and see a picture of her leaning over the kitchen sink, bathing him in a plastic tub with *First bath* scribbled underneath.

There are several other albums in the box, each filled with snapshots of my son and his mom—birthdays, trips to the dinosaur museum, and many moments captured at home. Amelia meticulously documented every important milestone in Caleb's life with handwritten notes below each photo. It's like she knew from the start that her time was limited and wanted to leave a piece of herself for him to hold on to when she was gone.

As I take out the last album, I spot a white envelope tucked at the bottom of the box. My throat tightens as I pull it free, running my thumb over my name written on the front in looping cursive. I've wanted closure since I found out about Caleb, but now that there's a possibility it's within reach, I hesitate, bracing myself for the endless possibilities of what could be inside.

I tug at my collar, trying to loosen the tightness in my chest. After a deep breath, I unfold the letter and begin to read.

Jensen,

By now, you've learned about Caleb, and naturally, you may be upset or have questions. I'll try my best to answer them.

As a teenager, I was diagnosed with Hodgkin's lymphoma. The road to remission was grueling but coming out the other side pushed me to chase every goal with relentless focus. I went to college, then law school, and spent years working long hours at my firm—all in pursuit of making partner.

I rarely took time for myself, and the night with you was a rare exception. You were charming, hot as hell, and had me laughing more than I had in a while.

A few months later, during a routine oncology appointment, I was shocked to discover I was pregnant. I'd always wanted a family, but never thought it was possible given that I'd been warned my chances of having a baby were slim to none. The excitement I felt was quickly overshadowed when my scans revealed the cancer had returned.

After Caleb was born, I went through multiple rounds of chemo and radiation, all in the hope of being around to see him take his first steps, say his first words, and start preschool. And by some miracle, I got to be there for all those things and more.

I was afraid that telling you about him would mean splitting his time between us. And that I'd miss out on important milestones, holidays, and daily routines. I couldn't risk that, not when I already knew my time with him was limited.

By hiding the truth, I know that I've failed you both, and for that I'm deeply sorry. I should have introduced you earlier, so it would make what comes next easier. More than anything, I regret not giving you the chance to be his father sooner, and I can only hope that you'll find it in your heart to forgive me.

We made the most beautiful boy. He's brought me more joy over the past few years than I ever imagined possible. I named him Caleb because it means "faithful," and when he was born, I needed faith more than ever.

Faith that I was strong enough to take care of him, even if our time was short.

Faith that he'd find the strength to keep going once I was gone.

And most importantly, faith that you would open up your heart and love him unconditionally.

He experiences emotions more intensely than most kids his age, and I worry how he'll handle my passing, so please be patient with him and guard his heart.

We might have only shared one night together, but it was enough to show me that you're kind, loyal, and hardworking—traits that will help to make you a great dad. I truly believe Caleb will be lucky to have you.

Though I'll be gone when you read this, know that I'm with you and Caleb in spirit—cheering you on from afar.

Yours,
Amelia

I blink back the sting in my eyes, as I stare at the letter, still in disbelief that it's real. In the past, I've wrestled with so many emotions directed at Amelia—anger, confusion, frustration—but now, all I feel is clarity. She asked for my forgiveness, and she's had it for a while now. With Briar's help, I've been able to make peace with the past, and having the full story behind Amelia's decision makes me realize I would have made the same choice she did—choosing to treasure every precious minute with my child before my time ran out.

The way Caleb came into my life might not have happened the way I initially had hoped, but if things had gone differently, I doubt we would have ended up in Bluebell, and I might have missed my chance to fall in love with Briar.

In a way, I owe Amelia everything.

It's only when the couch shifts slightly that I notice Briar has come into my office, settling beside me. Her hair is damp, curling at the ends, and the scent of my body wash clings to her skin. She rests her hand on my thigh, her brows drawn together in worry.

"Are you alright?" she asks.

I hold out the letter. "I found this at the bottom of a box of Amelia's things. She wrote it for me before she died. Would you like to read it?" I add when she doesn't move.

Briar nods, taking it from me, and lowers her gaze to the page. Her expression shifts with every line, and by the time she reaches the end, tears shine in her eyes.

"That was beautiful, Jensen. Thank you for letting me read it."

"I'm glad you're here to share it with," I say, wiping a tear from her cheek. "For a while, I convinced myself that the only reason Amelia left Caleb with me was because she had no other options. It was the only explanation I could come up with for why she hadn't left a note or reached out before she passed."

"Now you know the truth," she whispers.

"I'm grateful I do. Ever since I found out about Caleb, I've questioned if I'm enough for him," I admit softly. "So, having confirmation that his mom trusted me to do right by him and saw me as the best person to raise him is the reassurance I needed."

Briar takes my hand in hers. "I've believed in you from the start. All of us did. We were just waiting for you to believe it, too."

This is one of the many reasons I've fallen for her. She had faith in me as a dad before I had any of my own, and has been by my side through every uncertainty.

I lean in, kissing her on the lips. "I love you."

"I love you too," she murmurs.

I'll never get tired of hearing her say it, and I'm reminded how lucky I am that she's mine.

She tilts her head, motioning to the albums on my other side. "What are those?"

"Amelia left me a box of photos of Caleb. Want to look through them together?"

"I'd love to," she replies, a smile lighting up her face. "How about we bring them into the living room? I found some organic milk and top-shelf whiskey. We can make a city-boy version of spiked hot chocolate while we look through them."

I hold her gaze, returning her smile. "Perfect."

"Come on, then," she says, standing. When she turns toward the door, I give her ass a playful swat.

Briar glances over her shoulder, a smirk on her face. "You really do have an obsession, don't you?"

"With you? Always."

CHAPTER 34

Brian

WHEN CALEB WOKE UP THIS MORNING, HE WAS FULL OF questions about why we're going to the courthouse. While I made pancakes, Jensen explained that a judge will give him a special paper that says he's Caleb's dad. He showed Caleb his birth certificate with his mom's name and explained we need one that includes his dad's name.

He asked what a courtroom looks like, and when Jensen showed him pictures, one with a gavel on the judge's bench caught Caleb's interest. Now he's determined to use one himself.

I've just finished getting ready, and when I come out of the bathroom, my breath hitches when I see Jensen standing by his dresser, looking fine as hell in a white button-down, dark-wash Wranglers, and boots.

"Is that what you're wearing to the courthouse?" I ask curiously.

Part of me expected him to wear a three-piece suit and polished Oxfords.

He glances down at his outfit. "Yeah, why?"

I close the distance between us, straightening his collar. "You look very handsome."

He dips his head to give me a kiss before his gaze drops to my outfit. "You're absolutely stunning, and this dress is something else," he says, rubbing a piece of the fabric between his fingers.

It's a dusty rose chiffon with a cinched waist and a row of buttons down the bodice. I found it at Charlie's boutique last year, but haven't had a reason to wear it until now.

I smile against his lips. "I'm glad you like it."

We've been in New York less than twenty-four hours, yet Jensen is already more relaxed than when we arrived. I suspect it's because he's found closure he once thought impossible.

At first, I was worried when I walked into his office last night and saw him wearing a somber expression, surrounded by albums, with a letter clutched in his hand. After reading the letter, a sense of relief washed over me. Jensen's been drowning in guilt and confusion since learning about Caleb, doubting if he was enough for his son and wrestling with Amelia's choice to keep Caleb from him for so long.

Although her letter can't change the past, it provides Jensen with an explanation for her choices and a way to move forward without the weight of the past holding him back.

"Dad, Briar, can we go yet?" Caleb shouts from the hall. "I want to see the gavel."

We break apart seconds before he bursts into the bedroom, grinning. Our plan is to tell him we're together soon, but today is all about him. We also want to give him an opportunity to ask questions and take plenty of time to answer them.

I kneel down next to him, smoothing his hair. "Lookin' mighty fine, little man." He's dressed almost identically to Jensen, right down to the crisp white shirt.

"He wanted us to match as a surprise for you," Jensen adds, adjusting his cuffs.

Caleb throws his arms around my neck. "Are you surprised?!"

"Very," I say with a smile. "You both look very handsome."

He leans in and whispers in my ear, "Don't tell Dad, but I like my comfy shirts better."

I glance at Jensen who's covering his mouth to keep from laughing.

"Tell you what," I say to Caleb. "We'll bring one with us and you can change when we're finished at the courthouse. What do you think?"

He nods eagerly. "Can I bring Chompers?"

It was a big milestone when he finally shared the name of his beloved dino.

"Sure. You can hold him in the car, but while we're out, he'll need to stay in your backpack, sound good?"

"He won't mind," Caleb exclaims.

I stand as he rushes out of the room. Watching him find his voice and express himself has been a privilege. He's grown so much since the start of the summer, and every day brings new adventures and discoveries about his personality.

I turn back to Jensen. "You ready for this?"

"I've been waiting for this day since I met Caleb," he replies, voice thick with emotion.

Shortly after we arrive at the courthouse, a man in a charcoal-gray three-piece suit approaches us in the hallway. He looks to be in his thirties and carries a briefcase in his left hand. His piercing blue eyes flicker to Jensen, taking in his appearance with a hint of a smile.

Jensen grins when he glances over. "There you are. I was starting to think you might've bailed."

"Who are you, and what have you done with Jensen Harding?" The man observes, gesturing to Jensen's outfit.

"My dad's a cowboy now, just like me." Caleb chimes in proudly with his hands on his hips.

The man's brows lift. "No kidding? You both look sharp."

"Caleb wanted to match for our special day," Jensen tells him before motioning between us. "Briar, this is Dawson, my lawyer. Dawson, meet my Briar."

I hold out my hand. "Nice to meet you."

He shakes my hand, his eyes darting between Jensen and me. "Guess Bluebell gave Jensen more than just a change in scenery."

"Just helping him find his roots again," I respond, offering Jensen a knowing smile.

Dawson glances at his watch, and I catch a tattoo peeking out from under his sleeve. "We're next on the docket, so it shouldn't be long now."

He opens his suit jacket and takes an envelope from the inside pocket, handing it to Jensen. "Didn't want to steal the spotlight today, but I wasn't sure when I'd get another chance to give you this."

Jensen takes the envelope, and I peek over his shoulder as he takes out an invitation. At the top, printed in large, elegant script, it says: *The honor of your presence is requested at the wedding of Dawson Tate & Reese Taylor.*

His eyes widen as he glances over at Dawson "Wait. *You're* getting married? Never thought I'd see the day."

Dawson grins. "Reese graduated law school in May, and we're finally making it official."

"Congrats." Jensen claps him on the back. "I'm happy for you."

"Thanks, man. I can't wait to call her my wife," Dawson says with a spark in his eyes.

Jensen mentioned that Dawson is the top attorney in New York and has a reputation for being ruthless in the courtroom.

My first impression is that he's not someone you'd want to cross. But when Reese's name comes up, his whole demeanor changes, and it's clear she means the world to him.

Caleb tugs on Dawson's pant leg until he looks down at him. "What's up, kid?"

"I want to hold the gavel. Can you help me?"

Dawson blinks, caught off guard, his eyes darting to Jensen.

"I showed him some photos of courtrooms, and one had a gavel on the judge's bench. Now he's determined to give it a go."

Dawson chuckles. "You're in luck, kid. I know the judge handling your case, and I bet he'll let you hold his gavel and maybe even use it to call the court to order, as long as you listen to your dad while we're in there."

Caleb bounces on the balls of his feet, barely holding back his excitement. "I'll be the best listener ever, right Dad?"

"You bet, buddy," Jensen says, bending down to ruffle his hair.

Their exchange makes my heart swell. The bond between father and son is unmistakable, from their matching outfits to the joy mirrored in their smiles. Sharing this special day with them is a gift, and I'm beyond grateful to be the woman who gets to love them both.

"Did we miss it?" Mama Julie's voice echoes down the hall, and I turn to find her and Pops coming our way.

I'm stunned speechless, overwhelmed with gratitude at the sight of them.

I spoke with Mama Julie last night, but she didn't say anything about coming. I did mention how much I wished she and Pops could be here. They love Caleb like their own grandchild, and it felt wrong that they'd miss Jensen finalizing custody. They must have taken a red-eye flight to get here on time, and even though Pops isn't fond of leaving Montana, they made the effort because they knew how much this meant to us.

The hearing may just be a formality, but it marks a new

beginning for all of us, made even sweeter by the fact that Jensen and Caleb are staying in Bluebell for good.

"Mama Julie, Pops. You're here," Caleb exclaims, running straight toward them.

Pops bends down and scoops him up. "Hey there, buckaroo. Couldn't let you have all the fun in the big city without us."

"Did we miss the hearing?" Julie asks again, her heavy breathing hinting that they rushed here.

I shake my head. "No, we're waiting on the judge. I can't believe you came."

Mama Julie waves a hand like it's nothing. "There's no chance we'd miss out on Caleb and Jensen's special day."

"We're really glad you're here," Jensen adds with a grateful smile.

It reminds me that the Halsteads aren't just my family, but his as well. I'm so grateful we both have such an amazing support system. Judging by Jensen's expression, having Mama Julie and Pops here means the world to him, too.

"There's nowhere else we'd rather be," she replies, pulling him into a hug.

Dawson stands a few feet away, phone in hand, giving us space for our mini family reunion. But the second the courtroom door opens and the court clerk calls his name, he squares his shoulders, shifting back into professional mode. He bends down to grab his briefcase from the floor before turning to Jensen.

"It's showtime," he says before striding toward the open door.

Mama Julie, Pops, and Caleb trail closely behind, but before I follow, Jensen catches my hand and pulls me in for a quick hug.

"I love you. So much," he whispers in my ear. "And as grateful as I am for today, I can't wait until we're back in Bluebell."

"I love you most," I reply with a wink. "Let's go make this official."

As we enter the courtroom, my heart feels like it might burst.

I'm surrounded by the people I love most as the hearing begins. Jensen stands beside Caleb, his hand steady on his shoulder. Mama Julie, Samuel, and I sit in the row behind them.

After reviewing the will and legal papers, the judge asks Jensen a few brief questions, and within minutes, he grants him full custody, and extends his congratulations.

Next to me, Julie wipes away a tear as Samuel gently squeezes her hand. When Caleb asks the judge if he can use the gavel, Jensen looks back at me, grinning—happier than I've ever seen him. He mouths, "I love you," and I mouth it back with a smile.

I exhale slowly, a sense of peace settling over me now that the legal part of Jensen and Caleb's journey is complete. Whatever the future holds, I have my family—and that's what matters most.

CHAPTER 35

Brian

WHILE WE WERE IN THE CITY, WE SPENT A COUPLE OF days sightseeing. We kicked things off after the court hearing by surprising Caleb with a trip to the American Museum of Natural History. He often talks about visiting the dinosaur museum in Chicago with his mom, and while we couldn't make that happen this time, he still enjoyed it. One day soon, we'll take him back to visit all the places that were special to them. She may be gone, but Jensen and I are committed to keeping her memory alive, so Caleb will always remember how deeply she loved him.

We flew back from New York last night, and although we had a lot of fun, it's so good to be home.

I started the morning with a maintenance check on the cabins and covered the general store for a few hours so Ethel could take care of her housekeeping duties. Jensen picked Caleb up from summer camp today so he could take him for his first horse ride. He wanted them to start riding together and in the coming weeks, will teach him how to ride on his own. I can't wait for the day when we're all able to go out together as a family.

On our way home from New York, Jensen told Caleb that we're a couple and that they'll be living in the cottage for the foreseeable future. What excited him most was finding out that he won't have to say goodbye to Ziggy, and that he'll still get to see Mama Julie at school every day when he starts kindergarten.

The plan is for me to continue watching him in the afternoons. I cherish our time together and wouldn't trade it for anything. The only change is that I've told Jensen I won't accept payment anymore. It was never about the money anyway. I could never replace Caleb's mom, but I love him like my own, and I hope he knows he has a safe place with me—always.

It's late afternoon by the time I finish at the general store and head back to the cottage. With Jensen and Caleb still out, I decide to unpack. We got in late last night, and I haven't had the chance until now. I figured Charlie or Birdie would stop by today, especially after how many times they said they missed me while I was gone. But now that I think about it, the group chat has been silent today. That's unusual, considering we text constantly.

Backroads & Bad Decisions Group Chat

> Briar: Y'all have been awfully quiet today.

> Briar: Should I be worried you started another chat without me? *Face with raised eyebrow emoji

Charlie: Hi! We missed you!

Birdie: Welcome home! Earl drove me to town this morning and said he saw you coming in late last night.

Wren: Loved the photos you sent. Caleb is the sweetest.

I'm curious why no one's answering my question. They're normally upfront—Charlie in particular.

> Briar: He really is.

> Briar: Charlie? Birdie? Want to swing by later?

Charlie: Wish I could, but I've got inventory to handle at the shop.

Birdie: I'm still keeping a low profile, sorry!

My brows knit in confusion. Charlie did inventory last week, and Birdie just said she was riding in Earl's taxi earlier today. Something's going on, but I'm not sure what.

Wren: I'd stop by if I didn't live so far away.

> Briar: At least someone missed me. You're my favorite, Wren.

Charlie: Starts a new group chat…

> Briar: *emotionless face emoji

I giggle as I tuck my phone into my pocket, coming to a standstill when I enter my bedroom. There's a big white box tied with a red bow sitting in the middle of my bed. As I get closer, I notice a handwritten note on top.

SUGAR,

I KNEW THIS WOULD LOOK AMAZING ON YOU THE SECOND I SAW IT. WE'VE GOT A DATE TONIGHT, SO TAKE YOUR TIME GETTING READY, AND WHEN CALEB AND I GET BACK, WE'LL HEAD OUT.

I LOVE YOU,
JENSEN

My breath catches as I open the box to reveal a dress inside—a baby-blue A-line with a side slit and straps that tie into bows on the shoulders. I remember passing a boutique in New York where I'd admired it in a window display. Jensen must have gone back to get it for me.

God, he's the sweetest man. Not only is he an amazing father, but he's always finding little ways to show he cares through thoughtful gestures, and I'll never take them for granted.

After a long bubble bath, I do my hair and makeup, then head outside. I set up a pen for Ziggy out front so he can wait with me for Jensen and Caleb. After being cooped up in the barn while we were away—where Heath could keep an eye on him more easily—he's clearly thrilled to be back in the grass, happy and carefree.

It's not long before I spot a figure in the distance. As it gets closer, I see Caleb sitting up front on the horse, his small hands gripping the saddle horn, with Jensen behind him, one hand on the reins and the other wrapped loosely around Caleb's waist. They're smiling from ear to ear, and their joy is infectious. It makes me excited for all the memories we'll share on the ranch together in the years to come.

When they reach the house, Jensen gently pulls on the reins, bringing the horse to a stop, and climbs down before helping Caleb dismount.

I step off the porch just as Caleb races toward me, and I catch him in a hug.

"Hey, little man. How was your first horseback ride?"

"So much fun! The horse's name is Lucky and he moves *really* fast." He throws his arms out to mimic the motion. "Dad promised we could go again next week!"

"That's so exciting," I say with a smile.

"He also said I'm having a sleepover at Mama Julie and Pops' tonight, and we're making cookies and watching *Shrek*."

"Wow, sounds like fun."

Caleb nods enthusiastically before letting me go, and running over to Ziggy's pen to play with him.

I glance over at Jensen standing nearby, his gaze sweeping over me, taking in every inch.

"You're so beautiful," he murmurs.

Warmth rushes to my cheeks as I tuck a piece of hair behind my ear. "Thank you. I love the dress—it fits perfectly."

"The dress is very nice, but it's you that makes it shine," he says, stepping closer. "I have to take Lucky back to the barn and grab a shower. Then it's date night."

"You're always full of surprises, aren't you?"

He closes the remaining distance between us.

"Only the good kind," he says, pressing a kiss to my lips.

"Eww," Caleb groans. "Kissing is gross. Right, Ziggy?"

The goat bleats in agreement before looking our way. When he notices Jensen, he freezes, his legs locking straight before toppling over with a dramatic flop.

We all burst out laughing, Jensen included. I just hope Ziggy never stops fainting at the sight of him—it's comedy gold.

I couldn't be happier, and looking ahead, it's easy to see why—a swooning goat, Caleb's infectious giggles, and the urban cowboy who stole my heart. Nothing could be better than this.

After Jensen returned Lucky to the barn and got ready himself, we dropped Caleb off at Mama Julie's. She was already waiting on the porch, subtly blocking the front door, which makes me think she was in on whatever Jensen had planned. My curiosity grew as he led me around back, through the apple orchard behind the ranch house.

"You're really not going to tell me where we're going?" I ask as we weave through another row of trees.

Jensen squeezes my hand, a grin tugging at his lips. "No, but at least I left the blindfold at home tonight."

"Oh, I moved it to the drawer by our bed," I respond, playing it cool.

He stares at me, eyes wide. "Keep talking like that, woman, and I'll throw you over my shoulder and take you home."

"It'll be worth the wait," I say with a mischievous smile.

We finally come to a stop when we reach a small clearing. A translucent canopy tent stands beneath the fading sun, the distant mountains rising behind it like a painted backdrop. A rustic wooden table is set for two, adorned with flickering candles and fresh greenery, and two plush chairs are positioned next to each other. Nearby is a smaller table with a food warmer and miniature bottles of whiskey and water.

I spin in a slow circle, soaking in every detail. "Oh my god, this is incredible."

"Urban cowboy had help." I turn toward the house when I hear Charlie's voice, to see her approaching with a covered plate, Birdie right behind her with another.

I narrow my eyes playfully. "So *this* is why you two were acting suspicious when I texted you earlier."

"We were a little busy elbow-deep in decorations and making potato salad," Birdie says, setting her plate on the warmer.

I watch as my friends light the last few candles, putting the finishing touches on the romantic setup. I'm incredibly lucky to have their support. Their sincere desire for my happiness is overwhelming, particularly when they went all out after Jensen asked them to be involved tonight. It's like he knew exactly how much it would mean to me.

"Looks like our fairy god-matchmaker duties are complete.

Don't have too much fun, you two," Charlie says, shooting me a smirk as she passes.

When Birdie walks by, she gives my arm a gentle squeeze. "You've got yourself a good man."

I glance at Jensen, smiling. "I really do."

"Appreciate the backup," Jensen says to them with a grin.

"Love you both!" I add, blowing Charlie and Birdie kisses as we all burst into laughter before they turn and head toward the ranch house.

Once they're out of sight, I wind my arms around Jensen's neck, tilting my head to kiss him.

"Thanks for doing this."

"Anything for you, sugar," he says with a warm smile. "Why don't we sit down and enjoy the beautiful view?" He motions to the mountains and setting sun.

He pulls out a chair for me, and takes the seat beside me. "Before we eat, there's something I want to talk to you about."

I let out a playful gasp. "Uh-oh. Sounds serious."

Jensen clears his throat, and pulls a folded piece of paper from his front pocket. He smooths it out and places it on the table in front of me. It appears to be a sketch, covered in lines and measurements.

My brows knit together. "What's this?"

"Plans for your children's sanctuary," he says, his lips twitching with excitement. "I had a few different layouts drawn up so you'd have options, but if none of them are what you envisioned, we can have something new designed."

I barely process what he's saying. My mind stuck on the first part of his response.

"Sorry. I don't understand." My voice falters, thick with emotion.

"You've had this dream for years, always putting it on the backburner because you thought you had to do it alone." He takes my hand in his, rubbing my palm with his thumb. "You're not alone anymore, sugar. Having the privilege to see firsthand the difference you've made in Caleb's life made me realize that every child deserves someone like you—someone who's willing to advocate for them and honor their individuality." He pauses, giving my hand a gentle squeeze. "You have the ability to make a positive impact on countless kids who've been overlooked or misunderstood, and now, you finally have the chance to turn that gift into a safe space for those who need it."

My stomach flutters with anticipation as I use my free hand to trace the plans, trailing my finger along the lines on the paper. "These are amazing, but it might be a while before I can move forward. I just don't have the funds or time right now," I say with a sigh.

It pains me to admit it, but I haven't saved enough to start the project, and the little free time I have now will go toward finally finishing the cottage renovations.

"You don't have to do this alone," Jensen says, repeating his words from earlier. "I want to help."

"Are you really ready to walk away from the corporate world?"

"I accomplished what I set out to do in New York years ago—built a company I'm proud of. But even before you and Caleb came into my life, something about my career felt off. The rush of proving people wrong faded, and my routine became predictable." He straightens in his chair, adjusting his hands to rest on my hips. "I'm ready for a new chapter—one that centers around something far more important than anything I ever achieved at DataLock Systems: you and Caleb. That starts with helping you bring your dreams to life."

A warmth spreads through my chest. "Thank you for wanting to help but what if I mess it all up? I have no clue how to run a nonprofit. The whole process is overwhelming, and I think that's why it's taken me this long to get started."

Admittedly, having someone with experience and a genuine interest in my passions to guide me through the process would make the journey less intimidating and turn the uncertainty into an adventure we can share together.

Jensen's expression brightens. "You're in luck because when it comes to the business logistics, I've got you covered. I'm committed to making sure your vision comes to life, whatever it takes. Plus, if you can spare me now and then, Heath could use an extra hand on the ranch. I've enjoyed helping him and Walker more than I expected."

"Might do you some good. Maybe they'll teach you the difference between a non-adjustable wrench and an adjustable one," I tease with a chuckle. "Especially if you're planning to help me finish renovating the cottage, too."

"That's what I have you for. We're the perfect match." He reaches over, running a finger along the curve of my jaw. "We'll renovate the cottage together, and with the sanctuary, I'll be here every step of the way. But it's yours. You'll always have the final say, sugar."

I tilt my head, studying him. "Does that make me your boss?"

"You accept my help, and I'll gladly take your orders."

I nod. "I could get used to that."

A few months ago, I would have struggled to accept Jensen's help. But watching him return to Bluebell—a place he swore he'd never set foot in again—because it was the best decision for Caleb has taught me an important lesson: accepting support from the people who love you most isn't a sign of weakness. It's a strength.

My summer began like any other on the ranch, centered on work and moving closer to my dream of opening a children's sanctuary. Then Jensen and Caleb came to town, turning my world upside down in the best way possible. They've taught me that the greatest gifts often come when you least expect them, and I'll never take it for granted that I now have a family of my own—filling my days with love and purpose I wouldn't trade for anything.

I glance over at Jensen, his eyes filled with promise. "From here on out, it's you, me, and Caleb against the world."

"Nothing could be better," I murmur. "Now, shut up and kiss me, cowboy."

EPILOGUE

Jensen

Eight Months Later

THE WIND CARRIES THE SCENT OF PINE AND DAMP EARTH as we ride the worn trail. The mountain peaks in the distance still have a dusting of snow, but here in the valley, spring is already underway—wildflowers dot the ground and birdsong fills the air.

Briar leads the way, her hair loose beneath her hat, catching the sun whenever she glances back at Caleb and me. We're sharing a horse with him perched in front, my arm wrapped around his middle as he holds the saddle horn. I've ridden this path countless times, and it's always better when we're together.

Between working on the ranch, breaking ground on Briar's new children's sanctuary, and Caleb starting kindergarten, our weeks are hectic. Briar's foundation should be fully operational by this time next year. We've also begun designing a house that'll be built on the far side of the ranch. Julie and Samuel generously gifted us the land for Christmas, wanting us to have a home of our own and a place to grow our family.

With so much going on, we make sure to reserve every Saturday just for the three of us. We always enjoy ourselves, but I have something particularly special planned today.

Caleb twists to look at me, eyes sparkling with excitement. "Are we almost there yet, Dad?"

"We're close, bud," I promise.

"And then you're going to ask Briar your question?" he whispers loudly.

He tries to keep his voice low, but his excitement is obvious. Luckily, Briar is far enough ahead not to hear him.

I chuckle. "Yep, real soon."

Briar thinks the ride is the main event, but the real plan is to propose once we reach our destination. Caleb's in on the surprise, but with how giddy he is, he might blurt it out before I get the chance. Hard to believe he's the same quiet boy I brought to Bluebell last summer.

In March, I told Julie and Samuel I wanted to marry Briar, and they were thrilled. Julie said she had something special for me and returned with a ring that had belonged to her mother. Briar had admired it since she was a girl, so Julie offered it to me as her engagement ring if I wanted it. The moment I saw the oval diamond set in a gold bezel, I knew it was perfect.

Not only does it symbolize a new chapter in our lives together but it also reflects how the Halsteads have always seen her as their own daughter—and how they'll continue to give her the love and support she deserves.

For the past two months, I kept the ring hidden in the back of my sock drawer. Last week, I finally took it with me to New York for a quarterly shareholder meeting to have it cleaned. I couldn't risk taking it to the local jeweler and having the news of our upcoming engagement spread like wildfire before I even proposed.

I gently pull back the reins as we near the knoll where I brought Briar on our first date. It's become our sanctuary, and we visit often. Caleb loves tagging along, so I hung a tire swing from a sturdy cottonwood tree nearby, giving him a little piece of joy in our favorite spot too.

I lead our horse, Lucky, to a grassy spot and dismount, tying the reins to a nearby tree before helping Caleb down. He waits patiently nearby as I grab the blanket and picnic basket from the saddle.

He crooks his finger, and I crouch down beside him. "Yeah, bud?"

"Can I see the ring again?"

I let out a low laugh. "Just a little bit longer," I assure him.

At this rate, he's going to beat me to it if I don't act soon. I rub my palms against my jeans, my heart pounding with anticipation.

"I can set up the picnic," Briar says as she gets off her horse.

She makes her way over and takes the blanket from me, giving it a quick shake before laying it on the grass.

I'm still amazed that I get to call her mine. She's the most thoughtful, kind and loving partner, and treats Caleb with a patience and grace I'll never take for granted. The fact that I'll soon be able to call her my wife feels like one of the greatest gifts I'll ever receive—assuming she says yes.

"Caleb, can you bring me the basket? Your dad seems a bit distracted," Briar says with a wink.

I blink, offering her a sheepish smile. "Sorry—got lost in thought," I say, handing it to her.

"Thanks."

Briar opens the basket and lays out chicken salad sandwiches wrapped in gingham cloth, a bowl of fresh fruit salad, chocolate-covered strawberries, and a mason jar of sweet tea.

ANN EINERSON

She lets out a whistle. "Well, this puts my usual peanut butter and jelly sandwiches to shame. You really outdid yourselves."

"Glad you like it," I say with a smile.

Caleb and I made everything this morning with Julie's help. I told her I wanted to go all out, and she was more than happy to lend a hand.

When we don't move to sit down, Briar glances between us. "Don't you want to eat? It all looks amazing."

Caleb shakes his head. "Dad has an important question to—"

"Buddy," I interject. "Remember what we practiced?"

"Oh yeah. I remember now!" He moves to my side, smiling wide at Briar.

"You two are being so silly," she chuckles. "What do you have up your sleeves?"

Before I lose my nerve, I close the distance between us, and drop to one knee. Her breath catches as she watches me, stunned and speechless.

"From the moment Caleb and I stepped into the cottage, I knew things would never be the same." I take her hands in mine. "You've brought more joy and happiness into our lives than I ever thought possible. Beyond being Caleb's dad, nothing would mean more to me than making you my wife." I stare up into her beautiful brown eyes. "When I decided how to do this, I thought back to how it all began—with the three of us—and knew I wanted this new chapter to start the same, and in a place that's special to us."

My hand trembles as I take the ring from my pocket and hold it out to the woman who means everything to me.

"Briar Halstead, will you marry me?"

A quiet moment passes as she reaches over to gently squeeze Caleb's hand. He beams at her, practically buzzing with energy. Her eyes shine with affection before she turns back to me.

"Yes!" she exclaims, tears glistening in her eyes. "Absolutely, yes." She drops to her knees in front of me as I slide the ring on her finger. "Jensen... how did you get this?"

"Julie wanted you to have it."

"I've always loved this ring," she whispers in awe. "It's perfect."

I lean in and kiss her on the lips. "I love you, sugar."

"I love you too, cowboy."

My gaze lingers on the ring she now wears. I'm grateful for the journey that led us here and eager for the life we're building together.

I nod at Caleb, like we'd practiced. We went over this part several times yesterday with Heath and Walker while Briar was out with her friends, and he's been counting down the hours until he can ask Briar his own question.

He angles toward her. "Hey, Briar."

"Yeah, little man?" she asks.

"Remember how, when you went to live with Julie when you were a kid, you started calling her Mama Julie?"

Briar's face brightens. "I do."

"Well, I live with you now, and I was thinking maybe I could call you Mama Briar?" he questions, bouncing on his feet.

Caleb approached me about it last week, asking if he could have a special name for her like she has for Julie. And together we came up with the idea of Mama Briar.

Briar draws him in, her eyes finding mine as she replies, voice thick with emotion. "Yes, sweetheart. I'd like that very much." A single tear trickles down her cheek. "I love you so much."

"I love you too, Mama Briar," he whispers.

My heart overflows with gratitude as I watch Briar embrace *our* son. We've agreed to wait until he's older to decide whether he wants her to adopt him. Briar doesn't want to take away from the memory of Amelia and will respect whatever choice he makes. We're a family in all the ways that matter most, and that's all either of us could ever ask for.

The woman of my dreams is going to be my wife, we have the most amazing son, and our home is full of laughter and joy. I'm living proof that sometimes the best kind of life is one with muddy boots, starry skies, and a heart full of love. It's safe to say that I've been completely wrangled by love.

Caleb's first time speaking after losing his mom was one of the most emotional scenes to write. While the chapter is told from Jensen's POV, I felt inspired to share it through Caleb's eyes in this special bonus scene.
Type this link into the browser to read it.
https://dl.bookfunnel.com/9n5isdhe0u

Thank you so much for reading *Wrangled Love*. If you enjoyed it, please consider leaving a review on your preferred platform(s) of choice. It's the best compliment I can receive as an author, and it makes it easier for other readers to find my books.

OTHER BOOKS BY ANN EINERSON

If You Give a CEO a Chance (Harrison & Fallon)
*An enemies-to-lovers, second chance love story between a
retired hockey player and his new live-in private chef, in a
banter filled spicy romance.*

If You Give a Single Dad a Nanny (Dylan & Marlow)
*A swoon worthy, single dad/nanny, age gap, he's grumpy, she's
sunshine, banter-filled spicy small town romance*

If You Give a Billionaire a Bride (Cash & Everly)
*A marriage of convenience that starts with a Vegas wedding
between a reformed playboy and his best friend's sister in a banter-
filled spicy billionaire romance*

When You Give a Lawyer a Kiss (Dawson & Reese)
*A workplace romance between a grumpy billionaire and his new
assistant in an age gap, banter-filled, spicy love story.*

If You Give a Grump a Holiday Wishlist (Presley & Jack)
*A small town, fake dating, one bed spicy workplace
holiday romance.*

The Holiday Claus (Brooks & Lila)
*A holiday romance where a grumpy billionaire falls for
his best friend's sunshine sister, wrapped in an age gap,
only one bed spicy novella.*

The Spotlight (Conway & Sienna)
*A best friend's brother, opposites attract, dating in secret,
spicy rockstar romance.*

ACKNOWLEDGMENTS

So many people made this book possible, and I can't thank you all enough for your love, kindness, and support. *Wrangled Love* wouldn't have been possible without each and every one of you.

To Bryanna—For being my ride-or-die through this wild publishing journey. Part dev editor, part therapist, and full-time work-wife—you've stuck with me through every plot twist, late-night call, and looming deadline. This book exists because you never let me quit and believe in me, even when I didn't always believe in myself. You're the Charlie to my Briar and I love you most!

To Becca—Your feedback is invaluable, and I can't thank you enough for cheering me on from the sidelines.

To Jess—For being my creative partner from the start. Your talent for bringing each story to life with stunning graphics and videos never fails to inspire me. I'm incredibly lucky to have you in my corner.

To Tab and Kaity—I can't thank you enough for the time, care, and heart you poured into helping bring these characters to life. I'm so grateful for your patience with all my DMs, questions, and concerns. Forever grateful for you both!

To Logan—Thank you so much for your thoughtful feedback. It was incredibly helpful, and I truly appreciate your support!

To Emily, Jenny, Nikki, and Judy—I couldn't have asked for a better editing team. I'm grateful for your expertise and for pushing me to write a story worth reading.

To Caroline, Wren, Lauren Brooke, Kat, Jenna Lynn, Erica, Hunter, Ceilidh, Syd, and Morgan—Thanks for reading *Wrangled Love* early and providing the honest critique that challenged me to raise the bar and deliver my best work.

To Chelsea, Madison—For designing the most adorable

cover for this book. It was love at first sight, and it makes my heart so happy that my readers love it as much as I do.

To Kyler—Thank you for supporting my insane work schedule. Without you, my dream of becoming a full-time author wouldn't have come true.

To my ARC/Content teams—Thank you for all your thoughtful messages, posts, stories, reviews, and comments. Your endless love and support never cease to amaze me.

Most importantly, thank **YOU**. There are so many incredible books to choose from and I'm honored you took a chance on Jensen & Briar's story. None of this would be possible without you! Every single tag, share, and DM means the world and motivates me to keep writing on the days I think this might be for nothing. I hope you enjoyed your time in Bluebell, Montana!

ABOUT THE AUTHOR

Ann Einerson is the author of enchanting contemporary romance novels that will keep you hooked until the very last page, complete with heroes who fall hard and the heroines who keep them on their toes. She believes sometimes the best family is the one we find, curiosity is good for the soul, and a good book isn't complete without banter.

You can find Ann surrounded by her ample supply of sticky notes ready for inspiration and ideas. When she's not writing, Ann enjoys spoiling her chatty pet chickens, listening to her dysfunctional playlists, and going for late-night treadmill runs. She lives in Michigan with her husband.

KEEP IN TOUCH WITH ANN EINERSON

Website
www.anneinerson.com

Newsletter
www.anneinerson.com/newsletter-signup

Instagram
www.instagram.com/authoranneinerson

TikTok
www.tiktok.com/@anneinersonbooks

Amazon
www.amazon.com/author/anneinerson

Goodreads
www.goodreads.com/author/show/29752171.Ann_Einerson

Made in United States
North Haven, CT
26 July 2025

71033378R00208